THE WIND AND THE VOID

RYAN KIRK

THE WIND AND THE VOID

ISBN-13: 978-069268-797-0
ISBN-10: 0-692-68797-1

Cover art by Andrei Bat
Edited by Sonnet Fitzgerald
Interior design by Ryan Kirk

www.waterstonemedia.net

Give feedback on the book at:
contact@waterstonemedia.net

Twitter: @waterstonebooks

First Edition

Printed in the U.S.A

This one is for Kelly,
I'm proud of the woman you've become

Despite all my attempts to ruin your life as an older brother. . .

PROLOGUE

General Toro awoke to a cold, crisp morning, the third in a row. Despite the number of cycles he had seen, or perhaps because of them, Toro was fascinated by weather. In the Three Kingdoms, the farther south a traveler went, the warmer the weather became. But Toro was almost as far south as anyone in the Three Kingdoms had ever been, and though the autumn moon had just risen, already he woke to frost covering the ground in the mornings. It was as though the weather was broken. It felt as though the world was broken.

Toro picked up his sword and tied it around his waist. He pulled the blade out, just a little, to ensure it still came smoothly out of the scabbard. He needn't have worried. Toro was a man who took care of the details, and his blade, a family heirloom hundreds of cycles old, still shone as though it had just come from the forge. Its presence comforted him. The world around him might shatter, but the sword would remain, solid and unyielding in a world of chaos.

Toro was grateful even to wake up. Every morning fewer of them did. Every night they came. No matter how many torches were lit, they still found the shadows. They struck at random, and it was becoming commonplace to wake up to find your bunkmate with a slit across his throat or a stake through his heart. Toro had lost dozens of men, but the fear was an even greater threat.

He took a deep breath, calming himself before the day ahead. Then he stepped out of his tent, disguising his shock at how cold it was outside. All around him, men moved with practiced discipline, purposeful in spite of their fear. Toro took a moment to look around, to recognize and remember the faces in the crowd. When he rejoined the Great Cycle, a day he feared was not long in coming, he would go knowing he was proud of the men with whom he served. The First was the best of the Southern Kingdom, and he was humbled to be their general.

Toro began his morning routine. He went to a space in the camp dedicated to practice, an open area that messengers and soldiers avoided walking through. He was pleased to see the space was filled with men practicing. Although the area was crowded, the soldiers all made room for him. He drew a few stares, but by now his men were familiar with his routine.

Toro drew his blade. He never practiced with wooden swords. He hadn't for many cycles. Steel was all that mattered. He made a few cuts, warming up his body and mentally checking his form. For as long as he could remember he had been pursuing the perfect cut, the cut that would sing out as he struck. As his body, hardened by cycle after cycle of hard use, started to loosen, his movements and patterns became more intricate. His body remembered every cut, every step. The world around him shrank until it was just him and his sword, and then even that distinction became meaningless.

When he finished sweat was dripping from his body, but he didn't even notice. Sights and sounds slowly returned, and Toro was among his men once again. As sometimes happened, some of his men had stopped to watch. Toro still believed he was one of the better swords in the Southern Kingdom. He didn't have the speed or strength of the younger men, but his experience triumphed over their physical ability. His men were welcome to watch and learn.

His practice complete, Toro went about the daily business of commanding an army. His first task was to the walls. The First was stationed at Fort Azuma, the fort built by Lord Akira at the southern end of the Three Sisters. Toro walked with his back straight and his head up. Especially in these trying times, his men needed to see their general confident.

He was greeted by the same sight that had tormented him for the last few days. Out there, in the Azarian plains, beyond the reach of his strongest bow, was a sea of humanity. The Azarians had come with a strength no one in the Three Kingdoms had ever dreamed possible. There were tens of thousands of them, more than could be counted. Men, women, and children. The female nightblade, Moriko, had been right: Azaria had brought their entire nation to make war on the Three Kingdoms.

If it had just been the clans Toro and his men had gotten used to fighting, it would be different. Fort Azuma covered the entire pass, and during the summer without conflict, its walls had been strengthened and made taller. Though Toro's troops were outnumbered at least ten to one, they might have held. But the hunters changed everything. It was the hunters who came in the night, unseen, killing his men as though it were a game played among children, a lethal game of hide and seek.

Toro had no answer to the hunters. He had doubled and tripled patrols, and lit torches throughout the camp until he worried they would run out of fire before they ran out of food. His men still didn't sleep at night for fear their lives would be taken without a fight. The hunters would break his men long before the army beyond the walls would.

Toro stared in frustration at the army, thinking that if he just studied them long enough, a solution would come to mind. But none ever did.

As he watched, a youth ran from the camp towards the fort, bow in hand. The shouts of the warriors behind him carried to Toro's ears. He shook his head. They played this game every morning. The youth sprinted towards the fort, all alone on the plains that had seen so much death. Toro heard the grunts from the archers that held the wall, but their discipline held. He had ordered them not to shoot at these individual taunts unless their shot was sure. There was no need to waste arrows.

The youth got close, closer than any who had come before. They are getting bolder, Toro thought to himself. Were they restless in the other camp? The youth aimed at Toro, as they always did. His uniform was different than the rest, and if they didn't know he was the general, they knew he was important. The arrow flew, a lone dark streak against a cloudless and uncaring blue sky.

Toro watched the arrow, amazed again by the strength of the Azarian bows and archers. The youth was just inside the edge of his archers' range, and none of them felt confident enough to take the shot. The arrow dropped down, and Toro instinctively stepped back as the arrow clattered against the stone wall of the fort just below him. The boy had only missed by two paces. Toro shook his head, but waved nonetheless. He might as well torment them a bit while he could. They would come soon enough.

Toro sat in his tent, going over his correspondence and reports for the day. When he was younger he had thought the role of a general was to give inspiring speeches and lead men into battle. He had never guessed his greatest enemy would be day-to-day paperwork. The process didn't bring him joy, but it was his eye for detail that kept his army fed, supplied and prepared to fight the enemy who threatened the Southern Kingdom.

Toro ran his well-practiced hands through the papers, memorizing stockpile information, scouting reports of the surrounding area, and the number of troops and their distribution. He paused to consider the morale reports his commanders had given. The news wasn't surprising. The men were close to breaking, but Toro had no ideas for stopping the hunters.

He didn't consider himself to be an excellent strategist. Lord Akira's two younger generals, Makoto and Mashiro, were much better. But Toro had a lifetime of experience and could put together disparate pieces of information to create a whole picture of what was happening to his army. Unfortunately, the conclusions he was reaching weren't pleasant. They were holding, but unless something happened soon, discipline would break.

Since he had no grand ideas, he pushed the thoughts out of mind. He saved his personal correspondence for last, both because he looked forward to it and because he feared it. Toro opened the unfamiliar letter first, not surprised when he saw it came from his new lord, Tanak. He couldn't bring himself to put the honorific to Tanak's name. It was Tanak who had invaded the Southern Kingdom, killed thousands of soldiers, and left Toro alone in the south to defend against the much more dangerous enemy. The man didn't deserve the title of lord.

Toro read the letter once in disbelief, then a second time to ensure he hadn't been imagining the orders the first time. The letter ordered Toro to stand down and retreat from Fort Azuma. The First was to return up the pass, where they could meet with Tanak's advisers to discuss the new command structure of Toro's army. Tanak would send a small exploratory force down to the fort to meet with any Azarians and negotiate a lasting treaty.

Toro swore to himself. Tanak's decision was wrong, and he was placed again in a situation where he had to decide between his duty and the right action. The last time had been in the spring, when Lord Akira had left him here. At the time, Toro thought Akira was making a mistake, but that mistake was now the only thing standing between tens of thousands of Azarians and the Three Kingdoms. Or the Two Kingdoms, whatever they were calling it now.

The only reason that Toro could imagine Tanak would order the First back was because he didn't believe Toro's reports. He must think they were some part of a plot to give the newly merged kingdom into Akira's hands. But nothing could be further from the truth. If Tanak doubted the sincerity of Toro's reports, Toro would delight in stationing his new lord on the wall. Then when the arrows started to fall he would at least do some good as a shield.

He shook his head. Such thinking wasn't right. Personally, he might detest Tanak, but Tanak was his rightful lord, and as general of the First, he was sworn to obey. But if he did, the Three Kingdoms would lose their best defense. Tanak's letter implied any possible aggression from the Azarians was due to the Three Kingdoms' encroachment on their land, but Toro didn't believe that argument for a moment. You didn't bring fifty thousand troops to the field of battle to take over a single fort. You sent them to take over a new land.

Toro pushed his frustrated thoughts aside. The decision could be made later. He glanced with eagerness at the second letter. It bore Lord Akira's seal and was written in his hand. Toro opened it carefully and found the contents to be much different than those of the first letter. Toro was surprised when he read it. Lord Akira was asking Toro to come home. Not the army, just Toro himself. He knew the next cycle would be a time of great struggle, and he wanted Toro by his side, helping him lead the fight against the Azarians.

The letter ended on a personal note, discussing Akira's thoughts on his truce with Tanak. Toro couldn't fault Akira for his decision to surrender. He wished there could have been a different outcome, but Toro wasn't sure he could have done better. Lord Akira had made the best decision possible considering the circumstances. It wasn't ideal, but it gave them a chance to survive.

Toro gently put the letter down, scratching his long beard, lost in thought. The offer was a tempting one. It meant life instead of death, and his heart, still in love with the idea of a long life, begged him to take his lord up on his offer. It was easy to rationalize. He was the most experienced general in both the Western and Southern Kingdoms. His experience was invaluable. But the wiser part of Toro believed the decision and the order were wrong. He was not the best strategist in the Southern Kingdom. If a military solution to the problem facing them existed, it wouldn't come from him but from Makoto or Mashiro.

Toro believed a general needed to lead his army. It was a part of him, a belief which shaped his life. To abandon his army in the time of its greatest need would be tantamount to spiritual suicide. Even if only a part of his men stayed to defend the fort from the invading army, Toro knew he would remain with the men who stayed and fought. He could not ask any man to lay down his life if he wasn't willing to himself.

A single tear threatened to moisten Toro's cheek. He wiped it away dismissively, steeling himself for the reply he would have to make. Lord Akira's offer, generous as it was, had solidified his decision. He lit a new candle, knowing there would be much to say in this letter. It would be the last he wrote to his lord, a man he almost considered a son. He had much to say, and he knew his time was running out. He trusted Lord Akira would be satisfied with his decision.

Toro got to work, writing his final letter. He found that with his decision made, his soul was more at rest than it had been for some time. He wrote until his candle burned low, and just as night and darkness threatened to overtake his tent, he snuffed it out himself.

Another morning came, and fewer of his men were alive to see it. After his daily stint on the wall, Toro went down to see the pyre lit for the men who had lost their lives in the night. Toro shook his head. Dying in your bedroll at night, sleeping, wasn't the way to leave this life. A soldier should die with a blade in his hand, an enemy snarling in his face. This type of warfare had no honor.

Toro searched the faces around him as the pyre burned the bodies to ashes. The men were tense and afraid, more so than he had seen them before. He couldn't blame them. He felt the same way they did. It was one thing to know you might die in battle the next day, but it was quite another to know, deep in your bones, that if you went to sleep there was a very real chance you might never wake up. It was the fear of the elderly instilled in the hearts of the young.

As he watched, Toro knew his men only had a few days of discipline left in them. Unless their circumstances changed, it wouldn't be long before men tried to work their way back through the pass on their own. Here they died in their sleep having accomplished nothing. The worst part was, Toro couldn't change their situation. Leading a sortie beyond the wall would be suicide and would accomplish nothing, but for now it was the only way to inflict damage on their foe. Toro cursed Nameless, the commander of the Azarians. With hunters, Nameless could pick off his men one by one until they broke. It took longer than a direct attack would have, but it risked far fewer lives. Taking Fort Azuma would be a bloody battle if Nameless used traditional means.

That afternoon a scout came back from the pass with news. Toro welcomed him into his tent. The scout was obviously cold, and icicles still hung from his uniform. "Sir, there is a blizzard in the pass. It seems likely to stay, sir."

Toro considered the news. It was still early for the pass to have so much snow, but not unheard of. It opened up new possibilities for him. If the pass closed with snow early, no army would get through until spring, allowing the Three Kingdoms and Lord Akira more time to prepare a worthy defense after a summer full of war. Toro grinned maliciously. Nameless and his hunters might whittle down his men, but if they continued to take their time, they'd find their progress blocked by the pass itself.

"How much longer do we have?"

"Sir, we can't be sure, but our best guess is three days, maybe less. After that, no army will be getting through the pass."

Toro paced his tent. The scout came from a unit that specialized in the Three Sisters. They were older men, experienced in the ways of the mountains and their volatile weather. He had to trust their judgment. If they said three days, three days was all they had.

"Thank you. Make sure you get some warm food before heading back up."

The scout looked grateful. "Yes, sir."

Toro wandered the fort, studying his men carefully. They were determined, and they were proud, but they had never faced anything like the hunters before. Many of his men who weren't on watch were sound asleep, grateful to sleep during the hours the sun shone overhead, protecting their slumber better than their fellow soldiers could at night. With a deep sigh, Toro made his decision. He called the commanders together.

"Gentlemen, the last few days have been tough on us all. I hate to see our men taken in such a cowardly fashion. However, as you all know, events to the north have been dramatic, shifting the balance of power back in the land we call home. Our new lord, Tanak, has ordered the First back up through the pass."

Murmurs ran through the small group. Toro let them have a moment before he continued.

"It is clear to me politics are interfering with the safety of our kingdom. You all have seen the threat the Azarians pose. Too many of us have already paid the ultimate price, but Tanak would have us abandon our post, abandon the best defense of the Southern Kingdom."

Toro's voice had risen, and there were murmurs of anger matching his own. Toro let them stew for a moment before continuing, his tone now subdued.

"The fact is, gentlemen, as much as I wish it weren't so, Fort Azuma is lost. I don't question the bravery or the skill of our men, but these hunters are tearing us apart, and we are outnumbered ten to one, even without them. Even the most brilliant defense of this fort is doomed to fail. I won't mislead you."

"The good news is that the mountains themselves are on our side. As some of you may know, the pass is closing as we speak. Already the return will be treacherous. We only need to hold the enemy here for a day, maybe two, and we will succeed in giving the Three Kingdoms and Lord Akira enough time to mount a true defense of the land."

"Gentlemen, serving as your general has been an honor. I couldn't ask for a stronger, more honorable group of men. My orders are to march the First back to the Southern Kingdom, and I will see those orders fulfilled. Tomorrow morning I will officially order everyone north."

The murmurs became louder, and Toro knew he had them in the palm of his hand.

"That being said, I will not be going with you. I intend to stay here on the walls and give my life to protect your retreat. I will be disobeying orders from my rightful lord, and the punishment for that is death. I expect there will be those who will dishonor my name, and that I accept. If anyone would like to desert with me and man these walls, I would be grateful. There may be a few too many Azarians for me to take on by myself."

The joke was perfectly timed, causing a ripple of laughter to spread throughout the group. Toro would miss these men.

"Men, make it clear to everyone. If you stay with me, you will be considered deserters. That way, no one who returns will see trouble on our account. I don't need many men. A few hundred should suffice. There is no dishonor in following orders and returning north.

I expect each and every man of the First to show these Azarians what it means to be of the Southern Kingdom next spring. Make it clear that if they stay, there won't be any return. We will pay the price for desertion here in this fort. Are there any questions?"

The men looked at one another, silent. It began with one of the men near the front, who bowed all the way to the ground, his forehead against the cold ground of the fort. One by one the other men followed, until every man in the room had his face pressed against the earth. Toro looked out over them all and a tear came to his eye. At the end of his life he was proud. The Three Kingdoms were strong, filled with good, strong people like those before him. The Azarians would never win. Toro returned the gesture, holding his bow until every man had silently left the room.

Toro watched as the last of his men marched up the pass. It had been an orderly march, if one of the most heartbreaking he had ever observed. With him stood over three hundred men, those of the First who had elected to stay behind. There had been many partings, each of them made bittersweet by the knowledge they would never see each other again. Toro himself had wandered the camp almost all of yesterday, saying goodbye to each of the men. He was proud of them all, but none more than those who stayed behind.

He turned and looked over the men, grouped in formation. He had already assigned a command structure to them. Each of them knew what to do and who to report to. They would fight to the last man. Some had stayed to protect families. Some had stayed for honor, some for revenge, and a few because they felt they had nothing left to lose. Toro thought he should say something powerful, but found he couldn't speak without breaking down. So he nodded once instead. His men understood, and they went to the walls.

Toro had wondered how Nameless would react to so many of the First leaving the fort, and he didn't have long to wait to find out. That afternoon Azarian clans lined up to march towards the fort. Toro stood with his men. His armor shone in the cold sunlight. Today he was no more than another soldier. Today they were all bowmen, all swordsmen. When the charge commenced, Toro looked from side to side and said, "To protect our brothers."

The saying was passed up and down the line. The men drew their bowstrings back, and at Toro's command, the defense of Fort Azuma began.

The Azarians had little battle discipline. That had always been true, as long as Toro had fought them. But what they lacked in discipline they made up in bravery. Once they began their charge, they broke formation, each running fearlessly into danger. Toro launched his first arrow, and it was joined by hundreds of others, dark streaks of death against the blue sky. Azarians fell, but it made no difference as they ran for the walls. Toro and his men launched another flight just as an answering flight came up from the Azarian archers. While Toro's arrows came down on the Azarians in waves, their response was individual, each archer trying their luck against the soldiers of the First.

Men started to fall to each side of Toro, but most were protected by the stone of the fort. When the first Azarians started climbing the walls, a handful of men laid down their bows and picked up rocks to drop on them. Stone was plentiful in the pass, and a well-dropped heavy stone could take out two or three climbers.

It was only a matter of time before the sheer number of attackers overwhelmed Toro's troops. When climbers reached the top they would throw down ropes to assist others. Toro dropped his bow and drew his sword, rushing from place to place on the wall, hacking at ropes and slicing at opponents. Dozens of his men stood behind him in the courtyard of the fort, sending arrows into the Azarians who made it over the top of the walls.

Time blurred until it became meaningless. There was only the space in front of him. Twice, three times, the Azarians managed to get a foothold on the walls, and each time Toro's men surged forward in response. But each time there were fewer and fewer men to answer the calls for aid. Toro could hardly see the steel of his blade, it was covered in so much blood.

Evening fell early in the valley, and at first Toro was confused when there was no one left to fight. When his wits returned, he heard the call of the horn and saw the Azarians retreating for the evening. He was grateful. He had worried that Nameless knew the pass was closing. If he did, he would have never stopped, even if they had lost the light. Time was on Toro's side. If they could hold out for one more day, they would stop the Azarian invasion in its tracks.

The price had been high. Of the three hundred or so who had begun the fight, not even a hundred remained. Toro looked with pleasure at the Azarian bodies on the plains, but even though Toro's men had acquitted themselves well, they had barely reduced the sheer number of warriors Nameless had at his disposal.

That night the men were quiet around the fires. None of them would sleep that night. Between the combat and the fear of hunters, each would stay awake, maybe drifting off just for a moment or two before their partner next to them gently nudged them.

Toro worried the hunters would come to finish the siege, but it seemed that Nameless was holding them back. Toro wasn't sure why, but he was grateful. That night they rested undisturbed around the fires. Their food was simple, most of the supplies having gone back with the First, but it was still the best Toro remembered tasting.

He took in every breath, focusing only on the present moment. It was a beautiful moment, resting around a fire with the men he would die with tomorrow. They all knew, and all shared a look of calm acceptance. Above them, the stars were clear, and Toro could easily pick out the soldier and the princess, his favorite sets of stars. It was as much as he could have asked for on his final evening alive.

The sun rose over the peaks the next morning, but the only way Toro could tell was that he could see the faint outline of his shadow on the ground. The snow had come down from the pass and was starting to collect here in the valley. There was only a little on the ground, but the sky was gray and lifeless above them. It was a dreary day to die.

The snow must have warned Nameless that he had little time to get through the pass, because the entire mass of Azarians was on the move. Toro watched with a detached interest. It was an impressive feat to move so many so far.

There had been little to say this morning. Each man covered a section of the wall, and it was their responsibility alone. No help would come today. No archers stood behind them in the courtyard, and there were no reserves to call for aid. Toro's only command had been to take as many Azarians to the Great Cycle with them as they could. They had to hold the fort as long as possible. If they could delay even until the sun was high in the sky, it should be enough time. Toro hoped his own men had made it through the pass. The snow that came down whipped across the fort. Shooting arrows would be a matter of luck today. But that was better for Toro than for his enemy. Toro had far more targets to hit.

The Azarians approached. Again, Toro's men sent arrow after arrow into the crowd. They were to use as many as they could. Toro fired indiscriminately. The whole valley was a mass of humanity pushing against the fort. He fell into a rhythm. Nock, pull, release. Nock, pull, release. He didn't even aim, just sent arrows flying haphazardly against his enemy. There was almost no chance he could miss. Then he grabbed for an arrow and none were left. He dropped his bow and drew his sword, just in time for the first Azarians to break over the wall.

The fighting was close and bloody, but Toro moved like he never had before. There was no chance of surviving this battle, and when hope died, so did fear. Toro moved with a grace he had never before possessed, and Azarian after Azarian fell before his blade.

Then he was shoved off the wall, falling into a pile of hay below. As he came to his senses, he realized the last of his men were being slaughtered, and that he was alone in a circle of Azarians. They made no move to strike at him, though. Something held them back, and Toro began to dread meeting the only person with that kind of power.

Toro had listened to Moriko's tales of Nameless when she returned from Azaria, but he had never really believed her. She didn't seem like the type of person prone to exaggeration, but the description she gave of the commander of the Azarians was hard to believe. But when Toro saw Nameless in person, he realized she hadn't exaggerated, not at all. The man was huge, towering over Toro, a pillar of muscle and death. Even with his enormous size, he moved with grace and silence. Toro held his blade in front of him, but never had the action seemed so insignificant to him.

"You are the commander of this fort?"

Toro nodded. If he was going to die, it would be a legendary battle. He was pleased. He was a strong sword, and he was curious to see just how good these hunters were.

"Your men fought well. We will bring stories of their courage to your land."

Toro was surprised. He hadn't expected such magnanimity. "Thank you."

"Come, let us end this. I will give you the warrior's death you deserve."

Toro settled into his stance. He would show this Azarian the meaning of strength. If he could kill Nameless here, he could stop this invasion for good. Moriko had gotten a cut on him, so it couldn't be that hard.

Toro moved in, leading with a perfect cut, the cut he had been searching for his entire life. Then Nameless moved, too fast for Toro to follow. For just a moment, everything was in motion, and then the world stilled again. Toro stood there, confused. Had he cut Nameless? His opponent had been right there in front of him. How had Nameless gotten behind him? Had he won?

He tried to turn his head, but found he couldn't. The world started spinning as his head fell from his shoulders, a sensation his dying mind finally recognized. He wasn't afraid. He had lived his entire life in the shadow of death and had come to terms with it. He was only saddened he hadn't put up more of a fight. Nameless truly was a warrior of amazing strength. Closing his eyes, he smiled with pleasure at a life well-lived, grateful to Nameless for giving him a warrior's death. His world went black, and at the last moment he felt the presence of all life, and then he rejoined the Great Cycle.

CHAPTER 1

Ryuu woke up from a dream where Akira was cutting at him with a sword. In the dream, Ryuu felt like he was trying to move through water instead of air, every motion agonizingly slow. Darkness clouded the edge of his vision, creeping steadily inward. When his world went dark he woke up, covered in sweat. He closed his eyes again and sighed. The sounds of the village came to his ears, and he took a moment to enjoy the reassuring sounds of daily routine.

The village was small, a collection of a few huts in the woods. Ryuu had stumbled upon it as he wandered west. He didn't even remember its name. He had offered to help an older couple with chores in exchange for a place to sleep for the night, and they'd been delighted to oblige. They put him up in a room that had belonged to their son, off now fighting in the wars that ravaged the kingdom.

The hut was filled with sadness. The couple smiled often enough, and were very kind, but Ryuu could tell there was an emptiness in the house. It was the same emptiness he sometimes felt in his own hut, many leagues away. It was the void left when a loved one leaves and does not return. The couple missed their son and had no idea if he was alive or dead. He was a member of the First, stationed down in the Three Sisters. Ryuu didn't have the heart to tell them about the advancing Azarian invasion. He suspected everyone would learn of it soon enough, and he couldn't bear to bring more sadness to his hosts.

Ryuu didn't dare practice his forms in the village, and if he was being honest with himself, he didn't have the heart for it. It would only be a matter of time before riders came through the village with wanted posters bearing his face. He didn't need to help them by drawing attention to himself. Instead, he split wood for the couple, happy to help out in exchange for shelter. As he swung the ax he fell into a meditative rhythm, and he shut out the world.

It was past midday when he took his leave of the couple and followed the road again. Perhaps he should have been in more of a hurry, but he needed the time to think, and there was no better time than while on the road. Walking cleared his mind and allowed him to focus on the events of the past few moons.

As he walked he tried to use his sense, but it still refused to cooperate. It hadn't worked since his final fight with Renzo. His ankle still twinged a little when he walked on it, but it was nothing compared to the nakedness he felt as he walked through the woods without his sense. Ryuu didn't know what had happened. All he knew was that when he awoke from the battle he couldn't use his gift. He had tried meditating every day for a while, but when it hadn't created any results, he gradually stopped trying. Now he barely attempted it at all.

The woods were beautiful. Reds, oranges, and yellows were everywhere. It was almost winter, and most of the leaves had fallen, but there were still enough in the trees that one would have to be blind not to appreciate their beauty. Even so, the woods seemed stark and barren to Ryuu. He knew he was surrounded by life, but for the first time since he was a young child, he couldn't feel any of it. To his remaining senses, he may as well have been alone in the woods.

He was returning to Moriko, but he wasn't sure what would happen when he did. He was a different man than when he had last seen her. Not only had he been to the island, but he had found incredible strength and then lost it. Would she still care for him if he wasn't strong enough? The last time he had sensed her, he could tell she, too, had changed. She was stronger, more dangerous than ever before. And he was broken.

Ryuu's thoughts raced round and round as he walked. He thought of Shigeru and Takako, those he had loved and lost. He thought of Moriko, the love he was afraid he had lost. And he thought of Renzo, Shika, Rei, Tenchi and all the other nightblades he had met on the island. There was so much conflict, so many dreams colliding with one another in the Three Kingdoms. All he wanted was to live in peace.

He slept outdoors for the next two nights, not coming across any more villages. It was getting cold, but he had enough gear to sleep comfortably for a while yet. On the third day he crossed paths with a military unit, marching to the east. Their uniforms were those of the Western Kingdom, the new conquerors of the Southern Kingdom. He stepped off the road, careful to hide his face from their eyes. They paid him no mind. His sword was hidden on his back and he was dressed in poor traveling clothes. He would look to be no more than a peasant to them. In fact, he smiled grimly, he really was no more than a peasant anymore. Without the sense he wasn't a nightblade anymore. He found the idea didn't bother him as much as it once had.

As they passed, Ryuu had a strange thought. They couldn't call the land the Three Kingdoms anymore. There weren't three kingdoms. Would they call it the Two Kingdoms? Ryuu shook his head. It sounded wrong. And what would they call the land he was walking in? Would it be the Southern Kingdom or the Western Kingdom? He hadn't ever thought of it before, and wondered what was happening to the east, where the treaty was being signed.

The sounds of the forest returned as the troops marched away, and Ryuu pushed the thoughts out of his mind. It didn't really matter what they called the land. The only thing on his mind was Moriko. He needed to find her and figure out where they stood. The thought frightened him, but he had to know. He tightened the straps on his pack and kept moving forward.

The forest gradually turned into plains as Ryuu continued walking west. He knew if he kept going, he would eventually find woods again. As he expected, wanted posters started appearing, but they were few and far between, almost as though the effort to find him was half-hearted. He figured it was Akira's doing. He had to hunt Ryuu to satisfy the terms of the treaty, but his heart wasn't in it. Ryuu had taken the measure of Akira and found him to be an honorable man.

Ryuu had been on the road for almost a moon, and he guessed he was less than a hundred leagues away from the hut. He hadn't been moving fast, fear of his upcoming encounter with Moriko slowing his steps. But the day would come soon. He couldn't put it off forever.

Evening was falling, and a brisk wind told him it would be cold tonight. Ryuu could already feel it in his bones. He looked for some small hollow or brush he could spend the night in. As evening fell, Ryuu saw the flicker of a fire off in the distance. He walked towards it, hoping to share the warmth. When he approached, an older man invited him to join him by the fire. Ryuu gratefully accepted.

The old man was grizzled, long hair seeming to sprout at random from the tattered clothes that covered his body. He had the look of a man who had spent his life on the road, and Ryuu suspected the old man didn't have a place he called home. Even so, the man was kind and generous, and Ryuu immediately took to him.

"Where are you traveling to, young man?"

Ryuu hid his half-lie behind a grin. "To the south and west."

The old man shook his head. "Those are dangerous places. You would be better served to stay away."

Ryuu frowned. "What do you mean?"

The old man eyed him warily. "You haven't heard?"

Ryuu shook his head.

"There are all sorts of strange happenings west and south of here. Mind you, I've only heard rumors, but when one hears the same rumors from many different places, it's best to be wary. People say the roads aren't safe anymore, that travelers have gone missing. One of the crazier rumors I've heard is that an entire village disappeared."

Ryuu laughed. The old man had had him going for a moment. "Villages don't disappear, friend."

"No, but people do. The story I heard was from another traveler who had it from a village he'd been in. Apparently a little girl in the village went to sleep one night, and when she woke up the next morning the entire village was gone. Her parents, family, friends, everyone."

Ryuu served them each a bowl of stew that had been cooking over the fire. After the days of cold traveling, the warm broth was a welcome relief. They ate in silence for a few moments and Ryuu tried to decide if the old man was pulling his leg or if there was truth to the story.

The old man spoke again. "Anyway, you can believe me if you want. I'm heading north, away from the rumors, but you have the look of a man who can take care of himself."

Ryuu's eyes darted to the old man, suspicious.

The old man chuckled to himself. "I may be old, but these eyes have seen more than yours, and they don't miss much. You move silently, all the time, and that sword on your back isn't hidden from anyone who can use their two eyes."

Ryuu hesitated for a moment, wondering if he had walked into some sort of trap. But the eyes of the old man sparkled with mirth, and Ryuu accepted him at face value. He laughed softly and pulled his sword out and laid it by his side.

"You've sharp eyes, old man. I've traveled for hundreds of leagues and you're the first who has noticed."

The old man smiled. "People. They walk around all the time, but they don't see anything, not really. If people would just slow down and open their eyes, they would see an entire world they didn't know existed."

Ryuu nodded. He felt the same way about the sense.

Maybe it was the fire, or maybe it was the obvious mirth of the old man, but Ryuu found himself relaxing for the first time in over a moon. "So tell me, old man, if you're so observant, what do you see?"

The smile disappeared from the old man's face, and Ryuu knew he was looking at the old man as he was, not as he often appeared to be. Ryuu was reminded of Tenchi, cycles and cycles of wisdom hidden behind a grinning face.

"You're a warrior. The way you move can mean nothing else. But it's really your eyes that give you away. They never stop, they're always looking every direction. You've lived a life where you could be attacked at any moment. You've seen more than you should. There is little joy in your life at the moment, and if I had to guess, you are very lost."

Ryuu gave a short grunt in response, and there was a moment of silence.

The old man broke it. "And now you must return the favor. What do you see?"

Ryuu studied the man carefully. Despite his age, he moved with grace and strength. He handled a knife with a dexterity beyond a commoner. Ryuu gazed into his eyes, and he knew that at one time this man had been very dangerous, a soldier or a spy or an assassin. But not any longer. The old man had come to find peace with whatever was in his past, but he was always on the move, pursued by a history he'd rather forget. The old man saw Ryuu's gaze, and although Ryuu couldn't say how, he knew that the old man was aware Ryuu had guessed his past. Ryuu smiled.

"I think you're an old man who probably sees too much."

The old man laughed and served seconds of the stew. Ryuu had always believed food tasted better with friends, and the stew was excellent.

The next morning dawned cold, but Ryuu awoke more refreshed than he had in ages. He and the old man had talked late into the night. The traveler was already up and packing. Ryuu bowed to him as they left.

"May your journey north be safe."

The old man bowed in return. "And may you find peace."

Ryuu chuckled softly as the old man turned and walked away. He had decided the old man was right about the rumors, and he wondered what he was walking towards.

CHAPTER 2

Akira waited for Makoto and Mashiro to finish reading the documents. In front of them sat the final draft of the treaty that would merge the Southern Kingdom with the Western Kingdom. It was a long document, with hundreds of details that required close attention, and Akira fidgeted anxiously as he waited to hear what his two generals would think of it.

More than ever, Akira missed both Toro and Ryuu. The two of them couldn't be more different, but the one personality trait they shared was that they would tell him the truth, unconcerned about their status in his eyes. Makoto and Mashiro would get there, someday, but they still thought of him as a lord first and a person second.

When they had both put down the papers, Akira questioned them. "What do you think?"

"You have negotiated generous terms," Makoto answered.

Akira nodded. He agreed.

Mashiro, the more outspoken of the two, jumped in. "I don't trust any of it. These terms are too good to be true. He's allowing you to sit as second in line to the kingdom? And he's allowing it to be named the Southern Kingdom? I fear your life will be over not long after the ink is dry."

Makoto built on his friend's comments. "I agree. The terms seem too good for a victor to agree to. Is he worried about your people uprising against him?"

Akira shook his head. "No, he isn't that foolish. It's the military he worries about. His forces outnumber ours, slightly, but with the order for the First to return, the balance of power will shift. The First is our strongest army, and once they return, I could force his armies out of the kingdom. He knows his terms need to be generous for the alliance to work."

Mashiro stood up. "If that's the case, why don't we just use the First and crush his armies?" He paced angrily.

Akira raised an eyebrow. "You know we can't do that. If Toro's reports are true, and I have no reason to doubt them, we can't waste a single man on a civil war."

"It doesn't mean I need to like it. Your life will still be in danger."

Akira shook his head again. "Maybe someday, but not soon. If I die too soon after the treaty is signed, it will be suspicious. He'll need to keep me alive for a while, at least, if he wants this alliance to last. We have time."

Makoto spoke softly. "What do you think Toro will do?"

It was Akira's turn to stand up and pace the room. "I don't know. I asked him to return, but I've received no reply. There is a blizzard in the pass threatening to close it early. I fear we may not hear what happened to the First."

There was commotion outside Akira's command tent. A messenger entered.

"The First has emerged from the pass, my lord. News just came from riders, still covered in snow. They barely made it through."

Akira's initial reaction was one of joy. It would be good to see Toro again. But the news also meant the pass would be undefended for the first time in over sixty cycles. Akira feared what the next spring would bring.

The messenger continued. "There are letters from General Toro, my lord. He did not come through the pass with the First."

Akira's heart sank. He grabbed the letters from the messenger and dismissed him. Makoto and Mashiro watched in silence as Akira read the letters. He scanned them quickly and threw them to the ground in anger.

"That honorable fool!"

Silence settled over the small group as Akira raged. It was Makoto, the soft-spoken giant, who asked, "What happened, my lord?"

"He stayed behind with a few hundred soldiers to defend the retreat of the First. He knew they couldn't hold the fort against the Azarians. They were getting picked off one at a time by hunters. He sent the First back so they could better defend the kingdom, but he stayed behind, even though I asked him to return."

No one spoke, honoring Toro's memory with silence. He had been one of their best: experienced, thoughtful and strong.

Akira straightened. "I'm going to need some time. Would you two ensure the First is given the same orders as the Second and the Third? Give them time to go home and rest. They will be needed soon enough. Find out how solid their command structure is. I'll want recommendations for commanders in front of me before the treaty is signed."

The two generals bowed low and left the tent. Akira scooped up the letters he had thrown down and organized them neatly. He wanted to throw them in the flames, but they were the last words from a man who was as close to a friend as a lord could have. He couldn't bring himself to destroy them. Instead, he sat down and started reading them again, carefully, savoring every word. His eyes blurred with tears, but he wiped them away and kept reading.

Akira sat in the tent next to his own, looking down at one of the most beautiful women he had ever met. Today all he could see was her back, but even so, he still found her lovely. Her back was bare except for the makeshift bandages covering the deep cut that went across her spine and the back of her arm. Not only had the cut paralyzed her, it had also gotten infected. Several times a day Akira's best healers came in and cared for her, but still he wasn't sure if she would live or not. It had been almost a half moon since the attack, and still she clung tenuously to life.

Rei stirred slightly, and Akira knew she was awake.

"How do you feel?"

Rei turned her head to look at him. She grimaced at the pain the movement caused, but she didn't cry out. She was strong, although her voice was soft.

"I've had better days."

Akira smiled despite himself. Even in incredible pain, she still kept her attitude. He was humbled.

His thoughts were interrupted by her question. "How is your day going?"

"I've had better days."

She laughed and then sucked in her breath. "Oh, that hurts."

Akira continued, trying to distract her. "Tomorrow Tanak and I sign the treaty to join our two kingdoms. I know it is the right thing to do, but still the action pains me. It is a bitter task to give up my throne."

"Perhaps, but it is the only thing you can do to save your people."

A silence settled in the room. Akira had come here with purpose, but now that the moment was at hand, he found himself nervous.

"And what about you? What do you want to do next?"

Rei sighed. "I'm not sure. I miss my home, but I can't think of any way to return, not without betraying the trust of my people. I fear I'll never hold a sword again. It's hard to admit, but I'll need to find a new path for my life."

"Any ideas?"

Rei moved her head just a little from side to side. "No. Being a warrior is all I've ever known. I've forgotten what other dreams I used to have."

It was an impulse, but Akira blurted out, "You could stay here with me."

Rei shook her head again. "A nightblade and a lord? Our time has been enjoyable, and I wish it could be otherwise, but for the good of your kingdom we cannot continue. Also," she gave a mischievous grin, "I'm paralyzed from the waist down, and don't think I'd be as much fun as I once was."

Akira knew she was right. He didn't know what it was about Rei that made him take leave of his senses, but there was no way he could take a nightblade as a consort, much less a wife.

Akira stood up. "Rest well. I will come again before I leave to sign the treaty."

Rei smiled. "Thank you, for all your care."

Akira left the tent, thoughts wandering through his head, wondering how it had come to be the woman he cared for was a fugitive in his own kingdom.

The morning of the treaty signing dawned cold and cloudy. Akira worried that a storm was on the way. It was early for blizzards, but this season had all the marks of becoming one of the coldest in memory. Though it was only late fall, Akira was already bundled in layers of furs to keep himself warm. It had been a long time since he had felt so cold.

As Akira rode towards the field where the treaty would be signed, he realized he felt empty inside, as though giving away his kingdom meant giving away a part of himself. When he saw Tanak's banners snapping in the wind, a surge of hatred ran through him. This was the man who had ordered the slaughter of thousands of Akira's soldiers, the man who had broken a treaty that had protected the Three Kingdoms for over a thousand cycles.

As bitter as the task was, Akira had no choice but to move forward. The Azarians were a fearsome enemy, and he'd have to bury his hatred of Tanak to defend the people of his kingdom. He dismounted easily from his horse and motioned his honor guard to remain behind. The tent had been placed in the middle of an empty field, and while both Tanak and Akira had brought their personal troops with them, the soldiers stayed away. Rumors of the treaty signing had leaked out, and people were scattered around, watching the tent with curiosity. It was the first new treaty in over a thousand cycles.

Akira stepped into the tent alone and was immediately buffeted by the warmth of the space. Tanak had lit a fire and the tent was warm and cozy. Akira threw off his cloaks, grimacing in pain. When he tried to kill Ryuu, the nightblade had let him live, but his cuts had been deep. It still hurt to move.

"Akira."

"Tanak."

A tense silence hung in the tent, thick enough to cut. The two of them didn't like each other, but this treaty was necessary. Akira moved further into the tent and sat next to Tanak.

"Do you find the terms for the treaty acceptable?"

Tanak nodded. "I do."

"Shall we get this over with then?"

Tanak shook his head. "You may remember that part of our agreement was that you would kill the nightblade in your camp. I see you didn't bring any heads with you."

Akira silently stripped off his shirt, displaying the giant red scars that crossed his chest. "I honored our word. I said I would try to kill him myself. However, he left me alive. He escaped, but my men are hunting him. I have done all I can to fulfill the terms of our agreement."

Tanak sat and stared at Akira for a long time. Akira had a hard time believing Tanak would throw everything away over the fate of one nightblade. His invasion forces had retreated, a ways at least, and with the First up from the pass, Akira had more troops than Tanak in the kingdom. Time had passed and tables had turned. It was too late for Tanak to order Akira around, and he knew it.

"You wanted to die, didn't you?"

Akira glanced up, surprised at the question. He met Tanak's gaze. "I am the first lord to have lost his kingdom to invasion in the history of the Three Kingdoms. I am dishonored."

Tanak weighed Akira's answer. "And now?"

"The Azarian threat needs to be dealt with. Once I am certain my people are safe and well-governed, I may once again seek the Great Cycle. But until then, I am needed."

Tanak considered Akira's response. After a few moments of silence a smile broke out on his face and he started laughing. "Akira, you are too much. I will say this for you, your precious honor has been a great help to me."

Tanak looked over the treaties one last time. There were three copies. One for each kingdom and one for the monasteries. It was only a moment's work, but Tanak signed them all and turned them over to Akira. Akira scanned them himself, making sure the key terms of the treaty were unchanged, but everything looked to be in place. He held the quill in his hand, hesitating at the last moment.

Tanak watched with interest, but Akira was glad he maintained his silence. If the other lord had said anything it might have been too much for Akira. With a single stroke he would give away his entire kingdom, the work of his entire life. But there was no other way. He signed the papers, and the Western Kingdom and the Southern Kingdom became one new kingdom. It would still be called the Southern Kingdom, but it wasn't the land he was born or raised in. It was something new, and hopefully stronger.

Akira leaned away from the table. "It is done."

Tanak made as if to leave, but Akira gestured for him to stay. "What will be done about the Azarians?"

Tanak laughed. "They are your phantoms, Akira. I have sent spies down into Azaria, and they report the Azarians wanted nothing more than to reclaim the land south of the pass. Now that you have abandoned Fort Azuma, I expect hostilities will cease. My first act as lord of the Southern Kingdom will be to ride south and present a formal treaty to the leader of the Azarians."

Akira couldn't believe what he was hearing. "Are you serious? The Three Sisters is closed."

"Yes, but my scouts report some of the game trails are still open. It's not enough for an army, but a small party can get through. I will take a small force, but I have already sent envoys, and they have been well received."

Akira's head was spinning. "But they have hunters."

"And nightblades are clearly running all over our land, so we have nothing to fear. I will establish a new peace that will last for lifetimes."

Akira was trying to understand what Tanak was saying. If he was speaking the truth, it cast doubt on over sixty cycles of combat between the Azarians and the Southern Kingdom. Had his people really been the aggressors? It wasn't logical. Toro had written of a host of Azarians almost beyond count. It was much more than was needed to take Fort Azuma, especially if there were hunters in the party. No, Akira was missing something, but he didn't know what it could be.

"Tanak, I think you are making a mistake. We need to gather our forces and prepare for the upcoming war. The Azarians will be here in the spring and we need to be ready for them."

"We don't need to be ready for them. I will treat with their leader, and when I come back, we will have peace."

Akira saw he had no hope of changing Tanak's mind. He couldn't shake the feeling there was something more he was missing, but without any idea what it was, he had no options. As much as it pained him to do so, his new role was to obey.

"Very well. What would you have of me while you are away?"

"Lead the hunt for the nightblade. Work on the successful merger of the kingdoms. I want some of the goods from the Southern Kingdom sent into the Western Kingdom. If this is going to work, our people need to be united as one. I will station several of my closest advisers with you, and if there are any challenges, we can deal with them when I return."

"As you will, my lord."

Tanak laughed. "Have no fear, Akira. This partnership will work."

CHAPTER 3

Nameless stood on the walls of his newly-won fort and looked south into Azaria. He wondered what those who had stood here before him had thought. Had they believed they were looking on a savage and barren land? Nameless had never known any land but Azaria. Even as they made plans to depart, he would always consider it home. There was a part of him that felt regret. Not for the blood he had spilled or the battle that would come, but regret that the only way he had found to save his people was to leave their homeland. He wished there was another way, but nothing occurred to him.

The sun was high in the sky, but still the freezing winds blew down from the pass. The blizzard had been raging for days, and the scouts who braved the pass reported inhospitable conditions. Deep snow and avalanches had already cost Nameless some of his best scouts. In the plains below the fort his people were camped, but daily it seemed they retreated against the onslaught of the cold. Nameless feared the coming winter. The demon-kind were already ranging far and wide to bring in enough food for the camp, and he worried they wouldn't bring enough to maintain solidarity through the season. The People were not meant to stay in one place.

But those were decisions for another day. Nameless had to give credit to the man who had commanded this fort. His men stood firm against the demon-kind, refusing to break ranks though many were killed night after night. Even more impressive, the commander had held the fort for over a full day with only a few hundred men. He had given his retreating army time to make it through the pass before it closed for the winter.

Nameless could have killed them all that first day, but he had made the decision to leave the final assault of the fort to the clans, not the demon-kind. His first strategy had been to send in the demon-kind only. From what he knew of the people of the Three Kingdoms, he had expected the army to shatter after a few days of the attacks. He had hoped to take the fort without casualties to the clans. It had all gone to plan, except the army holding the fort had not broken as he had expected. There was a steel within the men he hadn't predicted.

Then the news came that most of the army was retreating and the pass was closing. Nameless decided to let the clans have their chance at taking the fort. It meant a greater loss of life, but Nameless assumed with only a few hundred men guarding the walls, the clans would be able to take it easily. The People needed to remember this wasn't just about the demon-kind. This was a victory for all of them. He had held his demon-kind back, but again he had underestimated his opponents. They had held for a full day. It hadn't been much, but it had been enough. Now he was stuck on the wrong side of the Three Sisters as winter settled in.

Nameless rolled his shoulders back and sighed. There was little to do about it now. Their only choice was to wait. With any luck, spring would come early. He had made a mistake, but the past couldn't be changed. Only this moment mattered.

He had sent twenty pairs of demon-kind through the Southern Kingdom over the game trails that were just barely open. Their orders were specific. They were to spread fear and terror throughout the Southern Kingdom. Nameless might not be able to lead the People across the pass this winter, but when they marched in the spring, he expected to find a land torn apart by fear. The army had held, but the people of the Three Kingdoms never would. They were too weak. Nameless smiled. He was delayed, but he wouldn't fail his people.

Nameless was out in the fields watching some of the clans train when a messenger came to find him. The messenger was one of his demon-kind, and from the snow still on his shoulders, Nameless assumed he'd come from the mountains.

"Yes?"

"An envoy comes from the Three Kingdoms. It is a small group, ten strong. They are taking one of the game trails through the mountains we have been watching."

"Is it him?"

The messenger shook his head. "We do not recognize any of the riders, and none of them are gifted. At least one is richly dressed though."

Nameless considered this for a moment. "How long until they are in sight of the People?"

The messenger thought about the question. "They are making slow progress. The trail is hard. Perhaps two or three days. More if the trail worsens."

Nameless debated what to do. His gut warned him against letting them see the mass of forces arrayed against them. If an enemy envoy was to reach the clans, it might spread further dissension among the ranks. He was already concerned about several clans after the escape of the female nightblade. Best to meet them in the mountains. "Can you guide me there?"

The messenger nodded, almost as though he was offended Nameless would ask the question.

"We will leave immediately. Find two others to come who have strong bows. I will meet you here."

It took little time for them to gather. Nameless approved of the other demon-kind who had volunteered. He had known both for many cycles, and their skill with a bow was excellent. Their quivers were full and their clothes were warm. Without a word they took off for the mountains.

The trail was hard, and it wasn't long before they abandoned their horses. Azarians prided themselves on their horsemanship, but they were riders of the plains, not of the mountains. Demon-kind could move faster on foot over the narrow trails that wound through the heights. Nameless set the pace, a steady march that ate up the distance between him and the envoy. His side still ached from where the accursed woman had gotten the best of him, but he relished the pain. It was a reminder that for a moment he had let down his guard. He had beaten her, but not by enough. Never again would he give anyone the chance to hurt him.

They ran through the day and night until they came to a place where they could see the trail for hundreds of paces. Nameless pointed to an outcropping of rock about a hundred paces ahead of him and about thirty paces above the trail. He spoke to the archers. "Go there. If needed, unleash your arrows. Stay hidden."

The archers nodded and trudged up the mountainside towards the rocks. Nameless saw their tracks and hoped the blowing snow would hide them by the time the envoy arrived. He turned to the original messenger. "Go further ahead and find a place to hide. You will be our last line of defense. If it turns to violence, ensure none of them find their way back home."

The messenger nodded and ran ahead. Nameless squatted in the snow and waited. If the messenger's estimate of the envoy's speed was accurate, he wouldn't have more than half a day to wait.

They came as promised, but when Nameless counted, there were only nine. His first suspicion was a trap, but when he studied their careful approach, he took a different guess. One had fallen on the trail. It was little surprise. The game trails existed, but they were dangerous, and for a group of ten, it was surprising only one had fallen.

The envoy halted in front of him, and Nameless took their measure. The one richly dressed was the one in charge, but his eyes were full of fear. The man tried to mask it, but Nameless could smell it on him. The other eight were warriors, and they handled their mounts well enough. But Nameless agreed with his messenger. None were gifted, and none would be able to match him.

The richly-dressed man spoke, "My name is Lord Tanak, Lord of the Southern Kingdom. Who are you, and why do you stand in our way?"

Nameless stared curiously at Tanak. The name he recognized, but the title was new. His sources had told him Tanak was the Lord of the Western Kingdom. He must have defeated the Southern Kingdom in combat.

Nameless' silence made Tanak uncomfortable, so he let it linger for a few moments longer than necessary. "I have no name, as is true of all my kind. However, I am the leader of the People, and I have come to hear what you would say."

Tanak looked around as though he disbelieved what Nameless was saying. They were in the middle of nowhere, a mountain pass used more by goats than by humans. It was not what the lord had expected.

"Are you going to escort me to your people? I come bearing terms of our truce."

Nameless stifled a grin. "We can treat here. I am the only one who must hear what you have to say."

Tanak looked doubtful, and Nameless saw in the lord's face that he considered the Azarians to be less than those of the Three Kingdoms. He considered the People savages. Nameless would delight in proving him wrong.

Nameless glanced at the men on horseback again. "Where is the one we dealt with before? The nightblade, Renzo."

Tanak shook his head. "He is dead, killed by another nightblade in battle."

Nameless was surprised. He had met Renzo once, and the man had been strong. For him to be defeated indicated there was greater power in the Three Kingdoms than he guessed. It must have been the boy. There was no one else capable. He pushed the thoughts aside. Right now all that mattered was dealing with Tanak. "What are the terms of your truce?"

"As you discussed with Renzo. All the land south of the Three Sisters is yours. The pass will be considered a no-man's zone. You will never have to deal with our attacks again. But we never have to deal with yours either."

Nameless laughed. It was the deal he had discussed with Renzo. Nameless would distract the armies of the Southern Kingdom, pinning them down in the fort while Tanak and Renzo swept through the Southern Kingdom. Unfortunately, it had taken Nameless longer than he expected to bring the clans in line, and his invasion hadn't begun until autumn. Fortunately, it had all worked out. He had promised Renzo peace, but what he really wanted was a land torn apart by war. Renzo had always seemed suspicious, but it seemed this lord had fully believed in their agreement.

Tanak frowned. "What's so funny?"

Nameless shook his head. "I will never treat with one as pathetic as you."

Tanak wasn't used to such treatment, and although Nameless saw the fear flash in his eyes, he acted as though he was courageous. "That's a bold statement when one stands against nine."

Nameless smiled. He felt the power flow into his limbs. Without a word, he drew his blade and darted among the horses. Every soldier seemed to be moving through water, unable to respond to his attack quickly enough. He intentionally left Tanak and a guard alive, but he wasn't quite fast enough to get through the entire line. The soldier who had brought up the rear of the envoy had turned his horse when they had stopped, protecting their flank. As soon as Nameless attacked, he spurred his horse forward, escaping Nameless' blade. Nameless threw out his energy, a signal to his demon-kind hidden up the trail. They rose in unison, sending an arrow each into man and beast.

Nameless cleaned his dark blade and turned towards Tanak. "Is my answer enough?"

Tanak looked terrified, and Nameless could see the dark stain spreading down his leg. The man was a coward. Nameless looked to the other soldier, frightened but standing firm. "Can you deliver a message?"

The soldier nodded, unable to speak.

"Good."

Nameless leapt easily onto the back of Tanak's horse. The lord hadn't even drawn his sword. Before man or beast could react, Nameless' blade sang one more time, and he caught Tanak's falling head with his other hand. He leapt down to the ground, landing softly in the snow. He took the head to the soldier and put it in his hands. "Tell your people we are coming."

CHAPTER 4

Moriko's sword cut through a snowflake as she finished her practice. The sword moved as an extension of her body; her mind and sword worked as one. She cut and turned and cut again, each move perfectly controlled. With a smooth motion she sheathed the sword and took a deep breath.

Something had changed inside her during her time in Azaria. It was more than just gaining the ability to "snap," as Ryuu called it. The ability was nice, but as Moriko breathed in the crisp winter air, her body felt more alive than it had ever been, tingling with energy. She felt like she could run for days and still have the strength to fight. Down in Azaria she had found a strength she hadn't known she possessed.

Finished with her practice, Moriko wandered through the woods. She had missed them dearly, but hadn't realized how much until she returned to them. It was quiet, the daily sounds muffled by the fresh powdery snow covering everything. The forest swallowed up even the sound of her footsteps, but she felt no hesitation wandering among old woods. They were places the people of the Three Kingdoms avoided, but to Moriko, visiting the old woods was like visiting a best friend. She felt refreshed and calm.

As often happened on her wanderings, her thoughts turned to Ryuu. It seemed hard to believe, but it had been over half a cycle since she had seen him last. She wondered if he had found the island, and if he had, what he had found there. But more than that, she wondered if he would return to her. She hadn't waited for him, and she didn't know how he would react. For all his strength, she still found him fragile in a way difficult to describe. His sword was strong, but his mind wasn't. Despite his age and experiences, Moriko felt like Ryuu still had to grow up.

She was making plans to leave the Three Kingdoms. There were trading ships that left from Highgate in the Northern Kingdom. If she could find her way onto one of those, they could take her to a new land, a land where she could put all the pain of her previous life behind her. The Three Kingdoms had fallen into war, and Moriko knew better than most that the challenges were just beginning. By next summer she was sure the entire land would be burning. She didn't owe the Three Kingdoms anything, and she didn't plan to be around to watch it burn.

The question she kept turning over in her mind was whether or not Ryuu would join her. He felt an attachment to the land and people that Moriko didn't. She wanted him at her side, but she feared he wouldn't want to run, that he would want to stay and fight in the middle of it all.

She shook her head, trying to clear it of unpleasant thoughts. The woods were too peaceful for such nightmares. She imagined the trees, here for time untold. They had seen so much more. At the end of time, all her problems were small and meaningless compared to the scope of the world. The thought brought her comfort as she wandered through the woods, her hand brushing lightly against the bark of the trees.

Although winter was just beginning, there was already a fair covering of snow on the ground. Winter had come early to the Southern Kingdom. Moriko wondered if it was some sort of omen for the coming storm. But her needs were more immediate. She and Ryuu had been gone all summer, and in their absence, most of their harvest had been destroyed. Moriko tended their garden as best she could upon her return, but the damage had already been done.

If she was going to survive the winter in comfort, she was going to need more food, and she was worried she might not be able to get it. She hadn't seen a soul since leaving the Three Sisters, and she had no idea what was happening in the rest of the Three Kingdoms. Had the Azarians invaded? Were the people of the Three Kingdoms preparing for war? If the whole land was prepared for invasion, it would be impossible to procure food.

Regardless, she had to try. She and Ryuu had plenty of money, as their needs were simple, and Shigeru had left a fair amount of gold behind when he died. Even if food was expensive, she should be able to get what she needed, if it was being sold at all. If nothing else, she needed to get out to learn what was happening in the world. Knowledge was safety.

She packed up their medicine kit. The nearest village was a two day's walk away, but she was known there as a wandering healer. It brought in some money while providing a backstory for a woman who came into town so infrequently.

The walk was cool but pleasant. Moriko had dressed in simple garb so she wouldn't be recognized, her sword hidden on her back, covered by the bulky medicine cabinet. It would be awkward to draw, but she kept her sense alive and expanded. She didn't worry about anyone sneaking up on her.

She arrived at the village without incident, but when she arrived, she thought for a moment that the village had been abandoned. It was small, about sixty people in all, mostly farmers. But though the village was small, it had always been lively. Most days people were outside working or talking with neighbors. People rarely stayed in. It wasn't their way.

When the village first came into view, Moriko couldn't see a single person. She worried for a moment, but when she extended her sense in the direction of the village she could sense the warm glow of life. Moriko frowned. It was cold, but not so cold people would stay inside. She didn't sense any danger, so she came down among the houses.

It was an eerie experience, standing in the middle of the village without anyone to greet her. She and Ryuu came through infrequently, but when they did, they had always been welcomed warmly. Today doors and windows were shut against the outside, and no one even knew she was there. Moriko wandered over to the house of the village matriarch. She had seen almost sixty cycles, and her house was the center of all activity.

Moriko knocked softly against the door. "Hello?"

She didn't hear anything, but she could sense the fear and panic in the house. She knocked softly again, and finally she sensed the old woman coming towards the door.

The door opened, just a crack, and Moriko saw a small fire burning in the center of the hut. When the old woman saw who it was, there was a commotion inside and the door opened all the way. Moriko was ushered into the house, quickly, and the door was shut behind her.

"What are you doing outside?"

Moriko wasn't sure what her best answer was. Something was happening, and if she was a wandering healer, she would be aware of it. She needed a story, but her mind didn't seem to work fast enough.

"I've been wandering for some time. I thought it was time to come to the village and see how you all were doing."

The old woman eyed her with a hint of suspicion. Moriko was surprised. They had always received such a warm welcome. What could be happening to make them act like this?

"I am sorry," said Moriko, "I have been in the deep woods for over a moon caring for an old man who behaves like a hermit. I have had no news in that time. What has happened? Why are you all inside huddled together with so much fear?"

The cloak of suspicion the old woman wore dropped in a moment. Despite her fear, she was still the matriarch of the village, and she believed in kindness and hospitality. "I am sorry too, my dear, but these are dangerous times, and no one travels the roads."

Moriko frowned. She had only been back in the Three Kingdoms for about two moons. How much had happened in that time to instill such fear in the people? "What do you mean? What has happened?"

The old woman looked around, as though the very mention of the danger might bring it into her household. "There are strange rumors going about. All we hear from everyone on the road is how entire villages are disappearing. The people in them vanish. Families have lost fathers, sons, mothers and daughters. Other travelers speak of horrible deeds, of villages massacred with no one left alive. They say that villages are red from the blood that has been spilled. I do not know what to believe, but we have heard the rumors enough times to know something is wrong."

Moriko shook her head. If what the old woman was saying was true, something was happening in the Southern Kingdom, something besides an invasion. Her mind raced, but couldn't come up with an explanation for the rumors.

"How long have these rumors been spreading?"

The old woman shrugged. "It has been a moon, maybe a moon and a half since we heard the first rumor. At first I dismissed it as the ravings of a lone traveler, but more and more we've heard stories from different sources, and now there are no travelers in this area. Whatever is happening sounds as though it started further to the south and is working its way north. We have thought about leaving the village and heading to New Haven. But it is hard to leave the land, and harder still to carry the supplies we would need for winter."

The old woman had said her piece, and a silence settled over the room. Moriko pondered what the old woman had said, but couldn't decide what was happening. It had to be related to the Azarians, but she wasn't sure how. Regardless, it wasn't why she had come.

"I'm sorry to hear such ill tidings, but I must be on the road again by tomorrow. Is there anyone who needs healing?"

The old woman nodded. "A fever has taken one of the older women, and one of our boys has broken a leg. Your services would be appreciated."

Moriko's presence in the village drew people from their homes, if only for a little bit. Children, tired of being cooped up in their houses, ran around the village freely, although Moriko could see their mothers kept a watchful eye on them to ensure they didn't leave the village, not even to play in the adjoining fields.

Moriko did what she could for the people of the village. The older woman's fever concerned her the most. They had already been doing everything they could to break the fever. Moriko gave them some herbs she hoped would help, but as she examined the old woman, she feared she had come too late and that the old woman would rejoin the Great Cycle soon. The young boy was a different matter. The break was almost brand-new, and Moriko was able to set the bone and splint it. Her work with the young man made her think of her time with the Azarians. In their culture, such a break could've been fatal. But here the boy would live to hopefully see many more days.

When she was done, Moriko went back to the old woman and bartered for some food. She wasn't able to get as much as she would've liked, but it was enough for now, and she could see the fear in the eyes of everyone she met. She couldn't bring herself to push for more.

They begged her to stay. In their eyes, being on the road was tantamount to suicide, but she was able to convince them that as a healer she was honor-bound to stay on the road and provide what help she could. It was clear they didn't agree, but they couldn't force her, and as the sun set on that day, Moriko left the village with a heavy heart.

Moriko was loath to admit it, but her visit to the village had made her nervous. There was no doubt in her mind something was happening in the Southern Kingdom, and if she had to guess, the Azarian hunters had something to do with it. They were the only warriors she knew of with the strength to eliminate entire villages and disappear without a trace. She thought about General Toro. Had something horrible happened down in the pass? She felt a twinge of guilt. Perhaps she should have stayed there.

Moriko shook her head. If the Three Sisters had fallen, there was little she could have done to prevent it. She was strong, but there were far more hunters than she could handle, and if the general had died defending the pass, she would've died there with him. She had made the right decision.

Nevertheless, her own safety was at stake. She had told Ryuu in her letter she would stay at the hut until spring came. At the time she had believed it would be safe to stay in the Southern Kingdom until then, but if the hunters were active in the Southern Kingdom, there wouldn't be any safety to be found.

Moriko was torn between her desire to leave the problems of the Three Kingdoms behind her and her desire to wait for Ryuu, to see what he would decide. Unable to choose, she chose a middle path, deciding to scout more regularly to the south of the hut. The rumors had placed the hunters, if Moriko was right, further to the south. If she was going to find them, that was the direction to search.

As the moon grew brighter in the sky, Moriko's daily pattern changed. Instead of spending her time in the old woods surrounding the hut, she wandered further south. There were two villages in that general direction, both about four days' walk from her hut. She traveled to both of them, scouting to make sure they were safe. She did not enter the villages, electing instead to remain hidden from sight. Both villages were quiet, sealed in like the one she had visited earlier, but were otherwise unharmed. Moriko was grateful. If the rumors were true, this meant the hunters were not yet nearby.

Moriko no longer traveled the roads. Instead, she followed game trails that kept the road in view or in range of her sense. In this way she was able to keep track not just of the villages, but of the travelers who roamed from village to village in these dangerous times.

It was on one of these journeys that Moriko encountered a pair of hunters. She sensed them long before she was in sight of them. She pushed down the fear that threatened to take hold of her. If there was anyone in the world who was still a danger to her, it would be a hunter. But she had faced them before, and they had joined the Great Cycle while she was still here, pursuing those who thought themselves invincible. They were dangerous, but so was she.

The afternoon sun was burning low when she sensed them, and she crept quietly towards them, making sure her own presence was completely suppressed. There was no way they would know she was watching them. She hid deep in the brush, keeping as much distance as possible between her and them. More than once she had been discovered by smell, and she had no intention of repeating that mistake.

Moriko squinted when she saw the hunters. The two of them were unmistakable in their Azarian garb. Their tall stature and easy grace made them easy to pick out. But they were meeting with someone who looked to be from the Three Kingdoms.

Moriko pushed her fear down. The hunters were in front of her, and it was she who was hunting them. They no longer had any power over her. She crept closer, trying to learn more. The person they were talking to didn't seem to fear them, and in fact seemed to be on equal terms with them. She felt like she was on the verge of solving a puzzle, the answer nibbling away at the edges of her mind, but she couldn't figure out why.

The man they were talking to was unremarkable as far as Moriko could see. He was of nondescript height, and his clothes didn't mark him as rich. His features were covered by a hood, and Moriko didn't dare get close enough to see if she recognized him.

She sat there as the hunters and the man conversed, debating what to do. Her instinct was to kill all three of them and be done with it, but it was full daylight, and she was most dangerous in the night when the shadows were her friends.

When it hit Moriko, she couldn't believe she hadn't noticed it before. The hunters were so strong that all her attention had been focused on them, but there was another person using the sense in the area, and when Moriko first noticed it, she realized it was coming from the third man.

The realization rocked her back on her feet, and she retreated to the shadows of the bushes and trees. If the hunters were meeting with someone who possessed the sense, it had to mean they were meeting with a monk. The more Moriko focused her sense on the third person, the more convinced she became. The sense manifested differently in different people, but all monks had the same training, using the sense in a very particular way. Moriko had grown up around such abilities, and now that she was focused, there was no doubt the man was a monk.

Moriko's mind raced through the possibilities. She tried to remember every memory she had of the monasteries. Never in her knowledge had a hunter visited, and she had never had any indication they were united in purpose. But she had been young. Perhaps she had missed the signs in the ignorance of her youth. Memories ran though her mind, but she couldn't come up with anything to make her believe the monasteries would work with the hunters. The evidence, however, was right in front of her.

The consequences frightened her. The monks were weak compared to nightblades, but they were still fearsome opponents, and the common citizens of the Three Kingdoms held them in reverence. If the monks cooperated with the hunters, the Three Kingdoms would fall. There wasn't a doubt in her mind.

The urge to jump out and strike was stronger than ever. Moriko had managed to move past the harms done to her while she was in the monastery, but she had never managed to forgive. The monks were as good as dead to her. But reason held her back. She was strong, but fighting three powerful opponents in the daylight was courting disaster. She would follow them until nightfall. Then she would strike and take their lives.

The hunters and the monk spoke for some time. Moriko waited patiently. Every moment they tarried was a moment the sun fell closer to the horizon, and the closer their deaths came. She hunted the hunters, and she was in no rush.

Moriko was disappointed when the hunters and the monk separated. She had hoped they would stay together so she could kill them all together. Unfortunately, their plans didn't coincide with hers. The monk turned to take the path south and the hunters turned to take the path north. Moriko was faced with a decision. She couldn't follow both of them. She suspected the hunters would be on the way to destroy another village, but the monk seemed important. He had been speaking with the hunters for some time, and they had treated each other as equals. The monk was carrying a bag, and if the bag held important information, it might be worth the price of several villages.

Moriko's hesitation lasted only a moment. She wanted to pursue the hunters, but alone, the monk was an easy target. She would kill him and track down the two hunters again. If she was fast, it wouldn't be difficult at all.

Moriko raced after the monk, staying well off the road. She wanted to get ahead of him and ambush him. She would have his bag and be away before the hunters got too far.

Eventually, Moriko cut towards the road. She found a tree that was easy to climb that stood near the path. She clambered up the branches, finding a perch about five paces above the trail. From her branch she would see the monk coming and surprise him. She wasn't well hidden, but no one ever looked up.

When the monk came into view, she thought she saw him slow down for a moment, and she was instantly suspicious. There wasn't any way he should be able to sense her, but if the past cycle had taught her anything, it was that she still had a lot to learn about what the sense could do. But the monk kept walking and her nerves were calmed.

The monk stopped a few paces ahead of where she sat. He looked up, and Moriko almost fell off her perch. There was no way it could be true, but the evidence was right there in front of her.

The face that looked at her was smiling, a ghost from the past, a smile that held no warmth. "Hello, Moriko. Come on down." His name was Tomotsu, and Moriko had thought he died many cycles ago.

She dropped from her tree, landing softly on the path in front of him. They stood a few paces apart. They were safe from each other for now, but were within a step or two of striking distance.

Tomotsu had been one of the first people she met when she had been taken to Perseverance. He was a cycle or two older than her, but she had been young and impressionable, and she had pinned all her hopes on him. He had cared for her after she'd been beaten, but she soon realized the monastery had him, heart and soul. When Ryuu had rescued her from the monastery, she had assumed Tomotsu had been killed with the other monks.

For a moment, she was glad her assumption was wrong. Even though Tomotsu had pledged himself fully to the monastery, he had always been kind to her, even when their viewpoints had been so obviously different. Even after Orochi trained her, Tomotsu still kept in touch. But as she studied his face, she knew something in him had changed.

"Hello, Tomotsu," she said.

"It seems the Great Cycle has brought us together again. It has been a long time."

She nodded. "It has. I am glad to see you."

Tomotsu barked out a harsh laugh. "You mean after you betrayed our monastery and the nightblade came and killed most of us?"

Moriko moved to speak, but Tomotsu held up his hand. "No. There is no point in conversation. This only ends one way."

Moriko interrupted him. "How can you be so blind? You saw what the Abbot did. How can you believe in a system that teaches such violence is justified?"

Tomotsu drew his sword. It didn't waver at all as he pointed it at Moriko. She understood, as she watched the point of his sword, how much rage he had carried for all this time. "I don't know how you can doubt the teachings of the Great Cycle," Tomotsu spat in her direction. "Even you have to see that the Cycle is coming to a close. What are the odds of you and me coming together, again, like this? The Abbot's teachings may have been hard, but it was the nightblade who established my faith. For the first time, I saw how dangerous the nightblades were, and I dedicated my life to killing them all. Those who don't believe must die."

Moriko opened her mouth to argue, but Tomotsu dashed forward, his blade eager for blood. Moriko dove out of the way and drew her sword, but she hesitated. This was Tomotsu, perhaps the first friend she had ever had in the world beyond her family. But as he came in again, there was nothing of the kind boy she had once known. He had been broken by grief. Moriko's sorrow was replaced by anger, and she attacked.

Tomotsu had no chance against her. He was well-trained and driven, but she was much stronger than him. In two passes he fell to her blade, his dying eyes filled with hate.

Moriko observed his passing into the Great Cycle. He deserved that much at least. When he was gone she closed his eyes and grabbed his bag. It was full of papers, a small fortune's worth. She stood for a moment over her first friend, and then the world came rushing back to her. There were still two hunters she needed to kill. The sun was setting, but if she hurried she could get to them before they caused any more destruction.

Despite her repeated checks, Moriko did not find any trace of the hunters besides the tracks they left, and even those were few and far between. Moriko began to wonder if they were moving faster than she had anticipated. Were they trying to reach the village during the day? If so, she didn't have a chance of catching them.

Moriko fought her urge to sprint after the hunters. It was possible they were moving much faster than she expected, but it was just as likely they were playing another game altogether. She didn't know what skills the hunters might possess, and there was certainly a possibility she was not the only person capable of hiding her presence from those with the sense. She had to be cautious, otherwise they could sneak up on her as easily as she could sneak up on them.

By the time the sun set, Moriko had not stopped for more than a few moments the entire afternoon and early evening. She was worried. If the hunters could maintain this sort of pace and still destroy a village without leaving a clue, they had physical capabilities far beyond her own. A shadow of doubt in her own abilities crossed her mind. Perhaps the caves had just been a fluke. Perhaps instead of all the skill she thought she possessed, she had just gotten lucky.

Moriko shoved the thoughts aside and focused on the present moment. Whatever doubts she had, she knew she would not be able to live with herself if she allowed a village to be destroyed when she could do something about it. As soon as the thought came to her, she stopped dead in her tracks. It was the type of thought she would've expected from Ryuu, a selflessness which would put her in danger. He was starting to rub off on her.

Moriko reached the outskirts of the village just as the sun was setting. At first glance, everything in the village seemed normal. She dared not enter and attract the attention of the hunters if they were nearby. Thinking quickly, she suppressed her presence and hid in some tall grass a few hundred paces away from the village edge. From her vantage point she could see the majority of the village, and sense all of it clearly. If the hunters were here, and if they attacked, she would be ready. She settled down into a comfortable position to wait.

The moon was high in the sky, and Moriko wasn't sure she had made the right decision. What if her tracking skills had misled her? What if the hunters had gone another way? Moriko was doubting herself, and after the encounter with Tomotsu, she was more shaken up than she cared to admit. Only her anger kept her on her feet. If the hunters weren't here, she would have to sleep for at least a day to be able to continue the hunt.

As the evening wore on, it became harder and harder to focus her sense on everything happening around her. Moriko allowed her sense to wander through the village and its surroundings, but nothing seemed out of the ordinary. Everything seemed quiet, a peaceful night and a sleepy village. The sound of crickets in the air was relaxing.

When Moriko awoke, she thought it was already morning. She blinked her eyes and shook her head and realized she was wrong. It wasn't morning, but the village below her was burning, throwing off enough light and heat to make her think the sun had come up. She cursed herself and bolted to her feet, but stopped before she ran into the village. She needed to think before she acted. Taking a deep, calming breath, Moriko extended her sense. She was late, but she wasn't too late. She could sense the two hunters, the center of everyone's attention. Marking them, she moved quickly.

Below her, several of the buildings were aflame, and there were shouts and screams from the villagers who were trapped inside their houses. Moriko debated whether to save them or to go after the hunters first. Her initial instinct was to go after the hunters. If she could kill them fast enough, she could then release the villagers without fear of them being attacked once again. But as she passed the first house, she couldn't do it. The screams and cries coming from within were too much for her to handle. She darted off to the side, and with a quick flick of her wrist, cut through the board the hunters were using to seal the door. She didn't stop to be seen.

Moriko hid behind a wall and threw out her sense. The two hunters had separated. They were acting as though they had nothing to fear. They had no idea they were being stalked. The thought of it made Moriko smile viciously.

Suppressing her presence as completely as she could, Moriko tracked one hunter circling around the village to the east. He was methodical, stopping in each house and killing the inhabitants within. Just from sensing him, Moriko imagined he was proceeding in a very nonchalant manner, as though killing was no different than washing his clothes. It made his movements easy to predict. She sensed him as he stepped into another house and began killing the inhabitants within. Moriko sprinted to the door of the house and hid just to the side of it. The hunter, confident in his ability to sense all those around him, wouldn't even be wary.

Her suspicions were correct. The hunter finished his work inside and turned to walk back out the door without a trace of suspicion. The moment he stepped through the door, Moriko made one cut, taking his head clean from his shoulders. The hunter had only had time to glance in surprise towards Moriko before it was too late.

Moriko didn't stop to gloat over her victory. The other hunter would realize his partner had been killed, and would know there was someone out there. He wouldn't allow himself to fall into an obvious trap. Moriko knew her second kill would be harder than the first.

Again, Moriko's assumptions were correct. The other hunter came towards her. Moriko moved from house to house, always staying in cover and never allowing herself to be within her opponent's line of sight. She circled around and worked her way behind him, watching the hunter's movements carefully with her own sense.

The second hunter stopped at the body of his companion, and Moriko risked a glance to see what her opponent looked like. What she saw surprised her. Her opponent was a hunter, and a woman. Thus far, Moriko had only met male hunters. She had never seen a female among them. She shook and cleared her head. Man or woman, it made no difference. She was one of the hunters who had destroyed more than one village.

A shrill cry of rage and grief rose from the hunter's throat, sending a chill down Moriko's spine. Clearly, Moriko had struck a nerve. The hunter cried out in the language of the Three Kingdoms.

"Come out! Come out, you coward, so that I may end your life for you."

Moriko debated her options. She was a strong fighter, but she also knew her strength relied primarily on stealth, not on one-to-one combat. The safest course of action was to hide in the shadows and wait until she had an opportunity to strike with a clean kill once again.

But some part of Moriko rebelled against the smart decision. She wasn't sure how long it would take to get another clean strike like the one she had gotten on the first hunter. While she waited for the perfect moment, this hunter could kill many more villagers. Moriko would have more blood on her hands. But what really drove her was the opportunity to kill the hunter face-to-face. She wanted the hunter to see her death coming for her.

Before she could fully think it through, Moriko stepped away from the house she was hiding behind and walked into the small square where the hunter was waiting. She said nothing, holding her sword ready in front of her.

The hunter's eyes took her in, running her up and down and trying to judge her worth as an opponent based on her stance. Moriko stood there calmly doing the same. It was easy to see that the second hunter was a formidable enemy. Moriko didn't detect any flaws in her stance.

"So you must be the one we were warned about, the one that escaped."

Moriko nodded.

"Good. Then I will gain much honor among the demon-kind for bringing them your head."

The hunter leapt forward, conversation at an end. Moriko snapped and hid her presence from the sense in the same moment. She easily deflected the first cut, and the battle was joined in earnest.

Her opponent was skilled, consistently pressing the attack, but always in balance and never leaving an opening for Moriko to strike. She may not have gotten any openings, but she also didn't feel as though she was in any danger. She could sense the cuts coming long before they arrived. If the hunter wanted to cut her, she would have to risk herself, and she wasn't ready to do that yet.

The two women fought back and forth in the square, and Moriko noticed there were some curious eyes peeping out from windows and doors. She had hoped to get through the evening without being seen, but a battle in the public square wasn't the way to make that happen.

Refocusing her attention, Moriko jumped two steps back, putting some space between her and her opponent. She didn't use the space to rest, but to launch her own attack, coming in with cuts as quick as she could make them.

If it had been a contest of skill, Moriko wasn't sure she would've won. The hunter was excellent, and maybe even a hair faster than Moriko was. But the difference lay in their ability to sense their opponent. Moriko's sense worked against the hunter, and she knew where the hunter's cuts were going to be a moment before they happened. Moriko, with her ability to hide her intent and her strikes, may have been a little slower, but the hunter was reacting on sight alone, and a mistake was inevitable.

In two more passes it happened. The hunter tried to strike at Moriko, not sensing Moriko's own cut. Moriko cut a blood vessel in the hunter's leg, and although the hunter still stood, she was losing too much blood to live much longer. Her return to the Great Cycle was inevitable. Moriko watched the hunter's last moments carefully. A part of her wanted to ensure the hunter died without hurting anyone else, but another part of her was curious if impending death would change the hunter's mind. Perhaps, as the end neared, the hunter would have some revelation, some change of heart towards the terror she had committed.

Moriko was sorely disappointed. The hunter glared at her and spat blood, even as she struggled to stay on her feet. She spoke loudly in the Azarian tongue, and although Moriko didn't know what she said, she was certain she was being cursed. It was, she reflected, a horrible way to spend one's last few moments. And then it was over.

Moriko looked around at the devastation. She had stopped the hunters. But they had already caused an incredible amount of damage, not just to this village, but to many of the villages in the area. Moriko shook her head. She still felt like somehow she was losing.

Since she had already been seen, Moriko went from house to house, checking to make sure people were okay and seeing if there were any injuries she could treat. By the time the sun rose, Moriko was tired enough to be a walking corpse, and gratefully accepted an offer of shelter for the day. She fell asleep and felt no more.

THE WIND AND THE VOID

CHAPTER 5

Ryuu's journey to the west became more curious every day. The old man had been interesting enough, and although Ryuu believed him, a part of Ryuu doubted how serious the situation had become. However, every day he traveled farther west and south it became more apparent to him the old man had not been exaggerating. If anything, he had understated the severity of the problem.

For three days after the meeting on the road Ryuu traveled in peace. The days were cold, but the sky was cloudless and the bright sun warmed Ryuu as he covered the leagues to the hut he had grown up in. There were few travelers on the road, and those he did encounter seemed to be going about their business as usual.

On the fourth day, the atmosphere on the road changed. It started in midmorning, as Ryuu was approaching a small village he had sometimes passed through growing up. He was three or four days of travel away from the hut, and the village had been one he and Shigeru had visited on occasion in the guise of wandering healers. They had not visited often, for it was a small village, with few goods to trade. But Shigeru had not liked to appear in the same village twice in a row, and this village was one he occasionally visited to break up the trips to the others.

Ryuu was only a league away when he encountered a large group of people walking towards him. He stopped and stood aside as they approached and began to pass. Even though it had been cycles since he had seen them last, he recognized the inhabitants of the village he was nearing. As near as he could tell, everyone in the village was on the road that morning. As the villagers began to pass, several of them recognized him, and they called a stop to the procession. Their greetings were friendly as one of the village elders shuffled up to Ryuu.

"Young man, it has been a very long time since you have visited our village. It is a pleasure to meet you again, although a shame in such trying times." The old man looked around. "Where is your father?"

Ryuu stared at the ground. "I am sorry I've not had the chance to tell you. My father passed away just over two cycles ago."

"I am very sorry to hear that. Your father was a great man, and brought much healing to my people. We will always be grateful for him. What sends you south today?"

Ryuu studied the old man, but there was no hint of guile in his demeanor. "I have received summons from a village farther south. I'm trying to carry on my father's work as best I can, and there are still those who need aid."

The old man shook his head. "Have you not heard?"

Ryuu gave the old man a quizzical look. "Heard what?"

The elder looked around, as though the very mention of what he was about to say would bring the demons from their hiding place. "It is a hard time. Villages to the south are disappearing. They are burned, and the inhabitants either disappear or are killed. Always, one survivor is left, one person to tell the story. The stories I have heard would chill your blood. With the war going on, there is no protection anymore. That is why we are on the road. We are going to New Haven, to tell our story and seek shelter until these horrors have been laid to rest."

Ryuu shook his head. "I have heard rumors, but I did not think they were true."

The old man nodded. "I once thought the same, but I've heard too much, and my people are scared. This is the only way to keep them safe."

Ryuu and the elder talked for a little longer, but Ryuu could see the villagers were eager to be traveling. With good conditions, it would still take them five or six days to reach New Haven from where they stood. Every moment seemed precious to them. Ryuu received many invitations to join them, but he begged their leave, and before long they were behind him, continuing their long, slow march to their new sanctuary.

As the day wore on, Ryuu encountered more and more people traveling towards New Haven. He didn't again encounter an entire village, but the number of people he saw could have filled many of the villages he knew. Ryuu estimated he had passed at least a hundred that day alone.

That night, Ryuu made camp with another small group of travelers, four families that reminded him eerily of the group he had been traveling with so long ago when Shigeru found him. Their story was no different than anyone else's. They had heard the rumors, and one of the men claimed to have met one of the survivors. Once the children were sound asleep the man related what he had heard first-hand from the survivor.

According to the survivor, they never expected their fate. One day everything in the village had been fine. The harvest had been good and the people were content. They went to bed unsuspecting, and many of them never woke up again. Bodies were pinned to walls and the village was painted red with blood.

Ryuu looked from traveler to traveler as the story was told and he could see that each believed completely in the story. That night he had trouble falling asleep, not because of fear or the story he had heard, but because of curiosity. There was no doubt in his mind something was happening to the south, but the stories he was hearing were grotesque, almost beyond comprehension.

The next day was more of the same. If anything, there were even more travelers on the road than there had been the day before. A mass exodus was occurring from the far reaches of the Southern Kingdom, but Ryuu saw no response from the military or the government. Though the sun was bright, the feeling on the road was one of dread. People were almost tripping over each other in their haste to escape. All were traveling to New Haven, expecting it would be a refuge from the horrors to the south. People seemed suspicious of everyone they met, and the kind greetings Ryuu had experienced the day became few and far between. More often than not, groups and families would walk past Ryuu without a word. More than once he received suspicious looks, as he was the only one traveling south.

Ryuu feared what would happen when all these people came to New Haven. It was a large city, but it was already full, and it couldn't handle the number of people seeking refuge inside. His thoughts traveled to Akira and Tanak, and he hoped they had a solution for their frightened subjects.

Ryuu considered leaving the road. If he still had his sense, it would've been the obvious decision. As it was, he was being seen by everyone; although he wasn't attracting undue attention, he was sure that once people saw his wanted posters in New Haven, word would get out about what direction he had traveled. He suspected there would be those who would connect whatever was happening in the outskirts of the kingdom to him.

But without his sense, Ryuu was blind. Off the road, away from people, he would be a sitting target for any who would take his life. He did not see or notice anyone following him, but he couldn't shake the feeling he wasn't safe yet. He picked up his pace. More than anything else, he wanted to get to Moriko. He hoped that once he did they could make some sense of the world as it fell into chaos.

There were two of them, because there were always two. One to track, another to kill.

It was the tracker who noticed the man. They had been hiding along the road for a day, debating whether to attack the villagers or to let them crush the nearby city with their overwhelming numbers. They had feasted on plentiful game while they argued. The warrior wanted to attack. If even the roads were unsafe, who knew how the people would react? He argued they would scatter throughout the land, easy to pick off in ones or twos.

The tracker disagreed. He liked the idea of everyone going into one city. That way, they would be easy to find. Also, they would carry the fear with them, causing riots and panic. Then they could walk into the city and cut it off from its miserable existence.

The two of them argued back and forth, neither particularly concerned about the outcome. The work was easy, almost demeaning.

Their leader had spoken truly, there were few, if any, who possessed any strength in this land.

The tracker sensed the man moving against the tide of humanity. They knew they were in the approximate area where this prey had been found previously, but they hadn't really expected to find him. The prey's hiding place had been discovered, and the man and woman should have moved on. But perhaps they were braver, or more stupid, than the demon-kind thought. Regardless, the man was moving against the tide, and he carried a blade, his eyes wandering back and forth restlessly. The tracker could not sense his power, but the way he walked gave him away. The man was a warrior, and even if he wasn't the nightblade their leader sought, perhaps he'd be strong enough to be a challenge.

The debate between the two was short-lived. Both of them detested slaughtering cattle. They would follow this man, and perhaps he would lead them to even more worthy prey.

CHAPTER 6

Akira sat at his desk, surrounded by stacks of papers he was convinced had no end. Ever since Tanak had ridden out to treat with the Azarians, his life had been nothing but an endless stretch of paperwork. Merging the two kingdoms was a simple idea, but the practicalities of combining two lands were enough to drive him to insanity. There were questions on how to merge the armies, who to appoint to new roles in the kingdom, and how to spread out food and supplies for the coming winter.

Even though Akira sat in his warm tent, daily he was reminded of the brutal nature of the weather outside. Though they were only in the first moon of winter, already snow swirled throughout the land, even in the remains of the Southern Kingdom.

Akira was predisposed to treat the people of his land better than those in Tanak's. His land had been torn apart by invasion, and he couldn't shake his natural impulse to give his people the best of everything. But he was wrong, and he knew it. As much as he detested the manner in which the new kingdom had been formed, it was a historic moment. For over a thousand cycles there had been three kingdoms, the remnants of one great kingdom held together by a treaty that had lasted much longer than anyone expected. Tanak had broken the treaty, but in so doing had created the opportunity for two kingdoms to become one. It caused the death of far too many good men, but Akira saw it as his duty to make their sacrifice worthwhile. He may have lost his kingdom, but he could do everything in his power to ensure this fragile peace would last.

So despite his desire to subtly sabotage the new treaty by providing his own people the best of everything, Akira worked to find solutions to provide for all. The problems were not trivial. As Akira looked over the ledgers and documents of the old Western Kingdom, he realized how close Tanak and his kingdom had come to utter ruin. If Tanak hadn't invaded, his kingdom would've fallen within the next five cycles. The papers in front of him were light, but the task in front of him was heavy. The Southern Kingdom had been a healthy kingdom, but Akira wasn't sure it was healthy enough to support so many new people.

To complicate matters, Akira could not bring himself to believe in Tanak's promises. He wasn't sure what Tanak knew or thought, but the last reports he had received from Toro made it clear the Azarians had come with an invasion force. Any other conclusion was preposterous. Akira hoped there was some chance Tanak would be able to create a peace, but in his heart he thought it would be impossible. He was certain that as soon as the pass opened, there would be tens of thousands of Azarians, hungry for land and blood, flooding the new kingdom.

It went against the orders Tanak had given him, but Akira was trying to balance the need to prepare for invasion with the needs of distributing supplies among all the people. It was a delicate task, but Akira did all he could within the freedom he had.

If the logistics of merging two kingdoms weren't headache enough, reports were beginning to trickle in from the edges of his old kingdom. The first one or two that crossed his desk he wrote off as unlikely. But as the days passed and new reports joined the old, the more certain he was the invasion had already begun.

There were at least a handful of hunters in his kingdom, destroying villages and spreading fear. The rational part of Akira's mind admired the diabolical efficiency of the strategy. At most, there were only a few dozen hunters in his land; but given enough time they would tear his people apart just as surely as an invading army. It was the same type of fear-based attack used in the siege of Fort Azuma, just on a much larger scale.

The worst part was that Akira didn't know how to respond. If they had been a more traditional opponent, Akira would've tasked squads and units to deal with the problem. However, he was certain they were dealing with hunters. If his intuition was correct, sending troops to fight and search for the hunters would be a waste of manpower and time. Any force large enough to kill a pair of hunters would be too large to spare, especially considering they had no idea where the hunters actually were. They were clearly working their way north, but they struck at random, and there was no predicting where their next attack would be.

If Ryuu had still been around Akira would have asked him. But thanks to Tanak, one of the only people who could help was a fugitive from the very people that needed his protection. Fortunately, there had been no sightings of him since he escaped the camp. Akira didn't know where he had gone, but a small part of him hoped Ryuu was out there trying to save the kingdom. It was a lot to ask, but Akira believed in him.

Without any good options, Akira was forced to do nothing, forced into inaction as the hunters slowly tore apart his land with fear.

Akira shook his head. If he let his thoughts go down this road, it was hard for him to turn back. There was a lot happening he couldn't control, but the papers and decisions in front of him were things he could influence, and strong decisions now could mean the difference between the survival and annihilation of his kingdom. He must not lose focus. Akira rolled his shoulders back and grabbed a new piece of paper. There was work to be done.

Akira was hard at work when the messenger entered his tent. Akira knew at once something horrible had happened, something important. Most messengers came into the tent with a crisp and practiced ease. This messenger looked as though he was walking towards his own execution. He was nervous, fidgeting in place as he waited for Akira to call for him. Akira eyed him carefully. He recognized the man, knew he was well respected as a runner throughout the camp. The man had been one of Tanak's, but Akira found no fault in his service. He always delivered his messages calmly and efficiently, and if Akira recalled correctly, the man also had a reputation for courage on the battlefield. Looking at him now though, it was hard to believe any of those things.

Akira motioned for the messenger to sit. "What is it? I fear you bring me terrible news."

"You are not wrong, my lord. The news is grave. One of Tanak's honor guard just returned from the mountains. He is nearly frozen solid, and the healers are not sure he will live, but he brought a message."

Akira waited patiently, although his heart beat faster.

"My lord, the guard was carrying Tanak's head. He told a story difficult to believe. They were ambushed in the mountains by the leader of the Azarians, even though they rode under a banner of peace. They were killed with very little conversation, and the leader handed Tanak's head to the guard. The only message he delivered was to tell us he was coming."

Akira took the news in as calmly as he could. A part of him leapt for joy. He hated Tanak for invading his kingdom, and he wouldn't shed any tears knowing the Lord of the Western Kingdom had met his end, particularly due to his own hubris. But at the same time, this was a clear message from the man Moriko called Nameless. The Azarians would come, and Akira was afraid his people wouldn't have the strength to withstand the forces arrayed against them. His mind raced, but he knew what he had to take care of first.

"Take me to his head."

The messenger hesitated. "My lord, there is no need. The head is frozen and grotesque, and those who knew him well have identified it. There is no reason for you to look upon it."

Akira thought about the messenger's words and their hidden meaning. It was no secret the men of the Western Kingdom and the men of the Southern Kingdom did not see eye-to-eye. Tanak's death was a blow to his men, and Akira would have to tread gently. He was now the Lord of the Southern Kingdom, but keeping it together would be far from simple.

Akira shook his head. "There is. I have no doubt about your report. Tanak and I may not have been friends, but he was one of the lords of the Three Kingdoms, and as such, was one of the two men who best understood me. He deserves my respects."

The messenger thought for a moment and then nodded. Akira let out a silent sigh of relief. With any luck, the messenger would spread word of his reaction throughout the camp. If he wasn't careful the armies would split in the next few days. With a gesture the messenger led Akira out of the tent.

The camp around them was abuzz with activity. One of Akira's first actions in Tanak's absence had been to work on merging the armies of the two kingdoms. Both were depleted after a season of warfare, and stragglers were still coming in daily. Everyone was organizing, meeting their new units and beginning to train together. Akira's two top generals, Makoto and Mashiro, had been instrumental in organizing the task. But even as they were so close to creating order, chaos reared its ugly head again.

The tent the messenger led Akira to was black, a place where corpses were stored until they could be properly honored. Even now, bodies were coming in from the battlefield to be identified, if possible. The men who worked in the tent were grim, but Akira was grateful for their service. Families deserved to know what had happened to their fathers, brothers and sons.

The messenger led him to the back of the tent, a place set aside and quiet. There on a bench was a blanket covering a lump. Akira had seen death before, and didn't shy away from the sight. He gently pulled aside the blanket himself.

The head was definitely Tanak's. Dueling emotions coursed through Akira. A part of him was elated, and he couldn't deny that. The man who had invaded his kingdom, the man who had brought death and destruction to his people, had rejoined the Great Cycle, and Akira was glad. Tanak's death made him the ruler of the largest kingdom the land had seen for over a thousand cycles. He had more men and more resources than any other lord in history. His mind raced with possibilities.

But he was also afraid. He was afraid for his kingdom, young as it was. They faced a threat stronger than any they had ever encountered. It would be easy to let the blame for failure fall on Tanak's shoulders, but all that mattered now was he was the lord standing between the Azarians and his people. He wasn't sure if he was up to the task, but he had to try.

He covered Tanak's head. There would be much to do in the coming days. He had full authority to make changes now, and he would. Tanak would be given a proper ceremony to mark his passing. The men needed to be organized. A thousand other tasks ran through his mind, but one stood at the front of them all. He needed to meet with Sen.

Akira rode on horseback through the Northern Kingdom, the second time he had done so within this cycle. His body was sore from his time in the saddle, but they pushed forward. Time was of the essence, every day a precious gift of preparation for the invasion Akira was certain was coming. They rode from sunrise to sunset, as long as the terrain around them was clear. Akira has pressed his men to ride in the evenings, but Captain Yung, the commander of his honor guard, didn't permit it. They weren't expecting an ambush, but the rumors of terror roaming the Southern Kingdom had made everyone nervous. They rode only so long as the sun lit their way.

Fortunately, the weather had held for them. It had been a winter marked by storms, but they encountered nothing more trying than softly falling snow on their journey. Akira was grateful. He had never been to the Northern Kingdom in the winter. Summers were challenging enough in the high mountains. He couldn't imagine how the people here survived the winters, and had little desire to find out himself.

Due in large part to the lack of storms, visibility was incredible, and Akira basked in the stark mountain beauty of the Northern Kingdom. Majestic peaks rose in the distance, gorgeous and hostile. Akira wondered at the men who lived near such mountains, and was grateful he wouldn't have to climb those peaks.

Sen had replied quickly to Akira's messengers, naming a different place for their meeting. Akira had expected to return to Stonekeep, the capital of the Northern Kingdom, but Sen had chosen a tea house much further south, making the journey quicker for Akira and his men. Akira wondered at the meaning of the gesture. Sen did nothing without reason, but Akira couldn't puzzle out the old lord's intent.

By all accounts, the last time Akira had been to the Northern Kingdom, he had failed. He had hoped to best Tanak at a Conclave, but his plan had shattered like fragile glass, and instead of unseating Tanak, he found himself the target of a coordinated attempt at the reunification of the kingdoms. He still questioned what had happened at the Conclave and hoped to have answers soon. In the eye of the public, Akira had done well, but he knew he had disappointed Sen, and that bothered him. He respected the old lord, almost as a father.

As he approached the meeting place, Akira considered his options. There must be a way to stop the Azarians from entering the kingdom. Toro had ordered the First all the way out of the pass. They didn't even man the high ambush locations throughout. Akira had been angry when he first heard Toro's orders, but on further reflection, they had been the right decisions. Hunters would find and kill any of the ambushers. If they had been fighting a traditional enemy they could have held the pass easily even in the summer, but an army reinforced with hunters was a very different beast. Akira would have lost more men with no benefit.

So now there was only one choke point at the northern end of the Three Sisters, where the pass opened up into the Southern Kingdom itself. Akira and his troops would have some small advantage when it came to terrain, but the kingdoms had never faced a force like this. They weren't strong enough.

Akira's plan was simple. They needed more troops to defend against the invasion, and the only troops available were Sen's. Not only did they represent more manpower, but their skill in the mountains was unparalleled, and Akira would give anything to have them assisting in the defense of the kingdoms. His primary goal was to convince Sen they were needed.

Akira and his honor guard crested the ridge overlooking the valley the tea house was in. Akira had never been here before, and he slowed his horse to a halt as he took in the view. The sun was bright and cold in the crisp blue sky. Off in the distance, perhaps a league off, Akira could see the tea house. Sen's own honor guard was stationed nearby. The mountains here were beyond gorgeous, hard snow-capped peaks stabbing the sky. Akira imagined the valley in the summer, filled with blooming wildflowers. It would be a wonderful sight. There was a peace in this valley, ideal for the meeting they were about to hold.

They were still some way off from the tea house when Akira ordered his honor guard to halt. There was no need for Sen or his guards to get nervous. Akira was here on a mission of peace, and if he couldn't trust Sen, there wasn't anyone left to trust. His guards didn't have to like it, and Captain Yung fixed him with a stare that would have frozen a lesser man, but Akira rode on alone.

As he tied up his horse, Sen emerged from the tea house to greet him. Like Akira, Sen was alone. They greeted each other as old friends, and Sen invited him into the tea house.

The house was warm and cozy, heated by a roaring fire and protected from the brisk winter air by surprisingly thick walls. They sat down and Sen served him tea. Akira watched with interest. Sen was old, but every movement he made was sure and precise. He had a great many cycles left to live, and Akira was glad it was so. When his tea was prepared, Akira sipped at it gently. It was a delicate blend, the best he had tasted in some time. Akira complimented Sen, and as was appropriate, they spent the first part of their time together speaking of trivial matters. A part of Akira wanted to hurry and get to the point, but a few moments here made no difference in the larger scheme of things, and the tradition was comforting. Akira found himself relaxing and enjoying his time with Sen. The tension fell away from his shoulders.

He had known the older lord since he was a child. He remembered trips to the Northern Kingdom every cycle with his father, meeting Sen and sitting on his lap. At the time, Sen had been one of the youngest rulers of a kingdom, although well into adulthood. Now, so many cycles later, Sen was still here, and he was the only other person alive who knew what it really meant to be a lord.

It was Sen who brought them to the point at hand, and Akira was almost disappointed when the peaceful spell was broken. "The world has been shifting. I was sorry to hear about Tanak."

Akira couldn't decide between honesty and politeness, so he kept his tone neutral. "It was a surprise to learn about his death."

Sen allowed the silence to grow between them. Akira considered several approaches to broaching the question, but Sen knew him well. Straightforward and honest was his best bet. "I would like nothing more than to sit and talk, old friend, but the time for decisions is at hand. I have come here to ask for your aid in repelling the Azarian invasion. There are no troops better suited for mountain warfare than yours, and we desperately need more men."

Akira let Sen have time to think. He suspected Sen had guessed Akira's purpose before the visit, but these weren't decisions to be made lightly. While he waited, he poured them each some more tea. Technically, it was rude for the guest to pour tea for the host, but Sen understood the gesture for what it was, a simple kindness. He sipped softly at his tea while he looked out on the snow-covered landscape outside. When Sen spoke, his voice was soft, as if he feared that if he spoke too loudly the fragile peace that existed would be torn apart.

"I do not know if I am willing to entrust my troops to you. My heart wants to believe you, but events of the past moons have made me doubt your motives. I would be a foolish lord indeed if I entrusted the safety of my kingdom to one who acted so rashly this past summer."

Akira controlled his reaction. He had hoped Sen had forgiven him, but there was no reason to. No words he could say would change Sen's mind. The old man always thought carefully, and if he said something, it was final. Akira had prayed it wouldn't come to this, but he couldn't leave the valley without Sen's troops. He hadn't even told his closest advisers of his real plan. "I understand. If you wish, I would be willing to cede the lordship of the Southern Kingdom to you if you would lend your aid. All I ask in return is that you work with my two remaining generals. They are experienced and have valuable advice to provide."

Sen studied Akira closely, the only sound in the teahouse the crackling of the burning wood. "You would relinquish your claim to the Southern Kingdom?"

Akira nodded. He knew the implication. The Kingdom would be whole again, but he wouldn't be king. "The last report I received from General Toro indicated several tens of thousands of Azarians ready to advance on our land, reinforced by an unknown number of hunters. They don't mean to retake Fort Azuma, as Tanak somehow imagined. They mean to take all our land. The only place we can stand against them is the northern opening to the pass. But we'll need every soldier we can get. The continuation of our kingdoms is all that matters. If that means giving up command, I do so gladly."

Sen sipped at his own tea, finally standing and pacing the room. Akira sat still, allowing the older lord the opportunity to decide on his best course of action. Sen was a strong ruler, and no words from Akira would sway his decision one way or the other.

Sen stopped and stared at Akira, as though it were some sort of trap. "Would you insist on being second in line to the throne?"

Akira shook his head. "The decision would be entirely yours. I would be honored to serve, but you can use me in whatever capacity you think best. You are well-loved across the kingdoms, and my people will follow you without question."

Sen continued his pacing. He spoke, and Akira was surprised, as it almost seemed as though he was thinking aloud. "You surprise me, Lord Akira. After the Conclave, I was convinced you were a man driven by pride. Your actions were desperate, and you didn't give up your land then, even though it would have reunited the kingdom."

Akira frowned, speaking before he realized he might offend the older lord. "You and Tanak were coordinated against me. I am proud of my kingdom, and I couldn't bear to lose it to such political conniving."

The older lord chortled to himself. "You believe Tanak and I were allies? That I knew and supported his campaign through my actions? That explains much."

"What do you mean?" Akira couldn't hide his confusion.

"I can see where you might have thought that. But this is the truth: I never coordinated with Tanak any more than I coordinated with you. I was willing to give up my kingdom because I desperately want to see the land reunited once again, even if it meant allowing Tanak to become our first king."

The whole world shifted for Akira, and in one moment he realized just how wrong he had been. He ran through the entire Conclave in his mind again, seeing it with a new perspective. He had underestimated Sen, terribly.

Akira bowed his head to the floor. "Forgive me, Lord Sen. I have been a fool."

Sen laughed, and Akira looked up. "If only we could have had this conversation several moons ago. We'd live in a very different world. Well, there's no point dwelling on the past. What would you say if I suggested we merge our kingdoms today?"

Akira was glad to already be sitting. It was the last thing he had expected Sen to say.

Sen continued. "Furthermore, I would take you up on your offer to relinquish your status. I would ask that you not be anywhere in line for the throne. Already, one lord has died with you underneath him. I would be foolish to become the second."

Akira didn't rush to speak. He had come for troops, but if there was a chance to reunify the kingdoms once and for all, wasn't that an even better solution? He breathed in deeply and replied with a question. "Would you defend the pass with all your strength?"

Sen nodded. "I believe your reports about the Azarians. My own shadows have echoed your concerns."

Now it was Akira's turn to stand and pace. He hadn't expected a gesture so grand. To be reunified, just when it was most needed, was the exact step they needed to take if they were to have a chance against the Azarians. He would be a fool to refuse the offer.

It would be hard to give up his authority, but he trusted Sen. Sen led his kingdom well, and his people were happy and prosperous, an even more incredible feat considering the difficult terrain they carved their lives out of. Handing over the Southern Kingdom was the right action to take. Sen deserved to be the kingdom's first king.

Akira nodded. "I accept your offer. It is very generous of you, and I believe you would make an excellent king."

Sen studied him again, and Akira felt like Sen could see right through him. Could it really be this easy? The Three Kingdoms had existed for over a thousand cycles, and now they may unify in less time than it took to drink two cups of tea.

Sen spoke. "Lord Akira, this is my suggestion. I have lived for many cycles, and I want to see our kingdoms unified. I was hurt this summer when the Conclave failed, but I believe you have the best interests of the land at heart. I will cede the Northern Kingdom to your care, and you shall become king of the Kingdom, reformed once again. War is a task for the young, and I wish to prepare my people for the imminent invasion. I will act as first in line to the throne, but my land and my troops are yours."

Words couldn't express Akira's emotions. Joy, pride, gratitude and hope all surged through his heart at the same time. He never could have anticipated the conversation taking the turn it had. He bowed to Sen, all the way to the floor. "I do not know what to say."

Sen smiled. "Sometimes it is best not to say anything at all."

Suddenly Akira was a child again, looking up to Sen and marveling at his wisdom. The man who was a lord fell away, and Akira faced Sen as he was. "Sen, I'm scared for our land. Even together, I'm not sure we can stand against the Azarians."

Sen nodded. "I am too, but we'll fight them together."

They sat and talked until the sun was high in the sky. There was much to accomplish, but they set out the basic terms of the treaty that would unify their lands. Both were willing to compromise, so the treaty was easy to form. The sun was setting when they finally finished. With another tremendous bow of gratitude, Akira left the tea house, eager to begin the return journey. He had entered the valley a lord, but he left it a king, the first the land had seen in over a thousand cycles.

CHAPTER 7

The cold wind blew down from the pass, but Nameless didn't care. He was demon-kind, and weather had no meaning to him. He was separate, above such small concerns as wind or rain. But his people kept to their shelters. It was not often so cold further south in Azaria, but despite their discomfort Nameless didn't dare allow the clans to spread too far from the pass. Their alliance was fragile as it was, continuing to exist only due to great need. The winter had barely begun and already food was an issue. They had found a little in the fort, and his demon-kind were scouring the mountains for game, but it would be a hard winter. It would destroy the weak.

Nameless did not believe in anything greater than himself. He held to no god and no belief system. There was only his own strength and skill. He stifled the urge to pray for the pass to open as soon as possible. He didn't know how much longer he could keep the People looking forward. Even his own demon-kind were having trouble following the narrow game trails which led to the Southern Kingdom. If the winter season continued its ferocity, he'd soon be completely shut off from news of the Three Kingdoms.

Today, however, Nameless was grateful for the wind and the snow. He wandered far afield of the collection of clans, allowing his abilities to guide him. He could feel the old man, a beacon in these desolate plains. Those of the clans wouldn't give him a second look, but his presence was as bright as the sun to Nameless and his gift.

He came upon the old man when the sun was high in the sky. The old man certainly knew Nameless was present, but made no move to recognize him. Nameless knew the old man's mind was wandering far and wide, seeing events far beyond the sight of a normal human. It was a useful skill, but one Nameless did not understand. It would be far too much to say that Nameless was scared of the old man, but being in the presence of such an unknown caused him discomfort.

The head of the Azarians sat down and waited patiently. He didn't know if the old man was actually focused elsewhere or if he just enjoyed making Nameless wait. For most, such an idea would be unthinkable, but the old man didn't fear Nameless. He knew he was too useful to be killed. Nameless wasn't a man known for his patience, but this old man was the only one alive who possessed the skill of far-seeing, and Nameless required him. Whether the old man was teasing him or not, he had to bear it for a while longer yet. The moment the Three Kingdoms were conquered, Nameless would end the old man and rejoice in his death.

When the old man opened his eyes, Nameless was ready. "What news, old man?"

"There is much happening to the north."

"I know that. I would hear of it."

Nameless' companion sighed, as if he wearied of such a rush.

"The young man, the one who strikes as fast as the wind, wanders back to the place he called home once before. But there is something different about him now. He is silent, and if I were to guess, I would say he has lost his gift."

The news startled Nameless. He did not know the lore of the nightblades in the north, but no demon-kind in his memory had ever lost the gift. He didn't think such a thing was possible.

The old man chuckled softly to himself. "It is not unheard of. You should spend more time studying and less time conquering. There is much to learn."

Nameless almost drew his blade then. Skill or no skill, he wouldn't tolerate such disrespect from anyone. But the old man was too useful, and he knew it. Nameless wondered if the seer had a death wish.

"You'll be pleased to learn two of the demon-kind have found him. They are on his trail now. I expect they believe he will lead them to the young woman who cut you."

"And what of her?" Nameless could barely control his anger at the thought of her. She would die at his hands. That was a promise he had made to himself.

"She is the void. I cannot feel her from here. I'm not sure I could if she was right next to me. But two more demon-kind have fallen, only a few days from the place the two of them used to live. I suspect it was her."

"How can you know?"

The old man shrugged. "There's nothing else that can kill us without me noticing it."

Nameless stood and paced, although his pacing was more akin to a light jog for most people. In his larger plan, the loss of two demon-kind was but a drop of water in a sea, but each one was valuable to him. Each one had a gift that should not be wasted. Never before had the demon-kind fallen as prey to others. If word were to get out, the fragile truce that held between the clans would melt like fat in a frying pan. The nightblades had to die.

Nameless turned and left the old man without a word. There was much more he needed to learn, but everything else could wait. He needed to meet with the other demon-kind and decide what must be done about the nightblades.

The far-seer watched the leader of all the clans rush off in a hurry. He shook his head, fearing for the fate of the People under such a fiery leader.

"You're welcome," he whispered softly to Nameless' retreating back.

It was evening when the council gathered. There were days when Nameless would have preferred to go without, but the trappings of tradition were strong. The People had never had a government, not like the sheep who lived in the Three Kingdoms. For as long as their stories went back, the People had always been a collection of clans. The closest they got to government was the Gathering, their once-a-cycle celebration.

The demon-kind were different, though. They were a clan without a clan. They took no names and served wherever they were needed. Each had been born into a clan, but now their only loyalty lay to each other and the People as a whole.

Long ago it had been decided the demon-kind needed control. Each of them was strong, and taken together, their strength was enough to shape the course of legends. That power had to be harnessed, and it had been decreed that no single person could decide the path of the demon-kind. And so the council of demon-kind had been born. When Nameless had decided to rise to power to save the People, his first task had been to convince the council his plan was necessary and right. If he had failed, he would have been killed by the demon-kind. He was strong, but not strong enough to stand against the combined strength of his brethren.

So even though he was the leader of all the clans, when it came to matters involving the demon-kind, he still had to approach the council and ask permission. If he lost the council, he lost the People. They would scatter to the four winds, declining in strength and numbers until they disappeared completely. No more stories would be told.

Nameless considered his words carefully. What he was about to propose was unheard of. When he looked at everything happening, it seemed a small and easy decision to make, but it was without precedent, and he knew his decision would be contested. He held the majority of votes in the council, but it was a slim margin, and there were several who would abandon him if they felt he was losing his strength.

Before he spoke he looked around the fire to see who had come. Many who he considered friends were gathered there, but they were almost matched by those who disagreed with him. They all had the best interests of the People at heart. They just had different ways of thinking about their problems. There still weren't enough people who saw the danger the People were in. Today the lack of game and food seemed like a temporary problem, but Nameless had ridden far and wide, and he knew there weren't enough animals left in the land to continue to feed their growing numbers. They needed a new land, a richer land. They needed the Three Kingdoms.

"Greetings, friends. I've called you here today because I have need of your strength. The two nightblades in the Three Kingdoms continue to be a thorn in our side. They bring hope to the land, strengthening it prior to our invasion."

Nameless knew the last part was his own fiction, but he had to convince the council their actions today would save the lives of the People come spring. He didn't believe the two nightblades could have that much of an influence on events, but they had to be eliminated. He had underestimated them too often. It wouldn't happen again.

"I propose we send four pairs into the Three Kingdoms to eliminate the nightblades once and for all."

The demon-kind were not known for dramatic expression, but Nameless took note of every raised eyebrow. There were many around the fire, even among those he considered allies.

One of the eldest demon-kind was the first to speak. Nameless respected his opinion. "Four pairs have never been sent on a single task before."

Nameless nodded. "I know how much I ask. But we sent two pairs against just one of them, and they never returned. It is more than we've ever sent, but the danger is greater than we've ever faced. The only way to ensure our success is to send more than we ever have before."

One of the younger members of the council spat into the fire. "It is disgraceful to send so many. Send one pair who knows which part of their sword to hold and we will be done with this foolish game."

Nameless eyed the youth warily. The young had never seen true hardship, not yet. Because of this, they felt they were invincible. They were a danger to his cause. If he reminded the youth that several demon-kind had already died at the hands of the nightblades, the youth would tell him the old men were getting weak and insist a pair of his generation be sent. Nameless considered the possibility. If these nightblades were as good as he thought they were, they would destroy a younger pair without a thought. The idea was tempting, if only to teach a lesson. But every demon-kind was precious, and he wouldn't waste them to teach others a lesson. He couldn't bring himself to be that petty. He kept his silence.

Several voices added their opinion to that of the youth. Nameless kept track of each, noting who was for the idea and who was against, and the reasons they gave. There was little duplicity in the council, and almost all spoke the truth of their opinions. There were some who supported Nameless in his plan, but many were against. Some were opposed because of the slight against their reputation. Others worried they were sending more and more demon-kind to their deaths. Time was a piece of the decision as well. The game trails were becoming more dangerous, and even seasoned mountain explorers were having difficulty making the trek from Azaria to the Three Kingdoms and back. Soon the mountains would be impassable.

Nameless made his last attempt. "I respect the wisdom and the voices that have spoken tonight. The problem in front of us is small, but we mustn't forget how it relates to the larger effort. The People must take the northern lands once the pass is open. Much more than our pride is at stake. The nightblades must be killed. We think of the deaths of our kind, as we should. But our lives and deaths mean little when we look at everything happening. The nightblades aren't dangerous because they kill us. They are dangerous because they inspire hope. Their very existence screams that we can be defeated. But if we break them, we are that much closer to breaking the Three Kingdoms."

One of the elders spoke. He hadn't added his voice to the discussion yet, but his quiet voice carried an air of command. Even

Nameless was attentive. "If you believe these nightblades are the threat you make them out to be, I am inclined to believe you. We know they have already killed too many of us. Four pairs is unheard of, but perhaps necessary. But you rush when no hurry is needed. Already twenty pairs cover the northern land, and the nightblades can't physically track them all down in the winter season. Fear will still spread, but give the trails time to open, then strike first in the spring. Allow our invasion to begin with the death of these heroes."

Nameless considered the old man's advice. In his heart, he wanted the nightblades dead, but he recognized his hatred for them was personal. They endangered the mission he had set before his people. Their lives were an insult to his, especially the woman's. He would have her head. That was a promise he intended to keep. But the advice was well-said. Sending pairs now risked their lives needlessly in the crossing. Besides, from the reactions he was getting from the council, they wouldn't approve sending pairs now. It was a compromise that pained him, but perhaps it was necessary.

Nameless nodded his agreement, and the decision was quickly made. In the spring four pairs would be sent to herald the invasion of the People. The nightblades would die, and the Three Kingdoms would fall.

CHAPTER 8

After the night she killed the two hunters in the village, Moriko never let herself stay too long in one place. The hut was still the center of her wanderings, and she came back to it from time to time to both drop off and gather supplies, but she never stayed for more than a night. Rumors of hunters in the land still flew from the lips of those she met, but it was becoming increasingly difficult to separate rumor from truth. She visited every village within four days of the hut, but she didn't encounter hunters again, even if the rumors implied she was surrounded by them.

Some of the villages were empty, deserted in the middle of winter. Visiting those villages spooked Moriko the most. They reminded her too much of the abandoned city she had encountered in Azaria. The emptiness was menacing, as though the silence held the promise of violence. Moriko trusted her sense, but it was still hard to believe a village didn't possess a single living soul. She walked through quickly and went on her way.

Other villages reacted differently. Many had seen people leave, but some citizens stayed. They didn't go outside often, but they would still open the door to a friendly face. Whether people stayed or left, the fear was palpable everywhere Moriko went. It was obvious the hunters were trying to spread panic, and just as obvious they were succeeding. It made Moriko want to scream, but screaming did little good, so she continued on her rounds, wearing herself out a little more every day.

It would have been easier if her mind wasn't on other things, like Tomotsu and Ryuu. Recently, it was Tomotsu she thought of the most. Her memories of him had been warm, and she had grieved privately when she thought he had died. He had never been the person she hoped he would be, but he had always been kind to her, and that was more than could be said for anyone else at the monastery. It had been a delight to see him alive after so many cycles had passed, but she still struggled to understand the events that forced her to take his life.

She tried to convince herself she hadn't had a choice, that he had forced her hand by dealing with the hunters and drawing his blade. But she knew it wasn't true. Ryuu was fond of saying that people always had a choice. It was a phrase he had learned from Shigeru, and it had seeped into Moriko's beliefs as well. She could have run away, could have tried to knock him unconscious. But in the moment she had killed him without much thought.

It was survival, Moriko thought. Tomotsu made himself a threat, and her survival was paramount. She would kill for it without hesitation. It was a truth she had learned about herself while traveling through Azaria. She was strong and would do whatever it took to keep living. As the Azarians would say, the strong survived. As soon as Tomotsu had drawn his sword against her, his life had been forfeit in her eyes.

Equally concerning were the documents Tomotsu had been carrying. Some of the documents were maps, maps of the Three

Kingdoms more detailed than any she had ever seen. They denoted mountains, villages, hiding places, and locations of strategic importance. The maps, combined with the actual meeting of Tomotsu and the hunters, painted a clear idea in Moriko's mind. In some way, at least some of the monasteries were working with the hunters to an end Moriko couldn't imagine.

Along with the maps were a pile of other papers, filled with writing Moriko didn't recognize. She figured it must be some sort of code, or a language she didn't understand. No matter how much time she spent looking over the papers, she couldn't decipher them. For all she knew, they could have been a collection of recipes. Given the context in which she had obtained them, she doubted it, but there was no way of knowing.

Her mind wandered with possibilities. At least one monk was collaborating with the hunters, but were more? It could be a single monastery, or it could be the entire system. Moriko wondered how deep the treachery ran and what it meant for the Three Kingdoms. The monasteries didn't have armies, but they were powerful nonetheless. The people held them in deep respect. The monasteries were the last remnants of the blades of legend.

Without answers, her mind circled upon itself more often than she circled the hut. When she wasn't thinking about the monasteries and their role in the invasion, she was wondering what had happened to Ryuu. She'd had no word from him, but she wasn't sure there would be any way for him to get word to her. Messengers were scarce in this part of the world. It had been almost half a cycle since she had seen him, and so much had changed for her.

As though thinking about him made it so, one afternoon as she returned to the hut she sensed him. She had just completed another circle of the surrounding villages and had come back with more supplies when she felt a presence within the hut. Her initial reaction was surprise. It had been so long, but it couldn't be anyone else. She paused and extended her sense carefully. There was someone within the hut, and it felt like Ryuu, but it also didn't. Moriko was hard-pressed to describe her sensations. It felt like Ryuu, but different. The power she was used to feeling from him no longer pressed against her mind. It was as though he were a normal person. Her heart went out to him. What had happened? Had he lost his strength just as she found hers?

Moriko moved to rush to the hut, but then she felt other presences on her sense. There were two of them, hiding well out of sight of the hut. She could feel the tendrils of the sense as they snaked towards the hut. They could only be hunters, and if Ryuu had lost his power, he was helpless before them. She sat on her heels, considering the problem. Was he bait? And if so, was he willing or unwilling?

There were no answers to her questions, but Moriko hadn't come this far to be intimidated now. She swallowed her fear and walked towards the hut, right into the trap.

When Moriko entered the hut, she saw it was Ryuu waiting for her. He looked up and grinned, a wide smile Moriko didn't realize how much she had missed until that very moment. It was hard to believe, after all this time, they were face to face once again.

Moments passed and the two of them looked at each other, each waiting for the other to make the first move. The last time she had seen him she had been riding south into Azaria as he was preparing to start traveling north. It had only been a half cycle, but so much had happened. Moriko had thought she was going to die at least half a dozen times, but she found a strength she didn't know she possessed. She came back a different person than the one who had left.

And she had no idea what had happened to Ryuu. He seemed fine, but there was a sadness in his eyes that hadn't been there before. As happy as he was to see her, nothing could hide the sorrow he was experiencing. And there was something else as well. She studied him closely. He was afraid. Of her?

Whatever was going through his mind, he stood up and approached her, cautiously. "I've missed you."

It was both a statement and a question, and in a flash of insight, Moriko understood. He felt abandoned when she chose not to return to Akira's camp. He had read her letter but he hadn't believed, and he was afraid he had lost her. Moriko wondered if he was right. If not for him, she never would have gone into Azaria, and although she was stronger for the experience, she wasn't sure she could forgive him, innocent as he was.

Ryuu took another tentative step, and for a moment all doubt was forgotten. Moriko stepped towards him and the two of them embraced tightly. Neither seemed to trust themselves to speak.

After a while they separated, and the words began to tumble out of Ryuu's mouth. "Moriko, there's so much I have to say. I'm sorry for everything that's happened."

Moriko didn't believe her eyes. In front of her one of the strongest nightblades in the land was acting like a blubbering idiot. She took a step back. She saw how his weight was off-balance, how his head tilted forward. She wasn't the only one who had changed in the past half-cycle. Ryuu had returned to her a different man.

Moriko's first reaction was disgust. Ryuu had been strong. As long as she had known him, he had always been strong. He was the boy who always wanted to do right, no matter the cost. Even when he lost Shigeru and Takako, he never lost the belief he could help others. But she wasn't sure the Ryuu in front of her believed in much of anything. He was weak and pitiful.

But all the same, her heart went out to him. Perhaps she had spent too much time among the Azarians, believing that strength was all that mattered. Maybe the Ryuu she had grown to love was still inside. He deserved a chance, if nothing else.

Moriko threw out her sense. She still didn't notice anything unique about Ryuu. Perhaps he was as broken as he seemed. The hunters sat outside the hut, still deep in the old woods. Moriko shook her head. If anything, they were predictable. They would wait until nightfall to strike. They had grown used to prey that relied on sight, but they didn't know, or had forgotten, that night was Moriko's domain. The moon was near-full, but in the growth of the deep woods, that wouldn't matter.

If the hunters weren't going to strike, they had time. Moriko went to put on tea, one part of her sense focused on the hunters to ensure they didn't surprise her. If her guess was right, Ryuu wouldn't have the ability to fight them. It would be up to her.

That afternoon they shared their stories. Ryuu went first. He spoke about his journey to the island and what he had found there. He talked about the strength and knowledge he had gained, the power he had felt. But he also talked about the division on the island, how one faction wanted desperately to return to the Three Kingdoms and another wanted to stay isolated.

Ryuu's story faltered when he reached the part about his decision to come for her. He told her how he had been able to sense what was happening to her, how he had originally left the island to come and rescue her. He spoke softly about Renzo's attack and how it had changed his mind, how he had known his only course of action was to go back to Akira. Moriko watched him as he explained his decision. There were hints of the Ryuu she had known there. He knew she might hate him for his decision, but there was no lie in his voice.

His story caused a flood of emotions to crash over Moriko. She was angry and upset, but also sad for the ordeals he had gone through. After Takako had died, he had hoped never to kill again. It had been a peaceful delusion until the hunters had appeared. But what tore him apart, more than anything else, was that he had been forced to kill a nightblade. She knew it felt wrong to him, and it had been the final weight that broke him.

Even though it had been the right decision, she was furious he had chosen to help Akira instead of continuing to ride south. The rational part of her mind knew it wouldn't have made a difference. According to his story, he wouldn't have reached her until she was already back at Fort Azuma. There was nothing he could have done, but still it angered her that he had chosen against her.

Silence reigned over the hut as she paced. Ryuu had told his story and would say no more unless prompted. He wasn't one to say more than was necessary. She glanced outside. Night was falling rapidly.

Ryuu broke the quiet. "I'd like to know what happened to you. You're . . . different."

Moriko glanced at him and glanced outside. She didn't have time to tell her story before the hunters attacked.

"Not now. There's something I need to take care of."

A look of fear flashed across Ryuu's face. "You're leaving?"

Moriko hadn't intended to tell him, but she was angry. "No, but two hunters followed you here."

Ryuu's look of fear was replaced by one of surprise. So it really was true. He couldn't use the sense and didn't know he had been followed. He knew if he fought them he would lose. But he stood up anyway.

Moriko shook her head. "You're in no condition to fight them. I will kill them and return."

Ryuu faltered for a moment. "By yourself?"

Moriko laughed. "I'm stronger than you can imagine." Not waiting to get into an argument, she stepped outside and slipped into the darkness.

Moriko's first hope was that Ryuu wouldn't try to follow her. Even without his sense he was an excellent swordsman, without doubt one of the finest in the Three Kingdoms. But it was foolish to attack hunters without the sense. They'd kill him in a moment.

She was grateful that Ryuu realized the same fact. Perhaps it had been the tone of her voice, or perhaps he knew he would be more a hindrance than a help in the upcoming battle. Whatever the reason, Ryuu stood just inside the door. It wasn't much, but it was the most defensible position around. If Moriko fell, it was the only place he stood even a hint of a chance at cutting a hunter.

Moriko strode confidently out into the woods. The moon was full, but in the shadows of the tall trees, her dark robes would be almost invisible. She let her presence seep out of her. She wanted their attention turned away from the hut. If they had been following Ryuu, it seemed reasonable to assume they had already figured out his weakness. If so, their first target would be her. Once she was dead, Ryuu would fall without difficulty.

But Moriko didn't plan on allowing them that chance. She had come out of the caves of Azaria reborn, deadly. Moriko frowned as she felt the hunters begin to move. One came towards her, the other towards the hut. She cursed silently. Either these two hunters were very confident or they didn't know who they were hunting. She guessed it was the former. Every hunter she had ever met had been proud. Despite all the hunters who had fallen to her blade, they still thought they were superior to her.

The decision put Moriko in a bind. She had hoped to lure both of them away from the hut, but if only one followed her it meant Ryuu was in danger. Fighting both at the same time would have been harder, but it would have guaranteed Ryuu's safety. It also meant she didn't get to fight the hunters on her terms. She would have preferred to creep up behind them and kill them silently, but if she tried that tonight, Ryuu would die.

It wasn't her style, but it was her only option. Moriko suppressed her presence completely and sprinted straight at the hunter following her. She crashed through the trees and leapt at the hunter. As she expected, the hunter wasn't surprised. His blade was drawn and the battle was immediately joined.

The hunter was strong, fast and experienced. To Moriko's frustration, he kept pulling her back, further away from the hut. In a flash of insight, Moriko realized their plan. They knew exactly who they were hunting. It wasn't the hunters who suffered from pride. It was her. The hunter in front of her was only to keep her busy, to draw her away from Ryuu. The second hunter would kill Ryuu quickly. They knew if he died she wouldn't be able to focus. She wouldn't be a match for the two of them. She had thought them prideful and headstrong, but instead they had planned their attack brilliantly.

Moriko was a stronger fighter than the hunter she faced. Her ability to suppress her presence, combined with her own strength, made her too strong for him. The problem was, he knew it. No matter what attack she tried, he was more than willing to give up ground. Every step he retreated was one step further away from helping Ryuu. Frustrated, Moriko attacked with renewed determination, her blade singing in the air.

The hunter didn't even try to block her attacks. He just kept moving backwards and dodging. Even when Moriko reached out in a desperate attempt to strike him, he didn't seize the opportunity.

Moriko paused her attacks for a moment, and the hunter let her. He didn't launch his own attack. It confirmed her suspicions. This hunter was in no rush to kill her. He planned on waiting for his partner to join him. Moriko's mind raced. Every moment she delayed was another moment Ryuu was likely to die.

She started walking backwards. She didn't dare turn her back to a hunter, but there was no reason for her to chase him. She could move back towards the hut, forcing the hunter into a decision. He could pursue or he could wait. If he pursued and attacked he risked exposing himself, but if he didn't, there was a chance Moriko would get back in time to the hut.

The hunter made his decision without hesitation. He leapt forward to attack, but he couldn't sense how Moriko would defend. She waited until he was close, then stepped inside his guard and cut. He tried to react in time, but without being able to sense her, he was almost blind. Her blade opened his chest from shoulder to abdomen. It wasn't a fatal cut, but he was out of the fight for a while.

Moriko turned and sprinted towards the hut. She hoped she wasn't too late.

Not since he was a young boy had Ryuu felt so helpless. He was five again, watching as his family and friends were killed all around him, unable to do anything to stop the massacre. If there were a pair of hunters out in the woods he was worse than useless. He was an added danger to Moriko. He stationed himself near the door of the hut, a place of cover where the cuts of the hunter would be hampered.

His heart froze when he heard the soft footsteps on the wooden steps. He thought back to his fight with Renzo, the technique he had tried to steal from Tenchi. Even though he couldn't use his sense, the technique should still work. He did his best to intend to strike in multiple places, confusing the sense of the hunter.

When he stepped out from the doorway, he was surprised by how close the hunter was. The surprise broke his concentration, and the hunter blocked Ryuu's cut with ease. Instinctively, Ryuu threw himself towards the hunter. Whether through luck or overconfidence, the hunter was caught by surprise. Ryuu tackled the hunter to the ground, dropping his own sword so he could get both his hands on the hunter's sword arm.

They rolled on the ground, and with a sharp jerk, Ryuu managed to disarm the hunter. He got a foot between his body and the hunter's and kicked him away from the swords. Ryuu knew he was no match for the hunter, but if he could make the match a fistfight, perhaps he would have a chance. If nothing else, perhaps he would live long enough for Moriko to come rescue him.

Ryuu had trained in empty-handed combat, but his life had been focused on the sword. He only hoped the same was true of the hunter. As the hunter recovered his balance, he went to draw a knife at his side. Ryuu charged him again, wrestling him to the ground and elbowing him in the face. They struggled against each other, but the hunter rolled and got on top of Ryuu.

The hunter lashed at Ryuu with a flurry of punches, knees, and elbows that Ryuu couldn't withstand. Ryuu couldn't respond fast enough to block the ferocity of the attack, and tried to curl into the fetal position. He got his arms up above his head, but the hunter kept his weight firmly on Ryuu's hips, and he couldn't raise them. Ryuu was being destroyed, the only good news being that punches alone wouldn't kill him instantly. But he wasn't sure how much longer he could last.

The hunter rose up to land a devastating elbow and Ryuu seized the moment. He grabbed the clothes of the hunter and pulled him down, rotating his hips at the same to get on top of the hunter. With a scream, he drove his fists furiously at any exposed part of the hunter he could. He lost all semblance of control, striking wildly.

The hunter collected his wits and lifted his hips, throwing Ryuu forward. Ryuu tumbled, coming to his feet in time to see the hunter pick up his blade. Ryuu's heart sank as he realized he had done all he could. He braced himself for the inevitable end.

Moriko's sense told her that both the hunter and Ryuu were still alive, but their presences were hard to separate. When she got within view of the hut she understood why. The hunter and Ryuu were rolling on the ground. Both of their blades were out of their hands, several paces away. They tumbled over each other, and for a moment Ryuu was on top, face bloody, fists driving into the face of the hunter. The hunter raised his hips and threw Ryuu forward, sprawling on the ground. The hunter scrambled away from Ryuu, grabbing his blade and standing. Moriko saw the hint of a triumphant grin on his face.

The hunter never knew Moriko had returned. He couldn't sense her, and all his attention was on Ryuu. She stepped up behind him and slid her blade between his ribs and back out again, smooth and easy. Her blade went straight through his heart, as she intended. The hunter let out a surprised grunt and collapsed to the ground.

Ryuu saw a shadow, darker than the others, break out of the trees. Ryuu could see it and knew it for Moriko, but the hunter had no idea his life was about to end. A blade pierced the hunter's heart and he dropped to the ground, surprise still on his face.

Ryuu looked at Moriko. There weren't any cuts or blood on her, and he assumed she had killed the other hunter. He wondered again what had happened to her. Back on the island, he had sensed a change in her. All afternoon it had been on his mind. She had always been quiet, but her silence held a different quality than it once had. When he had last seen her she had been strong, but not like this.

Moriko studied him, and Ryuu knew she was checking to see how badly he was injured. Without a word, she turned and melted back into the shadows of the trees. For a moment, Ryuu feared she was leaving him, disgusted by his weakness. As he picked up his blade and cleaned the dirt off it, he realized what it was about Moriko that was different. She was stronger, yes, but more than that, she was focused. Determined, even. Ryuu nodded to himself. That was it. She had purpose now.

Moriko turned and went back into the woods. The first hunter, the one who had tried to draw her off, was coming towards her. She had to give him credit for his courage. With the cut on his chest he didn't stand a chance, and with his partner dead, he knew it as well.

CHAPTER 9

Moriko declined to tell her story that evening, opting instead for rest. Ryuu didn't sleep well that night, nervous about what the new day would bring. He had loved Moriko once. Perhaps he still did, but he wasn't sure she was the same person he had once known. They slept apart that night, and the chill in the air that Ryuu felt seemed deeper than the winter's bite.

When Ryuu woke up the next morning Moriko was already awake, moving through her morning practice. Ryuu shook the sleep from his mind, amazed at the difference in her. When they had last been together, he had always been awake first. He watched her movement with interest, studying her technique.

The speed of her practice was startling. Moriko had always been strong, but her cuts today were crisp and fast. She was faster and perhaps stronger than she had ever been before. He was not the only one who had learned much over the course of the past six moons. He knew his perspective was altered due to the lack of his sense, but she was definitely stronger. Last night she killed the two hunters with little difficulty.

One thing was still true. Moriko was beautiful. She moved with speed, grace and strength; and although Ryuu had met many other nightblades, none were as attractive to him as Moriko was. Not even Rei, in all her perfection.

Moriko finished her practice and started heating water for tea. Ryuu said nothing, watching her carefully. Even in her daily rituals she was focused and completely present. He envied her. She was more alive than ever, and he was broken.

When the tea was prepared, Ryuu sipped at it gently. It was delicious, velvety richness blanketing his tongue. It was the best he had tasted in a long time, as long as he could remember. He thought back to Shigeru, who always claimed food and drink tasted better when consumed with dear company. Perhaps his surrogate father had been right about that too.

Moriko began her story without prompting. She spoke of the long days wandering south, the abandoned emptiness of Azaria. Although her voice was steady, Ryuu could tell those had been painful, fearful days for her. Ryuu regretted his decision then. She had gone south alone, and he was not without blame. It had been her decision, and he wouldn't take that away from her, but it had been influenced in no small part by his desires. He had caused her suffering, and for that, he felt ashamed.

Moriko paused for the first time when she spoke of the one-armed hunter she had killed, and Ryuu understood it was that decision that sparked this change he saw. She had broken her word and killed a man unawares. But as she spoke, Ryuu thought it wasn't the killing that tormented her. It was the fact she felt so little guilt over it. She had survived.

Ryuu listened with rapt attention as she described the Gathering. He was fascinated by the Azarians. His only experience with them had been in combat against the hunters, but Moriko had lived not just with their hunters, but with all their people. He laughed softly at her experiences at the tournament and her refusal to participate in the mounted archery portion. He tried to imagine her riding a horse while trying to hold a bow, and understood her refusal well.

Ryuu also paid attention to the tone Moriko spoke in. When she spoke of her time among the Azarians, of her hesitant friendship with Lobsang and Dorjee, he noticed a hint of admiration and longing in her voice. She had gone south to learn more about the Azarians and to find who hunted them, but she had discovered a people whom she held in great respect. Ryuu wondered at that.

"If there is one principal which guides them, it is the idea of strength. They are a hard people, and it is difficult not to think of the waste of life they create, but they are not cruel. They are disciplined and able to survive in a hard land. I think. . ." Moriko hesitated, as though the thought itself would bring Ryuu's anger upon her, "I think that here in the Three Kingdoms we could learn something from them. So many here aren't able to defend themselves. When villages are attacked, people don't stand and fight, they run and die."

Ryuu was angered by her words, but he forced himself to study her. Moriko was a kind person, though her kindness was often shrouded by layers upon layers of silence. It sounded as though she was dangerously close to condoning the burning of villages, but the thought would never occur to her. He tried to understand. She was upset by the carnage the hunters created, and only wanted the people of the Three Kingdoms to be strong enough to fight back, to not die needlessly.

He spoke softly. "If the Azarians come, there will be a slaughter, won't there?"

She nodded. "I believe so. It isn't because they are cruel or because they will view themselves as conquerors, but it will happen because they believe only the strong deserve to survive. It won't be overnight, but in a few moons, many will die as the Azarians cull the weak. There are few in the Three Kingdoms strong enough to survive. Our lives have been too easy."

Ryuu turned the conversation to a subject more personal. He didn't want to think about the fate of the tens of thousands of people scattered throughout the kingdoms. "And what will you do?"

Moriko answered him without hesitation. "I will survive."

Ryuu understood her now. Everything she had been through had stripped her of her other desires, her other dreams. She had become stronger in Azaria, but she had lost a part of herself. In her mind, survival was everything. But it wasn't, even if she didn't see it herself yet. If it was just an issue of survival, she would have left already. She wouldn't be roaming the woods, doing her best to protect the surrounding villages. He probed deeper.

"You plan to leave?"

She nodded again, and another silence descended as Ryuu thought about the woman in front of him.

"When will you go?"

Now it was Moriko's turn to study him. "As soon as I am able."

His final question was the most difficult to ask. "Will you stay here with me, at least for a while?"

There was much more he would have said, but the words were too difficult to say.

She stared at him in silence, and he worried he had presumed too much. Perhaps he had been wrong. Perhaps survival was all that mattered to her. But then she answered, and his heart was filled with a cautious joy.

"I will, for a while."

Moriko and Ryuu stood in a clearing facing each other, the same clearing they had been in so many moons ago when they were first attacked by the hunters. Prior to the attack it had been one of Ryuu's favorite places, but now the memories associated with the place made him wish he were anywhere else. It was why Moriko made them come here in the first place. He knew what she was trying to do, but his mind resisted.

It had been two moons since they reunited and Moriko killed the hunters. The height of winter had passed, and although spring was still far in the distance, the days were getting longer. In the time that had passed, they had tried to return to something resembling normalcy, but had failed. Ryuu's weakness hung between them like a curtain, preventing them from adopting their old lifestyle. He tried to train, tried to recover his strength and his ability, but no effort of his own brought it back to him. Every time he drew his blade he thought of all the lives that had been destroyed through his actions. Takako, Shigeru, Renzo, Rei, even Orochi. Their names and memories were a burden he wasn't sure he could shoulder.

Moriko had tried training with him a couple of times, but it was apparent there was little she could do. Instead, they spent their time together talking. Ryuu knew Moriko was listening closely to every word he spoke, and he knew she was trying to figure out why he was broken. He appreciated it, but after a moon together, they hadn't made any progress.

In fairness, Moriko didn't stay at the hut often. She still made her rounds, trying to ensure the safety of the nearby villages. Ryuu tried to teach her how to sense at a distance, but either he wasn't explaining it well or it wasn't possible for her. The only way for her to protect the villagers was to wander from village to village.

They shared a bed a few times, but even that wasn't the same. Without the sense, it was a different experience. It felt foreign and forced, and after a few attempts they slept apart, unable to bridge the differences between them. Every time Moriko left to make her rounds, Ryuu feared she wouldn't return.

Moriko had just returned from another trip, and it was obvious she had been considering the problem. With only a few words she handed Ryuu his sword, grabbed their wooden practice swords, and led the way. Ryuu followed without question.

The clearing was silent except for Moriko's voice. "I will be leaving soon."

Ryuu's heart sank. He tried to keep his voice steady. "I figured as much. I wondered how long it would take."

"You're a shadow of the man you once were. You can't focus, and without a clear mind and clear purpose, you'll never reclaim your sense. I think you've realized this as well."

Ryuu nodded. "But I can't think through a way to fix it."

Moriko shook her head. "I don't think you can think your way through it. Some things must simply be known."

Ryuu agreed. But knowing the solution was much different than solving the problem.

Moriko broke the silence. "Since the day I met you, you have been torn between two ideals. You want to protect everyone, especially those closest to you. But you also want to live a life of peace, a life where you don't have to harm others."

She drew her sword and looked at it. It shone in the early morning sunlight, casting reflections upon the snow.

"A sword is a weapon. A weapon designed to kill. In the hands of a nightblade, it is a weapon of unparalleled danger. You may want to use it to protect others, but if you protect them with a sword, it means you must kill. A swordsman is a killer. You know this, but you don't accept it. You want only to save, but you aren't willing to pay the price. The price of protecting the weak is the blood of those who would prey on them."

Ryuu's first impulse was to argue, but he realized she was right. Shigeru had said something very similar to him a long time ago, and he had accepted it at the time. But he had changed, and he had hoped he could protect the weak without killing others.

He was about to speak, but she held up her hand to stop him. She sheathed her steel and picked up the practice sword again. "I don't have time to continue to discuss what has happened to you. If I want to survive, I need to leave before the Azarians sweep through this land. But once I loved you, and I still care for you." Her eyes met his. "Deeply. And to honor that love, I will leave you with one last gift." She held her sword in front of her, pointed at him.

A hint of her purpose started to dawn on him. He feared what she would say next.

"Today we duel. I will give you a few passes to find your strength, but that is all. I will not kill you, because I don't know if I could live with that pain, but I will break your right arm and hand. You will never hold a sword again, and your path will be laid out before you. Perhaps you can save others in a different way. It will be up to you to find your fate. But if you want to hold a sword, if you are willing to kill to protect those who need you, you will need to find the strength to defend yourself. It's the last gift I can offer you."

Ryuu nodded. It was as he feared. She was leaving, and she was going to leave him shattered. He assumed a defensive stance, prepared for her strike. He remembered the horror of having his arm broken on the island, the physical pain meaningless compared to the pain of losing his purpose. He searched for that feeling again, the feeling of knowing what he was supposed to do.

Moriko sprinted forward, and Ryuu thought of Shigeru, his calm, weathered face as he patiently showed Ryuu a move one more time. He remembered when he had first met Shigeru, being scared and alone, surrounded by bandits. He remembered Shigeru sacrificing his life so Ryuu would have another chance. Shigeru had given everything to give Ryuu the opportunity to change the world. Ryuu watched as Moriko's hips rotated, clearly projecting her cut. He blocked her easily but didn't return the strike. He wasn't fast enough, and he needed to protect himself. Moriko went past him and turned. He had made it through her first pass.

Takako came unbidden to Ryuu's mind as Moriko cut again. Takako had been the most beautiful woman Ryuu had ever seen. He remembered his awkward first moments with her, the conversation they had shared. But mostly he remembered her death, the final hint of a smile on her broken body as she gave up her spirit. For cycles, Ryuu had wondered what her final thoughts had been, and in a moment of clarity, he found belief. She had forgiven him. She must have. Ryuu blocked Moriko's first strike, but she followed it up with a quick second cut. Ryuu blocked it as well, seeing it just in time. Moriko made as if she was going to retreat, but she struck again. Ryuu saw it and stepped away, her wooden blade passing harmlessly in front of him.

Moriko stepped away, giving him a moment of peace. Fear and anger mixed in his mind, a deadly milieu he couldn't escape. Moriko struck again, a series of cuts Ryuu struggled to keep up with. She was so fast, much faster than he remembered. Her last strike hit him in the upper left arm near his shoulder. The pain flared, but he pushed it down. Had she been using steel he would have lost his arm. It wasn't broken, but it felt horrible when he tried to move it. Her next pass would be her last. She would break his arm and there was nothing he could do to stop her.

Fury overrode his other emotions. He didn't know why Shigeru had trained him, but he believed he was meant to do something important. His gift was the blade, and that gift was about to be taken away. It was profoundly wrong, and every part of his body and mind knew it. Moriko shifted her weight, and in the back of his mind, Ryuu knew he only had moments to decide. Faces ran through his memory, and he looked at them for the first time without regret. Yes, he was sorry they had died, and he missed them dearly, but he had taken the best actions he could. It was all he could do. It was all anyone could ever do. And he was needed, perhaps now more than ever.

Moriko darted forward and all the doubt, all the hesitation in Ryuu's mind shattered. It was as though a cold wind blew through his mind, clearing out the debris that had built up over the past few cycles. His sense came flooding back to him, never gone, only hidden. Moriko contained her presence well, but Ryuu had spent too much time training with her. He could sense her as easily as he sensed himself. His mind was blank, and his body slipped into the energy that flowed through the old woods as easily as he slipped on his robes in the morning. He felt strength flood his limbs, and he exploded forward.

Moriko grinned and they met in combat in earnest. Their wooden swords snapped through the air as they spun around each other and the trees. Sweat poured from Ryuu's forehead as he met Moriko strike for strike. He was faster and stronger, but she had learned new techniques in their time apart. Her cuts came low and fast, and her body masked her movements well. If not for his familiarity with her, he would have been cut several times.

When he finally disarmed her, a wave of pride rushed through him. He felt whole and alive for the first time in many moons. He pressed her up against a tree and kissed her deeply, memories of their first kiss making him smile. She had pushed him away that time. Now she returned his passion hungrily.

The moment was over all too soon, and when he stepped back, he saw a light in her eyes that hadn't been there before.

He smiled. Their problems were only beginning, but in this, at least, he was whole. He didn't know what would happen next, but he knew it would be with Moriko, and that was enough for him.

CHAPTER 10

Akira, Sen, Mashiro, and Makoto sat around a table discussing the spring. Winter had come early, and it had been bitter; but spring was coming just as early, and with the change of the seasons the Azarians would come. Already some of the game trails were opening up in the mountains, and Akira worried they would soon be dealing with another flood of Azarian hunters in the old Southern Kingdom.

"My king?" Mashiro spoke, the lean general as impatient as ever.

Akira glanced up from the maps. He still wasn't used to the new title, even after several moons. They had held a ceremony, but it had been a quiet affair. There would be time for celebrations later, so long as they managed to keep their fragile kingdom alive. The unification had gone smoothly enough, but Akira hadn't instituted any major changes yet. For now, each of the old kingdoms managed themselves much as they always had. Akira had trusted advisers in each of the courts, but he was focused on the challenges ahead. Already he had summoned almost all the armies available. From the old Western Kingdom he had pulled two armies south to the Three Sisters. From the Northern Kingdom, another two armies of cavalry well-used to mountainous terrain. And from his own ranks, every man he could spare. Altogether, over thirty thousand men would be massed at the entrance to the pass. It was the largest fighting force assembled in the land for over a thousand cycles, and he still worried it wouldn't be enough.

Toro's last estimate to Akira had been that there were almost sixty thousand Azarians. By population the Kingdom was much larger, but all Azarians were trained in warfare. The sixty thousand Azarians would be over half women and children, but Akira didn't discount their effect on the battle. He knew they would fight well, and he worried his own men would hesitate to strike a woman, no matter how deadly she appeared.

But what worried him more were the hunters. Even with Moriko's journey into Azaria, they had no idea how many hunters the Azarians possessed. Perhaps it was only a few dozen. Or maybe it was closer to a few thousand. Akira had some of his best minds trying to guess what they might be facing.

Generally the sense was passed down by blood. A parent with the sense almost always gifted it to their children. However, in the Kingdom, the ability had been weeded out for dozens of generations. Monks weren't allowed to reproduce. The best guess of the scholars and the monks themselves was that the ability randomly appeared in about one out of every thousand children.

But according to Moriko, there was no prohibition against hunters reproducing in Azaria. The sense would be strong in some bloodlines, and it meant there could be many more hunters than they expected. Akira had read all the reports the scholars had written, but it all boiled down to one bare fact. They had no idea how many hunters would come through the pass once the snows melted. And that frightened Akira much more than the other sixty thousand warriors.

"My king?" Mashiro repeated, and Akira looked up from his thoughts. It was getting harder to control them. He needed rest.

"Mashiro, I see nothing in your plan I could improve on. Does anyone else have any suggestions?"

Those around the table shook their heads. Mashiro was a brilliant strategist, possibly the best military mind in generations. Nobody doubted him, even though he still hadn't seen thirty cycles.

Mashiro's plan was simple in its execution, which Akira was grateful for. In his experience the simple plans were often the best. They would hold the small gateway at the northern end of the pass as long as possible. It would be filled with archers and some infantry. They would make the Azarians pay for every step of ground they tried to cover. They wouldn't bother trying to man the small outposts along the pass. Mashiro agreed with Toro's judgment. Any soldiers stationed there would be sitting targets for hunters.

Mashiro hoped to hold the fort for as long as possible, but he knew it would have to fall sometime. The fort was too small and the numbers of their enemies too great. The plan was to draw the Azarians into the foothills of the mountains north of the fort. They would station a large force directly ahead of the Azarians to meet them head-on. Once the battle was met, men would swarm the Azarians from the hills to the east and west. They would come together and crush the Azarians in between them. Finally, Sen's mounted cavalry would stream down from the game trails in the mountains behind the fort. They would crush whatever stragglers remained.

As far as plans went, Akira couldn't think of one better. It used the terrain to their maximum advantage. If they were going to emerge victorious, it was by far their best way forward. But he couldn't shake his worry over the hunters. How would they affect the plans?

Akira looked around the table. "I believe we have the best plan laid here in front of us, and for that, I'm grateful. But I want us to put together plans for what should happen if we fail."

Mashiro looked as though he couldn't believe his ears. "My king?"

Akira met his incredulous gaze. "I hope more than anything that we emerge victorious from this battle. We are putting almost everything we can into this effort. But my heart urges caution. We need to be prepared for what should happen if we fail."

Sen nodded, and Akira saw he had been thinking along the same lines.

Akira continued. "Sen, my first wish is that you return to your homelands and find shelter there. Should we fall, your lands will be by far the safest. You can mount a resistance from there."

He could see the disagreement in the old man's eyes, but he didn't let the lord argue. "You are second in line to the throne. I will not risk both our lives in this battle, and a king needs to lead his people, even to the end."

Sen nodded again, and Akira was grateful. The older lord didn't need to like the command, but he had to follow it. The land couldn't be without leadership. Not for the first time, he wished that either he or the older lord had another to pass the command to, but neither of them had an heir.

Akira turned to Makoto. "I want you to organize a resistance. If we fall, what should the soldiers do? It is a delicate line I ask you to walk. Soldiers must be assured of their victory, but they must know what to do if it fails. This land will not fall peacefully to the Azarians the way the Southern Kingdom fell to the Western. Understood?"

Makoto nodded. His personality was better suited to the task than Mashiro's. Mashiro was the genius everyone looked up to, but Makoto was the one everyone followed. If anyone could inspire hope and help the men prepare for the worst, it would be the giant.

Akira stood up and bowed to all the assembled men. He thanked them and asked for Sen to see him before he left. Then, like a good leader, he stepped aside and let his men do the work that needed to be done. There was another task he needed to finish.

Unfortunately, the war wasn't the only item on Akira's mind. In his tent was one of the most unusual messengers he had ever encountered. The man wore a long dark cloak that didn't hide the scabbard at his side. By all outward appearances he seemed no different than most men, but Akira had watched him move with the cat-like grace that belonged to only one type of person. He had received a messenger from the nightblades.

Akira hadn't had time to speak with the man before he was to meet with Sen and his generals. More to the point, he needed time to think. Ryuu had indicated there were far more nightblades alive than anyone suspected, but he gave no clue as to where they were. If this messenger was from the same place Ryuu had gone, it was possible he was the most important messenger Akira would meet with.

The man sat exactly where Akira had left him, motionless. If Akira hadn't seen him move earlier he would have suspected the man was a statue. The messenger stirred when Akira entered his tent, lifting his hood and standing. It was the first time Akira had seen the man's face, and it was utterly unremarkable. Akira guessed the man had seen over thirty cycles, and was strong, but beyond that, there was little to identify the man as unique.

"Greetings, king."

Akira nodded. "Thank you for your patience."

The man gave him a look that indicated he saw right through Akira's discomfort. He knew the real reason Akira had gone to his meeting instead of receiving him. Akira straightened up. Nightblade or not, he wouldn't be intimidated in his own camp.

"You are welcome. It has been a long journey, and I am grateful for the opportunity to rest."

Akira wondered if they would have to go through the traditional pleasantries before the man got to the point.

"I see you have already intuited a fair amount about me," the nightblade said. "This doesn't surprise me. There are those who speak highly of you, and I see now they weren't entirely misled. You seem a man of integrity."

Akira was grateful for the compliment, especially from a nightblade. In his experience, they didn't often say what wasn't true. They had no retribution to fear for speaking the truth. "Why are you here?"

"I have come for Rei."

A mix of emotions ran through Akira's heart. On one hand, he was glad. Rei had told him they had greater healers where she came from, but with no way of contacting them, there wasn't any way to bring the healing to her. Perhaps this man would be able to take her back home. Akira was grateful she would be safe, someplace away from the coming war. But all the same, he was saddened. Even paralyzed, he would miss her company. She was beautiful, yes, but she also possessed a wisdom and strength far beyond her age. Akira had enjoyed his time with her.

"She is paralyzed from the waist down. I'll have a litter prepared for her as soon as you are ready."

The messenger smiled as though Akira had told a joke.

"Please allow me to see her first. I am aware of her injury and would like to attempt to heal her."

Akira glanced at the man quizzically.

"You have guessed that I am a nightblade, for that is all you know, but I am a dayblade, trained in the arts of healing. I have come to do what I can and bring her home. They already know she is injured. It is why I was sent."

Akira was surprised, and couldn't help himself from blurting out the first question that came to his mind. "You came just to heal her, knowing she was injured?"

The messenger nodded. "She is important to us. She is special."

Akira agreed. "Yes, she is."

The messenger cocked his head to one side, studying Akira closely. Again, Akira got the impression he couldn't keep any secrets from the man in front of him. "I see. We did not know."

Akira shook his head. "It's of no matter. I care deeply for her, and am glad you came to heal her."

The dayblade gave the king another knowing look. "You were expecting a different message."

Akira nodded. There wasn't any point in trying to hide the truth from the messenger. It seemed he could see directly into Akira's heart. "Your eyes see far, and the events shaping our lands are not secret. The land is reunited for the first time in over a thousand cycles, and yet we face an enemy more dangerous than we have ever met before. I know you know of the hunters. I hoped perhaps you had come with an offer of strength for us in our time of need."

The dayblade was silent for a moment. "And you would accept us with open arms?"

Akira nodded.

"And your people?"

Akira was about to nod, but then he thought about the question. He had become used to the idea of nightblades, but for almost everyone else, they were still considered the most deadly enemies the Three Kingdoms had ever known. "I don't know."

The messenger spoke softly. "We are no longer under the command of the king, but I will let your desires be known."

Akira didn't think he'd get any more from the messenger. It was as much as he could hope for. "Thank you."

Without another word, Akira led the dayblade to the tent where Rei was resting. When they entered Akira saw that Rei was wide awake. She had sensed another one of her people nearby.

"Rei," the dayblade's voice was filled with concern.

Rei murmured a greeting, and the dayblade got to work. Akira watched with unconcealed interest. The nightblades and the dayblades were legendary. He had been given the opportunity to see the skill of nightblades in some small part, but he had never seen a dayblade at work. The dayblade ran his hands gently and slowly along Rei's body, spending more time around the cut that had paralyzed her and left her right arm useless.

Akira wanted to question the dayblade. By sight alone there was little he could see. The works of the dayblades had passed into legend, and the reality of their skills was beyond his knowledge. He resisted the urge. Whatever the dayblade was doing, he was clearly focused on the task at hand.

The king stepped forward, risking the ire of the dayblade for a chance to see more clearly what was happening. The dayblade had his hand wrapped softly around Rei's arm, where she had been cut deeply. Time seemed to slow down, and to Akira's eyes, nothing seemed to be happening. But when the dayblade removed his hand, Akira saw that the scar on her arm had faded. It was still visible if one looked for it, but the change was dramatic. Akira shook his head to make sure he was seeing everything correctly.

The dayblade stood up and took a drink of water. He looked tired but determined. He glanced at Rei. "Do you want something for the pain? This next healing will hurt even more."

Akira was surprised. Rei hadn't let out any sign she was in pain. She was a strong woman.

Rei shook her head, and the dayblade nodded. "Then let us begin." He turned to Akira. "This will take some time. There is no need for you to remain."

Akira bowed. "I will stay for a while longer yet, thank you."

The dayblade seemed not to care. His attention was already focused on Rei as he sat down next to her, placing both his hands on her bare back. He closed his eyes, and again he went to work. Akira watched, but could see nothing happening. He did see that Rei was in pain, her face contorted and her teeth grinding against one another in an effort not to scream. Her will held for a time, but eventually the scream broke free, surprising and frightening Akira for a moment. Her scream was primal and uncivilized. It didn't seem to faze the dayblade at all. He just kept his hands on her back.

Akira took his leave as another scream was ripped from Rei's throat. The legends only told of the healing of the dayblades. They never spoke of the pain that accompanied such healings. Akira wanted to stay, but he could do no good, and Rei's screams rattled his nerves, as well as those around the tent. He was grateful her screams faded quickly.

Akira ran some errands, meeting with some of his commanders and signing a set of orders placed in front of him. He went about his day-to-day responsibilities with half a mind until the dayblade found him.

"I have done what I can."

"How is she?"

The dayblade hesitated. "My skills are excellent, but her hurts are grievous. Perhaps if I had been here sooner, but what is done is done. I have healed her spine as well as I am able, and I expect she will be able to walk again. In time, with more healing, she may fully recover from that cut. Her arm is another matter. There is only so much one can heal, and the cut across the back of her arm severed everything to the bone. I have done what I can, and she will have use of it, but she will never wield a blade again. I have given her the news and she grieves to hear it."

Akira could understand. He was a warrior too, and a warrior who couldn't fight lacked purpose. Akira was also a king, born to a family destined to rule. There was more for him than the sword, but Rei had grown up a nightblade. Her only purpose as long as she had been alive had been to fight. She wouldn't know who she was without the ability.

The dayblade interrupted Akira's thoughts. "Now that she is healed I am called to return with her to the place from where we came. She will have tonight to recover, but tomorrow we will leave."

Akira read into the dayblade's thoughts. "Thank you. I am grateful for all you have done."

He ordered a tent prepared for the dayblade and went to Rei's tent. He hesitated at the entrance, suddenly unsure of why he was even there. Not only was she a nightblade, but she was broken. How could he help?

She spoke even as he considered turning around. "I'm still here, you know. You don't need to be scared of me."

Her voice was stronger than Akira had heard it since the battle. It brought hope to his heart. "How are you?"

"I hurt worse than I ever thought I could. If it's possible, I think the healing hurt worse than getting cut in the first place. But look what I can do."

Slowly, as if she was uncertain of what her own body would do, she spun in the bed until she was laying on her back. It was the first time she had done so since coming to the tent moons ago. She looked up at the ceiling and sighed. Akira could see she was in pain, but it didn't stop her.

"Help me up."

Akira stepped to the side of the tent and got Rei her robes, slipping them over her shoulders to cover at least part of her nakedness. He grabbed her left arm, her good one, and gently helped her to stand. She got on her feet and fell forward into him. He embraced her gently and rearranged her robes, helping her dress. She was even lighter than he remembered. He didn't realize she had lost so much muscle while confined to the bed.

Rei took a few hesitant steps around the room, Akira never far from her side. It seemed ridiculous to him that as king of the land he would be spending time escorting around an injured nightblade, but his feelings couldn't be denied, inconvenient as they were. Rei flexed her right hand. It closed and opened slowly.

"Could you bring me my blade?"

Akira walked across the tent, drew the blade from its sheath and brought it to her. He handed it to her with a short bow. She grasped the sword with both hands and Akira stepped back. Rei tried a practice cut, but it lacked strength. She tried again and the sword slipped out of her right hand. She held it with her left, but the truth of the dayblade's comments were undeniable. Without a word she handed the sword back to Akira, who sheathed it for her. When he turned back to her he saw her crying.

He went over to her and held her gently. She returned the embrace and they stood there in silence, tears running down Rei's cheeks.

The next day Akira watched as Rei rode off with the dayblade. She couldn't keep her saddle well, and the dayblade had promised they would travel slowly. Her sword was still at her side, although it was now useless to her.

They had spent the previous night together. Akira hadn't expected to, but they had both felt the desire. He smiled and shook his head as memories came flooding back into his mind. It didn't make any sense at all, but there it was, all the same. He would miss her.

She turned and gave him one last smile as she rode away. Akira wondered if their paths would ever cross again. He hoped they would, but he wasn't counting on it. Spring was coming, and he didn't think he would see another summer.

The only way was forward, so Akira turned back to the camp and tried to push Rei out of his mind as best he could. The pass would be open within the next moon or two, and he had a campaign to plan, a battle to determine the fate of the Kingdom.

CHAPTER 11

Every day Moriko wondered at the change in Ryuu. For as long as she had known him, he had been conflicted in some way. He had always been torn between competing ideals. But their duel in the clearing had unlocked something in him. He was driven and focused; but beyond that he was strong, stronger than she would have believed possible.

She couldn't help but make the comparison to Nameless. Moriko still believed Nameless was stronger. His body and mind were almost consumed by the energy he possessed. He couldn't stop moving. Ryuu was something different. He lacked the sheer strength of Nameless, but it would still be a battle for the ages if they met. Ryuu was more focused than she'd ever seen him.

Unfortunately, that focus was entirely on saving the Three Kingdoms. He was ready to sacrifice his life, and thanks to her, he no longer suffered from any hesitation.

Moriko still wanted to leave. She had delayed her departure to see what Ryuu would do, and now the time had come for her own decision. She had no desire to save the Three Kingdoms, but she did want be near Ryuu. Once again he had become the man she cared for, and the idea of leaving him hurt her more than she cared to admit. At times she was angry at herself for allowing him to get so close.

To Moriko, retreating to the island had become the most important goal in her mind. Ryuu had discovered a place where they could be accepted. She had listened to him speak about the island, how different it felt to be someplace safe, a place where they could display their powers openly. When he spoke of the island, it sounded like a place Moriko could call home. Already her heart called for her to go, but she couldn't bear to part with Ryuu now that they were finally together again.

Every day they trained and discussed their next steps. Every day Ryuu would spend some time in meditation, expanding his sense. Moriko still couldn't believe his abilities. To be able to sense things at such a distance was incredible. It astounded her he had known what she was going through back when she was traveling through Azaria. She would have given anything for even a hint of what he was doing as well.

Spring was coming with alarming rapidity. The snows were melting, and every day Ryuu reported that the battle for the Three Sisters, the battle for the kingdoms, was approaching. Both forces had moved as close to their respective sides of the pass as they could. Ryuu expected the battle would commence within the moon.

Ryuu also reported other marvelous wonders. The armies of the Three Kingdoms had merged into a single fighting force of an incredible size. They didn't know what had happened, but somehow either Tanak or Akira had managed to bring together more people than the land had seen in over a thousand cycles. It was one of the best pieces of news they had.

The other news Moriko thought about often was the discord in the camp of the Azarians. Ryuu told her he sensed combat there. It was nothing on a large scale, but fights were happening more often. Moriko wondered if the alliance of clans Nameless had created was holding together. She thought of Dorjee and Lobsang and the other Red Hawks she had known, and she was surprised to find she hoped they were fine. They had brought the ire of Nameless upon themselves when it was discovered they harbored a nightblade, and she wondered daily what had happened to them after she left. She had cut their leader deeply, and she worried he might take out his wrath on them. She didn't hold out much hope for her friends.

Moriko knew she didn't have much more time to make her choice. Soon they would have to make a decision, and their paths would be set for good. She hadn't spoken much to Ryuu about it as he regained his strength, but she worried about the monasteries. They were tied up in everything happening, and she feared it wasn't for the best.

The hunters solved the problem for them. Ryuu sensed them as they split from the camp. The trails in the mountains had to be open enough for them to be willing to risk the trek. Ryuu counted eight hunters. Four pairs, all staying together as they made the hike through the rugged terrain. Both Ryuu and Moriko suspected their purpose, but it wasn't until they came through the mountains into the land of the Southern Kingdom that they were sure. The pairs did not split into separate groups, but kept together on a path towards their house. At the rate they were traveling, Ryuu figured they had five or six days before the hunters found them again.

Ryuu wanted to walk out to meet them, but Moriko urged him against it. Every step the hunters took in the kingdom was an affront to

Ryuu, but they were safest here in the old woods. As much as it pained him to admit it, she was right. In the woods Moriko would be even more difficult to sense, and it was here she could be the most use. In the plains they would be matched strength for strength, and despite Ryuu's power, Moriko was certain they couldn't face eight in open combat.

For five days they trained and rested. The waiting was hard, but every day the hunters came closer, unaware they would be expected company. Moriko was afraid, but she had never seen Ryuu like he was now. The kindness that defined him was still there, but there was a new hardness in his eyes. The last hints of childhood innocence had finally been stripped from his character, and he was more dangerous than ever, ready for this final war.

The hunters arrived on the evening of the fifth night, and Ryuu and Moriko were ready for them.

Moriko crouched in the shadow of a tree outside the clearing where they had first been attacked a cycle ago. She was saddened the clearing would have blood spilled in it once again, but it was the best place near the hut to hold the fight. The open space gave Ryuu room to use all his power, and the woods surrounding the clearing gave Moriko a chance to use her own special skills to the fullest.

Ryuu knelt in the middle of the clearing, meditating. He was bait, and there was no way anyone with the sense within fifty leagues of here would miss him. He was throwing off energy, almost enough to blind Moriko's own sense. It was only through force of will that she was able to focus on anything besides him. The hunters would find him, and he would lead them into combat near the edge of the trees. Moriko would dart in and out. In essence, his work was to stay alive. She would do the killing.

She was afraid, not just for herself, but for him as well. He had found his strength, and it was more than Moriko had dared to hope for; but against eight hunters, she wasn't sure it would be enough. Together was the only way they had a chance to live through the night, and even that hope seemed slim.

There was a soft rustle in the grass and the hunters came into the clearing. Each pair entered from a different direction, encircling Ryuu immediately. Moriko's breath caught in her throat as Ryuu dropped out of his meditation and stood up. He drew his blade and was answered by eight drawing steel in return. Ryuu's draw, normally a sound to strike fear in his enemies, seemed empty and hollow in comparison to the force against him.

Silence hung in the spring air. Moriko studied her opponents and saw that they were waiting for her. She was completely within herself, and in the old woods none of them had a hope of sensing her. But her absence made them nervous. She put herself in their shoes. By now they would know who she was and what she was capable of. She had probably killed more of their kind than anyone in their legends. They knew she was a danger, and they had expected her, but they had no way of knowing if she was even in the area. For all his strength, it wasn't Ryuu they feared. It was her.

If there was one thing that could be said about the hunters, it was that they did not lack for courage. They were wary, expecting a trap at any moment, expecting Moriko to appear at any time, but still they advanced. Moriko could tell that Nameless had not sent young, inexperienced hunters against them. These were hunters who had seen many battles, had seen many cycles of war and violence, and they would not make foolish mistakes. One pace at a time, the hunters closed in on Ryuu, a circle of certain death slowly closing.

Ryuu was as calm and steady as Moriko had ever seen him. She watched as he scanned the circle, trying to decide which adversary he would attack first. Against a group of eight, their best hope was to kill the weak first, reducing their numbers as much as possible before the battle began in earnest. From what Moriko could sense, it would be a difficult decision. Each of the hunters was strong, and none stood out as being weaker than their fellows.

In a moment, the clearing exploded into action, erasing the silence of the tense anticipation. It was Ryuu who struck first. It could be no other way. If he allowed the hunters to strike first and in unison, no amount of strength would keep him alive.

Even though Moriko and the hunters had been expecting Ryuu's attack, they were all taken aback by the violence of his first strike. It felt as though he had literally exploded into action. Ryuu dashed forward with incredible speed. A series of quick cuts sent one of the pairs of hunters reeling backwards, trying to keep their feet underneath them as an incredible flurry of blows sped their way. Ryuu scored a couple of small cuts on the pair, but they were too fast for him to land a lethal stroke on either of them.

Though it would have been better if he had killed at least one, what was most important was that he had broken through the circle that had threatened to entrap him. He had won his freedom of movement, and now all the hunters were approaching him from the same direction. Ryuu dashed and darted among them, landing a strike here and deflecting a cut there. His movements seemed to be random, but as Moriko watched, she saw the pattern unfold in front of her. Every pass he took brought the fight closer to the edge of the woods, closer to the deep shadows where Moriko waited in anticipation.

The battle raged closer and closer to Moriko, and although it pained her to stay in place, she forced herself to wait. So long as she was still she was completely hidden, and if she was able to take a pair completely by surprise, she might be able to kill one or even two hunters in a single pass. Not only would it reduce their number, the shock of losing two of their own so quickly could turn the entire battle in the nightblades' favor.

So Moriko watched and waited as Ryuu brought the battle closer to her with every strike. Every move and every cut Ryuu made was brilliant, and Moriko was in awe of both his speed and skill. Unfortunately, it was not enough to thin their numbers. The eight who attacked worked well together, and the pairs themselves were excellent. They were cautious, one pair staying on defense as another pair would attempt to attack. As soon as Ryuu moved his focus, the pairs would switch, another going on the defensive while the other attacked.

Ryuu was brilliant, and his strength was a sight to see, but he was still one warrior against eight, and everyone on the battlefield was an expert swordsman. It was only a matter of time. The hunters knew it, and Ryuu knew it as well. But every moment brought them closer to the edge of the clearing. Moriko watched in anticipation, trying to judge the moment best.

The battle seemed even until Ryuu made a mistake. He thought he saw an opening in one hunter's defense and he struck out, risking his balance to get a lethal cut. The opening was real, but it had been intentional. When Ryuu moved for it, the hunter's partner stepped inside for the block, surprising Ryuu just enough to throw him off balance. It wasn't much, but suddenly Ryuu was backpedaling, a flurry of cuts coming at him from the pair of hunters. They ran him into another pair eagerly waiting for him. Moriko almost left her hiding spot. He had lost any advantage he had. It would only be a matter of moments.

But she remained in place as she saw him allow a single cut through his defense to cut through his side. It wasn't deep, but the pain had to be incredible. She flinched for both of them, but by allowing the one cut through, he gained enough time to solidify his defense. The four continued to press him, but Moriko could see he was allowing them to press him naturally towards the woods.

Then the hunters made a mistake, not of skill, but of strategy. For some reason, a pair of hunters decided to make for the old woods and try and get around the battle and attack Ryuu from behind. She could imagine their thoughts. The old woods would mask their presence to some degree, and they hoped to get the drop on Ryuu. Any worry of a trap seemed to have slipped their mind in the heat of battle. And with Ryuu retreating straight towards Moriko's hiding position, it meant it would draw the pair right to her spot.

Moriko controlled her anticipation as the pair came towards her. They were silent, and if not for her sense, she would have wondered if they were trying to escape the fight. But in a few moments, the battle came right towards her, and there was nothing for her to do but make her move.

She attacked the pair who had come into the deep woods first. They walked only a few paces away from her, and for a moment she feared they would smell her presence. But they were too distracted by the thought of killing Ryuu, and walked by her without noticing her at all. As soon as their backs were to her, she made her move. With three quick steps she left the shadows. She drew her blade, a sound lost among the din of battle, and made her two cuts without hesitation. The first cut took the head off one of the hunters, the second was a thrust through the heart of the other.

Moriko couldn't have asked for a better effect. The six remaining hunters, so sure of their inevitable victory, were suddenly thrown a surprise. The four Ryuu was engaged with reacted by redoubling their efforts. Moriko went after them. Ryuu was holding his own, but with the pain of a cut, he would falter.

They saw her coming, even if they couldn't sense her. The moon was full and she still cast a shadow. One of the pairs attacking Ryuu broke off to face her, but they underestimated Ryuu's speed. The moment one of them stepped away and began turning towards Moriko, Ryuu saw an opening. He leapt forward and cut across the side of the hunter's neck. It wasn't a deep cut, but it didn't need to be. Blood starting pouring out of the wound, and the hunter sank to his knees as his life left him.

There were two reactions to Ryuu's cut. The first was Moriko's. The hunter's partner, momentarily distracted, dropped his guard, and Moriko took that moment to act. Another cut and another hunter fell. But Ryuu had also left himself open. He sensed the attack coming and threw himself out of the way, but another cut sliced across his chest. Again, it wasn't lethal, but Moriko feared he wouldn't be able to fight at his full strength much longer.

The two nightblades and four remaining hunters met on the edge of the clearing. Ryuu's speed and strength, slightly diminished, and Moriko's gifts met against the skill and steel of the two remaining pairs of hunters.

Time seemed to stretch and expand for Moriko. Both battle and the sense had a strange effect on one's perception. She couldn't tell if the fight lasted for a few moments or if they had battled through a whole passing of the moon. It felt as though they fought for a night and a day and another night, but perhaps it had only been the space of a few heartbeats.

Moriko's world shrank until it was just the six blades in the night. She tried to get the hunters to leave the clearing, but they wouldn't chase her into the woods. Their lesson had been learned. The moon was full, and they could see her so long as she remained in the clearing. She was strong enough that they couldn't kill her, but when they could see her strikes, and there were two of them, it was nearly impossible for her to land a killing blow.

Ryuu was in the same predicament. She could tell he was in pain, but he kept his speed up as best he could. But he wasn't as fast, and the pair he fought was willing to let him weaken. They kept a defensive front of blades, not giving him any openings to strike. They were hunters, and they were patient. It was much easier to kill a weakened opponent than a strong one. It frustrated Moriko, but she couldn't figure out a way to prevent it from working.

Time wore on, and Moriko feared they wouldn't be able to win. They were both wearing down, and the advantage was on the hunters' side. If they would just make a mistake, perhaps Moriko and Ryuu could seize the advantage, but these were some of the smartest hunters Moriko had encountered. They didn't underestimate their opponents, and there weren't any tricks Moriko could think of to save them.

They passed and passed again, swords glinting and clashing against each other in the light of the full moon. Moriko was getting exhausted, and she didn't know how Ryuu was still on his feet. Even now he would occasionally burst across her senses with a series of strong strikes and momentarily gain the upper hand, but the hunters would willingly give up ground and wait for the burst to pass. Once Moriko drifted close to Ryuu and for a moment they paired up against a single hunter, but the others leapt immediately to the one's defense. No matter what they tried, their efforts were stymied.

The result of the battle seemed inevitable. Each of them had been cut, and Ryuu had lost an alarming amount of blood. Moriko began to sink into despair.

It was Ryuu who saved them. She didn't know where he found the strength, but without warning he gave a yell which pierced even Moriko's soul. He exploded next to her, and to her sense, it was as though he were attacking from all directions at once. It shocked both her and the hunters, but it was the hunters who were on the wrong side of Ryuu's blade. Moriko watched out of the corner of her eye as a hunter blocked a strike that never came, opening himself up for the true strike. The hunter fell to Ryuu's blade.

Moriko felt a glimmer of hope, and then Ryuu exploded again, and to Moriko's sense he was striking in eight different places at once. She didn't understand the technique or understand where he found the power, but there was no denying how effective it was. Again, a hunter tried to block a strike that wasn't there, and again the real strike pierced the hunter's heart.

Moriko snapped back to the hunters she had been fighting. They were focused on Ryuu, and had forgotten temporarily about her. Moriko struck, their senses not giving them any warning. She sliced the neck of the first hunter, and the death of his partner shocked the other back to attention.

The tables had turned, and now it was two on one, but the two had pushed themselves past the limit of their endurance. Their strikes were slower, and their last opponent was still strong. Moriko summoned up all the strength and focus she had remaining to her, and Ryuu did the same. Their strikes came one after another, but the lone remaining hunter deflected cut after cut.

Finally Moriko got one cut in that struck flesh. It wasn't lethal, but she thought it would slow the hunter down. She was wrong. The hunter's blade moved faster than ever, and Moriko realized he was in a death frenzy. He knew his odds of surviving were slim, and he didn't hold anything back. His cuts were fast, but Moriko and Ryuu, exhausted, defended themselves well, landing cut after cut on the hunter. Both he and they were covered in blood, and still the hunter didn't fall. He kept attacking, his cuts becoming wilder, more dangerous. Ryuu eventually sunk his blade all the way through the hunter, but still the hunter kept swinging, unable to accept his demise. Ryuu scrambled backwards, sword-less, as the hunter swung wildly at him.

Moriko leapt at the hunter and tried for a cut at his neck. Maybe it was her exhaustion, maybe he had seen her shadow, but he sensed the strike and was able to dodge it, continuing to swing wildly at Ryuu. Moriko cut him twice across his back, frustrated and willing to settle for anything. The hunter finally fell to his knees, continuing to swing haphazardly. On his hands and knees he crawled forward, his focus only on Ryuu. He stabbed at Ryuu, but the nightblade was well out of his reach.

Moriko walked around the hunter. He was bleeding out, but slowly. She was moved to pity as the hunter continued to thrust his short blade into empty air. He had given everything and more. Moriko made one final cut, and it was perfect. The hunter's head fell from his body, and to Moriko's amazement, the hunter's body crawled forward one more pace before it fell.

Moriko dropped to her knees, allowing exhaustion to take her. Her eyes met Ryuu's, and there was pride there. They had defended themselves against eight hunters, well-trained and well-prepared. He had to be feeling the same elation she was. She smiled at him, an effort that took all her strength. He returned her smile, and then his eyes rolled up in his head and he collapsed in a heap in front of her.

CHAPTER 12

Nameless cursed his fate. The old man had reported the death of the four pairs he had sent. So many, and still they had fallen. He was made a fool by the nightblades, and he swore he would have his revenge. But for now, more pressing matters concerned him.

The winter had been a challenging one in the plains south of the Three Sisters. Game had been hard to come by, and the culling of the weak and useless had already begun. Nameless' demon-kind had been hard-pressed to find enough food in the area. But the end was in sight.

Nameless decided that once the People were safely in the land to the north he was going to give up his position as leader of the clans. They had been on their own for so long they were almost impossible to lead. Every day he dealt with new complaints from the assembled masses, and he knew there was a sizable number of the People ready to go their own ways. Only the strength and the threat of the demon-kind held them together.

The resistance was led by the Red Hawks, the same clan that had sheltered the nightblade woman. Nameless had confronted Dorjee soon after the woman escaped, and Dorjee had claimed he hadn't known of her strength. He had taken her word that she was nothing but a messenger. There was no lie in Dorjee. Nameless had hunted for the Red Hawks before, and though the mistake angered him, Dorjee was an honest and competent leader of his clan. Nameless had considered taking Dorjee's head regardless. At the time the Red Hawks possessed few friends among the clans. But Nameless couldn't bring himself to separate a clan from a strong leader. Dorjee had made a mistake, but he had done no wrong. He claimed he had tried to introduce the nightblade to Nameless much earlier, but hadn't received an audience. There were enough witnesses to testify to the truth of the story.

Nameless let Dorjee live, and since that day, those who disagreed with Nameless went to Dorjee, who heard all their complaints. The Red Hawks hadn't had many friends last fall, but now Dorjee regularly held council with at least a fourth of the clan leaders. Nameless wanted to take action, to kill those who rebelled, but Dorjee was a wise man. He brought the complaints to Nameless with a plain simplicity, and Nameless took responsibility for dealing with them as well as he could. Though Dorjee had become the leader of a rebellion, they had yet to take any action against Nameless' orders.

An uneasy truce sat between Dorjee and Nameless. Nameless had honored the Red Hawks by placing them front and center in the upcoming invasion, and Dorjee couldn't refuse without consequence. Nameless hoped that perhaps the soldiers of the Three Kingdoms would take care of the problematic clan if he couldn't.

Dorjee was one problem, but Nameless was frustrated much more by those who didn't possess Dorjee's patience and wisdom. Mostly it was young men who thirsted for fame and adventure. They formed groups ranging from a few individuals to a few dozen.

Usually they only caused minor mischief, running their horses through camps, practicing their archery too close to others, the sort of actions Nameless could overlook.

Sometimes, however, one of these small groups would go too far. They would lead a small raid on another camp, potentially steal some women. Cycles ago, it would have been permissible, but Nameless wanted as many of the People as possible to cross into the Three Kingdoms. They couldn't fight amongst themselves when they had a much greater task in front of them. So far the groups had remained small, and Nameless and his demon-kind had been able to step in. It would take a larger group to pose a serious problem. But Nameless hated every time he had to resort to violence against his own people.

Their problem was that they couldn't focus on the future. They saw only the suffering of the present moment. Nameless knew the winter was hard and that people suffered and went hungry. But if they didn't relocate, there was no future for them. The land to the north was rich in resources, and they needed that land if they were going to survive. Nameless knew it wasn't easy, and that their challenges weren't over; but if they didn't act now the People would continue to decline until they were but a memory in the stories of others, a ghostly threat to scare misbehaving children.

It was a thankless task he had begun, but he had hoped at least for understanding. The demon-kind understood, but only because it was their shoulders that had carried the burden of the People for so long. They knew how much harder it was getting to survive in the empty lands. They saw further than the rest of the People.

Nameless was grateful for their support. Without them, this joke of an alliance never would have existed. If he lost the demon-kind, he lost them all. It was a thought that ran through his head dozens of times a day, especially now as he approached their final conference before the invasion was to begin.

Nameless came to a small gathering of the demon-kind, just a little over a dozen. These would be the men and women who led them into battle. The clans would not fight as a single unit. They weren't the organized armies of the Three Kingdoms. Each clan fought for itself, with at least one pair of demon-kind to guide them, to be their eyes and ears. The demon-kind knew what waited for them on the other side of the Three Sisters, and if they could triumph in one battle, they could bring an end to the Three Kingdoms in one stroke.

Once the clans were safely in the Three Kingdoms they would disperse throughout the land and make it their home. Their alliances would be over. Their way of life would resume as it always had. The demon-kind would no longer rule. They would serve once again. It was the agreement he had made with each clan.

Nameless brought his mind back to the present. He could look to the future all he wanted, but to get there he needed to take the first steps. The old man had joined them at the fire. As much as Nameless detested his presence, the man had skills they needed. With a nod from Nameless they all gathered close together and studied a map drawn in the dirt.

The snow in the pass had melted, and it was time for Nameless and the People to begin their move. The scouts had determined the way was open, and furthermore had reported that no archers waited in the nooks and crannies that ran throughout the pass. Nameless approved. Had there been, he would have sent some of the demon-kind after them. They'd die without killing a single soul. Whoever was leading the defense of the Three Kingdoms had some wisdom at least.

The old man began, his voice strong but soft. He had spent the better part of the day wandering the northern areas of the pass with his gift. Nameless knew they would be expected, and he wouldn't lead his people into a trap. The old man and his gift gave them a decided advantage.

"Most of the soldiers are grouped directly in front of the pass. That will come as no surprise. However, they also have men waiting to the east and west of the opening of the pass. From what the scouts report, the land on the other side of the pass is very hilly, ideal for hiding many men. I expect they hope to funnel you towards their center and attack from both sides, surrounding you like the mountains you just came out of."

The old man paused for a moment to let the commanders consider his words. Nameless could find no fault with them. If he were commanding the opposing forces he would do something similar. He let the old man continue.

"I have also noticed there are troops and horses higher in the mountains, hidden from view. They will wait until we are committed, and then I expect they will sweep down the mountains and attack our flank."

Nameless shook his head. "Are you sure? Those mountains are steep. Our riders would never dare them, especially in combat."

The old man shrugged and gave one of his enigmatic smiles. "All I can say for sure is where they are now. What they will do is just a guess, informed by experience."

Nameless looked around the circle. One of the other demon-kind spoke up. "I think the old man is right. Our spies from the north tell us the horsemen of the Northern Kingdom are well-used to mountain paths. Perhaps they are the ones hidden up high. Our cavalry is used to the plains, not mountains. They will know this and seek to take advantage."

Nameless considered the advice for a moment.

"I agree. Now that we know how their soldiers are spread out, we know exactly what they plan. How shall we proceed?"

With that other voices joined in the conversation. Nameless was their leader and an excellent commander, but everyone present was skilled in the arts of warfare. He knew when to step back and let them work as they saw best. Their plan came together a piece at a time, and Nameless allowed himself to smile. They knew exactly what waited for them on the other side of the pass, while the Three Kingdoms would be taken completely by surprise. They would crush their opponents without a thought.

CHAPTER 13

The waiting was always hardest, Akira decided. There was a special type of fear one felt when an enemy was directly in front of you, a piercing fear a swordsman had to learn to overcome. But the fear that emanated from a silent battlefield was worse, somehow. It gnawed away at your courage one slow bite at a time, and Akira had never learned how to defeat it. Part of it was fear for his men. No matter how well they were led, many were going to die, and there was nothing he could do about it. He couldn't save everyone.

The pass had opened up two days ago, according to the scouts. But the information had to be taken with a grain of salt. Akira's scouts considered the pass open when a soldier on horseback could ride the entire distance without undue difficulty. Once that was true it was possible to push an army through. But Akira had no guarantee the Azarians considered the pass open at the same time. If he was in their position he would want to invade as soon as possible. But for all he knew, they would be content to sit at Fort Azuma for another moon.

Akira's men were in position. They had their instructions, and if the battle was lost, they were to break as soon as the word was received. Akira wasn't proud of the order, but he had the future in mind. If they couldn't stop the Azarians here, he would need every man alive to fight against an occupation.

Akira had tried to send scouts all the way into Azaria, but Nameless had already positioned archers in the pass. The archers kept taking positions closer and closer to the Kingdom, which seemed as good an indicator as any the Azarians were preparing to invade. Akira had sent scouts along the game trails, but they were watched as well. Whatever actions the Azarians were taking, Akira was fighting blind.

The sun hadn't yet risen when a messenger came to him with the news he had been waiting for. A scout had finally seen the Azarians moving. It had only been a short glance, but the pass was filled with them, and the scout predicted they would arrive by daybreak. Akira let out a sigh of relief. At least the waiting was over. He gave orders to rouse his generals and begin their final preparations. Then there was little else to do but sit and wait for the inevitable.

At daybreak the battle for the Kingdom began. Akira and his honor guard stationed themselves on a rise where Akira could see the battle unfolding. In the soft oranges of the sunrise, Akira saw for the first time the threat he had worried about for two cycles. Azarians filled the pass from side to side, advancing at a steady pace.

Akira's first line of defense were the fortifications at the edge of the pass. They weren't as well-built as the walls of Fort Azuma, and even the attempts to strengthen them in preparation seemed meaningless. It had been many cycles since there had been any need to fear an attack on this end of the pass, and most of the preparation had gone into repairing the fortifications instead of strengthening them.

The Azarians came close enough to the walls that they could shoot arrows over the top. Their lack of discipline was immediately apparent. Instead of waves of arrows, the sky was filled with a constant mass of death. Arrows flew as fast as the Azarians could string and shoot their bows. Akira's archers returned fire, the first tentative steps of outright war fought at a distance.

Akira watched with intense focus. The longer the Azarians were willing to fight at a distance, the better it was for his men. The soldiers of the Three Kingdoms were more disciplined with their shots, and they had the advantage of being behind a wall. Akira was certain that for every man he lost, the Azarians lost many more. He wondered how long it would be before the Azarians realized it as well.

It wasn't long. Approximately two dozen men and women burst from the Azarian ranks and sprinted for the walls. As soon as they did, the ranks of Azarians started advancing, and more and more arrows were sent towards the walls. Akira, standing safely in the distance, could see his men struggling to stay on the walls against the constant onslaught of arrows. Every time the front ranks of the Azarians advanced, more came through the pass and into bow range. His men never had a chance to catch their breath. Akira lost sight of the foremost Azarians as they dipped below the level of the walls. But just a few minutes later he watched as men practically vaulted up and over. He shook his head. He hadn't seen any ladders or siege engines. They had just climbed.

The first stage of the battle turned against them quickly. Akira saw his men fall off the wall in droves. It seemed like no time at all had passed before the Azarians had taken the wall. Although they were too far away to know for certain, Akira was sure he was seeing hunters for the first time. They dropped into the fort itself, and again

Akira lost sight of them. Akira feared what would happen inside. With hunters, fortified places of safety became death traps with very few exits. He couldn't imagine the terror seizing the hearts of those stationed inside the fort.

In the past few moons he had searched archives throughout the Kingdom for everything he could find on fighting nightblades. It was the closest he could come to learning how to fight hunters. What he learned made his head spin. Those who could sense and fight changed all the rules of warfare. Some of the greatest massacres in history had come from just a handful of nightblades entering a fortification. In close spaces each could kill dozens without difficulty.

Akira had cautioned the commander of the fort prior to the battle. He emphasized that it was better to retreat and save lives than remain and save their honor. He was grateful when the gates to the fortress opened and men came streaming out. Once the hunters were inside, the men didn't have a chance. Akira's orders had been to abandon the fort when it happened. He hadn't been sure up until this point the commander would follow orders, as it was strongly against tradition to retreat when you outnumbered the enemy. But the commander had swallowed his pride and called the retreat.

The men joined ranks with their fellow soldiers. Akira glanced to the east and saw the sun was just halfway over the horizon. He had hoped they would hold the fort a while longer, but he wasn't surprised. This battle would be decided on the open field. They had always known that.

For a while, an ominous silence fell upon the battlefield. Akira guessed the hunters would be opening the doors of the fortress, allowing the Azarians to pack in. It felt as though the world took a deep breath, the last calm before the storm broke upon their ranks.

Soon they would be opening all the gates on the north side of the fortress. If all went according to plan, they would charge straight down the center, where Akira stood with his men.

The sun had just finished rising when the doors opened again and the Azarians came flying out of the fortress. It was the most disorganized mess Akira had ever seen. There was no orderly advance here, just men, women, and children running from the fort in all directions. Akira's eyes narrowed. Although their movement seemed random, groups would form and head in specific directions. It wasn't organized, but there was a purpose to what was happening. Mashiro, standing next to Akira, noticed it too. "They are splitting into three prongs."

Akira nodded. "I agree."

Mashiro was the commander in charge. He and Makoto were equal in rank, but Mashiro was the better strategist, and it was his mind they relied on. Akira had learned long ago to trust his general. Mashiro sent messages to the armies waiting in the valleys to the west and east. "If the Azarians take the ridgelines, we won't have a chance. Attack now and hold the ridge." Messengers sprinted away to deliver Mashiro's commands. Akira approved.

The battle was met in front of them. The silence had been replaced by the war-cries of both sides, and those had been replaced by the ringing sound of steel on steel. It seemed there was no end to the numbers of Azarians pouring out through the Three Sisters. Akira watched with fascination as they funneled through the fortress and spread out again on the other side. The valley before him was full of them, but when he looked up, he saw the pass was still packed with Azarians, waiting eagerly to join the battle. Archers from the Kingdom loosed flight after flight of arrows into the advancing lines, and it seemed that everywhere Akira looked Azarians were falling. But still they kept coming, fearless in the face of the strength of Akira's armies.

For a time it seemed like a massacre. Akira's armies were prepared and orderly, and the sky was thick with arrows, the ground slick with the blood of the Azarians. Akira wondered if the Azarians would break and run back to their own people, but they kept pressing forward, a relentless pressure against Akira's troops. Akira had never seen so many people on a battlefield before.

Step by bloody step, the Azarians progressed, their ranks continually reinforced by the endless sea of humanity behind them. Akira could see areas of commotion in his ranks, and he feared a hunter was at the center of each. Arrows still flew through the air, but they weren't as thick as they once were. More and more archers were switching to their swords in order to defend themselves. Everywhere Akira looked the battle was joined in earnest, and he thought that even if he survived, the sound of steel would ring in his ears until the day he died.

In the midst of it all, Akira saw him. There was no way of being certain, but there was no denying the man fit the description Akira had received from Moriko. The man stood a head taller than anyone on the field, and he left a wake of effortless death behind him. He seemed to leap from point to point, always rescuing his people just as they were about to fall. Everywhere he went the Azarians redoubled their efforts, and he was making his way towards Akira.

Akira tried to follow Nameless, but the battle was too chaotic and he moved too fast. All Akira knew for sure was that their present location wouldn't be safe for much longer. He ordered his honor guard to switch to a different position to buy them some more time.

As they retreated, a hunter broke through their ranks. It was a woman, and she left a trail of bodies in her wake. Akira's honor guard jumped into action, spears at the ready. He watched with fascination. His honor guard had been training exclusively in tactics against nightblades, and Akira wondered how they would function against a hunter in the real world.

The biggest change they had made was that his honor guard had drilled extensively in the use of the spear for the past few cycles. The longer reach protected them from the speed of the hunters. If a single guard went up against them this way, a nightblade or a hunter would easily get inside the reach of the spear, rendering it worse than useless. But when they fought as a unit, the stories said spears were most successful at killing nightblades. Akira hoped the stories hadn't been lying, and that the same strategies would work against hunters.

The hunter saw Akira and leapt for him. Akira drew his own sword and deflected two cuts. He couldn't have stopped the third, but the hunter was stopped short by the spears of Akira's honor guard. Akira was proud, if just for a moment. He had crossed swords with a hunter and lived to tell about it, even if it was only because he had a hundred men backing him up.

The hunter backed up, and Akira's honor guard fell into a circle around her two rows deep. At first they kept their distance, ensuring their formation was set before advancing. The hunter saw what was happening, a trace of fear in her eyes. She darted towards one edge, trying to find a weak part of the circle. But even if she could knock aside a spear or three, there were always more spears there to protect their friends in the front of the line. Try as she might, she couldn't figure a way out.

Akira's honor guard didn't give her a chance. They advanced in unison, spears closing in. Akira forced himself to watch as she eventually fell under more than a dozen spear thrusts. He had always preferred the sword, but his men needed every weapon they had to fight back. War was no place for honor.

The sun was high in the sky and still the battle raged on. The sheer number of people in front of Akira was staggering, and he was impressed Makoto and Mashiro could keep any semblance of order in the combat. It was a day that would define their history. He had no doubt many legends would be born today.

Akira looked to the pass itself. He was further away than he had been this morning, but still, it seemed to him that fewer Azarians were streaming through it. Perhaps they were almost all through. Akira scanned the battlefield. If so, he thought his troops would hold. They would save the Kingdom.

Akira caught Makoto as he was giving orders to Akira's troops on the left flank. The giant was covered in blood and had a grim look on his face.

"How goes the battle? It looks like our lines are holding."

Makoto nodded, but he didn't smile. "They are for now, but I don't know for how much longer. Already our reinforcements are committed."

"Unless my eyes deceive me, there aren't as many Azarians coming through the pass."

Makoto nodded again, but Akira still couldn't see any relief in the general's face. Makoto turned to the pass and studied it. "Their hunters have killed and scattered almost all of our scouts and outriders. We don't know much of anything beyond what Mashiro and I can see right now, and that frightens both of us."

"Why?"

Makoto looked at his king as though he was missing the most obvious fact in the world. "We haven't yet seen any of their cavalry. The report from that nightblade said they were stellar horsemen, and we have yet to see a single horse come through that pass. It means their main blow hasn't fallen yet, and already we are close to breaking. Mashiro is considering ordering the northern cavalries to charge now."

Akira couldn't believe what he was hearing. It had been obvious, but he had missed it. But even he could see Mashiro's plan had flaws. "If we order the northern troops in now, we won't have anybody to flank the Azarian cavalry, if your guess is correct."

Makoto nodded. "You're right, but if we don't get help soon our lines will break, and once they do, we won't have any chance of winning this battle. Mashiro thinks the Azarians knew where all our troops were located before the battle began. Their attacks seem chaotic, but there is an order to them, and their movements have been too well placed to be coincidence."

Akira had to ask the tough question. "Have we lost?"

Makoto thought for a moment. He never spoke until he was sure of his answer. "Not yet, but it won't take much to push us past a point where we can't win anymore."

Akira let Makoto return to his duties, considering the words the giant had said. If they were going to lose, the smartest decision would be to retreat, but Akira wasn't sure he could give that order yet. The consequences of that decision were severe, and although it would save the lives of his men on the battlefield, it might cost far more lives in his kingdom.

The battle seemed to take forever and no time at all. The next time Akira noticed the sun, it was well on its way to setting. Still the lines held, but only through acts of valor that someday would become legends told to their descendants. Even Akira could see his men were close to breaking. They should have already, but they kept fighting and pushing harder than they ever had. Every man on the field knew what was at stake. All their plans had failed them, but still they fought. He was proud.

They still hadn't seen a single horse. Akira kept an eye out for them, as well as the one Moriko called Nameless. But neither appeared.

Makoto and Mashiro found Akira, and their look was grim. Akira could guess what they were going to say.

"We need to decide whether to call the northern armies down or not."

Akira looked at them. "I trust your decisions. Why come to me?"

"Because this is bigger than this battle, and it affects the whole kingdom. Our lines will shatter soon, and when they do the battle will be over. With the cavalry, we can break their advance. However, if our suspicions are right, and they are holding a large force in reserve, it could all be for naught. If we retreat now we'll have many more men to resist an occupation, but we'll have lost the battle. It needs to be your decision. Try to win here or win later."

Akira wished for a moment that leadership had never passed to him. He envied the life of a farmer, responsible only for his family and his own land.

"Even if you won't make the decision, what do you recommend?"

The two generals shared a look and grinned. They had been friends for a long time, although sometimes Akira forgot it. Mashiro spoke first, as he always did. "Fight."

Makoto spoke next. "Retreat."

Akira looked from general to general, unbelieving. For them to argue at such a time was beyond comprehension. It forced him to laugh. It wasn't a hearty laugh, but Makoto and Mashiro joined him in it, a brief moment of release from the fear and tension they all felt.

Perhaps it was wisest to retreat, but Akira couldn't swallow the idea. He didn't want his land invaded by the Azarians. It meant more death and suffering than he wanted on his soul. They had to try.

"Send the order. Charge."

The two men nodded and went to their work. They said nothing in judgment. Akira knew Mashiro would be pleased. He was more willing to take chances, but Makoto would be disappointed. He hated to see his men at risk.

Akira took a moment to look around. It was in the light of the dying sun that the fate of his kingdom would be decided. He saw the flags wave, relaying a message to the northern armies to charge. He saw his men in the valley were struggling valiantly, but they couldn't possibly last much longer.

There was a shout and a cry of alarm, and Akira ran to where Makoto and Mashiro were huddled with their commanders. Several of them were pointing towards the mountains. Akira followed their gaze but couldn't see what they were pointing at. But he heard snippets of their conversation and realized what was happening.

"No flags."

". . . been overrun."

He understood. The relays which were being used to send orders to the cavalry had been run over by the Azarians. Sen's First Army was in that direction, his best troops. Without them, it would be difficult to break the Azarian advance.

Makoto didn't hesitate. "Give me a set of northern flags."

The commanders protested. "Sir, allow one of us to go instead."

Makoto shook his head. "Do any of you know the flags for the Northern Kingdom?"

There was silence around the group and Akira cursed their lack of foresight. They had talked about having a single set of flags for all armies, but by the time the idea had come around, Makoto and Mashiro had been nervous about adopting a new system. Communication was vital. Instead, they had arranged for the flags to be operated by pairs of people, each trained in the flags of their own kingdom. They could translate messages back and forth, minimizing the possibility of mistakes.

Makoto prepared to leave, but Mashiro grabbed his arm. "Be careful."

"I will. But you always were the better strategist. Win this war."

They looked at each other for a moment, and Akira couldn't guess what was passing unspoken between them. It was Makoto who nodded and pried Mashiro's fingers from his arm. "Be seeing you."

With that the giant was on his horse, riding as far behind the lines as he could to get the message to Sen's First in time. Akira looked at the path he'd most likely take. It should be safe. He had already lost Toro. He couldn't afford to lose Makoto as well. It would be almost impossible to bear.

Shortly after Makoto left, Sen's second army charged over the eastern ridge of the pass, bearing down on the Azarians. Akira watched them, amazed by their skill in the saddle. Even though they were only at the edge of the pass, the mountain trails were still steep and treacherous, and few men dared them even on foot. But Sen's cavalry charged down the slopes, seemingly without concern.

A cheer went up from the men in the valley, and all pushed forward as one.

Akira dared to hope again. Perhaps there was another reason why they hadn't seen the Azarian cavalry yet. Perhaps there was none. Maybe Moriko's information had been wrong.

The Azarians seemed to panic as they were crushed between Akira's infantry and Sen's cavalry. The appearance of Sen's horsemen had changed the course of the battle. Akira glanced over at Mashiro, and even he seemed cautiously hopeful. It was enough to send Akira's spirits soaring.

There was a cry, and Akira looked to where the soldier was pointing. On top of the western ridge was a large man on a horse. Akira grinned from ear to ear. There was no mistaking Makoto, even at this distance. Not only had he delivered the message, he looked like he was ready to charge down with Sen's First. It was a bit foolish, but Akira could forgive him. It would be the killing blow. The Kingdom would be saved.

Makoto held flags in his hand. Suddenly, he started waving them vigorously. They were too far away for Akira to see what Makoto was trying to say. Mashiro rushed to a table and found a looking glass. His look was stern.

Akira couldn't bear the suspense. "What is he saying?"

Mashiro shook his head. "It's tough to tell without a relay. He's still a very long way away, but I think he's ordering a general retreat."

Akira's heart sank. From his vantage point high in the pass, Makoto would have a better view of both the pass and the battle below. If Mashiro was right, if Makoto was ordering a general retreat, it meant he was seeing something they couldn't down below.

Then Makoto was off, down the other side of the mountain, out of view. Akira was surprised until two other horses could be seen chasing him. Mashiro and Akira shared a glance. There was only one inescapable conclusion.

Mashiro's gaze was a question, and Akira nodded. Mashiro gave the orders. "Sound the retreat. As orderly as possible. Men should know what to do. Everyone, keep your swords sharp."

There was a look of dismay among the commanders, and Akira realized they hadn't figured out what was happening yet. To their eyes, they were winning.

The illusion didn't last long. Over the rise in the pass came horsemen. First just a few, but then more and more, until they numbered into the hundreds and into the thousands. They came charging down the pass, and the Azarians still in the valley raised a battle cry and redoubled their efforts. The men of the Kingdom saw the Azarian cavalry and all courage fled their hearts. Lines started to break.

Mashiro looked at Akira. "You must leave now. It won't be long. We'll need your leadership in the days to come."

Akira fixed Mashiro with a steely gaze. "We'll need you too. Don't you dare try to die on me. We'll meet in the arranged place, but don't you dare die. Save as many as you can."

Mashiro nodded and turned his back on his king.

Akira gave one last glance at the battlefield, but the outcome was no longer in question. He assembled his honor guard and they began their retreat from the valley.

Akira fought the urge to break down. He had just lost the battle for the Kingdom.

CHAPTER 14

The morning sun rose on Nameless as he stood on top of one of the peaks overlooking the Three Sisters and the land below. The land that would be theirs.

He had to give the warriors of the Three Kingdoms credit. They had fought well. Much better than he expected, in fact. The outcome had never been in question, but the People had paid dearly for this new land. Even when Nameless thought the lines had completely broken, they still maintained an orderly retreat.

Nameless had let them go. There was no reason to chase them further into the land. The People had fought hard enough, and they had a foothold in the land they'd never lose. They had set up camp on the battlefield last night, and many had mourned their dead. But they were in a new land.

Last night there had been a large council, something that had never been heard of outside of a Gathering before. Nameless had given up his leadership, as he had promised. The clans had known which direction they would head, and their plans were confirmed. Wild game was plentiful, and the Azarians would be fruitful and multiply. Nameless told them to go as they would. Perhaps there would be need to gather again in the future, but he did not think it likely.

They agreed to a location for the Gathering this fall. It was there they would discuss the future of all the clans. Until then, clans were to go as far and as fast as they wished. Nameless told the clans the demon-kind were again at their command, to use as they saw fit.

There had been much else to discuss, but Nameless left before the council concluded. His mission had been to get the Azarians into the Three Kingdoms, a land where they could grow and thrive. He had succeeded, and now his task was done.

Already he could see some of the camps breaking down below. Clans would spread in whatever direction they wanted. They had some maps of the land, rough as they were. More detailed maps were supposed to arrive, but they had never appeared.

Nameless debated what he should do next. While his mission had been accomplished, there was still much unfinished. He was free now, not beholden to the needs of the People anymore. None of the clans had requested his aid, so he could go as he wished. And although there were tasks that were perhaps more wise, there was only one task he wanted to finish.

She had shamed him by cutting him, though it was more his fault than anything else. He had gotten careless, and she had been strong. It was time for her and the boy to die. He would find the old man, who would tell him where they were. Then he would hunt again.

He smiled. It had been long since he had hunted, long since he had done as he pleased. He would kill the nightblades, and be rid of them forever.

CHAPTER 15

When Ryuu came to, he was home, on his own bedroll. He took a deep breath, causing his entire body to flare up in agony, and memories came rushing back to him. He remembered the blades in the light of the moon, the vast amounts of energy he used trying to defeat the hunters.

Moving as little as possible, Ryuu attempted to make a list of his injuries. He had been cut several times, and at least two of them were deep. He must have lost a lot of blood.

There was no point in moving. He assumed Moriko had brought him back to the hut, and Ryuu knew from personal experience it must have been an exhausting task. But if she'd been able to bring him this far, she would be alive and less injured than he was. He closed his eyes and let his sense expand, wondering if he could find her anywhere nearby. After a few moments of trying he gave up. He might be awake, but he still lacked energy. He wasn't able to focus enough to bring his sense to bear. Still, he hadn't lost it, and so he rested contentedly.

He didn't realize he had fallen asleep, but he awoke when Moriko came inside the hut. His eyes took her in. She moved stiffly, but he couldn't see any signs of a dangerous injury. A sigh of relief escaped from him. He had worried about her, but it looked as though she had made it out of the fight better than he had.

"I came back when I sensed you were awake."

"Thanks. How are you?"

A slight grin crept into the corner of Moriko's mouth. "Better than you, although not without injury."

Ryuu tried to sit up, concerned. "You're okay, though?"

Moriko shook her head as another wave of pain forced him to lay back down. "Yes, I'll be fine. You were cut much worse than I was. I worried about you for a while. You lost a lot of blood."

"Thank you."

"Well, life does seem to be much more exciting when you're around. Decided I'd keep trying it for a while."

Ryuu chuckled, and another wave of fire worked its way up his body. He groaned, but Moriko gave him no sympathy. He wouldn't have expected any from her.

"Rest, Ryuu. The woods are at peace right now. Rest, and we'll talk about what's next."

Ryuu did require rest. His injuries were the worst he'd ever sustained in combat. While none of the injuries would cause permanent harm, the healing process was long and slow. As much as he wanted to get up and move around, Moriko kept forcing bed rest upon him. She was often out, wandering the woods and making sure there weren't any dangers nearby. After a few days, Ryuu was strong enough to use his sense at a distance, but still Moriko left. He could tell she was anxious to get moving. As soon as he was strong again, they would need to make a decision about what was next for them.

To pass the time, Ryuu pored over the documents Moriko had taken from Tomotsu. Some of them were obvious. They were detailed maps of the Three Kingdoms, some of the most detailed Ryuu had ever seen. The rest were less clear. They were filled with text of some sort, but either it was a language Ryuu had never encountered, or it was in code. At first, he had thought perhaps the documents were in Azarian, but Moriko put that idea to rest. The Azarians didn't have a written language, so whatever was on these papers had started in the Three Kingdoms.

Before the hunters came, Ryuu had looked over the papers briefly, but he hadn't focused much on them. It had been far more important for him to train and regain his sense. But now he was healing and had little else to do to pass the time. It had been almost a quarter moon since he had been injured, and every day he sat up for as long as he could, studying the documents.

Looking at the nonsense made Ryuu think about language. In their language, every sound had a symbol associated with it. If you knew what sound the symbol stood for, you could read anything written on paper. Maybe the code held the same concept. Many of the symbols on the documents repeated, so perhaps the monks had just come up with new symbols for every sound. It would be an easy way to disguise what you were writing.

So Ryuu started looking for patterns in the documents. There were certain symbols more common than others. If these papers were in the language of the Three Kingdoms, it should mean the most common sounds would equate with the most common symbols, so he spent one day adding up how many times each symbol appeared on the page. Then he went to work at trying to match sounds with symbols. At times Moriko would come and help, but she had never cared much for mental puzzles. She preferred to be on the move, and so most of her days were spent outside. Ryuu knew part of it was that she knew they needed to make a decision soon, and she was afraid of what that decision might be. He didn't blame her. He was nervous about it too.

Ryuu distracted himself by trying to crack the code. It was slow work, full of false starts and retries, but he kept pushing forward, and in time he knew he was on the right path. He was deciphering word after word, and the more he completed, the easier it was to fill in the blanks. Eventually he made a key with every symbol on it.

Once he cracked the code, the next task was to translate all the papers. Moriko had acquired a hefty stack, and the work was slow and laborious, as he only memorized the most common symbols. The rest he had to look up every time they appeared. He split his time between using his sense to find out what was happening out in the world and using his mind to translate the pages in front of him.

The more he translated, the more horrified he became. Moriko had suspected the monasteries were up to something, but she had no idea the magnitude of their betrayal. Ryuu checked his work over and over, but he could find no fault with it. The code had been deciphered well, and the message in the papers was clear.

When he finished, Ryuu took the time to look over everything he had translated, reading it through from start to finish. Then he set it aside. The knowledge frightened him, but he wasn't ready to tell Moriko yet. Her reaction would be strong, and he wanted to be healthy when they discussed it.

It took Ryuu a half-moon to recover from his injuries. Even then he was still stiff and sore, but he could at least move without opening his scars, and he was able to resume light training once again. From then it was only a matter of time before he fully healed, but the moment had come for him and Moriko to choose their ways forward. Ryuu hoped they could continue on the same path, but he feared it would not happen. The upcoming conversation with Moriko made his stomach turn in a way battle never had.

It was a cool night when they lit a fire outside. The days were growing warmer, but the heat of the crackling logs was relaxing.

"We need to decide what to do next."

Moriko sighed. "I want to go to the island. That is all."

Ryuu shook his head. At least she didn't bother with polite formalities or dance around the question. "Will you allow me to try to persuade you otherwise?"

Moriko gave him a look which indicated she'd rather not, but she nodded.

"There are two facts I'd like you to know, which may change your mind. The first is that yesterday, the armies of the Three Kingdoms were defeated by the Azarians. The armies are in full retreat, and to the best of my understanding, it feels as though they are splitting up."

Moriko shook her head. "They never had a chance. I'm sorry to hear it, but it isn't a surprise."

Ryuu hadn't expected it would be. Moriko had been among the Azarians. More than anyone else alive in the kingdom, she had some idea of the power they controlled.

"The second fact will surprise you. I've finished translating the documents you found. The invasion wasn't random. In fact, it's been planned for a couple of cycles now. The Azarians always planned to invade, with the help of the Western Kingdom and Tanak. . . and the monasteries."

Moriko's eyes went up, and her eyes lit with fire. "The monasteries were involved in planning the invasion?"

Ryuu nodded. "From what it sounds like, there was quite the web of betrayal. Tanak wanted the Azarians to attack the Three Sisters last spring. His hope was that it would distract Akira and tie up most of his troops down in the pass. At the same time, Tanak would sweep through the Southern Kingdom. Tanak planned on a treaty between himself and the Azarians. He was led to believe the Azarians only wanted their land back."

Moriko shook her head. "No. From the first time I met Nameless, he made it clear his only goal was to invade and conquer the Three Kingdoms."

"I remember you saying that, and these documents have cleared it up. Tanak was deceived from the beginning. It doesn't say as much, but I assume Nameless wanted the kingdoms as weak as possible. With the Southern and Western Kingdoms at war, he could have walked right into the land without a fight."

Moriko continued the thought. "So Nameless wouldn't care that he was late to the pass. Maybe he never even planned on being there in the spring. The more the soldiers in the Three Kingdoms fought each other, the better for him."

"Exactly, but then his plan started breaking down. Akira surrendered without fighting the final battle that would have destroyed the remaining armies."

"And Toro held the pass long enough for the snows to settle in, allowing the Three Kingdoms time to regroup."

Ryuu was silent as he allowed Moriko to consider all the implications.

"But even if that's all true, Nameless still invaded, and we still couldn't stop him."

Ryuu nodded. "But they are hurt. There's no way for me to judge numbers, but our soldiers killed a large amount of their population. They are weaker than they've been in a very long time."

Moriko shook her head. "They won't think of it that way. In their eyes, only the strong survive. They'll consider themselves stronger than ever having come through such an intense trial. I fear for the land."

There was another silence. Ryuu wondered if Moriko was changing her mind.

"Regardless, I still want to leave for the island. The concerns of the land are not my own."

"You still haven't heard how the monasteries are involved."

She shook her head. "And I don't want to. I know you want to stay here and do something. And yes, we are strong, but we're still only two people against an entire nation. We can't change what's going to happen."

"The monasteries have always known Nameless was going to invade. Not only have they given him knowledge of the Three Kingdoms, they have a plan for taking over everything once he's here. That's what's in the documents I've found. Terms to be sent to Nameless regarding the ruling of the Three Kingdoms."

"What do you mean?"

"I mean that it looks as if the monasteries are going to take over the rule of the kingdoms. Nameless doesn't care about the people here. The monks are planning to make each of the monasteries its own little kingdom. Those who want shelter can flee there. It sounds like they plan to make monasteries into towns and cities."

Moriko stood and paced around the fire. "They are foolish if they think they can protect anyone from the power of the Azarians. I've met regular Azarian warriors more than strong enough to kill a monk."

"But the monks don't see themselves that way."

Ryuu watched as Moriko decided what to do. She didn't just dislike the monasteries, she actively hated them. If there was anything in the Three Kingdoms that would motivate her to take action, it was the idea of allowing the monasteries greater power.

When she finally stopped her pacing, Ryuu knew he had convinced her to take at least some action. "And what would you have us do?"

"At the very least, we need to let Akira know. If the monasteries are allowed to gather power, there's no way the Three Kingdoms will hold together. Maybe we help him, maybe we don't, but let's at least let him know. If nothing else, he's not that far away from the path we'd take to get further north anyway."

Moriko thought for a moment and then agreed. But she saw the look on Ryuu's face. "There's something else, isn't there?"

Ryuu nodded. "I wanted you to make the decision first. Hopefully this doesn't change your mind, but I think Nameless is hunting us."

CHAPTER 16

If there was one action Akira couldn't afford, it was to reflect on the past. It had been several days since their defeat at the Three Sisters, and still Akira couldn't bring himself to think about it. It seemed unreal, a nightmare he couldn't wake up from. There were times he thought, just for the briefest of moments, the battle had never happened and his land wasn't being conquered right in front of him. But he dismissed this fantasy, because if he allowed it to last for too long, the reality of their situation would crash down on him, and he wasn't sure he could handle the truth.

Instead, Akira focused on the day to day, completing one task at a time. Fortunately, there was always another task demanding his attention. Before the battle, Makoto and Mashiro had the foresight set up a system for surviving troops to communicate with one another, to maintain something resembling order even in defeat. So far, the system appeared to be working. Messages poured into Akira's tent day and night. Sometimes the groups were small, only two or three men. Sometimes they were large, headed by commanders who had gotten their men to safety.

They had been fortunate that the Azarians hadn't pursued their retreat. Akira was only two day's ride from the battlefield, but they thought they would be safe for at least another day or two. After the battle the Azarians had split into their clans. They were spreading in every direction. From everything they were hearing, the Azarian clans simply went where they wanted.

Akira and his honor guard were to the north and west of the Three Sisters, and so far, no Azarian clans had come this way. It was a small break, but one Akira was grateful for. His men weren't just physically exhausted, they were spiritually broken. The fate of the Kingdom had rested on that battle, and Akira and his men had failed. The knowledge took its toll on them all.

Akira's most pressing question was what had happened to Sen's First Army. Not only did Akira miss Makoto and his wisdom, but if the First was still around, they were the nearest whole army. Because the relays had been killed, Sen's First hadn't seen combat at the Three Sisters. They would have the strength to take actions Akira could only dream of with the troops he now possessed.

But they had no word of either Makoto or the army, and Akira feared the worst. If Mashiro was right, the Azarians had known where they would be, had known the exact layout of their forces. At times, Akira began to replay the battle in his head, wondering if there was anything else he could have done. But he had to push those thoughts away too. They had done everything in their power, but the strength of the Azarians had just been too great. Akira had heard dozens of horror stories from units who encountered a hunter in the battle. They had been hopeful in their stand against the Azarians, but their hope had been misplaced.

Amidst his regrets, Akira also grieved for Mashiro. The general and his men had covered Akira's retreat and had paid for it with their lives. His loss was most keenly felt when Akira studied his maps, trying to decide his next move. Mashiro had been young, but he had possessed a mind unlike any other.

But the past was the past, and Akira couldn't change it. There were supplies to manage and orders to give. He tried to put himself in the place of the Azarians, tried to figure out how they would expand through the land. He gave orders to the remaining soldiers to stop the Azarians however they could.

Time passed by like a swift river current, gone almost before he noticed it. He focused on the larger problems, and Captain Yung, the commander of his honor guard, worried about their personal safety. Most of Akira's honor guard were still alive, about ninety of his best warriors, all camped with him. Soon he needed to decide what to do with them. They were probably one of the largest fighting forces left in the land that used to be the Southern Kingdom. Akira studied his maps, marked all over with the positions of small units of troops.

Yung barged into his tent, interrupting Akira's study. "My king."

Akira waved his hand dismissively. "You can just call me Akira, Yung. We've known each other long enough, and I don't feel much like a king these days."

Yung shook his head and stepped up to Akira. "With all due respect, you are still the king. Act like it."

Akira straightened his back and Yung let out a slight grin. "Very well. News?"

"There is a clan moving in this direction. We've identified at least one pair of hunters with them."

"So it's time to move?"

"It does seem to be the wise decision, my king."

Akira studied his maps. They had been considering their next moves for a while now, but they hadn't settled on any specific plan yet. "Where do you think we should go?"

Yung stepped next to Akira and pointed at the maps. "My opinion hasn't changed. Sen is well defended with mountains and men. I think we should head west and lead a rebellion from that direction. That way the Azarians will always be between us."

Akira nodded along. It was the same argument Yung had made earlier, but Akira was uncomfortable with it. It meant retreating from the potential safety of Sen's strongholds and risking everything out in the open. It also kept their forces divided, and Akira wondered if it might be smarter to keep their forces together as much as possible.

But Yung seemed able to adapt more quickly to a new way of thinking. They weren't going to drive out the Azarians through brute force. If they combined their forces, all they would do was provide a larger target for the Azarians to attack. By staying separate, they could divert some of the Azarian attention from their allies.

Akira struggled to decide what to do next. The king in him wanted to go to Sen, to rule over what was left of their kingdom, but the warrior in him wanted to run towards death and danger, wanted to follow Yung's advice. The two sides of his personality warred, but there was little time.

"Very well. Let's send a message to Sen to let him know what's going to happen. He's to take over command of the Kingdom for now. We move west." He placed his finger on the symbol of a small village nearby. "We'll stop here for supplies and keep moving."

Yung grinned from ear to ear, perhaps the first time Akira had seen him do so. "Perfect. I'll inform the troops."

Just as he was about to leave the tent, Yung turned around, "By the way, it's the decision your honor guard wanted too. They want revenge."

Akira paced his tent and started packing his things, meager as they now were. He had the feeling his honor guard would have their revenge sooner than they expected.

Akira and his men rode down the trail in silence. They traveled the main roads, choosing speed over stealth. Besides, there were almost a hundred of them all together, and the idea they could hide from expert trackers like the Azarians was a foolish one. A blind man would be able to find their trail.

It was disorienting, to be riding through his kingdom like this. When he looked around, the last of the winter snows were melting despite the shade of hills and trees, the sun was shining, and birds flitted across the sky. It was a normal day in his land, and nature continued to follow its course despite the actions of the humans who made war on the land. If not for his memories, Akira could almost believe everything was right with the world. But then his memories would return, and all would not be right.

One of their outriders came back to the main group, a look of alarm on his face. Akira watched as the scout spoke with Yung, who then came and spoke to Akira. He knew the news would be bad as soon as he saw his captain's face. It was even more somber than usual.

"My king, the village we are approaching has been attacked. The scout reports that some terrible deeds have been done. I suggest we go around."

"Are there survivors?"

"Yes."

Akira considered, but only for a moment. "We go to the village. I am still their king, and if there is anything I can do for them, I will."

Yung studied his king and nodded. "As you will."

"And captain, let's make haste."

With that, Akira's entire caravan took off at a gallop. They were only a league from the village, and the distance passed swiftly underneath them.

Akira rode into the village and saw the scout hadn't been wrong. Several huts were burning, and blood was everywhere. Akira dismounted and looked around. Some of the blood was still drying. Whoever had attacked the village had done so recently. What happened here couldn't have happened more than half a day ago.

Akira ordered his men to provide what aid they could. They had hoped to stock up on supplies here, but they would be leaving with less than they came with. Akira didn't hesitate. They were his people, and he would protect them. Akira knelt down next to an older man who was surprisingly calm. He suspected the shock of the attack hadn't worn off yet.

Gently, Akira asked what had happened and got the story from the old man. It had been a small group of Azarians, young men by the sound of it, who had come for the village looking for cattle to feed their clan. They had gotten the cattle but had killed many. Some of the farmers and townspeople tried to fight back, but they had no skill and no blades. The young men didn't sound like hunters, but they made short work of those who stood up to them. They left not long ago with all the cattle from the area.

Akira told the man he would do what he could when a cry came out from down the street. "My king!"

Akira hustled down the street, eyes now following him. He had hoped not to be recognized, but his troops were too used to routine. He'd have to get them to stop using titles when speaking with him, for all their safety. When he got to the soldier, he saw his man was standing over an unconscious monk. Akira called for smelling salts, and soon the man came to.

The story he told was much the same as the old man's. He had been wandering when he came upon the village being attacked. He had rushed to try and aid the villagers, but he had been overpowered. While they spoke, some of the villagers came and thanked the monk for trying.

Akira stood up and conferred with Yung.

"We should follow them."

Yung looked with doubt upon Akira. "To what end? They'll return with the cattle to their clan, and then there will be little we can do. Even the smallest clan poses a significant risk to us. If they have a single pair of hunters, we'll be dead."

"Yung, this village needs hope. This land needs hope. I need to do something." He swept his hand across the scene and all his men. "We need to do something. This is small, but it's something we can do. They're moving cattle, so they'll be slow. We can catch them before they return to their clan."

Akira saw that Yung was swayed by his arguments. He nodded, and the debate was over.

"Good. Round up twenty men. Leave the rest here to help with repairs. We ride as soon as we're able. We'll bring back what was stolen."

Yung went about making it so. Akira told the old man what he planned. He figured the old man was the closest to a village elder they had.

"My king, you don't need to do this."

"Yes, I do."

Yung had no trouble rounding up volunteers. Each one of the honor guard wanted a piece of the action. He chose twenty and they returned to their horses.

Akira leapt on top of his horse, but Yung grabbed his reins. "You don't plan on going with them."

"Yes, I do."

"I know you want to fight, but you're no good to anyone dead."

Akira took a deep breath. "I know. But I need this. Then I'll listen."

Yung raised a doubtful eyebrow, but there was no stopping Akira. He nodded and went about giving orders to the men, and Akira rode off with the twenty soldiers.

They rode out of the village at a full gallop, and Akira could feel the frustration and anger pushing them forward. The tracks were easy to follow, and even Akira's untrained eye could see the Azarians were having trouble controlling the cattle. They didn't raise their food, so it would be a new experience for them. Akira grinned fiercely as he glanced up. The sun was still high in the sky. With luck, they could be back before the sun set.

It was mid-afternoon when they came upon their quarry. Akira took them in at a glance. There were six young men, and Akira was certain there wasn't a hunter among them. He ordered his men to charge, and he joined them with vengeance in his heart.

Akira spurred his horse faster, and he attracted the attention of one of the Azarians. The young Azarian turned around his own horse and charged at him.

Akira glanced at the blade the young man was holding. It was similar to the blades the hunters used, shorter than Akira's by the width of a hand. The king drew his blade and passed to the left of the Azarian. At the last moment, Akira turned his horse just slightly further to the left. Both warriors cut with their blades. The Azarian had tried for Akira's neck, and his cut was true, but the extra distance at the last moment caused the blade to pass harmlessly over Akira's shoulder. Akira's blade didn't miss, slicing into the side of the Azarian's belly. It was a fatal cut, but a slow death. He didn't care.

He looked around for someone else to fight, but everywhere he looked he saw only his honor guard. He took a quick count and saw they were all present. There were a few wounds between them, but nothing fatal. Akira grinned, and a flood of emotions surged through him, the familiar relief and regret of surviving another battle.

He glanced at the eyes of his men and saw the same emotions running through them. All were glad to have done some harm to the Azarians, even as small as this. An idea began to form in Akira's mind. He had almost a hundred of the best warriors of his kingdom near him. They could exact revenge wherever they went, so long as they were smart about it. The more the idea sat in his mind, the more he liked it. He thought Yung would as well.

With a single command he summoned his men to attention. They rounded up the cattle and began the short journey back. Akira grinned all the way.

"You want to do what?" The look on Yung's face was priceless.

Akira simply grinned and said nothing.

"That's a horrible idea. You'll be putting a target on your back, and if you haven't noticed, the Azarians are pretty great archers."

Akira just shrugged. "Admit it, you like the idea."

Yung paced back and forth, and Akira couldn't tell if he was going to explode or embrace him. Either seemed like reasonable possibilities.

"But you're the king."

"Which is exactly why this will work. It's far better than hiding in some dusty corner of the Kingdom and letting others die."

"What about your honor guard? How will they feel about it?"

"You know they'll be tripping over themselves to volunteer. I won't order anyone else along this path."

"You've really thought this through, haven't you?"

Akira nodded.

"It's a brilliant idea. We're all going to die, but it's brilliant."

"I'm glad you're with us."

The captain and the king were sitting around Akira's maps as he discussed his thoughts. His plan was simple. They would go from village to village, helping however they could, striking at the Azarians whenever it made sense to do so. They would harass and embarrass the Azarians, and as they did, word of Akira's movement would spread. Akira didn't plan on it, but he hoped the stories would inspire others to rise up against the Azarians. Already they had gotten a small taste of what life under the Azarians would be like. Small raids like the ones they had seen in the village were common among the invaders.

In short, Akira wanted to become an outlaw king. It meant they would probably die, but Akira couldn't think of a better way to make a larger impact in the next few moons. He could send out orders, but for the most part, the soldiers still alive in the land knew what they were supposed to do. The message had already been sent to Sen to take over the administrative duties of the Kingdom. He would be most useful fighting. It was also what he wanted to do. He'd rather fight than hide in the shadows and send more men to their deaths.

That evening the village held a celebratory fire for Akira and his men. One of the returned cows had been slaughtered, and the meat sizzled over the fire pit, eagerly devoured by Akira's men. Despite the pain the village had recently suffered, there was soft laughter around the circle, and several of his men were drunk.

Akira looked around, and for a few moments, he felt as though he was doing exactly what he was supposed to. He belonged around a campfire more than he did a map room.

Akira stood up and all eyes turned to him. He waited a few moments for silence.

"Men. When you were selected for my honor guard you gave up almost all that was dear to you. You swore to defend me, to forsake family and friends and maybe even life itself. I know I haven't always made it easy for you to guard me, but we live in tumultuous times, and I'm afraid I'm going to make it harder for you once again."

Akira paused for effect, taking his time to look around the circle.

"The Kingdom is in crisis, the worst it has ever seen. The Azarians have beaten us. They come for our land, but our lives mean nothing to them. We saw that firsthand this morning. Now the wise action to take would be to hide, to move from one secret location to another, issuing orders so that others may mount a resistance against our occupiers. It's what I should do. It's what any king should do."

Akira could see the discontent in the eyes of the soldiers around him, and he knew they would follow him. He hadn't been worried. Each of them was a good man, ready to do anything for their king and for the land.

"But that's not what I'm going to do. In front of me are almost a hundred of the best fighting men in the land. It was your skill and your character that earned you these positions, and it seems a mighty waste to not use both in service of our kingdom. This fight is much bigger than just my life. I have spoken with Captain Yung, and although he questions the wisdom of this decision, he fully agrees. Our plan is to make the life of the Azarians miserable. They may have come into the Kingdom, but they will find no warm welcome here!"

A cheer went up from the men. Akira waited for it to subside before continuing.

"I'm asking a lot of you all. This I know. We will be on the roads the entire time, and I expect that soon we will be hunted, if we aren't already. Perhaps even our own people will give us up for hope of reward, and when the sun sets on our lives, perhaps we were nothing more than an annoyance. I will not order any to join me, but I will ask for those willing to volunteer. Tonight we celebrate our lives, and tomorrow we go about taking back our land!"

Another cheer went up, and Akira knew that every single man would be coming with him tomorrow. Pride swelled in his chest. It was an honor to be able to command such men. Perhaps he wasn't worthy, but he would do everything in his power to make their skills and their lives mean something, even in defeat.

As Akira sat down next to Yung, the young monk they had found earlier in the day came up to him. "Excuse me, my king."

Akira glanced at the monk. "The people here in the village say you fought bravely against the Azarians. You have my thanks."

The monk shook his head, and Akira saw the shame on his face. "I tried, but I wasn't strong enough."

Akira placed his hand on the young man's shoulders. "Have no fear. All we can do is the best we can. There is nothing for you to feel ashamed of."

"Thank you, my king. I was wondering . . .," the monk's voice trailed off.

"Yes?"

"I was wondering if I might join you?"

Akira glanced over at Yung, who just shrugged. Akira saw nothing wrong with the idea. The monk was young and had clearly tried his best. He would be useful to have around.

"You would be more than welcome among us. We leave tomorrow."

The monk bowed his head in appreciation. "Thank you very much, my king."

Akira watched the monk walk away to join the celebration. Then he looked among his men again. He could not help it, but he was excited for the rising of the sun. To be on the road, a sword in his hand. He didn't realize how much he had missed the life of a soldier. It was a hard and short life, but it suited him best. He smiled at everyone and joined his men in the celebration.

CHAPTER 17

They had been on the road for a few days, and Moriko was glad to be taking action and moving forward. The spring season had always been her time for leaving, and if not for Ryuu, she would have left much earlier. His healing had taken time, first from the mental blocks he had put in place, then from the cuts he had taken during the attack on the hut. But he rode with strength now, and Moriko dared to hope their ordeal was almost at an end.

Their plan was simple. They would ride to where Akira was camped and let him know everything they had discovered. They would tell him about the monks and Tanak's betrayal. If he asked for their advice, they would give it, but they would not offer their help. After they were done, they were going to catch a boat traveling up the river. They would get off at Highgate and hopefully be on the island of the blades before summer even came to the Three Kingdoms.

Moriko feared it wouldn't be that simple. Every night Ryuu used his sense to understand what was happening all over the Three Kingdoms. He spoke little about what he sensed, but Moriko could tell from the expression on his face and his general attitude that life in the Three Kingdoms wasn't pleasant these days.

She didn't push the topic. If she did, he would try to dissuade her from leaving the Three Kingdoms. He wanted to help, to do something to keep the people safe, but he had agreed to go with her. It was foolish, but she figured that so long as they didn't talk openly about it, he would continue to travel with her.

That night was no different. They sat around their fire. Ryuu had his hands to the ground and was using his sense to travel far and wide. Moriko felt a small pang of jealousy. The skill was incredibly useful, and though she had tried many times to duplicate it, it wasn't within her ability. She took small comfort in the fact Ryuu could no longer even begin to hide his presence. He had gotten too strong, and no amount of effort would dim the energy emanating from him. They had each found their own paths towards strength.

When Ryuu opened his eyes, Moriko could tell it was even worse than usual. Though she hated to bring it up, she couldn't help herself.

"What's wrong?"

Ryuu considered her for a moment. "Perhaps it would be easier to show you."

Moriko frowned. They had tried it before, as it had been the technique Ryuu had used to learn the skill in the first place, but no matter how often they tried, Moriko hadn't been able to get it to work. There was no reason why tonight should be any different.

Ryuu read her thoughts. "I don't think it was anything you were doing wrong. I think perhaps the problem might have been more about me, that I didn't leave myself open enough. Would you like to try again?"

Moriko didn't, but her curiosity got the better of her. She nodded, stood up and walked to him.

"Try to stay focused on me. I remember that when it first happened to me, I wasn't able to maintain my focus because of the shock of it, but there's a lot to show you tonight."

Moriko nodded. He had given similar instructions before, but it had seemed silly after the fact. Nothing had happened no matter how much Moriko focused her attention.

She put her hand on his shoulder, and felt a small thrill of satisfaction. It had been a long time since they had come together. Despite all the time they had spent living together in the past few moons, there was still a barrier between them, and neither Moriko nor Ryuu knew how to break through it. As she held on to him, she realized how much she missed him, and wondered if they would ever figure out how to live together like they once had.

She focused her thoughts as Ryuu brought his hands down to the ground. She narrowed her sense down to only one target, and that was Ryuu. Everything else fell away. There was no forest, no land around them. For all her sense could tell her, they were in a void, just her and Ryuu. For a moment her thoughts wandered, and she thought such a future wouldn't be all bad.

At first nothing happened, but when the shift hit, Moriko almost lost her focus completely. She suddenly understood what Ryuu had spoken about. It was as though she was traveling at a high speed, much faster than the fastest horse could gallop. The land sped underneath her, and she struggled to keep focusing on Ryuu. It was a strange sensation. On one level, she knew he was there, that she was standing next to him at a campfire, but everything her mind was telling her was different. In her mind she was flying, free and without care. She knew that if she focused on the freedom she would lose her connection with Ryuu, and she kept her focus.

She couldn't tell where they were going. The speed was too fast. But in just a moment they stopped, and again Moriko almost lost her focus. She was fighting the sensation of both moving very fast and not moving at all. She sensed the village surrounding her. People were dying, being killed by Azarians. There was no hiding for anyone. All those who fought died. They had no training or skill. But even those who hid were often killed, as they were considered too cowardly and too weak to live by the Azarians.

As quickly as they arrived, they left again. This time Moriko was ready, and the sudden speed didn't shock her sense again. They went to another village. This one was more peaceful. Azarians were there, but it wasn't a slaughter. The village was in relative peace, but still Moriko could tell something was wrong. Then she sensed the villagers serving the Azarians. It didn't feel like slavery, exactly, but it wasn't that far off.

Again they left, and Moriko sensed Akira, surrounded by loyal soldiers. They were on the move, leaving behind a village that had seen many dead. There was a bright flash of power, and they left Akira and his men behind. They didn't travel far, but there was an Azarian clan with two hunters. The hunters were turned towards the north, and Moriko realized they were going to hunt Akira.

They kept moving faster now, and in the back of her mind, Moriko wondered if the effort of this was exhausting Ryuu. It was as though she was on his back and he had to carry both of them. More and more flashed across her sense and her mind, but finally they stopped at one last place. Moriko had no problem identifying where they were. As long as she lived, she would remember the sense of that man.

It was Nameless, and he was searching for them.

With a gasp, Moriko's focus finally broke, and suddenly she was back around the fire again. The disorientation was intense, and Moriko threw up her supper, light as it was. When she cleaned off her mouth and stood back up, she felt better. She glanced over at Ryuu and saw he was coming out of his trance. Sweat glistened on his brow, and she knew she had been right. It had been an effort for him to carry her.

They sat in silence for a few moments as Moriko took in all that she had sensed. It was so much information, and so much of it had just been fleeting impressions. But it was all true. She didn't even know where to begin.

The effects of the Azarian invasion didn't surprise her. It was difficult to experience firsthand, but it wasn't surprising. To the Azarians, the people of the Three Kingdoms would be weak. They killed all those they didn't consider strong. In their minds, it wasn't even murder. There would probably be those who would even consider it a favor. They were killing the weak so the strong could survive. It was the way of life they brought to the land.

Likewise, it wasn't surprising that Akira was being hunted. Nameless was a smart man, and he wouldn't allow any resistance to form. Akira had already gathered many troops to his cause and would be a danger. Nameless would seek to eliminate it as soon as possible.

She also wasn't surprised that Nameless would be hunting them himself. She had cut him in front of his men, and that would not be forgivable. No matter how long it took, he would find her. Of that she had no doubt. She had made an enemy for life.

None of it changed her mind though. She still wanted to go to the island, to leave it all behind. She had known the consequences of her actions back when she made the decision. It was difficult to face those consequences first-hand, but she was strong enough to keep moving forward. She was more worried that Ryuu would turn away from her and try to help the people of the Three Kingdoms.

Moriko looked at Ryuu and saw that he understood her mind. There was a look of sadness on his face.

"My mind isn't changed," she said.

"I know. I worry both about Akira and us, though."

"If we ride hard, we can get to Akira in time. The hunters are just starting out."

"And Nameless?"

"He is far away still. If we ride hard to Akira, he will still have to track us. Once we make it to the river, he can't catch us."

"I fear he will follow us to the island."

"That's fine. What better place to fight him than when we have thousands of nightblades at our back?"

Ryuu glanced up at her. "You know he won't come alone. He is many things, but stupid is not one of them."

Moriko sighed. "I know. But let's take it one step at a time. Akira first?"

Ryuu nodded. "Akira first."

As the fire died down they went to sleep. Come morning they would have a hard ride in front of them.

They moved quickly, as fast as their legs could carry them. Both of them were used to the steady trot that ate up the leagues, and they moved without rest, their feet constantly churning. Moriko's mind wandered, as though it had separated itself from her body. She knew her body was running, but inside she was focused on completely different questions.

At night they stopped to take a short rest. Ryuu focused and sent his sense out. His worry was evident. They made good time, but they were further away from Akira than the hunters. The hunters were taking their time, but even if they continued at their current pace, Ryuu worried they wouldn't make it. Regardless, they needed rest. They were able to run the entire night, but they needed strength to fight the hunters.

Moriko wondered if Ryuu was overreacting. Akira had almost a hundred men with him, all of whom were highly trained. But as he lay down, Ryuu explained his concern.

"Did you feel the flash of power last night?"

Moriko nodded. She hadn't thought much of it, thinking it was some sort of side effect of the technique Ryuu had been using.

"There is a monk with them, and he's flaring his energy."

Ryuu didn't have to say any more. In a normal situation, Akira would be well protected, but if there was a traitor in their midst, a monk who was guiding the hunters to Akira, the situation was more complicated. He could lead Akira away from his protection or set any number of other traps for him. That was Ryuu's true worry.

They slept for only a little time. They needed to keep running. The moon was still half-full, providing plenty of light to guide their way, and again Moriko fell into a running trance.

The morning came, clear and bright, the sun lighting up the blue sky. The two of them pressed forward, continuing to get closer to Akira. Every once in a while Ryuu would call a halt and place his hands on the ground. They would alter their course slightly and keep running. Moriko kept glancing at Ryuu. He was strong, but he had been recently injured. He was demanding a lot from his body. Not only was he running, he was using a technique which required a significant amount of mental focus. She was worried they would get to the battlefield and he would be useless.

The sun was high in the sky when Ryuu called for another halt. Without even catching his breath, Ryuu put his hands down on the ground. He was focused only for a few moments. "It's going to be close. We're about a league away, and they're about half that distance. But they are cautious. We have no need to be. Let's go."

Again they altered their course slightly and took off, now at a mad dash. Moriko brought her focus back, not allowing herself to fall into a trance. She needed to contain her energy perfectly so they wouldn't sense her coming.

Time and distance passed, and soon her own sense came alive with feelings of life. She could sense Akira's troops easily. For a while now she had felt the pulse of energy the monk had been releasing, and she felt now that the monk was right in the middle of the troops, probably next to Akira. But she could sense the hunters too. They were close, preparing to strike. Their focus was entirely on the prey in front of them.

Ryuu sensed it too, and put on a burst of speed. His energy burned against her mind. Despite the hunters' focus, there was no way they wouldn't know they were being approached. She wondered how they would react. Would they turn and fight or make the attempt on Akira's life?

She didn't have long to wonder. The hunters attacked the caravan while she and Ryuu were still about two hundred paces away. Ryuu abandoned all pretense and his energy flared even brighter. Moriko was stunned. She didn't know where this energy came from. She was sprinting as fast as she could, but he pulled away from her.

It was only a few moments, but they stretched into eternity. Moriko could both sense and see the combat being joined. She had to give credit to Akira's honor guard. Even though they were taken by surprise, they fought well, and stopped the hunters' advance. The hunters had needed to break through the guard in one pass, but they had both failed, and were forced to stop and deal with the threat. If they didn't, they would leave their backs open to the blades of the guards.

Two guards died, but their sacrifice hadn't been in vain. They gave Ryuu the time he needed to reach the battle, and he exploded on the scene, his blade glaring in the midday light of the sun. Moriko thought Ryuu was even stronger than he had been before, fighting in the clearing by the hut. After two days of running, she didn't know where he found the energy and the strength.

The two hunters had no choice but to engage Ryuu. If they turned their attention away, even for a moment, they would die. Blades flashed and came together, and the ring of steel could be heard across the plains. Despite being outnumbered, Ryuu had the upper hand. Akira's honor guard formed a circle of spears around the battle but hesitated to strike, unsure of what was happening in front of them.

Moriko felt Ryuu's power flicker, a momentary dimming of the energy he possessed. The hunters must have as well, for they redoubled their efforts. Ryuu switched from attack to defense. He was still fast enough to stay in front of their cuts, but he wasn't fast enough to strike back.

Fortunately, he didn't have to be. With all the attention on him, no one noticed Moriko. The circle of guards around the hunters was tight, but they were all still mounted. Moriko slid under the ring of horses, kicking up dust as she entered the circle. The hunters never sensed her approach. She came to her feet, drew her blade, and made her cut all in one smooth motion. Her blade sliced through the neck of a hunter, and Ryuu was suddenly freed from having to defend against two attackers. His power flared with renewed effort, and the other hunter fell under the speed of his blade.

Almost as soon as it had started, it was over. Ryuu and Moriko looked around, their incredible effort shocking Akira's honor guard. They had a host of spears pointed at them, and they looked to Akira for guidance. Akira grinned widely. "Ryuu, Moriko, it's good to see you again!"

The absurdity of the situation almost made Moriko laugh. All of Akira's honor guard sat in their saddles, unsure if the two strangers meant them harm, and Akira was greeting them as though they were old friends.

Ryuu looked up to Akira. "Good to see you too, Akira."

Then he collapsed to the ground, his face in the mud of the trail.

It felt a little strange to be walking when everyone else was on horseback, but Moriko didn't let it bother her. She had had enough of horses in her time in Azaria, and if she didn't have to ride a horse again in her life, she would be happy. She felt better when she was walking on her own two feet. The distances they traveled didn't bother her, and they were traveling at a pretty slow speed. She felt more connected to her sense, and she could fight much better on her feet than on a horse. Despite their history together, Moriko couldn't bring herself to fully trust Akira. He would keep his word if he could, but if he had to kill the nightblades to protect his kingdom, he wouldn't hesitate.

The sun was setting as they made camp. Moriko didn't want to admit it, but she was grateful. She had run through most of the night and the entire morning, and fought at the end. Granted, it had been a quick and easy battle for Moriko, but the effort still wore on her. She had sat for a while at the scene of the battle, but had been on her feet ever since. She was ready to rest for the night.

Ryuu was carried on a makeshift litter behind a horse. He looked comfortable, but was still unconscious. Moriko had checked to see if any of his scars had opened, but nothing had. Physically, he seemed fine. She suspected he had just used his body too hard and needed rest. His heartbeat was strong and his pulse was steady. Though she could barely sense his presence, she wasn't too worried about him.

There had been a good deal of confusion following the battle. The attack had come as a surprise, but the rescue even more so. Akira explained that Moriko and Ryuu were some of his best shadows, but he saw the looks of doubt on the men's faces. They suspected the truth, and it was only loyalty to their leader that allowed Akira to get away with it. Moriko wondered how much longer the lies could last. Time and time again the nightblades were making their presence known in the Three Kingdoms, and it wouldn't be too long before someone started to connect the rumors together.

The monk had certainly known it was a lie. Moriko sensed the fear emanating from him after the battle, but she pretended not to notice. Her instinct had been to kill him on the spot, but she didn't know how the situation stood. Indecisive, she feigned ignorance and paid him no mind. Once Ryuu woke up he could discuss it with

Akira. The two of them were closer, and Ryuu wouldn't get them killed through rash actions.

There was no way the monk wouldn't have felt Ryuu's strength, and Moriko suspected word of their existence was common knowledge among the monasteries. But the monk had also seen Akira's casual greeting of the nightblades and knew they had a previous relationship, so he said nothing. Each party was silent, waiting for the other to make the first move. Moriko worried what the monk might do, but figured they would be safe until Ryuu woke up.

They made camp in the prairie. A fire was lit, and Moriko was grateful for its warmth. She sat with the rest of the men and listened to them tell their stories. Many of them were about the fellow soldiers they had lost that afternoon. The burial had been done before they remounted, but grief wouldn't be so easily buried. The soldiers took turns telling stories about the men who had died. Most were funny, but some spoke of the men's courage in battle and kindness to other soldiers.

Moriko listened with half her mind. She was moved by the companionship of Akira's honor guard. Besides Ryuu, she had never had anyone she could trust, anyone who she knew would fight for her, come to her aid when it was needed. Beside all these men, willing to die for one another, she suddenly felt alone. More than ever she wanted to go to the island, to a place where her secret wouldn't get her killed, where she could be herself.

The talk went late into the night, and Moriko was surprised to see Akira joining in the stories. He knew the members of his honor guard personally, and he shared a funny story about a night one of the young soldiers had fallen asleep on duty. Akira had caught him, but the soldier, who had always had a quick wit, told Akira he had been guarding Akira's dreams. The soldiers chuckled, fond memories of their departed brother in their minds.

Moriko fell asleep to the stories, and slept more soundly than she had in several moons. When she woke up, the sun was high in the sky, a blanket was laid over her, and Ryuu sat next to her, his eyes alert and shining. Moriko snuggled up next to him, laying her head on his lap. They lay like that for some time before Moriko started to wonder about their situation. The camp was alive around them, but the day seemed late and they weren't preparing to leave.

"Akira ordered a day of rest. They've been riding fairly hard the past few days. He said it was for mourning, but I think more than anything he just wants to figure out his next steps."

"How are you?"

He brushed her hair with his hand. "I'm fine. I pushed myself too hard."

"You were stronger even than when we fought the eight."

He was silent for a moment. "I think it's becoming easier for me to draw power in. But it also burns me out. When I let go of it, the recovery is hard. I worry that if I pull too much, I won't recover from it."

Moriko grabbed his hand and held it. His gift was a powerful double-edged sword. He could accomplish spectacular feats of skill, but it might kill him. She wanted to escape, to go to a place where he wouldn't need to draw on his strength.

They rested for a while together before Moriko was ready for the day. They needed to speak with Akira. It was easy enough to find his tent, and the guard let them in after a brief conference with Akira. As they entered, Ryuu spoke softly to Moriko. "Keep your sense open. I don't want any ears to hear what we are about to say."

Moriko knew he meant the monk.

Akira greeted them with open arms and served them tea as they sat down. It was the most comfortable Moriko had felt in days, and she relaxed herself. She was as safe here as she could be, at least for a while.

Ryuu wasted no time getting down to the matter at hand. As soon as they were settled he told Akira everything, from Moriko's encounter in the woods to the translated documents. Ryuu had carried them and laid them before Akira as he spoke. Akira let him go on without interruption, but his frown got deeper and deeper as he learned more about the betrayal of Tanak and the monks. He looked like he was about to explode when Ryuu told him about the monk among them.

"I can't believe it, but at the same time, everything is falling into place. I had forgotten how Renzo passed the tests at the Conclave. It was because the monks knew what was happening. They all sensed him, they just lied about it."

Ryuu nodded.

Akira turned to them and gave them a look Moriko knew all too well. She dreaded what would come next. It would tear them apart.

"Ryuu, I can't believe I need to do this again, but I must. Will you help me stop what the monasteries are planning?"

Ryuu looked at Moriko, and her heart dropped to her stomach. It was just the same as it had been last spring. He wanted to help. She knew he was going to accept, and if he did, she would leave him forever. She wouldn't allow herself to go on another errand for a lord ever again. But she kept her mouth shut. If that was his decision, so be it.

"I'm sorry, Akira, but I can't accept. Not this time."

Akira was surprised, as was Moriko.

"Before you argue, let me explain. The first reason I cannot help you is that in my heart, I feel that my direction lies elsewhere. Moriko and I are traveling to where the nightblades live. My hope is to bring them back to the Three Kingdoms."

Akira corrected him absent-mindedly. "You mean the Kingdom."

Ryuu's jaw dropped to the floor. "What do you mean?"

Akira looked at both of them and saw the shock on their faces. "You mean you don't know?" He laughed loud and hard, a sound that Moriko found pleasant. Despite herself, she liked him. As much as she wanted to hate him, she couldn't. He was a good man.

"You are talking to the king!" Akira kept laughing, mostly at the shock on Ryuu's face. When his laughter wore off, Akira told his side of the story, how Tanak had been killed and how he had met with Sen, forming the Kingdom once again. Ryuu was speechless, and when he was able to find his words, they came slowly, but were congratulatory.

"I never thought I would live to see the day. Well done!"

"Thank you, but our kingdom is at risk, and it needs your help."

Ryuu returned to the argument he had been making before Akira's surprise. "Akira, though you may be able to harass the enemy, you can't defeat them. You know this. They are too strong. If we are looking at the future, we need to bring the nightblades back to the Kingdom."

Akira thought through Ryuu's proposal. "I suspect you are right. On our own, I'm sure we don't have the strength to turn the tide, but to be honest, I'm not sure even the nightblades will. By the time you get to them and back, the Azarians will have swept over most this land."

"It will be up to you to prepare the way. If I could, I would help you try to solve the problem with the monasteries, but I suspect that is a problem of diplomacy more than a problem of strength. You need to convince them not to undermine you. If the nightblades come back, everything is going to change, and the monasteries are going to need to be part of that. They have too much power not to be included, and if they aren't on board, you'll have a civil war and an invasion to deal with. You'll need to get the land ready for us."

"Say I believe you, what's your second reason?"

Ryuu laughed. "Nameless is hunting us. So long as we're with you, you'll have one big, mean Azarian hunter after you."

Akira gave Ryuu a questioning glance. "I've seen your skill, and there's none like it in the Kingdom. Surely you can defeat him?"

Ryuu shook his head. "I'm not sure. Moriko was lucky in her fight, and even she barely escaped with her life. He won't underestimate us again, and I suspect he's stronger than me."

"That's hard news to hear."

Ryuu raised an eyebrow. "And he's not even after you. Think about how unhappy I am about it."

Akira considered his options for a moment, but he hadn't become king without being decisive. "Very well. I don't like your plan, but your reasoning is sound, and I agree with it. I will wish you the best. When do you leave?"

"Today, as soon as I've dealt with the monk."

"What do you plan to do?"

Ryuu looked Akira straight in the eye, and Moriko could see how much he had changed. "I'm going to torture him for information and then kill him."

Akira met Ryuu's gaze, and it was hard. But Akira was a hard man, used to unpleasant decisions. "I see. Your road will be a tough one, but I wish you well on it, friend."

Moriko started. He had never called them friends before. Ryuu nodded, acknowledging and returning the status in kind. Akira smiled and bowed deeply to the two of them.

After they left the tent, Moriko stopped Ryuu. "Do you want me to come with you?"

There was pain in Ryuu's eyes, but also determination. "No. You'll kill him before he talks."

Their eyes met, and Moriko saw that Ryuu hated what he had to do, but would do it anyway. He was driven forward by his purpose now. And he was right. There was no love lost between her and the monks, and one wrong word from the monk would bring her wrath down on him.

Ryuu went towards where the monk was resting and walked with him off into the distance. He went over a small rise in the land, and then Moriko had to rely on her sense.

The sun was almost touching the horizon when Ryuu came back. Moriko had sensed the entire proceedings, but she asked him anyway.

"I didn't need to hurt him. He was young, and his anger was quickly replaced by fear. He told me everything. The entire series of events had been preplanned. The attack on the village, the monk getting knocked unconscious. Everything was designed so the monk could lure the hunters to Akira. I need to let him know. The monks can't be trusted, not at all, not if they are going to go to such lengths."

Moriko could see the pain in his eyes. He hated every moment of this, but he pushed himself forward. She had felt him kill the monk.

He had given the monk a warrior's death, which was more than she would have granted him. But still it hurt.

That night, Moriko offered what comfort she could. It was under the stars, with no tent to shield their actions from prying eyes, but neither of them cared. Moriko felt him give himself up completely to her, seeking some sort of escape. She returned his desire, and the stars turned overhead. She didn't know how much it helped, but he slept peacefully after.

In the morning there was a fresh look of determination on Ryuu's face. Whatever would come, he seemed ready for the day. They bid their farewell to Akira and were off. They had gratefully accepted the horses of the soldiers who had died protecting Akira. Moriko wasn't pleased, but they needed speed now. Nameless was horsed, and he would gain too fast on them otherwise. The rode north while Akira and his men rode west, into an uncertain future.

CHAPTER 18

It took longer for Nameless to find the old man than he expected. It was likely the old man had tried to avoid Nameless' grasp, but he couldn't escape that easily. He was too useful. After inquiring around a number of camps, Nameless discovered the old man had left with one of the first clans to leave. That clan had been heading northeast the last time they had been seen. Nameless had no choice but to ride after them. Without the old man's help, there was no way he'd track down the two nightblades.

His search was further complicated when the first clan he tracked down was the wrong one. Several small clans were traveling in the same direction, and Nameless followed the wrong set of tracks to the northeast. Fortunately, the clan pointed Nameless in the right direction. He followed their directions, surprised at how fast the clans were moving. If they kept this pace, they'd cover the entire land within the summer.

Nameless also noticed he wasn't welcome among many of the clans. The reactions he received were mixed. They were grateful to be in a new land, but many, many people had been lost. Far more than Nameless expected. The defense the Three Kingdoms had put together surprised him. There was still strength left in this land. Not enough to stop them, but enough to make their advance painful.

Nameless received assistance from the pairs of demon-kind with almost every clan. They were the ones who welcomed him, who realized what the move to the new land truly meant. He was surprised how much the lack of gratitude frustrated him. He had never chosen to lead the People because he wanted praise, respect, or power. But all the same, he had led the clans to a new life, a life which would sustain them for many generations. The price had been steep, but inaction would have cost even more. The People couldn't look beyond their current suffering. They couldn't look into the future and see the disaster that had been averted.

He puzzled over this as he rode towards the clan harboring the old man. When he did finally reach them, the old man was waiting for him. Of course he was. The old man would have felt him coming days ago, and there was only one reason Nameless would come this direction.

The clan the old man had joined was a small one, not much more than three dozen people strong. They had no demon-kind with them besides the old man, and he hardly counted. As Nameless approached the old man, he received many more stares of hate than of respect. He pushed the matter aside. They could say what they wanted to about him, but he had saved them. Hopefully someday the stories would reflect the truth.

When Nameless rode close, the old man grinned. "Can't blame a man for trying."

Nameless felt a sudden compulsion to explain himself, to get the old man to understand why he was needed. "I need to track down the nightblades. On my own it would take too long. I need your help."

Nameless stopped suddenly. He may no longer be in charge of the People, but he wouldn't fall to begging.

The old man was watching him carefully the entire time, and his eyes seemed to see more than he let on. His face was blank, but he nodded. "I will come with you. I had hoped to get away and live peacefully, but there's no use escaping fate. Allow me to say my farewells."

Nameless looked at the old man with confusion. To hear him speak of it, they were heading to some great doom, but in reality they were just hunting two nightblades. Nameless had little doubt he could defeat them. The old man wished the clan well and joined Nameless shortly. They turned their horses around and took off, stares of hatred burning into Nameless' back.

They made good time. Despite his companion's old age, he still rode well. In many ways, his skills with a horse were superior to Nameless'. He did not complain, but when the day's ride was done, it was clear he was exhausted. Despite the physical exertion of riding, he still used his power every night to keep Nameless updated on what was happening in the land. He spoke not just of the nightblades and their actions, but of everything he could sense.

Nameless was grateful for the information. Even though he had relinquished leadership of the People, he still cared for them deeply and wanted to see them succeed. He was pleased they moved so quickly into the new land. The People had been through many trials in the past few seasons, but those who survived were strong, and the people of the Kingdom couldn't resist them.

There was a limit to how much the old man could tell him. Nameless could learn about the movements of groups of people, and with the aid of a rough map, he could see how the People were spreading. Most of the time the old man could tell him which groups were clans and which were not, based on the presence of the demon-kind. But without personally knowing who many people were, the old man couldn't tell him where all of Nameless' most important adversaries were.

Nameless knew Akira had taken the crown of the Kingdom, and he knew Akira hadn't been killed at the battle of the Three Sisters. But on his own there was little he could do about it. The old man didn't know Akira, so he couldn't pick out his energy from anyone else's. But the old man could find the boy, the one as fast as the wind, so he was perfect for Nameless' hunt.

One night, as the old man was using his sense, his eyes opened suddenly. "They are on the move, and fast."

Nameless fixed him with a stare that doubled as a question. The nightblades had been on the move for days.

"We'll need to change the way we are heading. Be patient. I'll find out more."

The old man closed his eyes and returned to his meditative posture. Nameless quenched his frustration as well as he could. He accepted the old man's skills were not easy to come by. At one point he had tried to learn them and failed. But patience was not a quality he possessed, especially when the old man teased him with information.

"I see." The old man had opened his eyes again.

"There are two of us heading towards a group, maybe a hundred people or so. It seems the nightblade is trying to intercept them."

"Can you tell if the girl is with him?"

Nameless' companion shook his head. "I have not been able to detect her in many seasons. Not since she was in our land. But they were together when the four pairs attacked, and I see no reason why they would have separated."

Nameless considered the information carefully. Something important was happening. Two demon-kind wouldn't attack a group of over a hundred, especially if the group was made of soldiers. Victory wasn't out of the question, but it was highly unlikely. Even with all their strength, there was a limit to what they could accomplish. If they were attacking a group that size, they had a good reason. It would be a very good reason if the nightblades were trying to stop them.

"There is something else."

Nameless glanced up.

"I believe one of the monks is with the group. He is flashing his power on a regular basis."

Everything became clear to Nameless. If one of the monks was acting as a beacon for the demon-kind, they would be with someone of importance. Given the location, it was most likely Akira, or maybe one of his top generals. But about a hundred people would be the correct size for an honor guard. It had to be Akira.

"Can we get there in time?"

The old man shook his head. Nameless was going to barrage him with more questions, to ask if they pushed their horses all night, but he knew the old man had already taken it into consideration. If he said there was no chance, there was no chance.

"When will they meet?"

"Tomorrow, late morning to mid-day, perhaps."

Nameless didn't rest well that evening, his mind on the conflict about to occur. The next day he called an early halt. "Even if we can't make it, I need to know what happens."

The old man obliged, assuming his meditative posture on the ground. Nameless paced all around him, but the old man opened his eyes soon.

"Are we too late?"

The old man shook his head. "Not for a while yet. You should leave and give me some space. You can't affect the outcome, and the presence of your energy so close does make this more challenging. Come back at mid-day."

Nameless, lacking options, took the old man's advice. To keep his mind occupied he went hunting, finding plentiful small game in the area. When he came back, the sun was high in the sky, and he had killed four rabbits. He was looking forward to the meat they would provide.

His companion was in his meditative state, so Nameless set about making a small fire at a distance. If he must wait, it was best he make himself useful. At the very least, they could have a good meal when this was over.

The rabbits were nearly finished roasting when the old man came and joined Nameless. "I'm glad you have found ways to make yourself useful."

"What happened?"

The old man turned somber. "We've lost two more of our kind."

Over bites of the rabbit, the old man told what he had sensed, how the demon-kind had attacked, but the boy who was the wind was there just moments later.

"He is strong, you know, and keeps getting stronger every time he fights. And I am sure the girl is with him. One of us died and I couldn't sense anyone near him. I suspect it was her. No one would loose an arrow in the middle of a crowd."

Nameless chewed on the information and his rabbit. It wasn't a surprise, although it was disappointing. Those two nightblades were strong, and the only way they would be killed was if he did it himself. Nameless and the old man finished their meal and returned to the hunt.

Two days later they came upon the battleground the old man had sensed. The trail of the men and the blood on the ground were all the evidence Nameless needed. That and the two bodies lying right next to the trail. He recognized the pair, and he grieved their loss. They were young, but they had been talented and dedicated.

They dismounted, and Nameless began preparing the rites of passage. He stacked what small wood he could find and cleared the brush from the area. Then he stacked their bodies, gently, on the kindling. He and the old man observed a minute of silence, and Nameless went to work starting a fire. The kindling caught easily, and in only moments the bodies were burning. From nothing they had come, and to nothing they would return. It was the way of all life.

After the fire had died down, Nameless caught a whiff of another scent, another body left out in the open. He walked for a ways, following his nose. The scent was strongest when the wind blew from the north. Nameless moved that way, coming over a small rise and seeing the body he had smelled. It was another young man, dressed in the robes of a monk.

Nameless didn't care about this body. The man had been weak. There were no signs of struggle, only a head detached from its shoulders in one clean cut. Nameless could imagine what had happened. The monk had spilled everything he knew, and he had still been killed. The secrets meant nothing to Nameless. He had no intention of honoring any of the promises he had made to any of the people of the Kingdom. It was unlike his kind, but survival meant more to him than his honor. He was already vilified among his people, let them have one more fact to stoke their rage. They were alive, and that was all that mattered.

What did matter to Nameless was discovering that his opponents were ruthless. The monk had posed no physical threat to them, and from the look of it he hadn't even put up a fight. But they still killed him. Nameless approved. They too, were willing to do anything necessary. They would be worthwhile opponents.

Nameless returned to the old man. He could tell something was on his companion's mind, but he hesitated to speak.

"Out with it. You haven't held back much before. Why start now?"

"Fair enough. I can see you know what happened here. This was an attack on the king."

"So?"

"You can also see the paths diverge here. We know the nightblades are heading further north. The king is heading further west."

Nameless indicated he had better get to the point.

"If you were interested in regaining your honor with the People, the head of a king would be a good way to start. He will cause chaos if left alive."

Nameless was surprised that he didn't reject the idea out of hand. The old man was right. If left alone, Akira did seem to have the ability to cause trouble. Nameless had imagined the king was directing troops from someplace hidden, coordinating small attacks that would annoy and disrupt the clans. Now that they knew Akira was with the group, the old man would be able to track them, no matter where they went. Nameless could stop Akira before he caused too much damage. Bringing the head of Akira would go a long way towards repairing his relationship with the clans.

But Akira wasn't the greatest danger to the clans. He was the easier target, the one that would bring Nameless back into good standing with the People, but he wasn't the one Nameless had to truly protect the clans from. It was the other two, the wind and the void, who would change the course of events. Akira was an annoyance, but if the two nightblades continued to kill off the demon-kind, or summoned the other nightblades from wherever they hid, their occupation of the land might come to an end. Nameless knew there was only one path forward.

"We ride after the nightblades."

The old man fixed his stare on the younger man. "We ride towards death, then."

"So be it."

The old man sighed, and without further attempts at persuading Nameless, turned his horse towards the north and towards the nightblades.

CHAPTER 19

Akira was disappointed to have the two nightblades leave his company. It was more than the fact that they were strong. He was surrounded by strong warriors, and although none of them had the skill or ability of either of the nightblades, it was not their combat prowess he missed. He missed their attitude and levelheadedness. Neither of them were particularly interested in gaining his favor, and their advice to him had always been above reproach. They didn't always see things the same way, but Akira knew he could trust them to speak their minds.

Besides that, he considered the two of them to be friends. It was hard to believe, considering they were nightblades and he was the king of this new kingdom. But fate seemed to make for strange acquaintances, and there was no doubting there were few others that Akira would rather have by his side.

Akira pushed away the thoughts as they rode off. There was no use questioning the decisions of either Ryuu or Moriko. They were going to do what they thought was right. They always had and they always would. And although he missed them, he had to admit that he agreed with them. If Nameless was out hunting them, it was safer for everyone if they were separated.

The information about the monasteries had disturbed Akira more than he let on. He hadn't wanted to say as much in front of the two young warriors, but if the monasteries were to lead their own faction or divide up the land in any way, there was no way the Kingdom could stand against the Azarians. If the land was to have any hope at all, they needed to remain united. The time for petty differences had passed the moment the Azarians came into the Kingdom. Akira didn't want to believe the report, but it made sense, and it explained a lot that had happened over the course of the past two cycles.

Akira conferred briefly with his men, but his decision was made. If Ryuu and Moriko had brought him the truth about the monasteries, he needed to act on it immediately. They were five days ride from the nearest monastery, a small one named Hope. Akira searched his memory for any information about the monastery, but all that came to his mind was that it was one of the smallest monasteries in the land, holding less than a dozen monks the last time he had checked.

It was as good as place to start as any, so Akira and his men headed that direction.

Akira and Captain Yung lay in a dense patch of grass less than a league away from Hope. To say the monastery had changed would be an understatement. Akira had only visited it once before, but his memories of the place were of a small, welcoming monastery. It was located in the middle of the plains, and once you entered its walls, it was easy to believe you had found a place of true peace. It had been a silent and relaxing visit the last time he had come, and Akira remembered he had regretted leaving so soon.

Hope was no longer a center of peace. All around the monastery people were swarming about in activity. From what Akira could tell, the vast majority of people were preparing and planting land. For hundreds of paces, fresh black dirt stood in stark contrast to the green grasses of the prairie. Akira was no expert in farming, but it looked like the monastery was trying to raise enough food to feed dozens, if not hundreds of people.

The walls had changed too. The last time he visited, the walls had been beautiful wooden structures, the wood brought in from a small forest many leagues away. The walls had been more symbolic than defensive, a symbol of separation between the everyday world of the Three Kingdoms and the world of the sense. But now the wall was reinforced with stone twice as high as Akira stood. There was little doubt the monastery was no longer focused on peace.

Nothing that Akira saw made him happy. The monastery was preparing for war, preparing to last for a siege, reinforcing what Ryuu and Moriko had said. To make matters worse, they only rarely saw monks partaking in the labor. When Akira did see a monk, the monk would wander around the workers, clearly providing supervision. From their distance, the workers didn't seem happy.

Anger built in Akira. Those were his people, and no one should be forced to work against their will. The monks thought they were superior. They always had.

Akira looked at his captain, "I need to get closer to see what is going on."

His captain shook his head, and Akira suppressed his frustration. There was no one better at defending Akira, but a large part of that was because Yung was a cautious man. Akira appreciated his caution most days, but on others, like today, the caution could be infuriating.

He knew what his captain was going to say even before the words left his lips.

"I do not think it is a good idea, my king. If it is more information you seek, let me send one or two of the men. Their loss would mean little compared to yours."

"This is something I need to see with my own eyes. If the monasteries have betrayed our trust, I need to see it myself. I will only go and observe. I will return in the morning."

"If you are set on this course of action, at least allow me to accompany you."

Akira gave his captain a mischievous grin. "I'm afraid not. You need to stay here and remain in command of the troops. If something does happen, I need to know somebody will come and rescue me."

The captain cursed under his breath. "I might just leave you there."

Akira laughed out loud. Such humor was rare from Yung. "It will be fine. You worry too much."

The captain ordered one of his best swordsmen to join Akira. Together they changed out of their riding clothes into peasant garb. They didn't have any way of concealing swords, so instead they hid knives and daggers wherever they could. Akira's captain watched the proceedings with a disgruntled eye, but he said nothing. He had served under Akira for many cycles, and was well used to the behavior of the man who was his king. There were some battles he wouldn't win.

Without fanfare, Akira and the swordsman, named Yuki, left for the monastery. The sun was setting by the time they reached the gates.

There was a monk stationed there. He had, of course, seen Akira and his retainer approaching from a long ways off, but he made no move to greet them, waiting until they approached close to the gate. "Who are you, and what brings you to Hope?"

Akira and Yuki gave fake names, claiming to be farmers who were seeking sanctuary at the monastery. Akira figured this to be the most likely explanation for why the monastery was so crowded. People had to be running to them as places of refuge. The monk eyed the two of them carefully. "I do not recognize either of you from around here." It was half a statement, half a question.

Akira wasn't prepared for the increased scrutiny, but Yuki was. He spun a story, saying they were from lands further to the south, driven north in front of a clan of Azarians. It was a good story, and by the time the soldier was done, Akira half-believed it himself.

The story seem to assuage the monk, and he gave them a welcoming smile. "I am sorry I had to ask, but these are hard times. I hope you will forgive me."

Yuki replied, "No offense has been taken. We are simply grateful to find a place where we can be safe."

The monk nodded. "If it is safety you seek, you have come to the right place. Have no fears on that account, we are strong enough to withstand the might of the invaders."

The monk led them into the monastery, crowded as it was at night. There were dozens of people here, all of them with a look of fear in their eyes. Akira wasn't sure if the fear was of the Azarians, or of the situation they found themselves in now. The people were dirty, and the monastery smelled much worse than Akira remembered. They were huddled close to one another, and at night they shared a common sleeping space far too small for all of them.

That evening, Akira struck up conversations with many of those at the monastery. The stories they told were much the same as the one Yuki made up for them. They were farmers, villagers, traders. In one way or another, each of them had been driven from their homes and their lands by the advance of the Azarians. They had heard from flyers, traveling monks, or from family and friends that the monasteries were places of safety. While the stories were all slightly different, they were all at heart the same.

Safety, they had. But the safety that was promised came at a price. As soon as they arrived, they were put to work. As Akira had seen, many of them were out farming the lands around the monastery, trying to grow as much food as possible. Those who had been farmers were put in charge of these groups, under the supervision of at least one monk.

Others were assigned the task of building the wall. Anyone with expertise was tasked with helping to lead the efforts. Stones were taken from soil that was tilled by the farmers and brought to the wall for construction. It was a haphazard business, but day by day, the wall grew higher and thicker.

There was another group Akira hadn't seen from his scouting. They were the dirtiest and the most unhappy with their stay at the monastery. The monks were digging underneath the monastery, trying to create more room both for people and for food. Those who were not able or willing to help with the farming or the building of the wall were tasked with digging, a task in which they saw no sunlight for almost the entire day.

As Akira looked around at his fellow disheveled occupants, he saw the signs of strain already written across their bodies. Skin was hanging from several of them, and almost everyone had a haunted look about them. They had found safety, but they had not found peace. Akira's anger was kindled. He couldn't believe the monks would be so bold and so callous in the treatment of the others. He had never been overly fond of the monasteries, but he had always assumed their best intentions. As he looked around the room, it became harder and harder to do so. This was a blatant grab for power. Like the others, he desired rest, but as he struggled to find sleep, he was not thinking about what chore he would be assigned the next day. He was thinking how he could save his people.

When the sun rose the next morning, Akira was still unsure what he should do. On one hand, his people had a level of protection and safety here they wouldn't were they out on their own. Even though the monks' behavior angered him, he couldn't believe that they fail to protect people within their walls should the threat appear. He wasn't pleased. No one should have to exchange their freedom for their safety.

His final decision was to make no decision at all. They would leave immediately. Everything he had seen confirmed the report Ryuu and Moriko had brought to him. The monasteries were making a grab for power, and they were doing it on the backs of Akira's people. But Hope was not the center of the problem. As near as he could tell, there were still less than a dozen monks inside the monastery walls, and if change was going to begin, it wasn't going to start here. The Chief Abbot of the monasteries was in the land that used to be the Western Kingdom. If Akira was going to change anything, that had to be his next destination.

He whispered his plan to Yuki as soon as he was up, and the guard agreed. Even though there were only a handful of monks here, they were well known for their martial prowess, and should the situation turn violent, Yuki wasn't sure he could protect his king.

As the monastery woke up around them, Akira and his guard packed their belongings. They would attempt to leave with as little commotion as possible.

As soon as people started going about their daily tasks, Akira and Yuki made for the exit. Akira glanced left and right, looking to see if their exit was drawing any attention. As near as he could tell, none of the monks seemed concerned about them.

Their success lasted only for a moment. Akira heard a voice behind him. "Excuse me, but I don't think I've had the pleasure of meeting you yet."

Akira turned around, and his heart sank as soon as he saw the speaker. Of all the monks in the land, the one that stood in front of them was one who had been at Stonekeep for the Conclave. It was one of the monks who had lied to Akira, who told him Renzo was not a nightblade. Akira knew his face would not be known by everyone, but this monk certainly knew who he was. He threw off his hood, all pretense of hiding done for.

The monk did not seem surprised to see Akira. He had probably been spotted yesterday when he came in. He cursed himself for his stupidity and not listening to his captain. He should learn to trust his men more.

The monk let out a sly grin, and all around him Akira could feel the other monks closing in a loose circle. "Lord Akira. What a pleasant surprise."

Yuki burst out, before Akira could stop him. "He's your king now."

The monk didn't seem disturbed. "He might have been our king, once, but - I don't know if you've noticed - the land has fallen, and there is no order now except that which we provide."

Yuki was about to draw his sword, but Akira laid a restraining arm on his shoulder. "Let it be. We did not come here for a fight."

Akira squarely faced the monk. "Your treachery runs deep. I hoped not to believe it, but I needed to see it firsthand."

The monk shrugged. "What you call treachery, others may call our best hope for survival. You were not strong enough to stop the invasion. The only people left who can defend this land are the monasteries. We only saw what was coming and prepared for it."

It was hard for him to contain his anger. "You only knew what was coming because you helped plan the invasion."

The monk's look turned stern. "That is a terrible accusation to make."

"It's easy when one has intercepted the papers between your monasteries and the Azarian invaders."

The monk seemed startled by the fact. He glanced around the circle. "Come now. I know you did not come to argue trivialities." Akira looked around and saw what the monk saw. Their argument was attracting the attention of all the people in the yard. Akira held out hope. If he could sway the people to his side, they would far outnumber the monks. Already, many of them would've overheard his guard state that Akira was king.

"I know you have betrayed us to the Azarians," Akira said, his voice echoing in the small monastery. "I know you helped them plan this invasion, telling them where our forces were weak and where our supplies were. Perhaps, just perhaps, forgiveness can be found for that treachery. But I will not stand by as you enslave my people under the pretense of safety."

There was a silence all around them, and Akira knew the situation was balanced on the edge of a blade.

"I do not know about what you speak, Akira. But I do know this. We are here to provide safety for the people. We are the only ones who can stand up against the Azarians, and you are only angry because you have not yet understood this truth. Yes, this is a hard life, but each man, woman and child here is doing everything they can to promote their own safety. We did not tell them that life in the monasteries would be easy, we only told them we would keep them alive. They, at least, have better things to do with their time than run around shouting baseless accusations at everyone."

Akira could tell the crowd was swayed by the monk's arguments. It was easy to underestimate how much power the monasteries had over the common person in the Kingdom. He had to force the issue. "You've not heard the last of me. It seems I have business with the Chief Abbot."

Akira turned to leave, daring the monk to try anything in front of everyone watching. He was surprised when the monk didn't even hesitate.

"My brothers, the king is feeling unwell. Perhaps an honest day's labor scares him too much. Make sure he makes it to my chambers." The loose circle of monks closed in tight, and Akira's guard looked at him for direction. Each of the monks was armed with a staff, giving them a much longer reach than the short knives Akira and Yuki had. The skill of the monks was well known, and although they might be able to defeat one or two, there was no way the two of them could defeat all the monks. Akira gently shook his head.

He looked around to see if any of his people would stand up for him, but already people seemed to believe the conflict was at an end, and they all started going their own ways, ready to start their daily chores. Akira had a hard time believing what he was seeing.

His people wouldn't stand up, not even for their king. It was a blow harder to take than the monasteries' betrayal.

Without argument, Akira and Yuki allowed themselves to be prodded back towards a small room near the back of the monastery. Once they were in, a bolt slammed shut on the outside.

Akira had been captured.

Chapter 20

Ryuu and Moriko rode as fast as the horses would carry them. Moriko had never been a big fan of horses, but in this case, every bit of speed was a help to them. They wanted as much distance between themselves and Nameless as they could get. All day long they were in the saddle, stopping to rest only once the sun dipped completely below the horizon.

Each night, Ryuu would spread out his sense, trying to understand what was happening in the Three Kingdoms. By the time he was finished, Moriko would have a small meal ready to eat, and the two of them would rest and fill their bellies as Ryuu told Moriko everything he was sensing.

Most of what he could sense wasn't surprising. The Azarians continued to push further and further into the land, and they moved quickly. Ryuu had thought it would take more time for the clans to move their entire population, but that didn't seem to be the case. He supposed that when there was no resistance, the clans were able to move as fast as they could ride. The clans seemed to go where they pleased, but Ryuu noted they expanded in a fairly uniform manner. Their expansion wasn't quite as chaotic as he would have expected, and he wondered if they had planned this expansion before they crossed the Three Sisters. It would explain why they were able to move so quickly and spread out so fast. By the end of the summer, the Azarians would cover almost the entire land.

At the moment, the advance of the Azarians wasn't Ryuu's main concern. He spent most of his time focusing on Nameless, judging to see whether or not they put any more distance between themselves. Even though two days of hard riding separated them, Nameless always seemed to know exactly where they were going. It was a problem Ryuu desperately wanted to figure out.

They were only a day's ride away from the river. Once they arrived, they would follow it until they reached the nearest town. Then the plan was to hire a boat to take them up the river to the northern sea, where they would then find transportation to the island of the blades.

As Moriko cooked, Ryuu sat down and tried to find Nameless once again. It was not a challenging task. Nameless let off more energy than anyone Ryuu had ever met, and he never bothered to contain it at all. He was like a bright light shining in the darkness against Ryuu's sense. Tonight, again, little had changed. Nameless continued to follow them, and he had even gained a little bit of distance. Ryuu and Moriko rode their horses as fast as they could, but Nameless was faster.

Ryuu wasn't too concerned about the distance between them. There had been some days where they had gained, and some days they had lost, but altogether both the hunter and the hunted remained about the same distance apart. Ryuu was trying to figure out how it was Nameless was able to track them so easily. Just to be certain, two days ago Ryuu had turned them further towards the west. It meant extra distance to reach the river, but he had hoped it would shake their pursuit. However, that night when Ryuu had used his sense to find Nameless, he was right behind them, the same distance he always had been. No matter which way they turned, Nameless was always following them.

Tonight, instead of focusing on Nameless, Ryuu focused on the space surrounding the hunter. It was difficult, as his attention kept wandering back to Nameless and his energy, like a moth driven towards the light. But there had to be someone else, he just wasn't able to sense them so close to Nameless. Again and again his attention drifted back to Nameless, and once more he would try to spread his attention further away. When he found what he was looking for, he was surprised. The man he found had little strength himself, but Ryuu could feel the tendrils of the sense emanating far and wide from the man. Ryuu knew what was happening.

He returned to himself and opened his eyes and looked at Moriko. There was a grin on his face, and Moriko saw he had figured something out. "What is it?"

Ryuu leaned forward. "We know the hunters always travel in pairs. This has always been true. But you never said anything about Nameless' partner."

Moriko scrunched up her face, as though she had never realized this fact for herself. "I never thought about that, but now that you mention it, it seems rather obvious. I never saw him with a partner."

She closed her eyes, imagining the scene between herself and Nameless, the closest she had ever come to dying. How many people had surrounded her that day? Nameless had been in the center of the circle, and if a partner had been with him, there should have been an odd number of hunters. Moriko's memory was far from perfect, but her memories of that day were forever burned into her mind. She was sure there had been ten hunters in the circle. She searched all her other memories of the leader of the Azarians, and slim as they were, she couldn't remember him with another man or woman as his partner. She shook her head. "I don't remember him ever having a partner. From everything I saw, he was alone."

"Regardless, I think I know how he is able to track us," Ryuu said. "You told me that in Azarian culture, among the hunters, there is always one who is considered the warrior, and one who is considered the tracker."

Moriko nodded.

Ryuu continued, "I don't know if they are partners in the way we are used to seeing, but doesn't it make sense the best warrior of the Azarians would have the best tracker at his disposal?"

"I suppose. But who is it?"

"I don't know who he is, but I can tell you this much. There is another man with Nameless, and he has the ability to sense at a distance, just like I do. He keeps a fair distance away from Nameless, but I think it is only because of how strong Nameless is. He is the reason why Nameless is always able to track us no matter which way we go."

Moriko gave Ryuu a look he wasn't able to decipher. "You have an idea, and I'm not sure I'm going to like it."

Ryuu grinned and shook his head. "No, you're not."

Moriko couldn't believe she'd been persuaded to do this. Two days ago, when Ryuu had sold her on the idea, it had seemed like a good one. The heart of it was simple. Ryuu would act as a distraction, drawing Nameless away from the man who was his tracker. Ryuu would have a chance to fight Nameless, and there was a chance many of their problems would be solved with one decisive action.

It was the decisive action that appealed to Moriko. She was tired of running from place to place trying to figure out what to do. Instead they would attack their problem head-on and finish it.

But now, in the middle of executing the plan, Moriko wasn't so sure. Doubts assailed her mind. She had no concerns about tracking and killing her target. She was invisible, and if she was smart the hunter would never even know she was there. But she was worried about Ryuu. He was strong, stronger than she had ever seen him, but she couldn't help but think he wasn't strong enough to fight Nameless.

She had objected, lightly, but not enough to change the course of their actions. The plan had become a reality.

Moriko pushed the thoughts out of her mind. What was done was done, and they had set themselves upon a course from which there was no return. They were as prepared as they could be. There was nothing left to do but to trust their skills and hope for the best.

They camped next to the roaring banks of the river for two days, practicing and training, acting as though they hadn't a care in the world. Each night, Ryuu would extend his sense and confirm that Nameless and his partner continued to get closer.

As the sun set that evening, Ryuu threw out his sense one last time. Their plans had been made, and there was no turning back. Nameless was only three leagues away, and would be at their camp by the time the moon was high. Moriko suppressed any nervousness on her part. It was Ryuu who had the more challenging task. They kept a tense watch that night, Ryuu in a meditative position almost constantly. For the plan to work, he had to let Moriko know where

Nameless' partner was going to be. And so they waited for the two of them split up. Ryuu was certain Nameless wouldn't bring his partner into the battle. He would not risk his tracker.

As soon as Nameless and his partner separated, Ryuu gave Moriko directions as best he could. So long as he got her close it would be good enough. Once nearby, Moriko would be able to sense the man herself.

Moriko crept through the brush. There was a partial moon, casting dark shadows as clouds passed overhead. Her progress was slow. If the hunter was one of the best trackers of the Azarians, his other senses would be sharp as well. Moriko stayed downwind of the hunter, moving so slowly she didn't even rustle the grass. Her muscles burned and screamed for relief, but she was an expert at ignoring them.

She could sense the person she was stalking. His sense spread far and wide, and she knew he was gathering more information than she could ever imagine. But the tendrils of his sense ran over her without notice, and that was all that mattered. For all his knowledge, he wouldn't see his own death coming.

Moriko crept closer, and the man she was tracking came into view. He was old, one of the oldest men she had ever seen. All of a sudden, she hesitated. It wasn't that she couldn't kill him, but a man this old deserved respect. Killing him without warning seemed wrong somehow. He had to die, but it should be with honor.

She drew her sword, the ring of steel leaving the sheath cutting through the night air. The old man startled, stood up, and turned around. He faced Moriko with a look of calm serenity up on his face. "The void has come for me at last," he said with a smile on his face.

Moriko frowned. The words of the old man didn't make sense to her. "You know why I'm here."

The old man nodded. "Yes, I've seen your coming for some time now. I tried to warn him, but he would not listen. You are the one who will bring death to us all."

Moriko was confused, but the words echoed in her mind, and she couldn't let them go. What was the old man talking about? Did he somehow see the future?

The old man seemed to be able to look inside of her mind. "No, I cannot see the future, and would not wish that curse on anyone. But I can see the way the pattern forms, and I can see the way this world continues to turn, day after day. It does not take the gift of sight to see what will happen. I warned him, but he would not listen."

The old man's words shattered Moriko's confidence, but she had come with a singular purpose, and nothing would turn her aside from that. "Take a few moments. Make your peace."

The old man smiled. "Thank you for your kindness. You've shown your quality, but I have always been at peace. This world has always been enough for me. Do what you came to do."

With that, the old man spread his arms wide, opening himself up for Moriko's attack. She suspected a trap, but her sense gave nothing away. The man fully intended to allow her to strike him down where he stood. She hesitated only for a moment and then dashed forward. Her blade came back and made one cut. The old man didn't move a muscle, and the cut was clean.

Moriko couldn't be sure, but she thought she heard the old man whisper as his head fell from his shoulders. "A beautiful cut."

Moriko didn't want to admit how much her encounter with the old man had shaken her. She cleaned her blade and sheathed her sword. She had both horses, and the next steps in their plan were clear. She mounted the horses and was off.

Ryuu waited on the banks of the river. They were only a few days away from the confluence of the largest rivers in the Kingdom, and here, the stream that originated in the mountains of the Northern Kingdom had become a quick and powerful river. Where he stood the river had worn away the banks for more lifetimes than Ryuu could imagine, carving its way deep into the earth. The drop was three or four times his own height, and if the worst came to pass, Ryuu planned to make that jump. The water was dark and fast, but still less dangerous than Nameless' blade. He wouldn't die. Not here. Not tonight.

A strange mixture of nervousness and excitement coursed through his body. He had always sensed how strong Nameless was, even back when he was on the island. To come face to face with that strength made him nervous. He had fought strong opponents before, but never anyone like this. As much as he tried to push the thought out of his mind, Ryuu was certain Nameless was stronger than he was.

But that knowledge also excited him. He remembered a conversation he and Moriko once had. She told him she was never truly alive unless she was facing an opponent stronger than her. At the time Ryuu had disagreed. He wanted to believe there was more to life than beating the next strongest opponent. But as he stood on the banks of the river he wasn't so sure. His blood raced and all his senses were sharp. He had to admit, he was eager to face the man who came his way.

Either way, there would be some sort of conclusion tonight. Once Moriko killed the man who was tracking them, getting away from Nameless would be much easier. Ryuu hoped he might defeat Nameless tonight, but he suspected he wouldn't be able to. His primary goal was to live, and to distract Nameless long enough that Moriko could finish her work. He still needed to get back to the island. The only hope for the Kingdom was for the nightblades to return.

Ryuu's thoughts were interrupted as he felt Nameless get closer. At any moment now he would come over the last small hill separating the two of them. He was eager to see the man who had changed everything for the Kingdom. Moriko had made him out to be larger than life, and Ryuu was curious to see how he stacked up in reality.

When Nameless finally crested the hill, Ryuu almost laughed. Moriko, if anything, had been understating Nameless' qualities. Orochi had been big, but this man was a giant, and Ryuu couldn't see even the smallest part of fat on him. He wore nothing but a ragged shirt and pants, and both looked as though they were ready to rip off him at any moment.

The second thing Ryuu noticed was the way he moved. Despite his size, the man moved like a cat, his body always perfectly balanced. Ryuu's heart was racing. He had known, in his mind, he had never faced an opponent like Nameless before; but now he knew it in his bones. The man was so large it was almost a joke.

Ryuu stood in place, fighting the urge to jump straight into the river. As frightened as he was, he had to know.

When Nameless stopped, he stood about five paces away from Ryuu. The two men studied each other, taking each other's measure before the battle began.

When Nameless spoke, Ryuu was surprised by how soft his voice was. "So, you are the other one that has caused us so much trouble. You do not look like much."

Ryuu looked up at Nameless. The man stood at least two heads taller than him. "No, I suppose I don't."

"Where is the girl?"

"She went on."

Nameless cocked his head to one side. "I don't believe you. You people don't value honesty."

Ryuu met his challenge with a straight look. "I do. This is between you and me tonight."

The two stood in silence for a few moments, and Nameless nodded. "Very well. No games?"

Ryuu took his stance. "No games."

Within the blink of an eye, Ryuu fell into the way of all things, feeling the energy flow into him. He drew it into his body. There would be no cautious exchange of passes in this battle. The two of them would go at each other with everything they had, right away. Ryuu approved. It was the way warriors should fight.

Nameless exploded into action, but Ryuu was prepared. He had sensed the attack and its ferocity. He leapt forward as well, and their swords met on a moonlit night.

Ryuu wasn't surprised by how fast Nameless moved, but it seemed impossible when seen firsthand. The man was so big, it seemed like there was no way his body could be so quick. There were three passes where no one struck, each dodging the cuts of the other, and then their swords struck.

Ryuu had been well balanced, and his cut had been true, but Nameless was much stronger than he was. The cut knocked Ryuu back several paces, and his feet quickly shifted so that he could stay on them. Nameless didn't give him any chance to recover, and again the hiss of the blades could be heard in the night.

Ryuu cut low. He was closer to the ground and hoped he could get Nameless off-balance. But Nameless danced out of the reach of his blade, trying to cut down Ryuu from above. Ryuu had to disengage or risk a sword to the top of his head.

The two fighters separated for a moment, and Ryuu fought the urge to grin. He had never met a swordsman like Nameless. He was strong, fast, and smart, and he didn't make the mistakes that so often meant death on the battlefield. Ryuu wasn't sure how Nameless would fall, but he was excited to try and find out.

Nameless seemed to feel the same way, and the two came together again. This time, Ryuu tried getting inside of Nameless' guard. He was smaller and hoped to punish Nameless with a close-in sword fight where he couldn't use all the strength of his arms. Nameless cut down on Ryuu, and he deflected the blade up high, allowing it to slide down his own blade behind him in an umbrella block.

Ryuu was inside of Nameless' guard, and he drove his knee into his opponent's stomach. He wasn't expecting to hit a wall, but his knee told him Nameless didn't have a weak stomach. All the same, the blow had been true, even if the only effect was Nameless taking a half-step backwards.

Ryuu didn't give Nameless any space. He rotated, striking at Nameless' stomach, this time with his elbow. His elbow confirmed what his knee had told him: there wasn't any soft space on Nameless to strike. Ryuu saw the opening as Nameless took another step back. He dropped his shoulder and cut flat across his chest. Nameless somehow managed to dance backwards fast enough to avoid a deadly cut. Ryuu's blade gently sliced into the outer layers of Nameless' skin, but it was far from lethal, and Nameless used the moment to get some space between them and bring his sword down into a defensive stance again.

It had been close, but Ryuu wasn't going to get a good cut in. He recognized it would only be a moment before Nameless could bring his strength to bear, and he leapt backwards, keeping his defense up.

The two opponents circled each other warily. Ryuu tried to draw in more energy as Nameless attacked. Both attack and defense were true, but Nameless was still faster than Ryuu was. It might have been by the width of a hair, but that extra speed was a chasm Ryuu couldn't cross. Ryuu recognized it as he kept falling back a pace at a time. Distance was his only defense.

Nameless stepped in close to him, and Ryuu sensed the kick coming, but there wasn't much he could do about it. He tried to shift with the kick to lessen its impact, but there was little he could do otherwise. It sent him flying backwards, and for a moment he thought he could keep his feet under him, but he saw that would be a mistake. It would take him a moment to regain his balance, and in that moment Nameless would strike. Nameless pursued him relentlessly.

Instead, Ryuu allowed himself to fall. Nameless tried to cut at his head, but Ryuu rolled backwards quickly enough for the cut to pass harmlessly overhead. As he came back up, Ryuu brought his sword straight up, strong and steady. Nameless must have sensed it in time, because his body was already reacting. He was able to just deflect it with his own, shorter blade, but now he was off-balance.

Ryuu summoned all the energy he could and launched himself at Nameless. For just a moment he had the advantage, and he used it for all it was worth. His blade cut the air cleanly, seeking Nameless' flesh. But for all Ryuu's speed, it still wasn't enough. Nameless was just a little faster, and in the space of a few heartbeats he had regained his balance and the edge again.

After another pass the two fighters split apart. Ryuu was exhausting himself quickly. He was bringing in a lot of energy but expending it at the same time. He looked at Nameless and saw the big warrior was also sweating profusely. That was good. At least he was making the hunter work for it.

Nameless was also looking for a chance to catch his breath, and Ryuu was more than willing to let him have it.

"Your strength is remarkable. I've never fought one as strong as you. It was a mistake for me not to come and kill you earlier. I will not underestimate you again."

Ryuu looked at Nameless, a strange feeling of pride and companionship rushing through him. "Thanks. I'm still not quite as fast as you, though." There was no disappointment in his voice. He was just stating a fact. Both of them were experts, and both could acknowledge the truth.

Nameless nodded. "No, you are not quite as fast, but when this battle is decided, it will be by the narrowest of margins."

Ryuu thought quickly. He didn't think that he'd be able to win this fight, and as much as he wanted to finish the battle here, he didn't think he could. He still needed to get stronger. And right now Nameless was between him and the river.

Ryuu bowed slightly to Nameless. "It has been an honorable duel."

He didn't give Nameless the time to figure out what was happening. He launched himself at Nameless, summoning all the energy he could. Nameless was prepared, but Ryuu had expected him to be. They passed each other three times, and finally Ryuu saw the opportunity he was looking for. He had worked himself into a place where he was closer to the river, and he cut at Nameless with strength. Nameless stepped back, and it gave Ryuu the moment of space he needed.

Ryuu turned and sheathed his sword, sprinting straight towards the river. He leapt, falling straight into the freezing cold water. As he drifted downstream, he managed to turn around against the current, and saw Nameless silhouetted against the moon, deprived temporarily of his prey.

CHAPTER 21

Nameless watched as Ryuu drifted down the river. For a few moments, he debated chasing after the nightblade, but ultimately decided against it. The current was fast, and although Nameless was certain he could pace the river for several leagues, it seemed to be more work than it was worth. He had enjoyed his fight with the young swordsman more than he cared to admit, and did not want to see it come to an end so soon. At his core, he was a hunter, and he was tracking the most dangerous prey he had ever had the privilege of tracking. He wanted to savor it while he could.

More pragmatically, Nameless was worried that if he left the old man he would never find him again. The old man helped because he was required to, but Nameless was certain that given the opportunity, the old man would be much happier finding his own way. If he was going to track the nightblades, he needed the old man's assistance.

Sheathing his sword, Nameless wandered back towards the old man. He had left him a safe distance away. He wasn't sure how far the two nightblades could sense, but he needed the old man out of danger.

Concern started to build as he approached the place where he had separated from the old man. Although his tracker did not leave much of a presence, Nameless thought he should be able to sense him by now. His first thought was that the old man had taken the opportunity to run off. It surprised Nameless. He knew the old man had no desire to be in his service, but at the same time, he had also known that Nameless would not be gone for long. To leave with such a short window of opportunity was a bold move.

But as he got closer, a suspicion snaked its way into his mind; and with every step, the suspicion wiggled deeper and deeper into his heart. He had been foolish and had underestimated the nightblades once again. How could he have been so blind?

In a few more steps Nameless was running at full speed, more and more certain of what he would find. When he got to the old man's body, all his fears were confirmed. The old man had a smile on his face, and he had greeted death like the old friend it was. The cut that had separated the head from the body was sharp and well-executed. Nameless' first thought was that at least it had been a clean death. He had no doubt his companion had died quickly and painlessly.

He was surprised by how much emotion he felt at the old man's passing. He had cared little for him when he had been alive, but somehow his death, happening right under his own nose, was more than Nameless could take. Grief, anger and confusion ran through his mind, battling for supremacy.

It was rage that won. A white-hot burning anger settled into his gut, and tears streamed down his cheeks, burning his face with their intensity. It wasn't enough that the nightblades had killed so many of his brothers and sisters and had hounded his steps at every turn. They also had to kill his partner right under his nose. Nameless had no doubt it had been their plan all along. The boy was the one who would distract him. He had never fought to win, only to give the girl enough time to sneak up on the old man and cut off his head. Although a small, silent part of Nameless understood it had been a brilliant decision, the greater part of him raged at their insolence. Didn't they realize he was stronger than they were? Didn't they know their place was to die?

Nameless fell to his knees next to the old man's body. All thoughts ran from his mind, replaced only by a rushing torrent of anger. For a few moments he lost all reason, and screamed into the sky, so all the world would know his rage.

When Nameless woke up, the sun had already risen above the horizon. He glanced about in a daze as the events of the previous evening came back to him. Anger, grief and embarrassment fought side-by-side in his mind, but their intensity had lessened from the evening before. Instead, what Nameless felt more than anything was emptiness, a lack of purpose or direction. Until last night his purpose had seemed clear, his path straightforward. His only goal had been to hunt the nightblades, but now that they were gone he was not sure what to do next.

He could continue the hunt. If his guess was correct, the two nightblades had planned this out and would most likely meet in a village downstream. Nameless would be able to pursue them by picking up the trail at the nearest village. But he would not make the same mistake of underestimating his quarry once again. They would continue to elude him, and although Nameless was stronger than either of them, he was not sure he was stronger than both of them. He also suspected at least one of them could use their gift at a distance, just like the old man had been able to. Nameless could not think of another way they could have discovered the old man. Nameless was a hunter who had pursued dangerous game before, and he knew there sometimes came a moment where the hunter became the hunted. He was afraid that if he pursued the two nightblades much further that would be his fate.

Nameless looked at the body of the old man, and decided his first step should be to send the old tracker properly on his way. There was a small grove of trees nearby, and Nameless made short work of a few of the smaller ones. He formed a mighty pyre, much larger than the one he had built for the two of his brothers that had fallen several days before. He had not always liked the old man, but his gifts had been unique, and he had served the clans well. Without his help, the battle of the Three Sisters would have been a much bloodier affair. With the strong defense the Three Kingdoms had mounted, without the old man they might not have won. It was his knowledge of the positions of the armies of the Three Kingdoms that allowed them their victory. Nameless believed he deserved an end fitting of his deeds.

The work took the entire morning, but when it was over there was a stack of dry wood half as tall as Nameless was. He positioned the old man gently on the wood, and sat in silent meditation for a few moments, honoring the man's memories and deeds.

When he was done, Nameless took out his gear and lit a fire on the first try. The fire was slow to catch, but grew quickly. Nameless took a few paces back, watching the wood and the body burn, life returning to wherever it had come from. He watched with a strange sense of detachment, like his mind was half there and half somewhere else, wandering paths his consciousness couldn't follow.

The fire burned down when the sun was low in the sky. Nameless felt relief, as though all burdens had been lifted from his shoulders. He realized that his work for now was done. He could not pursue the nightblades with any hope of success, but even if they escaped, he was not sure they were the problem he once thought they were. Nameless knew there were other nightblades, rumors of an island far to the north. But from everything he had learned, they had long ago distanced themselves from the Three Kingdoms. In the cold light of day, Nameless realized there was no reason for them to return.

The People were far more important right now. As he and the old man had traveled, the old man had kept him abreast of events happening far and wide. The People were spreading out quickly, as the plan had asked of them. But although they spread quickly, there were still challenges and struggles. The clans had lost far too many good people coming into this land, and though they would be stronger for it, they still needed all the help they could get.

Nameless thought back to his days when he had been much younger, when he had both seen and experienced far less. He thought about his days roaming the land, going from clan to clan, seeking to aid them however possible. A slight hint of a smile played upon his lips. Those had been long and grueling days, but he had lacked the care and concern that he carried with him this season. He had simply gone from place to place, doing all that he was able, moving on when there was no further need of him.

It occurred to him there was no reason why he could not relive those days. He was a demon-kind, and although for a time he had led the clans, that time was now over. His duty was no longer to lead, but to serve.

The more he thought about the idea, the more merit it had. He wanted to be remembered well, and if his decision to lead the clans into this new land would be controversial, perhaps the least he could do was to help those of his people who needed it.

Nameless had always been decisive. In a few moments, his course was settled. He knew what he would do, and his heart felt much lighter. He would find the clans and help as he was able, living off the land as he had in his youth.

Nameless decided he would follow the river to the west. From the maps he carried, he knew that a mighty confluence of the rivers was only a few days' walk away. Water was sparse in Azaria, and he marveled at the opportunity to see two great rivers come together into one monster river. Perhaps along the way he would find a clan and ask if they needed help.

With a smile on his face, Nameless went on his way.

CHAPTER 22

Akira studied his cell with a great deal of curiosity. He suspected the small building they were in had been designed as a storehouse. The walls were thick and sturdy, and there were no windows to the outside world. When he examined the door he saw there had never been any way of locking the door from the inside, so he could guess that the building had been designed to keep things in. Assuming that taking prisoners was a new tradition for the monks, it made the most sense to believe they were in a storehouse.

Although Akira spent a substantial amount of time evaluating his surroundings, he could see there was no way they could effect a stealthy escape. If they were going to get out of here on their own power, it would have to be when someone opened the door, and from the caution the monks had taken with them, Akira was certain it would be a long time before that plan worked.

They had been stripped of what weapons they had soon after being thrown in the cell. Although the room was dark and time had no meaning, Akira assumed it was about mid-afternoon when one of the monks came in with a bowl of soup and some rice for each of them. Akira studied the monk's entrance carefully, having already decided that if they were going to escape these times were their only chance. The monks knew it, too, and took precautions. While one of the monks brought in the food, another was at the door, and Akira could see there were two behind him as well. If they were going to escape they would have to fight their way out, and Akira wasn't sure they had the strength, particularly without weapons.

Once he had decided escape was unlikely, Akira spent his time wondering about the events that had transpired. He was surprised by how not surprised he was by the accuracy of Ryuu and Moriko's reports. He had hoped they would be wrong, but he had suspected the monasteries of duplicity for some time now. Many cycles ago, he had been warned by his advisers that the monasteries were becoming too active in local politics, but Akira had bigger worries on his mind and had brushed the concerns off. He hadn't concerned himself about the small, petty deals the monasteries made. Now he wondered if he had been wise in overlooking those acts.

He sighed. There was nothing to be done about it now. The monasteries had made their choice, and he had to decide how he was going to react. He wondered idly what the plan of the monks at Hope could be. It was a small monastery, and had little strength or renown on its own. Akira also had no idea what type of authority the Chief Abbot had entrusted the other abbots with. Would they try something here at Hope, or would they send him to the Chief Abbot in the old Western Kingdom?

As Akira pondered, Yuki worried. Though Akira could just barely see his outline in the near perfect darkness of their cell, it was clear from the sounds of the guard's frantic pacing that he was frightened. Akira tried to reassure him.

"Have a seat. You're making me nervous."

Yuki sat down, but Akira's respite was short-lived. Soon, the soldier was up again, pacing back and forth. When he spoke, Akira could hear the hint of desperation in his voice. "What are they going to do to us? We're outnumbered and have no weapons."

Akira frowned. His honor guard consisted of the best trained and most competent troops of his kingdom. For one of them to start to crack so easily was concerning. "Rest yourself. What is it that concerns you so?"

"My king, give me an enemy I know how to fight, and nothing will stop me. My blade is sure, and should I be disarmed, my hands and feet are just as effective. But these are monks. For all the skill I possess, I am not sure I could best any of them in single combat, much less the dozen that stand between us and freedom."

Yuki helped Akira to understand. Akira had never held the monasteries in high esteem, but he was unique in that regard. They were heroes of the people. They had a power completely separate from his own, and they owned the hearts of his subjects. That was why they were able to get away with what they did, and people would thank them for it. For a moment his mind wandered to the bigger problems facing him. If he was going to break the power of the monasteries, he had to figure out some way to break the power of their hold over his people. It was a hard question, and one he didn't have the answer to yet, so he focused his attention on the present.

"They are good fighters, but they can be bested. I have seen it happen."

The last part was a bit of a lie. He knew monks had been defeated, and knew that a nightblade like Ryuu held the monks and their training to be worthless, but he had never actually seen a monk defeated. A part of him was curious to see it happen.

The soldier seemed calmed a little by Akira's words, but still he paced. "My king, I always believed I would die on the battlefield, but this is too much to bear."

Akira shook his head and then realized Yuki couldn't see the motion in the darkness. "I do not think you have much to worry about. This is a small monastery, and I doubt they will take any action rashly. I expect that Captain Yung will resolve the situation soon."

Akira's demeanor finally calmed Yuki, and Akira laid his head down to get some rest. If nothing else, this was an opportunity for him to get some much-needed rest and relaxation. He only hoped that rescue would come soon.

Akira wasn't sure what time it was anymore. It felt as though the two of them had been imprisoned for days, but the rational part of Akira's mind knew that not even a full day had passed. But whether it was now night, morning or midafternoon, Akira had no clue.

He fared better than the young soldier who was with him. Perhaps it was his age, perhaps it was his experience, or perhaps it was his unshakable faith in the captain of his guards, but he did not pace endlessly the way Yuki did. After a while, he gave up trying to convince the young man to relax. They were certainly in danger, but there was little they could do about it, and it was no use worrying about what they could not change.

The cell was a very quiet place. The thick walls muffled the sounds coming from outside, so Akira was surprised when he heard a bell ringing. He couldn't tell how far away the bell was, but he suspected it must be close. He smiled to himself. A bell could mean a great many things, but he suspected it meant the captain of his honor guard was finally on his way.

After the bell rang, Akira placed his ear by the door of their cell. Although the sounds were muffled, he was able to make out the dim sounds of the monastery in confusion. He could hear shouts, some of which sounded like commands, and others that sounded like panic taking root. He frowned. There was a possibility he didn't want to consider, that perhaps the Azarians had already made it this far north. He pushed the thought aside. Either way there was nothing he could do except wait calmly.

After the initial turmoil died down, there was little that Akira could hear. He gave up his post at the door. Whether the alarm was due to the Azarians or to his own captain, Akira assumed they would come for him soon. When they did, he didn't want to get knocked on his tail when the door opened.

The waiting was the hardest part. It was one thing to wait when one knew they might have to wait for a long time, but to wait when something was happening right outside was its own unique form of torture.

It seemed like half the day had passed, although it had probably only been a few moments, when the door to the cell opened. Akira was blinded by the early morning light streaming through the door. Standing in the door was a tall silhouette that Akira immediately recognized as Captain Yung. Never before had he been so grateful to see the captain of his guards.

It was Yung who spoke first, "I think I've come to rescue you."

Akira noted the sarcasm in his captain's voice, but he was so glad to see him, he played along. "You think?"

Captain Yung nodded. "Yuki is definitely free to go. He listens to orders. I've spoken with the monks, and we have come to an understanding. I'm only bringing you out of here if you agree to listen more closely to my suggestions in the future."

As Akira's eyes adjusted to the light, he looked behind Yung. The courtyard was filled with his honor guard, and many of them had blades drawn. He could guess the kind of understanding they had come to. He smiled at his captain. "I cannot guarantee I will listen much better, but I will certainly make an effort."

His generally stoic captain laughed. "Well, that will have to be good enough for now. Come on, let's get you out of here."

When Akira stepped out of the cell, he took a long look around the courtyard. His men held their position well, forming a corridor of safety leading to the main gate of the monastery. It was clear Captain Yung had decided this was going to be a smash and grab operation. Akira was supposed to walk out and his guards would follow.

As tempting as the idea of simply leaving the monastery was, Akira paused. Even though he had had plenty of time to think while he was locked up, his thoughts had never wandered past what would happen after he was rescued. He looked around at all the people who had come to the monastery seeking shelter and had only found pain and servitude. Akira couldn't stand to see his people treated in such a manner, and now with his honor guard here, he felt compelled to take some action.

But he wasn't quite sure what he should do. He could order the deaths of the monks, but he was afraid of the repercussions of such an act. The monks were strong fighters, and although it looked as though they had peacefully allowed Akira's honor guard to enter, if their lives were at risk they might fight and kill many of his men. Not only was Akira disturbed at the prospect of losing some of his men, he couldn't stand the idea of any of his people killing each other when there was a much greater enemy camping a hundred leagues to the south. His short visit had also reminded him how revered the monks actually were. If he took direct, violent action against the monks, there was no telling how the people would react.

He could also order the monks bound. There was a slight chance of resistance, either from the monks or from the people seeking shelter in the monastery, but it was a much more attractive option than killing them. But then they would have six additional mouths to feed, and there was a good chance the monks would use their skills to act as a beacon to bring other Azarian hunters to their location. Akira shook his head. No matter how fast he thought, he couldn't think of what to do with the rebellious monks.

Captain Yung had been about to remount his horse when he saw his king stop and think. "Sir?"

Akira looked up at his captain. "I cannot leave my people here to be forced into servitude by the monks. They deserve better, especially in these trying times, but I do not know what to do."

Akira watched as Yung thought through the problem for himself. He could see the veteran trying different ideas and discarding them, just as he had moments earlier.

Akira decided to put the question to the people. If he did not know how to save them, perhaps they had some ideas. He raised his voice and spoke. "My people. All your eyes are open, and you can see what is happening here. The monks make you work night and day, with little rest and little food. When your rightful king comes within these walls, he is detained like a common criminal instead of king over all the land. But I do not know how best to help you. I do not know how best to ease your suffering."

He let a silence settle over the monastery. For a moment, it seemed as though the Abbot of the monastery was going to speak, but Akira stopped him with a stern gaze. The people would have to make their own decision, not influenced by the rhetoric of the monks.

The silence dragged on, and Akira wasn't sure any among the people would ever speak up. Had they become this afraid? Akira looked from eye to eye, trying to catch the gaze of just one who would stand and speak. But one by one, each person averted their gaze.

Finally, a woman stepped forward. Akira took her measure quickly. She appeared to be the type of woman who could be found all over his land. Her hands were calloused from work, her skin had seen many cycles of sun, and she held tight to her husband's hand as she spoke, her voice clear in the crisp air of the morning.

"If you wish to help, please leave."

Akira physically took a step back, surprised by the woman's request. It was the last thing he expected to hear.

The woman found a little bit more courage and continued. "You seem like a decent man, and all of us here believe you think you are doing what needs to be done. But our armies have failed us, and our young men aren't coming home. The monks say they can protect us, and we believe them."

Akira looked around the courtyard and saw many nods of agreement among the people. Rage, anger and grief welled up in his heart, and he was barely able to contain himself. How was it that his people would choose servitude to the monks over a chance for freedom and a new start? His mind struggled to comprehend, but he wasn't able to put a rational thought together. He was moments away from losing his composure when he heard the calm voice of his captain. "Akira, we should leave."

Akira looked in surprise at his captain, who never used his name, and saw the same pain and sadness that he felt reflected in his captain's eyes. It sapped all the anger from his bones. "Very well. I shall do as you ask."

He mounted the horse that had been provided for him, and took one last look around the monastery. "I know that right now you are scared. I know, because I am too. But know this. We're still fighting, and we will continue to fight until we have peace. Hide behind these walls today if you must, but one day you will be free. You have my word."

With a silent curse, Akira spurred his horse to motion, refusing to look back at the monastery as he left.

CHAPTER 23

At one time, Ryuu thought jumping in the river would be a great idea. Now he was far less sure. Moriko had taken their gear, but all the same, Ryuu was weighed down by his sword and clothes as the river took him downstream. He had never realized how many rocks and downed trees were in the river. In short, swimming and drifting downstream was not the relaxing experience he had hoped it would be.

Eventually the water slowed, and Ryuu saw he was approaching a village. With a few powerful strokes, Ryuu swam in the right direction, ensuring the current would push him up along the banks of the river.

It was mid-afternoon by the time Moriko found him. He had started a small fire outside the village, warming himself and drying his clothing and gear. They each updated the other on the status of their tasks. Ryuu wasn't surprised to hear Moriko had accomplished her task without difficulty.

Ryuu was hesitant to talk with Moriko about his own experience, partly because he was still figuring it out himself. He had fought with all the power he had, and it still hadn't been enough. But there was a nagging sensation in the back of his mind, a doubt that would not go away. Had he fought with everything he had? Was he as good as he was going to get, or was there still more for him to learn? He did not know the answers to the questions, but hoped he could find them before he met with Nameless again.

Once they were all caught up and Ryuu's clothes were decently dry, they continued on their journey. Moriko had brought the two horses they'd gotten from Akira, and they continued to follow the river at a decent pace. Ryuu knew they had shaken Nameless momentarily off their trail, but he wasn't sure how far Nameless would pursue them, and he wanted to put as much distance between them as possible.

That evening they came upon village that was small, but had a dock. There was a decent sized boat moored there, and Ryuu figured it was as good as any. They rode into the village to find the ship's captain.

The man was easy to find, and fortune smiled upon them. The man was leaving for Highgate in the morning, and was more than happy to take on two additional passengers in exchange for their horses. As Ryuu suspected, everyone who was able to head north was doing so, trying to avoid the Azarian advance for as long as possible. Everyone was waiting for a miracle, but none was forthcoming.

The next morning they were off, and the days that followed were some of the most relaxing in Ryuu's memory. He and Moriko didn't train, worried that word of their skills would spread. Instead, they spent most of the day lounging around the ship, watching the land pass behind them quickly. The wind was from the south and the currents were strong, and Ryuu was amazed by how quickly they sailed up the river. It was his first time on a ship on the river, and he delighted in the speed of the vessel. After two days of traveling, the captain picked up on Ryuu's interest, and the two of them formed a loose friendship. The captain would instruct Ryuu on the nuances of the ship, and on occasion even gave him a chance to steer the vessel. Ryuu was thrilled, and Moriko simply shook her head and laughed at him.

As they traveled north, it felt like a weight was lifted off their shoulders. Ryuu couldn't use his sense very well while on the boat, but even if Nameless was pursuing them, they had left him far behind. For a while, at least, they were safe, and for the first time in several moons, both of them felt completely at ease.

They continued to dance around the question of what they would do once they got to the island. Ryuu wanted to convince the nightblades to make a return to the Kingdom. Moriko wanted to make their home there. Sometimes it came up in conversation sideways, but every time it did, they changed the subject quickly. The time would come when they would have to make a decision, but both of them enjoyed a temporary truce, enjoying their days on the river as a simple and carefree time.

It only took them a few days to get all the way to Highgate. Ryuu couldn't believe how much faster water travel was. He would never ride a horse through the Northern Kingdom again if he could help it.

When they reached Highgate, Ryuu barely recognized the city. The last two times he had been through, it had been one of the most exciting places he had ever seen. Markets had flooded the city, and you could hardly turn a corner without running into a vendor willing to give you the best deal you'd ever heard of. The city had been alive, full of an energy all its own. As they journeyed up the river, Ryuu told Moriko about it, about all the people and the wonderful types of food they had.

But when their little ship pulled into dock at Highgate, it felt as though they had sailed into a ghost town. Last summer, Ryuu could hear the city from leagues away, the combined voices of thousands of people all living, breathing, and selling next to one another. Today Ryuu could hear the sound of old paper blowing across the streets.

There were people about, but far fewer than Ryuu had believed possible. The docks were nearly empty, where once they had been filled with ships of all shapes and sizes. The people who remained did not seem friendly, and indeed, as they disembarked from their ship, Ryuu felt as though they were being actively avoided.

Moriko stood next to Ryuu and looked up at him. "Quite the city you've got here."

Ryuu looked around in wonder. "I don't understand. The Azarians haven't made it this far north. How can the place be this deserted?"

Moriko didn't know the answer either, so together they walked deeper into the city, trying to understand what happened. Everywhere they walked the windows had shutters over them, and the silence was almost oppressive. After a little bit of searching they found an inn that was still open. When they walked in, they drew stares from the two patrons in the hall. They took their seats as the innkeeper came up to them.

"How can I be of service?"

"Food to start. But perhaps you could also tell us what has happened here. The last time I was here, the city was full of people," asked Ryuu.

The old man gave them a suspicious look, but Ryuu deflected it easily. "We have been on the road for a long time, and have not heard news in several moons."

The innkeeper shrugged, apparently unconcerned about any danger they might pose. "It's no secret. The land has been invaded to the south, and people are running scared. It is said the invaders are moving north quickly, and will be here within the moon. The monasteries have offered shelter, and most have left to live within those walls."

Ryuu nodded his appreciation at the information. The Azarians were expected to be here within a moon? It seemed hard to believe. The distance between Highgate and the old Southern Kingdom was large, and groups of people moved more slowly than individuals. The Azarians might be coming, but he didn't think they would arrive so soon.

All thoughts of the Azarians fled from their minds as the innkeeper brought them food. Perhaps it was because they had been on a boat for the past quarter moon, but the food was delicious. Both Moriko and Ryuu helped themselves to hearty portions, and when they were done, just for a moment, everything seemed right with the world.

After their meal the two nightblades found a small place that was out of the way. Moriko guarded the area while Ryuu sat down to extend his sense as far as it would go. They had been many days without accurate information, and there was much they would need to know to move forward. Ryuu closed his eyes and placed his hands on the ground, sending his sense far and wide across the land. He sensed the advance of the Azarian clans, moving forward at a pace that continued to surprise him. In the back of his mind, he thought that perhaps the innkeeper hadn't been as wrong as he had thought. It would be more than a moon, but at the rate the Azarians were advancing, it would not be much longer than that, not unless something stopped them or slowed them down.

Ryuu also found Nameless, surrounded by other Azarians. Ryuu didn't spend too much time focusing on what was happening, but simply confirmed the gigantic hunter wasn't on their trail. Satisfied they were safe for the moment, Ryuu focused his attention on the docks. He was worried that with Highgate as empty as it was there would be no ship to the island. His fears proved to be unfounded. He sensed two nightblades at the docks and made a mental note as to their location.

Ryuu was about to stop his roaming when one other thought occurred to him. He sent his sense to the south, searching for the nearest monastery. What he found was almost enough to knock him free of his meditative state. The monastery was there, and it had grown enormous. Ryuu couldn't even guess how many people surrounded the monastery. Whatever the monasteries were doing, they were attracting incredible numbers of people. To his sense, the monastery felt almost the way Highgate did last summer.

Shaking his head, he came out of the trance. They were safe for now, and they had a ship, but Ryuu did not like the way events were moving in the Kingdom.

After Ryuu finished his scan of the Kingdom, they decided it was best to get to the docks. With all the chaos the city seemed to be in, Ryuu wasn't sure how long the nightblades would stay in the area. He could see Tenchi withdrawing the boats back to the island until events had settled.

Their trip to the docks was short and uneventful. The few people who were on the streets skittered out of their way, and it seemed as though everyone in the city was afraid of one another. Ryuu couldn't help but continue to be surprised. He had never thought about how a large city would react to an invasion, but never in his wildest dreams had he thought it would be this way. He would have expected fortification and militias, but instead the citizenry had fled as fast as their feet could carry them.

They advanced onto the docks cautiously. Ryuu had left the island with Tenchi's blessing, but there was no telling whether or not he'd be allowed back. A lot had happened in the cycle since he had left, and he worried he might have used up all of Tenchi's goodwill.

The two nightblades on the docks stood in almost the exact same position as Ryuu remembered them. To the unobservant eye, they looked like hired help lounging about on the docks, but Ryuu could sense the two of them paying attention to everything that happened nearby. Their vigilance was commendable.

As was his style, Ryuu decided the straightforward approach was the easiest. He walked right up to the nightblades, grateful they didn't draw their blades on him. That, at least, was an encouraging sign. He looked from one nightblade to the other, but their faces might as well have been made from stone. He had no idea what was running through their minds.

"I've come to see Tenchi."

The nightblade on Ryuu's left spoke. "And what is your purpose?"

Ryuu looked from one to the other, wondering what was going on. He had hoped to be able to get to the island without any questions. A thought crossed his mind. What if Tenchi wasn't in charge anymore? Shika had been determined to seize power, and although Tenchi had been confident in his authority when Ryuu had left, a lot could have changed in that time. Tenchi was old, and he could have passed away while Ryuu was gone.

Ryuu decided to answer as safely as possible. "I need to know what the nightblades intend to do. The land is falling apart and needs our help. I need to find out if the nightblades will come and aid the Kingdom."

A grin broke out on the faces of the two men, and one flipped a coin to the other. Ryuu looked quizzically between the two of them.

The nightblade on the right explained. "We have a bit of a pool back home on when you would return, Ryuu. This is just the start of my winnings."

The two nightblades laughed, the sound carrying far over the empty docks. The tension fell from Ryuu's shoulders, and the three of them shared a bow.

"We couldn't help but mess with you a little bit. You're always so serious about everything."

Ryuu shook his head. That much was true.

"Come on and get in. You're pretty much the only reason we're here at all anymore. These docks aren't as welcoming as they once were, and when you're one of the only ships coming in and out of the harbor, you tend to draw a lot of attention to yourself."

Ryuu and Moriko got in the boat, and before the sun set they were on the water again. Ryuu tried to question the two nightblades about events on the island, but they were reticent to share too much.

"I apologize, but I'm not sure how much to say. Some is pretty obvious, but I imagine Tenchi will want to fill you in on most of the details. I can say this. The old man is still in charge, but the island is definitely reaching a point where a decision will have to be made. I've never seen the people so divided. Shika, as you can guess, still wants to return to the mainland in force, and Tenchi continues to hold us back. I'm not sure what effect you'll have on everybody, but I do know this. When you arrive, you're going to force the issue to a point."

Ryuu nodded. Nothing the man said was particularly surprising, but it was still worrying to him. He knew the decision was important, but he didn't want to see the blades torn apart by it. That would be the worst possible outcome. There were too few of them left, and they needed to be unified in purpose.

The journey was otherwise uneventful. The seas were as calm as they ever got, and although Ryuu still didn't like being out of sight of land, it could have been far worse. Moriko seemed to take to the sea naturally, and sometimes Ryuu was envious of how she simply seemed to adapt to everything that happened to her. It was one of her greatest strengths.

They pulled into the island two days later, and as Ryuu had expected, Tenchi was there to greet them.

Ryuu surprised even himself by sweeping Tenchi into a big embrace. He was sure Tenchi had sensed it coming, but it seemed to take the old man by surprise.

Afterward, Ryuu looked Tenchi over. He was old, but still seemed vigorous. Ryuu had never met anyone as old as Tenchi, and even at his advanced age, the man had beat him in a duel just a cycle ago. He wasn't sure Tenchi could repeat the feat again, but it had been impressive at the time.

Ryuu introduced Tenchi and Moriko formally. They each knew of each other, and the introductions were short.

Tenchi fixed Moriko with his gaze. "It is a pleasure to finally meet you, Moriko. I have heard much about you from Ryuu, and you must be strong indeed to hold the affections of such a warrior. However, I must ask one task of you before you come onto the island."

Ryuu groaned inwardly. He had forgotten about the trials. Moriko was going to be very upset soon.

Moriko said nothing as Tenchi continued. "I know that out in the world you have accomplished great things, but as I'm sure Ryuu has told you, this island can only be entered by blades. To become one, there is a set of three trials you must complete."

Tenchi pointed to the wall that Ryuu remembered having to climb the first time he had been on the island. His fingers ached at the memory. "You will find your first challenge there. The next two will be self-explanatory."

Moriko fixed Tenchi with a hard gaze. "No." Ryuu had to contain a laugh as Tenchi involuntarily stepped back a pace.

Tenchi looked confused, and Ryuu again had to stifle his mirth. The old man had no idea what he'd stepped into. He had expected the trials to be a minor formality, but Moriko wouldn't bend to anyone's rules.

Tenchi looked as though he was about to reply when Moriko continued, her voice soft but clear. "I know you mean well, but I won't go through your trials for the sake of propriety. I know Ryuu has spoken about me, and you know what I'm capable of. I couldn't care less whether or not you consider me a nightblade, but I am coming onto this island."

The leader of the island was torn between anger and astonishment. Ryuu wondered how he would respond. Moriko would never give in, though. He felt foolish for having forgotten about the trials.

Tenchi finally laughed, his mirth evident. "Well, I suppose you've forced my hand. There's no doubt of your abilities, and these are trying times for us all. Welcome, welcome."

With that, they were admitted to the island, and they began the long journey up to the top of the plateau. As they left, Tenchi pulled the two of them aside and whispered, "I'll give you a little bit of time, but your arrival has stirred up quite the hornet's nest of expectations. You won't have more than a few days to prepare, and then we will summon a council to determine the fate of both the nightblades and the Three Kingdoms."

CHAPTER 24

The hunting party was larger than any they had encountered before, and it made Akira's decision more challenging. Most of the parties they had encountered over the summer had been small, no more than ten to fifteen men on average. But either this group had joined with another, or their information had been wrong. Either way, there were almost thirty Azarians ahead of them, and Akira had to decide his course of action.

The summer had settled into a pattern. Akira and his men traveled through the Kingdom, bringing what aid they could whenever it was in their power to do so. They would attack small groups of Azarians, pressing their advantage whenever they outnumbered their enemy by a healthy margin. It wasn't a courageous strategy, but Akira figured there would be time for courage later. Now he needed men, and that meant attacking easy targets.

His plan was slowly starting to work. Word of his deeds was starting to spread throughout the land. It had taken several moons, but they had worked their way to the border of the old Western Kingdom. They could have made much better time, but Akira's focus was larger than the monasteries alone. He needed to protect everyone he could. So they wandered back and forth across the land, doing what they could for the people behind enemy lines. It also gave him extra time to decide what he would do about the monasteries.

The home of the Chief Abbot would be well defended. Although there were only several hundred monks scattered throughout the land, Akira assumed many of them had been called to their primary monastery. It would take more men than Akira had to break through the monastery with force.

His experiences at Hope haunted his memory. Even if he did try to break the monastic system by force, he wasn't sure the people of his land wouldn't turn on him. He had underestimated the hold the monasteries had on the people. There was no compelling reason for the monasteries to cooperate with him, either. In short, he was out of ideas.

So Akira and his honor guard continued along, slowly, towards the monastery. They were gathering power among the people. When they came to villages, more often than not word of their arrival had already spread, and he and his men were welcomed as conquering heroes. Akira was grateful for the support, but he felt as though he was selling them a lie. His men might make a difference for a little while, but in the grand scheme of events happening in the Kingdom, they were but a thorn in the side of the Azarians.

The actions they took did help, even if it was only for a little while. It wasn't much, but it was all he could do, and for now that was enough for him.

He stopped his mind from wandering and focused on the problem in front of him. His men had been told by a nearby village there was a small hunting party nearby, but instead they had found either a large hunting party or small clan. Akira's scouts reported at least thirty men. It was one of the largest collections of Azarians they had encountered yet.

Akira's men vastly outnumbered them. The entire summer they had only lost six men, but taking on a group of Azarians this large almost guaranteed Akira would sentence some of his honor guard to death. It was a risk he wasn't sure he was willing to take. Too many had died for too little already.

Akira held conference with Yung.

"I think we should attack them."

Akira was surprised. "I thought you would be more cautious."

"No. There's no doubt it's more dangerous than anything we've done yet. I know you are thinking about the men, but I am too."

Akira's eyes rose up with a question written across them. "What do you mean?"

"We've been successful all summer. We've hurt the Azarians in many small ways, but the men want to hurt the Azarians in bigger ways. They are content now, but I don't know how much longer that will last. They need something more they can be proud of. Maybe this isn't it, but if nothing else, they will learn the cost of taking a bigger risk."

"You're willing to let men die to teach others a lesson?"

"No, but I'm afraid we'll lose more if we don't do something soon. They're chomping at the bit. Our success has gone to their heads. They think they're capable of more than they are. This attack is dangerous, but we know that even if we make a mistake, this won't stop us."

Akira considered the advice of his captain. It wasn't how he felt, but he had come to rely on Yung. The man was born to serve in the army, and it showed in everything he did. He was reliable, level-headed and never impulsive. He was a good man to have by your side.

"Very well. Draw up the plans. We'll attack at dawn."

The sun was just beginning to rise when Akira and his men launched their attack. It began with a well-coordinated flight of arrows from the east, striking throughout the Azarian camp. Some were normal arrows, aimed at those in the hunting party who were up and moving. Others were flaming arrows, aimed at the tents that comprised the Azarian shelters. Some Azarians died in their sleep, and Akira felt no guilt over it.

Even though the Azarian party didn't have any hunters in it, Akira had learned long ago not to fight the Azarians in the evening. Moriko had mentioned in her report that nighttime raids were common among the Azarians, and Akira and his men had learned that lesson the hard way on one of their first missions. Their enemies from the south were experts in fighting by moonlight, and their guards were always at their most alert when the sun was down. Experience had taught Akira and Yung it was much better to strike by the first light of the sun, when the Azarians were usually less watchful.

The arrows had the desired effect on the hunting party. They felled several warriors and lit some of the tents on fire. More importantly, it sowed confusion among the Azarians. Akira could well understand. It would be disorienting, to say the least, to wake up and have arrows pouring down around you.

But he had to give the Azarians the credit they were due. Despite the initial shock, it only took them a matter of moments to organize themselves. They separated to the north and to the south, attempting to circle around the archers who were attacking their position.

If there was one aspect of the Azarians Akira had learned in his summer campaign, it was that most of them didn't think in terms of military strategy. Nameless did, which is how the Azarians had been able to beat his men at the Three Sisters, but most of your day-to-day Azarians did not. They thought like hunters, trying to circle around their prey and sneak up behind it. One of their fatal flaws was that they didn't stop to think how they were hunting prey that fought back.

Akira and Yung had predicted the Azarian response perfectly, and men were hidden along two shallow draws to the north and south of the Azarian camp. When the Azarians split up they followed the draws and walked right into the ambush.

Akira was grateful for his success. The wind had been from the west the entire evening, and they had spent an inordinate amount of time worrying about their scent. Several reports had already come to them about the abilities of many of the Azarians. It was said that some of them could smell their prey from hundreds of paces away. Akira didn't want to lend the rumor any credence, but he couldn't be sure, and it was better to be safe than surprised.

At Yung's signal, Akira's men launched their second ambush in the draws. His honor guard rose to their feet and charged the Azarians, surrounding them in moments. The Azarians were heavily outnumbered, but they didn't run. That was another thing Azarians had in common. They never ran. The battle was fierce but short-lived. It was only a matter of moments before they broke through the Azarian hunting party.

Akira watched the battle with a detached eye. He listened to the battle cries of the Azarians and watched as their energy and enthusiasm clashed against the cold discipline and training of his men. The Azarians were excellent fighters, and Akira saw at least one of his men fall to a cut, but the Azarians didn't have a chance.

He watched and was taken by a deep sadness. Everything was meaningless. They would win here today, even though it cost them valuable men. Men who could have had full lives. They would buy the villagers some safety for a time, but the Azarians would return. They always did. Akira shook his head. He couldn't allow himself to think like that. He had to keep thinking about moving forward.

He turned his horse around and rode back to camp. Akira had wanted to take part in the battles, but Yung had flatly denied his king's request. There was no need for him to participate, and they risked far, far more than they gained. Akira understood the argument his captain was making, but it didn't mean he liked it. He wanted to take part in the fight, to be alongside his men when they risked their lives.

Akira rode back to camp. He would start their meal, doing what he could to aid the fight. They would rest nearby for one evening, but they would be on the move again tomorrow. They hoped to reach the next village soon to rest there and trade for supplies.

Yung and the men rode in not far behind him. As Akira examined their faces he saw a mixture of sorrow and pride. They had won the battle, but they had lost friends.

Yung stopped next to Akira. "We lost three."

There was nothing else that needed to be said. Akira bowed slightly to Yung, who rode in silence towards his tent. If he took a step back, three soldiers weren't a tremendous loss, especially considering they had killed over thirty Azarians. But his men were the best warriors in the Kingdom, and the loss of any one of them was hard to swallow. He still had most of his men, but it wasn't enough. Not against the flood of Azarians coming into the Kingdom. He would miss his men. He reminded himself to ask Yung to tell him who had fallen in the battle.

As his men rested together the next night, Akira reflected on the events that were starting to change the shape of the Kingdom. Everything he had known, everything he had grown up believing, was changing under the Azarian threat.

The first fact, more obvious than any other, was that his people were suffering. Everywhere they went, Akira and his men heard stories of tragedy and pain, stories of families being forced from their homes, forced to serve the foreign invaders. Some places seemed better than others, but overall the story was the same. It was a bad time to live in the Kingdom. There was no guarantee of safety, and absolutely no guarantee of justice.

Moriko had warned them, and her predictions were becoming reality every day. There was a story of one clan that wandered the Kingdom seeking strong warriors. When no one stood up to them, they would slaughter the entire village. Another clan had enslaved a village. New Haven had become a center of misery. Many had fled there when the rumors had first spread, and the city had rapidly grown overcrowded. Now two clans sat outside of New Haven, blocking any entrance or exit. There were rumors the starving people locked in the city had resorted to cannibalism. Meanwhile, the clans sat happily outside, enjoying a never-ending feast.

But along with the suffering, there was hope. It was a small pinprick of light in a blanket of darkness, but it was there. News of Akira and his deeds was starting to spread throughout the Kingdom, and more and more often he and his men were receiving a hero's welcome. It wasn't much, but knowing that his people knew he was out there fighting for them made the struggle worth it.

The village they were in had so far been unharmed by the advance of the Azarians. They were near the far northern borders of Akira's old kingdom, and Akira wondered whether they had escaped notice because they were small or because of their location. Ultimately, Akira didn't care why they had been spared, he was simply grateful the Azarian menace hadn't touched all his people yet.

The village welcomed them with open arms. They slaughtered one of their cows when they heard of Akira's arrival, a valuable gift for his men. That night the beast was roasted, and the storehouses of the village were opened to them. As tempting as it was to feast, Akira's men took little. They knew resources were scarce, and although they appreciated the support of the people, every bite of food they took was one the village would not have available in their hard times.

Akira spent most of the evening listening to stories being told around the fire. He and his men had become almost as popular as legendary outlaws, a role his men seemed to relish. The stories they told around the campfire were full of embellishment, and if Akira hadn't been with them during their engagements, he would've thought that each of them had slaughtered hundreds of Azarians. But he did not stop his men. They enjoyed being heroes, and their stories built their little unit into a legend, which was what Akira was really hoping for. As a man, he could only do so much, but as a legend, there was nothing they couldn't accomplish.

So Akira let his men tell their stories, even joining in on occasion.

As the evening wore on, there was a short lull in the conversation, as though the conversation hit a wall. It was the wall that signified the villagers were done hearing about what Akira and his men had accomplished, and became interested in understanding what they were going to accomplish next. Akira had gotten used to that particular silence, had come to look forward to it. In that silence he started to spread a new message.

"Everyone, thank you for your hospitality. Our life on the road is one of struggle, but every time we come to a village we are greeted with a warmth that reminds us why we do this. We'll leave in the morning, for it is unsafe for us to spend too much time in any one place. What I would leave you with is this: Our times are changing. It is a painful change, one that none of us wishes to live through. But it is happening all the same, and we must be ready."

"I come to you today with a message, a message which may be difficult to hear, but one that needs to be heard nonetheless. Do not give up hope. There is still more strength in the land than you would believe. I'm going to tell you a secret, a secret that has only been known to the lords for hundreds of cycles. It is about the nightblades."

Akira waited a few moments. He had given the speech a dozen times, refining it each time in the telling. At the first mention of the nightblades, he saw the uncertainty in the eyes of all the villagers. He understood. He knew how they had grown up in a world where nightblades represented everything that was evil, and changing that perception would not be easy. But he had succeeded before, and he would again. He had to.

"The nightblades still exist, and they are still in the Kingdom. While we hunted them, they remained hidden. Yes, they were responsible for the shattering of our Kingdom over a thousand cycles ago, but they have learned from the error of their ways, and now exist to serve our people once again. I know this is hard to believe, but it has been true for a very long time. In this, our time of greatest need, the nightblades will return to save us."

Akira gave everyone a moment to allow the message to sink in. There was always a moment of silence, followed by a flurry of questions. He was ready. If the nightblades were going to come back, the land needed to be ready for them, and that was his mission.

Now he only hoped he wasn't lying to his people.

CHAPTER 25

Moriko couldn't believe how large the island was. She had heard stories from Ryuu, but it was another thing altogether to see the island in person. It seemed impossible that an island so large would remain undiscovered. However, as their small ship neared the island, she saw firsthand just how impregnable it was. The cliffs were impossibly high to scale. As they sailed into the hidden bay, Moriko knew there was no way anyone would find the island and get on it on their own. If they were lucky enough to do so, Moriko had little doubt the nightblades would make sure they never left.

She had been angered by Tenchi's attempt to get her to take the nightblade trials. She wouldn't be a part of any system, no matter how well intentioned it might be.

Her anger had passed quickly though. The old man meant well, and did not know how much Moriko detested the systems the nightblades had created. The novelty of the island was amazing to her. Ryuu had been here before, and thought nothing of it, but for Moriko, it was a wonderful experience. There were other nightblades. Everyone knew who and what they were. And they were safe. The island was everything Moriko had dreamed of for the past few moons, and it didn't disappoint. It was impossible for her to hang on to her anger.

They were accompanied by a small party as they hiked the long tunnel which led to the top of the island. On their way to the top, Ryuu and Tenchi exchanged news. Moriko tuned out as Ryuu told his half of the story. She had been there and knew everything Ryuu was going to say. His story held no interest for her. But her ears perked up when Tenchi started to talk about events on the island.

"It has been a tumultuous time since you left, Ryuu," the old man said.

Ryuu was instantly alert. "What happened?"

Tenchi gave Ryuu a look that Moriko couldn't decipher.

"I'm sure you are aware your first arrival here threw this island into an uproar. Now you force the question of our return. We didn't reach a decision while you were with us before, although the conversation has been continuing ever since, and at times it has become rather heated."

Ryuu nodded. There seemed to be something more that Tenchi was saying that Moriko wasn't picking up on, but Ryuu was. "Has she done anything she's going to regret later?"

Moriko realized the two of them were speaking of Shika, the leader of Tenchi's opposition on the island.

"Not yet, but I fear your second arrival will put us to the test. The question must be answered, once and for all."

This time, Tenchi fixed Ryuu with a stare that was unambiguous. "But that is why you returned, isn't it?"

Ryuu nodded. "The need for the nightblades has never been greater. And never before has there been a time where our return could have the impact it would now. With the Three Kingdoms reunited, it only seems right the nightblades return to protect the land as they once did."

Tenchi stroked his long beard. "Perhaps it is as you say. I still have many fears and concerns, but this decision is bigger than me. This is a decision for all of us to make."

Ryuu nodded again. "I agree."

With that, the discussion about the future of the nightblades was at an end. There was nothing else for the two of them to discuss, but both men seemed content to walk together in silence. Moriko was fascinated by how the two of them could disagree on such an important topic and still be friends.

She didn't have much time to wonder about that as they neared the top entrance to the island. The transition to daylight was sudden, as heavy curtains had been placed over the mouth of the tunnel. Moriko blinked away the tears and was astounded by what she saw.

Ryuu had told her what to expect, of course, but it was still different seeing it in person. There were small homes as far as the eye could see, dropping off suddenly into the infinite blue expanse of the sea. There were so many of them! Moriko's eyes drifted from the houses to the people, and she could see evidence of the daily training and work which defined life on the island. It was the training that drew her eye more than anything else. She watched the smooth cuts, the expert blocks, and she knew with a certainty she was someplace she not been since she was very young. She was home.

Moriko studied her opponent. He was taller and stronger than her, but that wasn't unusual. She had never been a tall woman, and the men on the island seemed to delight in holding that fact over her head. It was probably because none of them had found a way to beat her in combat yet.

The man in front of her held his blade with an easy grace. He had seen several more cycles than Moriko, but she wasn't worried. At first, they had trained her against younger opponents, young men and women who were still reaching adulthood. The young men had been full of energy, and as she started to defeat them, they became more and more focused; but day after day they still fell beneath her wooden blade. She started giving private lessons to some of the younger women, showing them how to turn an opponent's strength to their own advantage.

It hadn't been long before she was matched against older opponents, men and women with more skill with the sword. Moriko had been excited to see what they were capable of, but again, every opponent she faced fell with barely a struggle. She had known she was strong, but it was only on an island filled with other nightblades that she began to realize just how strong she was.

Her reverie was interrupted when the nightblade she was fighting moved forward. His approach was cautious. He had seen her fight several times, and was under no illusions as to her ability. If he was going to fall, it wouldn't be through overconfidence or a silly mistake.

Moriko was completely inside herself, and knew there was no way this nightblade would be able to sense her intent. She felt his strike coming far in advance, and at the last possible moment, took a small step back to allow the wooden blade to pass harmlessly in front of her.

The nightblade was surprised, but his cut had been a cautious one. He wasn't going to over-commit and leave himself wide open.

He cut again, and again Moriko took a slight step back at the very last moment.

The pattern continued for two more passes, Moriko allowing his cuts to slice through empty air. Despite his training, she could see he was starting to get frustrated. It would only be a matter of time before he made the mistake that would end this game.

He struck again, this time a little harder than he had before, a little faster, hoping to catch her unawares. Moriko dodged the cuts, and sensed him about to step forward, putting his full weight into another powerful strike.

It was exactly what she'd been waiting for. She abruptly reversed course, moving suddenly towards him instead of away from him. He was already committed to his attack, and Moriko saw that he knew he had lost already. She batted aside his blade before he could generate enough force to be a danger to her, and in one simple move, she was inside his guard. She could have gone easy on him, but that wasn't in her nature. Moriko trained to kill, and if she ever lost that, there was no telling how long she would last in the outside world.

Moriko cut with all her strength, striking the nightblade with a strength and violence he wasn't expecting. The air went out of his lungs, and Moriko watched with pleasure as he collapsed, struggling to catch his breath. She looked around for any other challengers.

There were none, and Moriko wasn't surprised. They all wanted to be stronger than her, but none of them had what it took, and most of them knew it. There were some who would try their luck, but those who did always felt her blade.

Ryuu and Tenchi were there, as they often were, watching her fight. She had trained against Ryuu, and was fairly certain he was the only one on the island who had any chance of striking her. When they dueled, it was anybody's guess who would win. Ryuu was faster and stronger, but Moriko's ability to hide from the sense and to snap gave her a fighting chance as well. Ryuu was always capable of a good fight.

Moriko went to join Tenchi and Ryuu. Tenchi, as he always did, seemed to know what was in her mind without her having to say a word.

"Moriko, I do not know if we have anyone on this island who is a match for you. Perhaps myself, on a good day, but I'm getting older, while you are getting stronger. Even I don't know if I can teach you anything else."

Moriko shook her head. "I find it hard to believe there isn't anyone here who can challenge us. There's so many of you. It seems unlikely that Ryuu and I would have such an advantage."

Tenchi shook his head. "I, on the other hand, don't find it surprising at all. You need to remember, Moriko, that you and Ryuu grew up in a hostile environment. You have always known that your skills were the only thing keeping you alive in the land you grew up in. You were in constant danger, and your life was always on the line. It's not to say that you aren't gifted, for both of you certainly are, but that gift has been tempered in the fires of life and death. You fight because your life depends on it. Here they train because it's what is expected of them. Your experiences are something the nightblades here don't understand. It is no surprise to me you have become as powerful and as strong as you have. If you hadn't, you'd be dead."

Moriko thought about what Tenchi said. She'd never thought of it in that way, but his idea seemed right to her. Whenever she dueled any of the nightblades on the island, there was always a hesitation, a particular softness in their strikes. Neither she nor Ryuu had such a softness. They trained and fought to kill, and it was a very different experience than training and fighting simply to get stronger.

It made Moriko wonder if Ryuu's goal of getting the nightblades to return was worth pursuing. The hunters were like her and Ryuu. Their skills were forged on the battlefield of life, and all their softness had been burned away under the merciless Azarian sun. All that was left was strength, strength Moriko worried the nightblades on the island wouldn't be able to match.

She looked up at Ryuu, and from the look on his face, she figured he was thinking something very similar. The nightblades were strong, but she didn't know if they were strong enough.

Moriko and Ryuu sat across from each other in the small home Ryuu had been given when he first came to the island. They were eating the evening meal, and Ryuu brought up the topic she had hoped never to discuss. They had already been on the island a half moon, and Moriko knew every day was a hard one for Ryuu. He had wanted to go to the island and bring the nightblades back to the Kingdom the next day. But Tenchi wouldn't allow such haste. He argued that the nightblades faced the most important decision of the past thousand cycles of their history. It would be foolish to rush to an emotional decision.

Moriko had met Shika and found that she liked the leader of Tenchi's opposition. She was strong and outspoken, two characteristics Moriko valued. Shika was a frequent visitor as Moriko and Ryuu made plans to return the nightblades to the Kingdom. Ryuu was using the time given by Tenchi as an opportunity to set up meetings with small groups of blades on the island, holding intense discussions as to the future of their people.

Moriko had attended one of the meetings and found it boring. The arguments were predictable and obvious. Ryuu and Shika didn't coerce people. They simply asked that everyone think carefully on the arguments both for and against returning to the Kingdom. Moriko decided she had better things to do, and she spent her days training, escaping the political nonsense Ryuu engaged in.

They hadn't settled the question between themselves yet, and it was a question Ryuu was ready to force.

It was an unfair question for him to ask. She knew he wanted to bring the nightblades back, and he knew she never wanted to leave the island. But they both wanted to stay together, and that was where their problem lay.

"What do you hope to accomplish with the nightblades? Even if you get them to return, what will you do?" Moriko asked.

Ryuu thought for a moment before answering. "I want the nightblades to figure out a way to attack the hunters. If we can break the hunters, we can break this invasion."

Moriko shook her head gently. "The Azarians are more than just the hunters. Everyone who rides with them is a strong and capable warrior, and I don't think just killing the hunters will be enough. Also," she hesitated, "I don't know if the nightblades are strong enough to overcome the hunters."

Ryuu almost objected, but Moriko stopped him.

"Come on, Ryuu. You have fought both hunters and nightblades. Tell me you think the nightblades are stronger."

Ryuu looked like he was about to, but stopped. Perhaps he wasn't willing to admit it, but he had to see the truth of Moriko's statement.

Moriko pressed her advantage. "So if you aren't sure you can win, why are you even trying?" She thought about her next statement before continuing, deciding it needed to be said. "What if all you are doing is sending all these nightblades to their death?"

A tense silence hung over the room as Ryuu considered Moriko's questions. When he spoke, he spoke slowly, wanting to make sure every word was exactly what he meant. "I have thought about that, too. I think about it every day. The fact is, I don't know if the nightblades coming back is the right thing to do. However, it is the only thing I can do. I don't have any other way to help."

"But why? Why do you feel the need to protect people who wouldn't lift a finger to help you?"

Ryuu spoke softly. "Because all life is worth fighting for. It's not about trying to save only those people that I care for, or those who care for me. It's about trying to save everybody, as many people as I can."

"You can't possibly save everybody. You know that."

"I know. But to me, it is like pursuing perfection in swordsmanship. There is no way to be perfect. There will always be some little thing that you can do better. But that doesn't mean I don't try every time I train."

Moriko didn't agree, but she understood what Ryuu was trying to say.

Ryuu continued. "You're absolutely right. I don't know what's going to happen if I succeed, but I have to try something. I couldn't live with myself if I didn't."

Moriko hated Ryuu then. He had always been willing to sacrifice himself to save others. Why couldn't he just think about himself for once? Ryuu's next question froze her mind solid.

"The only question I have is this: What will you do?"

Moriko wished desperately this moment had never come, that she would never have to answer this very question. She knew what she wanted. She wanted to stay on this island, to hide from the world and live out her days in peace.

Suddenly, her time back in the monastery returned to her. Again she was naked and tied to the floor, and Ryuu came into the scene. That evening, he had been willing to sacrifice himself to save her. Every time she drew breath, it was because of the type of man he was. For the first time in a long time, she felt guilty about her selfishness. She couldn't ask him to change, not now when everything was at stake.

Her next words surprised her. "Will you come back to the island, if you can?"

Ryuu nodded. "If I can."

With that, Moriko's mind was made up.

"Then I will come with you."

Ryuu's face lit up. It seemed like he was a new man, and Moriko realized how much her answer meant to him.

She gave Ryuu a small smile. "Somebody has to keep you alive, so you can come back. And knowing you, I'm the only one strong enough to bring you back safely from whatever mess you get yourself into."

Ryuu laughed as she spoke, yet she couldn't help but feel her words were far too accurate.

CHAPTER 26

If there was one thing Nameless was certain about, it was that the land the People had moved into was a rich land. Losing the old man had been hard, and Nameless hadn't forgiven himself yet, but now he was able to wander the land freely, hunting and wandering as in the days of his youth.

Everywhere he went, Nameless was amazed by the diversity and quantity of the wilderness he explored. Almost all his previous life had been spent wandering the plains of Azaria, and while his homeland held an austere beauty, it paled in comparison to even the most desolate sights of the Three Kingdoms.

For almost a full moon Nameless lost himself in the beauty and wonder of their new land. He wandered back and forth, and although he sometimes encountered a clan, he always avoided them. He told himself he wasn't shirking his responsibilities, that he was scouting out the land to ensure it was right for his people. But it was a thin lie, and he knew it. He wanted to be alone, to focus only on his own survival. It was pure living.

From time to time he would be visited by some of the demon-kind, and they reported on the progress of the invasion. For the most part, it had gone as expected. The People, although vastly outnumbered by the citizens of the Kingdom, were much stronger warriors; with the aid of the demon-kind, the People had made tremendous progress into the land. But despite this, there were problems beginning to bud, challenges to be solved immediately. The alliance with the monasteries, which had given Nameless much of the information they had used to plan their invasion, was on unstable ground. From the reports Nameless heard, it sounded as though the monasteries were using the invasion as an excuse to assert their authority. Nameless had always expected this, but he hadn't expected that they would try to do so by attacking his clans. The reports were scattered at best, but Nameless worried they were indicative of a growing problem. The monasteries would need to be dealt with.

And their king, if he could even be called such, was still a problem. He was wandering the land, much like Nameless. But instead of exploring, he was harassing and killing the People. For a single man, he was causing an impressive problem. Had Nameless felt like exerting the authority, he would have sent two pairs of demon-kind hunting him, but none of the clans could look beyond their own survival.

His People were also having trouble settling in the mountainous regions which had once been known as the Northern Kingdom. Apparently the military there was still powerful, and their riders had superior skills in the mountains. It was unfortunate to hear, but Nameless couldn't bring himself to care too much. Even if they weren't able to make progress into the Northern Kingdom, they would still have over two-thirds of the land, which was more than enough space for them to grow and become stronger. In time his warriors would learn how to ride in the mountains, and they would decimate the armies of the Northern Kingdom.

At times, the demon-kind inquired as to what his intent was. His answer was always the same. He had done his duty as he saw fit. The People did not need a leader anymore. The only reason he had seized power was because of the necessity he had felt. Now that his people were across, his duty was done. He planned only to serve individual clans as best he could, much as he had before he came to power. At times, the demon-kind were disappointed in his answer, but none dared to question his strength, and Nameless continued his wanderings.

After a full moon of exploring their new land, Nameless decided it was time to rejoin a clan. He would wander until he found one, but once a clan accepted his service, he'd be happy to join them as their demon-kind.

Once his decision was made, it only took Nameless a matter of days to find a wandering clan. Here, in the land that used to be known as the Southern Kingdom, the clans were already widespread. They were still moving north through the Western Kingdom.

When he came upon the clan, the first thing he noticed was that it wasn't very large. There were probably no more than three or four dozen members. He wondered if they had always been so small, or if it was the move into this new land that had killed so many of them. There were none of his kind with them, which surprised him. There should have been enough demon-kind for one pair to go with every clan. He wondered if a pair had fallen to violence, or if something else had happened to cause them to leave.

Nameless decided that in the tradition of his people, he would come bearing a gift. Instead of going directly to the clan, he went on a hunt. Here, hunting had almost become a trivial task, and before half the day had passed, the carcass of a deer hung over his shoulders.

By the time he entered the camp dusk was beginning to fall. There was a short cry from one of the women as he was first spotted, but Nameless made no move to react. The old man had said he was not loved by all the clans, and that was something he must live with. Perhaps someday they would see what he had done for them.

Nameless stopped about two dozen paces away from the camp. If they did not want him, so be it. It was their decision to make.

A man separated from the rest of the clan, and Nameless could see from the way he walked that he was the leader. His balance indicated he was a strong warrior, and he exuded confidence. He stopped two paces away from Nameless. Nameless made no move, aggressive or otherwise. For all the clan leader's strength and confidence, Nameless towered over him, and could have crushed him without a thought.

"Why are you here?"

It was a ritual greeting, one asked to any demon-kind when they first approached a new clan. Nameless responded with the ritual words, "I come to serve."

Nameless fought the urge to say anything else. Words were cheap, and intent could only be discerned through action. The leader of the clan looked upon the deer carcass and upon Nameless, and in a moment his decision was made.

"You are welcome at our fire. We would welcome your service."

Nameless nodded and followed the clan leader forward, surprised at how relieved he felt. With some help from the young men, Nameless quickly skinned and prepared the deer for the fire, and prepared to feast with his new clan.

For the next few days, Nameless could almost believe everything was right with the world. He acted as a scout and hunter for the clan. During the days he ranged far and wide, and at night he returned to the campfire to be among the People, those who had survived the harsh transition from the lands of Azaria to the lands of the Three Kingdoms.

In bits and pieces, Nameless learned the story of the clan he traveled with. They had always been a smaller clan, for as long as their stories went back. They were an offshoot of an older clan, but had never numbered more than two hundred members. It had not been the battle at the Three Sisters that had reduced their numbers, but Azaria itself. Many cycles had passed since the founding of the clan, and every cycle was a greater struggle than the last. Food had become scarce, and as the clan dwindled, fewer and fewer others were willing to trade women, causing the clan to diminish even more quickly.

Prior to the battle of the Three Sisters, the clan had been fervent supporters of Nameless. They had experienced the danger he had foreseen and knew he spoke the truth.

The Battle of the Three Sisters had been brutal to their clan. They had already been reduced to less than fifty, and the battle claimed the lives of several more. When the demon-kind had come to guide them on their journey through the new land, they had politely declined help. It was not that they held anything against the demon-kind, but the clan had decided that if they were going to survive and grow in this new land, they needed to do so on their own. It was a belief Nameless agreed with. Their story touched him, and although they made it clear he would not travel with them permanently, he was welcome to join them on the journey for a little while. He couldn't have found a better clan to serve.

Nameless was grateful for his time with them. The clan might be small, but each of them was hard and strong. If all the clans were made of warriors like these, there was nothing they couldn't accomplish.

He traveled with the clan for almost another full moon before trouble struck.

The clan had been traveling west, hoping to find the bridge that spanned the old Southern Kingdom and the Western Kingdom. Their final goal was the plains of the Western Kingdom, and they were eager to be on their way. But as they approached the bridge, Nameless realized something was not right. The Kingdom, to his gift, was a loud and bright land. It was always full of life and energy, and the land practically sang to him. But today the land was quiet, as though a hush had fallen over every living thing. The hairs on the back of his neck stood up, but he could sense no danger. Nameless didn't warn the clan because he was not confident of what he felt, or more accurately, what he didn't feel. He knew something was wrong, but unless there was something solid he could bring to the clan, he would remain silent.

When the attack happened, it happened with a suddenness and ferocity even Nameless didn't expect. He felt them at the edges of his awareness, but they approached quickly. Men charged over the hill, and it took Nameless only a moment to realize his clan was being attacked by monks.

Quickly, he cleared his head of disbelief. It was hard to imagine monks attacking, but here they were. There wasn't any time for thought, only action. Nameless drew his sword and leapt into the battle, summoning all the energy he could.

His gift told him there were almost a dozen monks altogether. In the moment Nameless had to think, he realized that no matter how fast he acted, he wouldn't be able to kill all the monks before they reached the clan.

Then the battle was upon them and there was no more time for thought. Nameless rushed into the melee, his sword singing in the air. Three monks fell before they even had a chance to react to him.

Four monks turned to face him while another four ran towards the clan.

The four who remained surrounded Nameless, but he had no fear. He knew the monks of this land were stronger than the average person, but they would not be able to touch him.

They attacked as one, their blades moving to strike in well-rehearsed unison. But Nameless wouldn't give them that chance. He moved in towards one of them, forcing them all to react. The monks were good, but they had no idea what they had brought down on themselves. Nameless was faster and stronger, and in only a handful of passes, all the monks had fallen to his blade.

He didn't take any time to gloat. The other four monks were wreaking havoc within the clan. The clan had strong fighters, but they had been taken by surprise, and the monks were strong themselves.

By the time Nameless reached the battle, several clan members had already fallen, but so had one of the monks. When Nameless entered the fight, everything changed. Two of the last three monks fell in quick succession, a look of confusion plastered up on their faces. Nameless severed the spine of the third, causing him to collapse in a useless heap on the ground.

Nameless lifted the monk's head from the dirt. "Who sent you?"

The monk tried to summon up the energy to spit, but Nameless felt it coming and slammed the monk's head into the ground. He pulled at the monk's hair and brought him face to face. He waited for his answer.

"You'll never have our land."

Nameless pushed the monk's face into the dirt, holding him there until he almost suffocated. The monks were beyond foolish. They had helped Nameless and the People enter, and now they thought they were stronger? His rage could barely be controlled. He stood and let the clan know they could treat the monk as they wished. His death was certain to be slow.

A silence descended upon the party as the clan started to take care of their dead. Every death was keenly felt in the small clan.

Nameless watched them work with anger rising in his belly. It was one thing for the people of the Kingdom to resist the advance of his people, but the monks had been allies, promising aid and assistance once his people came into the land. Now they had betrayed him, and betrayal he would not stand.

He thought about offering to help the clan with the care of their dead, but he knew it was a task they would want to take care of on their own. He respected this clan. Respected their strength. They deserved better. It was time to show those monks they weren't in charge of this land. Nameless walked over to the man who had first greeted him, the man who led this clan.

"Forgive me, but I must go. I must have vengeance for this act."

The leader of the clan nodded, and Nameless could see the fire of vengeance burned in his eyes as well. As he left, he could hear the final words of the clan leader echoing in his mind. "Make them pay."

CHAPTER 27

Akira and his men rode in silence. Not because they were hunted, or even because they were hunting. It was sorrow, pure and simple.

He understood how his men felt. He battled the same emotions, and when he was honest with himself he had to admit he was losing the fight. All summer long he and his men had fought valiantly, but the situation seemed worse than ever.

The village they passed two days ago was the third in a row devastated by the Azarians. It was getting worse. In the spring, it had seemed like there needed to be some pretense for the Azarians to attack. Now they simply walked into villages and started the slaughter.

Despite a life on the battlefield, Akira was still surprised by how much blood a human could lose. In the last village, dried blood covered every surface that wasn't burned down. As they always did, the Azarians left one alive to spread the tale. In this case, it did them no good. Akira didn't think the young man would ever speak again.

In the village before the last, the sights had been even more gruesome. There was a grove of trees outside the village, and every villager but one had been hung from the trees. Not by their neck, which would have been a relative mercy, but by their arms. Their skin and organs had been removed. There had been no survivors. The body of one young woman wasn't hanging with the others, and Akira suspected she had ended her own life rather than live with what she had seen.

That time, Akira's men were able to track the clan, and they had attacked. Perhaps it hadn't been wise, but it had been right and necessary. They caught the hunters out scouting, before they could raise the alarm for the clan. It had taken almost all his men to encircle the two hunters with spears, but eventually they fell. They attacked the rest of the clan in the middle of the day. The clan was taken by surprise, their confidence in their hunters misplaced.

Revenge had been exacted, but the price was steep. Between killing the hunters and attacking a large clan, Akira was down to just over seventy men. They were being whittled away, slowly but surely.

Even though they found revenge, their hearts were still empty. Tensions were rising between the Azarians and the citizens of the Kingdom, and the citizens were paying for it with their lives. Too many didn't know how to fight.

No matter how much they did, no matter how hard they fought, Akira and his men were learning a brutal truth.

Nothing they could do was enough.

Since the last village, Akira and his men had stayed off the road. They were wanted men, and he decided to call a halt to their wanderings for a time. He told the men it was so the wounded could recover, but he had not been completely honest.

In truth, Akira had to decide what he was going to do next. He had hoped, at the beginning of the summer, that his small group would ignite a spark of rebellion, but now he understood it had always been a foolish dream. His men had fought well, but it was going to take much more to ignite the will of the people against an oppressor as strong as the Azarians. For rebellion to take root, hatred of the enemy had to overcome the fear of the enemy. There was plenty of hate to go around, but much more fear.

Akira considered different options. They could keep fighting, but even his honor guard wasn't strong enough to make a difference in the Kingdom. They would continue losing men slowly until they were all gone. But the other option was to disband, and that was just death in another mask. Akira would much rather go out fighting.

His reverie was interrupted when a messenger burst into his camp. The man was breathless and looked as though he hadn't eaten or bathed in days. His horse didn't look much better. Akira sat up straight, his heart full of fear. There was no way they would receive good news in a time like this. He wasn't sure how much more he could bear, but he wouldn't let his men see his despair.

The messenger was welcomed around the fire, but Akira could see he was not alone in his fears. His honor guard glanced about at each other, worry in their eyes. He hoped this would not be the piece of news that ended all their intentions. His imagination ran ahead of him, creating different scenarios that meant the end of them all.

After the messenger had caught his breath and been fortified with some food, he looked straight at Akira to deliver his message. He didn't seem concerned that everyone could hear him. "My king, I've traveled long and hard to find you. Although word of your deeds has spread throughout the land, you are still remarkably difficult to track down."

Akira allowed himself a slight grin. "Good. If we are hard to find, it is safer for us to strike. Tell me now, my men have ridden long and hard, and we have little stomach for polite conversation. What is your message?"

Akira was grateful when the messenger got right to the point. "My king, I've been sent by General Makoto. He and Lord Sen's armies still hold the lands of the Northern Kingdom. To this day, no Azarian has entered there. I come with information and a question. General Makoto has tasked me with informing you of our troop distributions and our logistics. In return, he wants to know what you plan next. He wonders if you are going to continue to run around the land like a beggar king, or if you are going to come to your senses, join him, and fight."

Akira couldn't believe what he was hearing, but the messenger misunderstood why. The poor man thought he had offended.

"Those were his exact words, my king. Not mine."

Akira looked around the campfire. Perhaps it was just the light of the fire reflected in the eyes of his men, but he thought he saw a spark of hope that hadn't been there before. Ever since the Battle of the Three Sisters he and his men had thought they were the only ones left, but in a single moment, they found out they weren't alone.

Ideas started to race through Akira's head. Makoto was alive. With armies at his disposal and the whole of the Northern Kingdom at his back, there were still possibilities. They had options once again.

Akira's heart, starved for so long for hope, suddenly surged forward. He didn't know exactly what they were going to do, but they were going to make a statement, a statement the Azarians couldn't ignore.

CHAPTER 28

Ryuu wasn't sure how much more he could take, but fortunately the time of waiting was almost over. In a few days Tenchi would call a meeting of all the blades on the island, and a decision would be made. Despite his best efforts, Ryuu wasn't sure which way everyone would vote. In some corners of the island his message had been well received, heard by blades eager to return and assume their rightful place in the Kingdom.

But for every person he met who was excited, there was one who wasn't, one who was either attached to the life of the island, or afraid the blades' return would spell their inevitable doom. Ryuu didn't agree with them, but many would not be swayed, and many shared Tenchi's opinion that the Kingdom was not ready for them to return. For too long the blades had been the stuff of nightmares.

Ryuu was certain he had already presented his argument to everyone on the island, so there was little left for him to do but to be present and answer questions and concerns the people would raise. He only hoped it would be enough.

He was training with some of the older nightblades when Tenchi found him. Tenchi watched their practice with interest, but gave no advice. When Ryuu finished, he went over to Tenchi to see why he had come.

"You fight well. You have become even stronger since you left the island."

"I still need to be stronger."

Tenchi nodded. "Yes, you do."

"That's all? I know you sensed the battle between Nameless and me. You know he is stronger than me. You know how much will depend on the outcome of our next meeting. All you're going to do is agree with me? What comes next? What technique will I use to defeat him?"

Tenchi shrugged. "I have taught you all the combat skills I know. I wish it were otherwise, but you have already mastered every technique we know." He turned and stared directly at Ryuu. "You either get stronger and beat him, or you don't. I wish there was more help I could offer, but that is the truth of it."

Ryuu rolled his shoulders back. The sun was shining brightly, and it was hard to think of the dark future when the present moment was so beautiful. "Well, why find me if not to teach me? I know you didn't come here just to rain on my day."

Tenchi grinned, and Ryuu was glad to see he hadn't lost his cheerful disposition. "You're right, of course. There is someone who would like to see you, and I've come to escort you to them."

Ryuu looked around. It was an unusual request, for the island was small, and he was certain he had visited everybody since his return. He couldn't think of anyone on the island who would be able to send Tenchi as a messenger.

Ryuu had learned not to ask questions of Tenchi when he wasn't in the mood to answer them, so he sheathed his sword and turned to follow him. Moriko, who was nearby, did the same. Tenchi turned around and motioned for her to stop. "I'm sorry, Moriko, but I think this is a meeting best held by Ryuu alone."

Moriko gave Ryuu a questioning glance, and he shrugged to indicate he didn't know what was going on either. Moriko made her decision quickly, turning around to continue training.

Tenchi escorted Ryuu in silence, content to not provide any further clues. Ryuu followed suit, knowing any questions he had would not be answered. Soon they reached a hut right next to Tenchi's. Ryuu frowned. He had been to visit Tenchi several times, and every time, the small house next to his had been empty. Ryuu had never sensed anyone inside. But Tenchi motioned him in, and Ryuu followed without question. Tenchi did not come in with him.

Inside, the house was delightfully cool. It was dark, with all the windows and the door covered. There was a little light, but the shadows in the house were long, and Ryuu couldn't sense anyone inside the house. He wondered for a moment if this was another test of Tenchi's.

But then a familiar voice spoke out of the darkness, and Ryuu couldn't believe who he was hearing.

"Hello, Ryuu, it has been far too long."

Ryuu's heart leapt for joy. It was a voice he hadn't expected to hear on the island, but one that made his day even better. "Rei! I didn't even know you were on the island. If I had, I would've come much sooner."

"I know. I have hidden my presence on this island ever since I returned. But I wanted to see you, and I suppose I owe you an explanation."

Ryuu shook his head. "You don't need to explain anything to me. I'm just glad you're here. But why the secrecy?" Even as they spoke, Rei was cloaked in shadow and he couldn't sense her.

"You will see soon enough, but first, I wanted to explain what happened to me and how I felt."

Ryuu nodded. His initial surge of excitement had been replaced by apprehension. When he last saw her, Rei had been crippled from a cut. But it had been over half a cycle since then, and apparently much had happened in her life. There was something in her voice he couldn't quite place. It was as though she had grown old in the past few moons.

"When we left this island together, I was so eager to see the Three Kingdoms. I wanted to see the land we came from, the land so many of us still call home. You warned me, but still I didn't believe. Then I saw with my own eyes. Yes, there is a tremendous amount of good in the Three Kingdoms, but they are also weak and scared of us, and I see that now. There is some strength left. Lord Akira is a worthy man. But there aren't enough like him in the Three Kingdoms."

Ryuu listened closely. He heard the change in her tone when she spoke of Akira, but he also heard a sadness that had never been present in her voice before. When they left the island, she had been the most optimistic person he had ever met. Now she had seen the true state of things, and Ryuu worried the Rei he had left with would never return again.

She continued. "When I was first brought back, I was grateful to be here. I wanted to run away, wanted to hide from everything happening. I am safe, and here my concerns are very limited. But while I've been back, I've been thinking about you. You see, you've grown up in the Kingdom, and you've experienced all that it has to offer. You've seen the good and the bad. Knowing everything, you still want to do all you can to save the people."

"For the longest time I didn't understand. But now I think I do. Our error is the same as the Azarians. We think our strength makes us better than the people in the Kingdom. But it doesn't, does it? Though we are stronger, we're no different than any other citizen of the Kingdom. The blades need to remember that. They need to return to the Kingdom, they need to stop hiding. To that end, I will help you convince everyone to return."

Ryuu tried to follow her argument, but she was explaining it to herself, not to him. All that mattered to him was that she was alive and she would support him. She would be an influential voice in the debate, but he had to push that aside. He considered her a friend, and she was clearly still in pain. "Rei, I'm more grateful than you can imagine for your support, but right now I'm more worried about you. Are you okay?"

Rei didn't respond, but Ryuu could sense her as she began to allow her presence to escape. Like Moriko, she could hide from the sense. She wasn't nearly as good, but still good enough to escape casual detection. As Ryuu began to sense her, he realized something was off. They weren't alone. There was someone else in the room with them.

Then Rei stepped out of the shadows, and Ryuu understood everything. Her belly was large, and the energy he had felt was a life inside her.

He didn't know how to respond, but his feelings took over, politics aside. "Rei! Congratulations."

He rushed forward and embraced her tightly.

She returned his embrace and Ryuu felt as though he was going to tear up. All of a sudden the enormity of what was happening dawned on him. "Does he know?"

Rei shook her head. "When the dayblade came for me, not even I knew. He didn't tell me what he sensed until we were well on our way back. I haven't been sure what to do, so I've just been taking it one day at a time."

Ryuu shook his head. "Wait, do you even know everything?"

"What do you mean?"

"You said you've kept yourself isolated from events. Did you know Akira has reunited the kingdoms and become king? You're carrying the heir to the entire Kingdom."

"Yes. That thought has been first in my mind."

Ryuu couldn't help but be amazed by the turn of events. The more he thought about it, the funnier it became. He started to laugh, a slow chuckle that grew into uncontrollable laughter.

"I've seen it all. You are carrying the heir of the king as a nightblade. I don't think that's ever happened."

Rei frowned. "It hasn't. In the time of the Kingdom, it was against the law for any blade to bed a royal family member. It was punishable by death."

They looked at each other for a moment, and the absurdity of life was too much for them to handle. They both laughed until they cried.

A few nights later a full assembly of the island was held. They were in the same amphitheater where Ryuu had dueled Tenchi, a large depression in the surface of the island perfectly conducive to the mission of deciding what would be next for the blades.

Everyone Ryuu had become close to was sitting up front with him at a low table. Moriko, Rei, Tenchi, Shika, and several other members of the council were there. After the evening meal the amphitheater filled up quickly. The murmurs that filled the space were loud and intense, almost as though there was a hive of insects among them.

The excitement and nervousness were easy to feel, and Ryuu felt it most of all. Everything he was came down to this vote. By himself, he was strong, but not nearly strong enough to turn aside the Azarian invasion. Even if he managed to somehow kill Nameless, he wasn't sure it would be enough. He needed more strength. He needed the nightblades.

In the time since he had come to the island, he had become convinced his purpose wasn't to become the strongest fighter in the world. Swordsmanship was a skill, not a purpose. His purpose was to bring the nightblades back to the Kingdom. That was what he had been born to do, and it all came down to tonight.

When Tenchi was convinced everyone had entered the amphitheater, he stood up. The crowd, despite the energy crackling throughout, was silenced almost immediately. Tenchi's voice was both soft and strong, carrying well throughout the space. Ryuu admired the sheer presence of the man.

"Everyone knows why we are here tonight. I won't restate the obvious. I only ask this favor of you all. Make your best decision tonight. Listen to the arguments, and however you make your choices, make them well. We all know we aren't simply speaking about the decision in front of us. The decision to return to the Kingdom or not will echo down for generations, and it is our responsibility to make sure those echoes ring truly in the hearts of our grandchildren."

Tenchi paused to let his request sink in.

"We'll get right to it. All of you know Ryuu. No one here can question either his strength or his integrity. You know his arguments, but here's a last chance to hear what he has to say."

Ryuu stood up and bowed towards Tenchi. He had thought for a long time about what he was going to say tonight. At one point, he had almost memorized a long, rambling speech. But as he stood here in front of all his peers, the words seemed empty and meaningless.

"This is not a time for words. I have argued for the return to the land, and I believe that time is now. The Kingdom is whole again, for the first time since we left the shores of Highgate in search of our new home. A king rules who would welcome us back. And most importantly, the people of the Kingdom face a threat from an enemy they do not have the strength to fight."

"I understand Tenchi's concern. He thinks of the safety of those on the island, as he rightfully should. And he's right. I can't stand before you today and tell you that every citizen of the Kingdom would welcome us back with open arms, even if we did come in and save them all. There are many who would still fear us."

"But this is the question I would leave you with: If not now, when?"

Ryuu paused to catch his breath. "No, it is not the perfect time to return, and there are risks, but if we don't return now, when will we? We have waited almost a thousand cycles, and we have never had an opportunity like this. If we don't return now, we never will."

Ryuu sat back down, his speech greeted by a deafening silence as the blades considered his words.

Rei stood up next.

"I don't have much to say that hasn't already been said. I have been to the Kingdom, and Ryuu speaks truly. I would only add this:

Back when we lived in the Kingdom, nightblades took an oath to serve and protect the people of the Kingdom. We don't say that oath anymore, but I think that perhaps we should. They may not deserve our help, but that doesn't mean we shouldn't give it to them."

Finally, Tenchi stood up to speak.

"I also don't have much to say. You've heard my arguments before, and neither Ryuu nor Rei have sought to deceive any of us. They have the truth of it. You know I've spoken of my concern about what will happen if we return. I worry that the persecution and the hunts will begin again. But I'm not just worried about how they will react to us. I'm worried about how we will react to them. We have gotten used to a certain way of life, and even this question has threatened to tear us in two. Renzo, one of our best, betrayed our location to try to kill Ryuu. I wonder if perhaps we aren't ready to return. Perhaps we haven't reached the necessary maturity our powers demand. We are strong. Strong enough to take life and strong enough to change the course of history. But we have heard what comes of strength. We know it from our own histories and we hear it happening now in the Kingdom. Strength corrupts, and those who are weaker suffer. How will we act when we are placed in a position of power over another? Will we uphold our oaths to protect life? Or will we be all too willing to take it? I don't know the answers to these questions. I only know the questions need to be asked."

Tenchi allowed his words to sink in. He would be the last to speak.

They had each spoken at length regarding the procedure for conducting the vote. The question that had been most on people's minds had been whether or not to make the votes public. A private vote would prevent bias, but Tenchi had argued for a public vote.

He argued that this decision wasn't one to be made privately, but in front of all.

They had talked as a council and in small groups around the island, and the final decision was that the vote would be public, a show of hands. They would do it at a glance, and if the vote seemed close, they would argue some more.

All of Ryuu's work came down to this moment. Tenchi looked throughout the crowd and called the vote. "All who wish that the blades return to the Kingdom, please raise their hands."

For a moment, no one stirred. No one wanted to be the first to voice their opinion, to vote for a course of action they couldn't return from. The time for talk had passed. Ryuu's breath caught in his throat. Perhaps all of it had been for nothing.

But then a single hand rose above the crowd. Ryuu tried to see who it was, but their face was lost among a sea of people. One by one, hands started to rise, and soon hands were going up throughout the crowd. It was more hands than Ryuu had ever seen in one place, but as he looked around, he wasn't sure it was enough. It wasn't a decisive vote.

Tenchi waited patiently, the silence in the amphitheater deafening. When it looked like no further hands were going to rise, he glanced back at Ryuu. Ryuu took a mental image of the hands in the air and nodded. He couldn't tell for sure, but it appeared as though they didn't have a decisive majority.

His fears were realized when Tenchi called for the votes to remain on the island. This time, there was no delay. Hands began to rise throughout the crowd, and Ryuu felt his stomach and his hopes drop. There were just as many hands in the air as before. From just a glance, Ryuu couldn't tell which side had more votes.

Tenchi looked at Ryuu with a frown on his face. Of all the possible outcomes, this was the one they had feared the most. They had wanted a decisive mandate from the people, but the people were almost evenly split. Tenchi motioned for the people to put their hands down and turned to Ryuu, his voice low. "Our people are split."

Ryuu was at a loss. "Do we ask for more debate?"

Tenchi shook his head. "It would be insulting. You know as well as I they have had plenty of time to think about their vote. Further arguing only makes us look weak."

Ryuu's mind was spinning. All this time he had felt that he were driven by a larger purpose. For the past few moons, he thought he had found it. He would be the one to lead the nightblades back to the Kingdom. But with a single vote that dream had been crushed. He didn't know what to do next.

Behind them, he heard a rustle of robes. He turned around to see Shika standing up. Ryuu raised his eyes in hope as he looked at her. When she stood, she drew all eyes to her. She was a natural born leader, a skill Ryuu had never possessed. When she stood up, all the murmurs and conversation stopped, and she had the full attention of everyone present.

Her voice was soft, but it carried. "There is another option, one that hasn't occurred to others. We talk as though our return needs to be either everything or nothing, but perhaps neither option is what we should be looking at. You all know I want to return to the Kingdom, but even I don't think it should all be done at once."

"I propose we send an expedition to the Kingdom. You've heard Ryuu's arguments. The people face a danger they cannot stop. Rei was also right. At one time, we were the protectors of the Kingdom, and we should be once again. But that doesn't mean we all go. Instead, let's send an expedition of volunteers to aid the Kingdom in their fight. Perhaps we will be welcomed, perhaps not, but we can take the first step towards our return while maintaining a safe population here."

She paused, but not long enough to allow anyone to interrupt her. "I know there are those who fear revealing our very existence to the people who have sworn to hunt us down, but it is foolish for us to think our secrets are safe for much longer. Ryuu's battles have been seen by many, and the leaders of the lands already know we exist. It is time for us to take the first step out of the shadows."

Tenchi glanced at Ryuu, and he shrugged. He hadn't expected anything from Shika tonight. She had gone with him, often, to rally support, but he hadn't expected her to speak this evening.

Tenchi gave the assembly time to converse. When he stood, it quieted down. "We have another vote before us. As with the earlier votes, it must be decisive, or none of us up here will feel comfortable taking action. The question in front of us is this: Do we send an expedition to the Kingdom, comprised entirely of volunteers?"

Tenchi gave them a few moments to decide, but then he called for the vote. Ryuu forced himself to breathe evenly as he watched the hands go up for a third time. But this time there were more. Many more. Tenchi didn't wait for Ryuu's confirmation. He then called for the vote against, and it looked as though fewer than a hundred voted against it.

Tenchi turned to Ryuu, and for a moment, it looked as though the old man was going to collapse. Ryuu understood the enormity of what had just happened, but it didn't strike him physically the way it did Tenchi. Still, the master of the island stood up straight when he addressed the audience.

"It has been decided. We will mount an expedition to the Kingdom to save it from the Azarians."

CHAPTER 29

Nameless fingered his sword as he looked down at the monastery below him. Before he took another step, he needed to get his anger under control. For three days he had raged at himself, but it would do him no good when it came time to draw his blade.

He had heard rumors of the audacity of the monks. He understood they believed they could withstand the Azarian invasion by hiding behind their walls and bringing the people in, and their plan might have worked. Nameless didn't think his people would have cared about what the monks did so long as they stayed out of the way. But hiding behind walls hadn't been enough. They had to prove their strength, so they sent out these foolish raiding parties.

Nameless had stopped the clan from being completely slaughtered, but too many had died. The clan was already small, and this blow might be the event that undid them. Nameless had tried to help with the healing, but his hands were meant to shed blood, not to stop it.

What he couldn't understand was why the monks had attacked with him there. If they were gifted, there was no way they didn't feel his power. And still they had attacked, rushing headlong to their own deaths. There were only two possible explanations. Either their pride was so great they ignored what their gifts told them, or they weren't gifted in the first place. Either way, they were weak, and he couldn't abide the knowledge they had killed part of the clan he had sworn to serve.

He had tracked the trail of the monks easily, leading him to the monastery below.

He laughed at their excuse for protection. The walls were tall, but they were rough and easy to climb. A small town of tents had sprung up outside the monastery, and Nameless imagined the tents were filled with the people running away from the invasion. They would discover they had run to the wrong place.

There was no hesitation in his mind. The monks were weak, and they needed to be shown the error of their ways. It never occurred to him to pursue a different path.

Nameless summoned the energy around him and felt his being infused with strength. Were he wise, he would have waited for nightfall, but the message would be clearer in the light of day.

As soon as he started walking towards the monastery the peal of a bell could be heard. The tents started to empty as people ran desperately for the main gate. Nameless didn't bother to hurry. He could smell the fear coming off of them, the weakness. One bold monk ran for him, trying to give the people more time to get behind the gate. The monk was armed with only a staff. He swung, but Nameless stepped closer, allowing the blow to bounce off his shoulder. With impossible quickness, he grabbed the monk's neck and squeezed. He felt the monk's throat crush beneath his fingers, and he dropped the lifeless body to the ground.

A pair of archers attempted to fire on him, but he could tell they were untrained. When they had coordinated the invasion with the monasteries, Nameless had learned something of the monks. Most of them trained primarily in the staff, a weapon which could be lethal or not. They believed it suited them as defenders. Few trained in the sword or the bow, weapons meant only to kill. Nameless planned on demonstrating the weakness of their philosophy. Strength without the will to kill was meaningless.

He drew his short blade to knock aside one well-aimed arrow. Then he was inside the tent city, and he ducked out of the sight of the archers. He didn't fear them, but he didn't want to worry about them either. He found an untended fire and started blazing a path through the tents, putting everything he found to the torch. When he was confident everything would catch, he turned his attention to the monastery itself.

He first looked to the gate. It would have been nice if it had remained open, but it was shut and barred, and there was no way he could take the gate by himself. The walls were twice his height, but their construction was poor. Nameless grinned viciously to himself. He chose his place and sheathed his sword.

There was no use in a sneak attack. If the monks had the gift, they would know roughly where he was all the time. He ran at the wall, his first step against it propelling him upwards. He grabbed the first hold he'd seen from the ground and pulled himself up, helping propel himself with his legs. His fingers reached the top of the wall and found purchase, and in a moment, he had scrambled to the top.

A monk was on top of him almost immediately. Even with his speed, he didn't have time to draw his sword. But there was no need. The monk was charging, and it was an easy matter to grab the end of the monk's staff and redirect him off the wall towards the crowd huddled below.

Nameless watched with pleasure as the monk fell and crushed several others beneath him. At the Battle of the Three Sisters, the commander of the fort had possessed the good sense to evacuate the fort when the demon-kind got inside. These monks weren't as clever. With a glance around, Nameless drew his blade and dropped into the crowd.

He didn't even think about what happened next. He didn't need to. His opponents weren't even opponents. He felt nothing more for them than he'd feel for cattle. His sword moved of its own accord, and he didn't even hear the screams of the people he cut. He was in another place.

The gate that had once been the symbol of their protection was now the symbol of their entrapment. Nameless advanced towards the gate, blocking any from lifting the bar. His work was methodical and perfect. One cut per person, his stance steady even as blood pooled on the grass beneath him.

The monks were no challenge. They were nothing compared to him. One even dared to lift a sword against him. That monk earned himself several cuts and was granted a final gift of seeing his entrails slowly leaking from his belly.

When Nameless was done there was only one monk left. Nameless gave him what little credit was due to him. Despite everything, he stood his ground. Nameless looked for something to wipe his blade on, but everything was covered in blood. Frowning, he walked towards the final monk. The monk swung his staff, but Nameless caught it in a one-handed grip. He easily yanked it out of the monk's hands and tossed it away. Such a useless weapon. He took a step closer to the monk and used the monk's robes to clean his blade. It wasn't perfect, but it would do for now.

The monk smelled, and when Nameless looked down, he saw the monk had lost control over his body. It was disgusting.

"Tell them all what happened here." He thought about elaborating, but there wasn't any point. His blade had done all the talking necessary.

Nameless turned and left the monk alive. He left through the front gate, perfectly calm for the first time in many moons.

CHAPTER 30

Akira was beginning to forget that he had once lived a life that didn't involve riding in the saddle every day. He was forgetting what it felt like to sleep in the same place more than one night at a time. That other life was a fond memory now, his body well-used to the rigors of daily riding. He and his horse were one, gliding over his land with ease.

He and his honor guard were heading east, out of the old Western Kingdom, towards the borders of the old Northern Kingdom. The decision to rejoin the remainder of the armies of the Kingdom was an easy one. For the first time in a moon, his men rode with a sense of purpose. Comments and questions flew back and forth, and Akira felt as though he was among his honor guard once again. They had come close to breaking.

As they rode, Akira's mind wandered. The messenger had brought them hope, but now Akira struggled to decide how to use that hope to his advantage. Learning they weren't alone had been life-changing, but as his mind continued to work through the challenges they faced, he still wasn't sure what he could do.

His heart wanted to take command of whatever troops were remaining and lead an assault against the Azarians. But that was foolish. He didn't know where to attack. The Azarians were spread throughout the land, and no single surprise attack would break their occupation. All he would succeed in doing would be making them angry. They would retaliate and more of his people would suffer.

He wasn't numb to the suffering his people had undergone. Everywhere they went, the stories were the same, and Akira carried them all. Villages burned. People slaughtered like cattle. Women taken as though they were possessions. The Azarians might be outnumbered by citizens of the Kingdom, but they held the land tightly. If Akira took any action worth doing, they would just squeeze tighter.

Akira's real worry was that he was too late. The land and the people had already been scarred. The Azarians were already spread throughout the land. Perhaps there was no going back to the way life used to be. Maybe it would be best to start again in the Northern Kingdom.

His melancholy thoughts were interrupted by a commotion near the rear of the line. He looked back and saw a group of monks trying to reach him. His honor guard had their swords drawn, surprising the monks. Given Akira's recent experiences, he wasn't surprised his men had reacted with such force. The monks briefly tried to defend themselves, but one of them spoke in a commanding voice, and the monks laid down their weapons. Akira studied the speaker carefully. There was something familiar about him, but he couldn't quite place it.

The men were brought forward, Akira's honor guard holding spears at the ready should any of them attempt anything. Akira studied them. Four of them looked perfectly unremarkable, but one was dressed in clothing of very high quality. Realization struck Akira suddenly. He was looking at the Chief Abbot of the monasteries.

Akira sat across from the Chief abbot, wondering what would happen next. The last time he had seen the abbot had been at his father's funeral, and they had both been much younger then. Akira had always observed the basic formalities when dealing with the monasteries, but he had never really believed in their power. When he was lord, he had as little to do with them as possible. The abbot was just about the last person he ever expected to see outside the walls of a monastery.

From the way the Abbot was carrying himself, it was clear he had no idea Akira knew of his treachery. Akira was content to let him play the fool. Perhaps he would hang himself on his own words.

Akira's men stationed themselves around the two leaders, but Akira had no real fear of the man he was meeting. The abbot was a man in love with the finer things in life, and he had none of the lean hardness that denoted a man used to hardship or war.

Akira let the abbot set the pace of their discussion. He was elated when his unexpected guest got right to the point.

"My king, I was very surprised by the welcome we received when we found you. I know the times are tough, and your men are wary, but I will admit I expected a more generous welcome."

Akira managed to force out a smile. "Well, they have been through a lot. They have seen things no man should have to see."

The abbot ignored Akira's remarks. "Perhaps, but it hardly seems a valid excuse for the treatment we received."

Akira shook his head. "I don't know. If you had seen some of the things my men had seen, I think you would understand why they are so nervous." He looked around the circle and saw several of his men snickering to themselves.

Akira was surprised when the Abbot continued his line of questioning. A wiser man would have realized something was wrong the moment their arrival was greeted by swords. But the Abbot was too offended to recognize the danger he was in. "I am sure you have seen terrible events. But our opponents are the Azarians. There's no need to draw steel against the monks. It is behavior unworthy of the king's honor guard. I am surprised your men have fallen so far."

Akira had enough. "You would also be suspicious if monks took your king hostage. I hear it's a fairly common reaction."

The Chief Abbot's offended look dropped from his face, and a look of pure surprise replaced it. He tried to recover. "I am sure I don't know what you mean."

Akira interrupted him. "I'm in no mood for games. We know you cooperated with the Azarians, and we know you're trying to establish the monasteries as the new protectors and rulers of the Kingdom. So, why don't you tell me why you're here, and we can get right to the point."

The abbot was thinking fast, realizing he had placed himself in a danger he hadn't anticipated. After a few moments, all pretense dropped and he looked at Akira as directly as he was able. There was disgust in his eyes. "I won't deny the truth. I've come here because our plans have failed. The monasteries need your help."

Akira laughed at the Abbot. "This had better be good."

The Abbot glowered at him, and Akira managed to remain silent while the Abbot told his story. He admitted to passing information along to the Azarians to help them with their invasion, and told Akira that in exchange, the monasteries were to be treated as safe zones for people to remain. The abbot tried to explain that it was a way to protect people against an imminent invasion, but Akira brushed his explanation aside. There was no doubt about what motivated the monasteries, and it wasn't benevolence.

It was only when the Abbot spoke about recent events that Akira's attention was focused. One of their monasteries had been completely destroyed, the victim of a bloodbath of unbelievable proportions. Akira had seen the destruction Azarians visited on those weaker than them, but even he was surprised by the behavior. Moriko's reports had told him that if nothing else, the Azarians were a very honest and straightforward people. It seemed unlikely they would break an agreement they made.

Akira pressed the Abbot, who finally admitted that the monks had been raiding Azarian clans in violation of their agreement. The monks had thought themselves more powerful than the Azarians. It made sense to Akira. If the monks were the ones who broke the agreement, the Azarians would have no hesitation about breaking their half of it too. But it was surprising one man could destroy an entire monastery. Akira didn't hold the monks in the same esteem they held themselves, but they were strong warriors.

From the description, the man had to have been Nameless. His strength was incredible.

The action forced the monks to reconsider their plans. If one Azarian could do so much damage, they realized that they didn't have the power to hold back the invaders the way they once thought they could. They had realized their error was too much pride.

Akira was saddened to hear the news of the monastery. For as much as he detested the monks, he could imagine the pain and suffering of the people who believed they would be protected by thick walls and strong monks, only to find their beliefs were misplaced. He thought of the people at Hope, who had been working so diligently in exchange for the promise of protection. That hope was no more. The monasteries had been exposed, and while Akira was grateful for that, he wished it hadn't come at the expense of so many lives.

He said as much to the abbot, but finished with a question. "As sorry as I am to hear this, I still don't know why you are here. What do you want me to do against such a threat?"

The leader of the monks responded, "I come because I know there are still men willing to fight, and we need to fight back if we are going to survive. My monks are willing to help, and now that our crimes are known, I hope it will help us atone for what we have done. But our betrayal has one benefit. We have been close to the councils of the Azarians, and I know how to strike them. I know how we can hit them so hard they will leave the Kingdom forever."

CHAPTER 31

Nameless was able to sense them coming, a pair of demon-kind. He sighed to himself. A part of him had hoped they wouldn't find him, but there was no chance of that. He was too strong, and there was no way he could hide his power from those who had the gift.

Ever since the monastery, Nameless had refused the company of others. He didn't feel guilty for his actions, but he had no desire to rejoin the People. When he traveled with the People, he invited complications, and he had enough of those. He had done what was necessary for them to survive, and at the moment, all he desired was solitude. He craved the simplicity of survival.

There was a certain beauty to wandering the earth alone, a beauty he'd forgotten in his effort to bring the People to a new land. It was just you against nature, and nature wasn't plotting against you. It just didn't care about you. It was simple and he understood the rules. Survive or die. There was nothing else to it.

It hadn't been very long since he had destroyed the monastery, but in that time he had traveled a great distance. At least it felt like it. The geography was varied in this new land. He had experienced the awesome power of a thunderstorm as it rolled across the plains, and as he rested in the woods he had sensed a diversity of life he had never before experienced. Their new land was an incredible place, and Nameless felt as though he could wander for the rest of his life, always finding something new to discover.

But it seemed he would not be so fortunate. He knew why the pair of demon-kind came searching for him. The autumn moon was approaching. There was only one message they could bring. Nameless thought long and hard about what he would do when this moment came, but he still hadn't decided on his answer.

It didn't take long for the demon-kind to reach his location. They moved even faster than Nameless expected. But when they came into view, he understood. He knew the pair, and they were one of the best pairs for tracking alive. They had been staunch supporters of his campaign to bring the People into this new land. He wondered if they had volunteered for this task or if someone had sent them, knowing their previous relationship.

Nameless greeted the pair warmly. Whatever their reasons for coming, they were a worthy pair, and deserved all the respect he could offer.

They never stopped walking as they spoke. It wasn't their way. Demon-kind knew that life was movement, and all important discussions were best held on the trail. It was refreshing to return to the way after so many meetings held around fires.

The pair did not bother with polite trivialities. "The time of the Gathering is almost upon us. There are many who ask what your plans are."

Nameless kept his peace for a while, and they walked in silence. He still hadn't decided one way or the other, but didn't know how to say so. Finally, he decided the truth was his best strategy. "I'm unsure. The People are in their new land, and I feel that my work is done. My presence brings no joy to many clans, and it seems best to me that it is time for the clans to lead themselves, as it has always been."

Nameless saw the pair exchange glances and wondered what was being said about him among the demon-kind. He realized with a surprise that he cared deeply about what his peers thought. He was cared little about losing the love of the clans, but he still desired the respect of the demon-kind. They had been the ones who understood that the People needed to move.

It was the tracker who spoke. "You know as well as any of us this has been a great trial. Our people grow stronger every day, but still, they need the guidance you offer."

Nameless was surprised. "And whose will is this?"

"The will of all of us." Nameless knew the tracker was referring not to the clans, but to the demon-kind. "Lend us your strength one more time. Then the People will find their way."

Their argument persuaded him. As much as he no longer wanted the burden, he felt in his bones that they were right. His strength was still needed, at least for one more Gathering. He would set them on their way and then disappear into the land forever.

His assent was nothing more than a small nod of his head. It was all the sign they needed, and the three of them turned in a different direction, walking together towards the Gathering.

CHAPTER 32

As the island faded from view, Moriko felt a chasm open up in her heart. She hadn't said much to Ryuu, but she was going to miss the island far more than she admitted. For the first time since she was a little girl, she had been home. In her time there she had felt welcomed and safe, but more importantly, she had felt whole. She never realized the toll it took on her to always be hiding part of her identity in the Kingdom.

She and Ryuu left the island first. It was going to take some time to put together an expedition and land them discreetly on the shores of the Kingdom. The past few days had been full of discussion and debate as the leaders of the island figured out how best to mount the expedition. Ultimately, they decided on a simple strategy. They planned to use almost every ship at their command, including many of those hidden around the island in case of emergency. While they were on the way to Highgate, many of the other boats would take different routes, mapped out long ago. The leaders of the island had always known such a day might come.

The expedition looked to be over three hundred blades. Once landed in the Kingdom, they would meet inland at a designated place. Their goal was to avoid detection as well as they were able.

Moriko and Ryuu had a different task. They had been assigned the job of meeting and coordinating with Akira. Ryuu and Tenchi could sense the king was still alive. If anyone could guide the nightblades upon their return to the Kingdom, it would be him.

Moriko glanced back towards the island. It had dipped below the horizon, but at the moment she wasn't thinking about the island. In a few days, the sea would be filled with ships setting sail for the Kingdom. Each ship would hold over a dozen blades. She was struck senseless by the enormity of what they were about to accomplish.

The journey across the sea was uneventful, and when they got to Highgate, it was even more desolate than before. Several sections of the city had burned, and if people ever returned, it would be a long rebuilding process.

The streets were almost entirely devoid of life, and the only people still in the city were scavengers seeking valuables families had discarded. People were dirty and grimy and hadn't seen a bath in some time, but everyone carried their discoveries with them.

At times, Moriko worried someone would be foolish enough to attack them. Although their clothing wasn't the finest quality, it was far superior and more durable to anything being worn on the streets. They had to be tempting targets. Fortunately, no one dared. Moriko was relieved. She had no desire to fight citizens of the Kingdom.

At the outskirts of the city they found horses for sale. The prices were extravagant and the horses poor, but Ryuu didn't argue. Speed was of the essence, and it was important they arrive at Akira's location ready to jump into whatever happened next. They mounted the horses and were off, beginning Moriko's first adventure through the land that had once been the Northern Kingdom.

As they rode, Moriko was astounded by the beauty of the land. Like Ryuu, she had been a child of the forest, and she wasn't used to mountains. Her only previous experience had been in the Three Sisters, and that pass paled in comparison to the peaks they rode by. It was hard to keep going when all she wanted to do was stop and stare at the majesty of the jagged rock.

Despite Moriko's reluctance, they made good time towards Akira. Every night before they went to sleep, Ryuu would extend his sense and find exactly where they were going. In less than a half moon, they were looking down upon Akira's camp.

When they arrived, Moriko noticed the size of the camp. Ryuu had told her Akira was traveling with a small contingent, but she had assumed it was at least several hundred men. Instead, he was traveling with less than a hundred, and each of them looked haggard and worn. Time had not been kind to Akira or his men since she had last seen them.

They rode into the camp, where they were recognized by Akira's guards. The guards allowed them to pass, and in just a matter of moments Moriko found herself in the tent of the king.

Akira greeted them warmly. "Come in, come in. I had hoped I would see you two before too long."

Moriko was grateful to see Akira as well. She was amazed he had gone from a man who had ordered her death to a friend, but the world was a strange place.

Ryuu was about to leap into the reason they'd come, but Akira held up his hand for a moment of silence. "Wait. Knowing you, you'll want to get right to the heart of the matter. Please indulge me. I have a gift for you. I wasn't sure I would ever see you again, but I had these made for you just in case I did."

Akira handed them each a parcel, and Moriko looked at Ryuu suspiciously. The package was soft, and she had no idea what was inside. Ryuu shrugged, indicating he had no idea either.

They opened their gifts, and Moriko's breath was taken away. Inside was a beautiful set of robes, made of the blackest material she could imagine. She could tell right away the quality was far beyond anything she had ever worn, and she recognized immediately what it was. It was the robe of a nightblade.

Akira chuckled, delighted at the effect his gifts had on his guests. "I hoped you would like them. They are made from drawings from the time of the Kingdom long ago."

Moriko looked up, a question in her eyes.

Akira answered her unasked question. "While you've been gone, I've been busy. I have been preparing the way for you. It is time for the nightblades to return."

As soon as she and Ryuu stepped into the command tent the situation became charged. A large man in fine robes started at their appearance. Akira had asked them to come to the meeting in their new robes, and both of them had been happy to do so.

It was a strange sensation, to be wearing the black out in the open, surrounded by men who would have been more than happy to kill her only a couple of cycles ago. But now they nodded their respect to her. It wasn't a full bow yet, but in time, perhaps it could be. Maybe Ryuu was right. Maybe there was a chance for the nightblades to come back to the Kingdom. Maybe the people were ready.

But not all of them. The well-dressed man drew a dagger and lunged at her. She sensed the strike coming, and with one hand she deflected the blow, while the other delivered a strike to the man's face, open-palmed. Blood erupted from the man's nose, and the look of horror on his face was almost amusing.

With a curt shout from Akira, guards separated the two of them. More accurately, they moved the large man further away from Moriko. None of them ventured too close to her.

The man sputtered, and Akira gave him a rag to stop the flow of blood. "That was a foolish decision."

The man finally managed to find words to express his rage. "I had heard you were spreading rumors, but I never dared believe they were true! I will have your head!"

Akira glanced around the room. "You are welcome to try, but I don't think my honor guard is going to help you."

The man looked around and saw that if there was an enemy in the room, it was him. He settled back into his cushions, considering his options.

Ryuu leaned over and whispered in Moriko's ear. "I think you just punched the Chief Abbot."

The pieces fell into place for Moriko. She could feel the sense emanating from the man, but it lacked power. She hadn't noticed at first, her own sense largely contained in the larger group of people. Ryuu was better able to use his sense in crowds, so he knew better than her what they were stepping into. He probably hadn't told her on purpose, to see what would happen.

Moriko didn't feel any guilt. If she had known who he was, she might have drawn her sword instead of using her fists. Perhaps that was why Ryuu hadn't said anything.

Akira knelt to the ground, and everyone else followed suit. "Let's get introductions out of the way. You all know me. To my left is my top general, Makoto. The man over here is the Chief Abbot of the monasteries, and he's the reason why we are all here today. To my right are two nightblades whom I'm honored to call friends, Moriko and Ryuu."

The Abbot started at the mention of Moriko's name. He fixed her with an angry stare. "You're Moriko?"

Moriko didn't realize her name had become so well-known in the monastic system, although she supposed it was understandable. The Abbot turned his gaze to Ryuu and a look of understanding came over his face.

"My king, these two nightblades are responsible for the massacre at Perseverance several cycles ago. They must be killed. I know you consider our work with the Azarians a betrayal, but if you must know, it was only because of the actions of these two that we even sought the partnership."

Moriko's head spun at the news. The Abbot wasn't lying. She and Ryuu had been responsible for the massacre at Perseverance, but it had been the fault of the monks. All Ryuu had done was help her escape. The monks had attacked them. It had resulted in the deaths of several monks and one Abbot. How had that one event driven the monasteries to betrayal of the entire Kingdom?

Then she understood. The monasteries had thought they were the seat of true power. They had thought they were the only ones gifted with the sense, and maintained absolute control over it. They had thought all nightblades extinct. But then one breaks into a large monastery and kills their best warriors without a problem. Of course it would have shaken their system to its core. In the Azarians they would have seen an alliance to both protect themselves from the nightblades and put themselves in a position of power in the Kingdom. The monks had overestimated their strength yet again.

Akira spoke, and Moriko brought her attention back to the moment. "Trust me. I know what they have done, and although I don't condone it, I understand it. Since then they have been instrumental in aiding the Kingdom, and I believe they will continue to do so."

He silenced the outburst from the Abbot. "It's time for us to be realistic. We all want the Kingdom to survive this threat, and each of us has a part to play. Yes, under the old treaty, cooperating with nightblades was punishable by death, but that treaty ended with the coronation of Tanak, our first king. Abbot, you know the monks don't have the strength needed to resist the Azarians. We need the nightblades, now more than ever before. You need to accept the times are changing."

The Abbot looked for a moment as though he was going to leave the tent, but then he thought better of it. The cynical part of Moriko's mind knew that if nothing else, if they were successful, this meeting would lay the foundation for future work together. If the Abbot left and their effort was successful, the monasteries wouldn't receive any support from the new Kingdom. He had to stay, whether or not he liked it.

In the end, the Abbot nodded his acquiescence. "Very well."

Akira smiled, and Moriko thought it was genuine. She realized he really did want everyone to work together. It was more than just necessity. "Good. I am glad. Now, if you would be so kind, please tell everyone here what you told me. I think they will be very interested."

The Abbot looked to the group. "As everyone seems to know, we made the decision to cooperate with the Azarians several cycles ago. We were mistaken, and know that now, but if there is any advantage to our error, it is that we have been close to their councils and have some idea of what they plan."

"Right now, all the clans of the Azarians are spread throughout the land. This was by design. The clans as a whole were given a mandate to spread out. They never really trusted us, and they wanted to see the land they'd conquered for themselves. But they aren't settling, not quite yet. There's one more thing they need to do. This autumn, they will come together in an annual celebration called a Gathering."

Moriko nodded. She had been at their Gathering during the last cycle, and she had a fair number of good memories to go along with the nightmares of those days. She had wondered if they would hold to their traditions in a new land.

"At this Gathering, the clans will decide where they are going to settle. The People, as they call themselves, are nomadic, but they do recognize vague territories. Apparently, it keeps inter-tribal disputes to a minimum. Normally, they wouldn't worry much about it, but the clans are under stress. They lost far more people than they expected when they invaded, and clan dynamics are very different than they once were. The Gathering will be very important, and everyone will be there. I know where this Gathering is going to be held, and if we strike it hard enough, perhaps we can send them all back into Azaria."

Akira let the idea sink in and then turned to Moriko. "Moriko, of all the people here, you know the Azarians best. What do you think?"

It took Moriko a moment to realize her name had been called and all faces were turned to her. She hadn't come to the meeting expecting to become a key source of information. She thought in silence for a few moments.

When she spoke she was hesitant, as though she was testing the words for herself before letting others in on them. "I think the Abbot is right about one thing. If we are going to strike the Azarians in any meaningful way, this will be our best opportunity. They haven't settled too well into the land yet. If we wait for a future Gathering, no matter how hard we hit, they won't budge. I'm also not sure the Kingdom will be able to mount a resistance if we wait another cycle."

Everyone seemed to know there was more, and Moriko was uncomfortable with how closely everyone hung onto her every word. "However, I don't know if we have the ability. The Azarians will view any attack as a test of their strength and will, and they'll believe the only way to pass that test will be to remain. If we truly want them to retreat, we can't just attack them. We need to break them, and I'm not sure we have the strength."

Ryuu spoke softly into the resounding silence that followed Moriko's statement. "Do you think that's true even with the nightblades coming to help?"

Moriko nodded.

Everyone seemed disappointed until Akira spoke. "Thank you, Moriko, for your honesty. I believe Moriko is right about the timing, which means we absolutely must seize this opportunity. If we wait another cycle, or for any other opportunity, I fear our strength will have diminished too far. Ryuu and Moriko have told me several hundred nightblades are on their way, and I intend to make full use of them, along with every soldier and citizen who can stand and fight. I do not know if we'll be successful, but it is the only chance we have; if we give up, we give up the Kingdom."

Those around the table pondered Akira's words, and one by one, everyone nodded their consent. The decision was made, and they settled down to make their plans.

CHAPTER 33

Akira and Ryuu rode together near the head of the column. Behind them were thousands of men, the vast majority of soldiers who were left to fight for the Kingdom. As far as the column stretched back, Akira knew their numbers paled in comparison to the full number of Azarians. But it had to be enough. It was all they had.

It had been almost a full moon since they had come together and decided to attack the Azarian Gathering, but it felt as though it had only been a few moments. Entire days passed almost without Akira noticing. All of his energy had been directed to organizing the attack. Unlike the Battle for the Three Sisters, there was no contingency planning for the soldiers. If they failed, nothing else would matter. There would never be another attempt.

Some days had been pleasant, filled with reunions. Meeting again with Makoto had been a sweet moment, one Akira treasured. They mourned together the loss of Mashiro, who had been as a brother to Makoto. Akira hadn't realized how much he missed his general until they met again. Makoto's gentle nature inspired him and kept him focused on the task ahead. Together they worked endlessly to plan the best attack on the Gathering.

Sen had come into the camp, and meeting with him had been particularly bittersweet. The old man had come down from Stonekeep to visit Akira, and together they made plans and reminisced about times gone by until the moon was high in the sky. For many cycles Akira had kept the older lord at a distance, but now the practice seemed foolish. Once, Akira had thought Sen was a potential enemy, but he had rarely been more wrong. Sen was the strongest ally Akira could imagine, and he regretted the cycles of wasted time.

Sen had offered to ride into battle alongside Akira, but Akira had refused his kind offer. They couldn't risk both of them. Akira was younger, stronger, and a better soldier. He would be more useful on the battlefield than the older lord. If Akira was to fall in battle, it would be up to Sen to take on the role of king. Akira wasn't sure what good it would do. If they failed, the Northern Kingdom was vulnerable and would soon fall. But it was important to maintain their pride. Even if they were all to fall, they would do so with dignity.

Initially, Sen had been resistant to the idea of staying back, but Akira had persuaded him. Neither of them had any living heirs, and to leave the land completely without leadership was irresponsible. It had to be Sen, at least until another ruler could be determined. It was frustrating to plan for a future Akira didn't hope for, but they had to be prepared.

When they began their march, Sen had been the hardest to leave behind. Akira was humbled by the old man's courage and generosity, and wanted to do nothing more than sit and talk with him for as long as time allowed. Memories flashed through his mind, his childhood visits to Stonekeep and Sen's small castle. Sen was the only tie Akira had to the days of his youth. He openly wept when the old man rode with his honor guard back to Stonekeep. Akira couldn't shake the depressing thought that he might never see the lord again.

It would be beneficial if they could wait longer to make their strike. Akira and Sen had both sent out calls throughout the Kingdom for volunteers, sending riders from village to village to recruit anyone who was willing to risk life for their land and their families. People had been trickling into the camp for several days, and every day they delayed they grew in numbers. But it was a risky game they played.

They couldn't be sure how much longer the Gathering would last. Moriko had told them the celebration lasted an entire moon when she had been among the Azarians, but she had no idea if that was tradition or not. They had waited as long as they dared, and they couldn't risk another day.

Ryuu had been instrumental in the planning of the attack. Every day he spent the entire morning meditating, his sense wandering throughout the Kingdom. He kept Akira updated on the status of the Gathering, and every day Akira worried he would come back with news the Gathering was breaking up. But he never did. The nightblades from the island approached and volunteers trickled into camp. The time would never be better.

Their battle plan, again, was simple. They would attack the Gathering from different directions. The Azarians had formed their Gathering at the confluence of the two great rivers, but they stayed inside the boundaries of the old Southern Kingdom. In other words, their backs were to the river. Akira and his men would attack from the southeast and Ryuu and the nightblades would attack from the southwest. With any luck they would drive the Azarians into the river and out of their land.

Akira spent much of the journey lost in his own thoughts. Ryuu rarely spoke, and their plans were laid, so there was little to do but ride and think. Akira had always dreamed of becoming king, but he never thought it would be like this. More than anything, he had wanted to bring peace and prosperity to the land. He had never expected he would be forced to save it. Unfortunately, it didn't seem to be his fate to lead in a time of peace. He would have to settle for doing all he could to save his people.

The king looked over at Ryuu, the nightblade who had sparked so much change in the land. But as much as the land had changed, Ryuu had changed even more. Akira remembered when he had first met the nightblade. He remembered the day well, thinking at the time it would be his last. He had been disarmed easily, his own sword held against his throat. Ryuu had been so young, and so naively idealistic.

But those ideals had cost the young man, and had burned away much of who he had been. Akira understood the nightblade better than he thought. Ryuu was still idealistic, but in a different way. He had been forged in difficult trials, and his idealism was more realistic now. He rode forward with purpose, something Akira had never really seen from him before.

He spoke softly. "What is on your mind?"

Ryuu glanced over at him briefly. There was no deception on his face. "My battle with Nameless."

"You must have fought well to still be alive."

The nightblade shook his head. "Not the battle I've already had. The one I will have in three days."

Akira frowned. "I know you have never been in a large battle, but I can assure you, the odds of you two actually meeting on the battlefield are slim."

Ryuu disagreed. "No. We will meet. His rage towards Moriko and me is bottomless, and although she can hide from him, I can't. Even several days away, I can sense him as clearly as I can see that tree over there. I have little doubt he can do the same. He knows I'm coming, and that she'll be with me. We will meet."

Akira thought about the nightblade's words. "You're that strong, then?"

Ryuu nodded. He was never one to talk much about his own strength. He was so much like the warriors Akira had idolized in his youth. The strongest warriors had no need to boast. It was the silent swordsman that Akira feared most.

Akira continued his thought, trying to get to the heart of what Ryuu was telling him. "But despite your strength, you fear you aren't strong enough?"

Ryuu nodded again.

Akira wasn't sure if there was anything he could say to make Ryuu feel more confident. The young man had an accurate assessment of his abilities, and if he thought he wasn't strong enough, he probably wasn't. The thought disturbed Akira, but it wasn't his place to question the nightblade.

"All we can do is all we can do." It was a saying his father had used all too often.

Ryuu rolled his shoulders back, as though he was trying to shed the weight of responsibility he felt. "That's true. It doesn't make it any easier, though."

That evening, as the rest of the men set up camp, Akira watched as Moriko and Ryuu prepared to leave to meet up with the nightblade expedition. It felt as though a fist was grabbing his heart and squeezing. Up until this moment the march had seemed like a dream, the sort of heroic exploit he imagined himself leading as a child. But as he watched the two nightblades efficiently pack up their gear, it became all too real to him.

They were marching to a battle they had little hope of winning. They were hopelessly outnumbered, and Moriko, who knew the Azarians best of all, thought that even the strength of the nightblades wouldn't be enough. There was an excellent chance he would never see the two of them again, and just for a moment, he was seized by the desire to tell them to run, to leave the Kingdom and never return. They had done enough.

He kept his silence, and it wasn't long before they were ready. The two nightblades turned to face him. There was so much he wanted to say. He wanted to express his gratitude for all they had done, wanted to tell them to be careful, wanted to tell them to escape the madness that was coming. But none of the words could escape his lips. To speak about his feelings would be to demean their import.

Akira met Ryuu's gaze, and although they said nothing, they understood each other. Akira knew what Ryuu was thinking, and he believed Ryuu understood him also. There wasn't anything to say.

In a surprise gesture, Ryuu knelt to the ground and bowed all the way down, his forehead pressing against the floor. After a moment of hesitation, Moriko did the same.

Akira fought back tears. He had known the two of them for cycles, and never had they given him more than a nod. Coming from the two of them, a simple nod had always been enough. This was more than he deserved. He knelt down to the ground across from them and returned the gesture. None of his men were around, but he wouldn't have cared if they were.

He remained in his bow, even after the rustle of their robes reached his ears. He knelt, the cold ground reassuring against his forehead, a few tears watering the grass beneath his face. The sound of two horses trotting away came to him, and it wasn't until the sound faded into silence that he rose.

The two nightblades were gone, and Akira was certain he would never see them again.

CHAPTER 34

There were days where Nameless wished he had taken different actions in his life. It wasn't quite regret for his choices, but it was close. These days, he wished he had stayed far away from the first Gathering in the new land. When they crossed the Three Sisters, their plan had been simple. Defeat the armies of the Kingdom and explore the land. At the first Gathering they would share information and let other clans know where each was planning to settle. It had been so simple when they spoke of it back in Azaria.

There had been some complaints. Some felt they should skip the exploration phase and go straight to settlement. They had fairly detailed information from the monasteries. But he had convinced them otherwise. It wasn't that he distrusted the information from the monasteries, although the thought did cross his mind. Nameless had pushed for exploration for two reasons. First, it introduced all the clans to the land that was going to be theirs. If they were going to live here, they needed to know it, deep in their bones. They needed to see just how perfect this land was for them. Second, although the information from the monasteries was most likely accurate, the monks didn't see the land the way one of the People would. If this land was to be their new home, they needed to understand it from their own perspective. For example, the monks would never consider the mating or migration habits of large game.

The purpose of the first Gathering was to take all the information the clans brought back and combine it into one coherent whole. Then clans would discuss where they would settle. Any clan was welcome to settle wherever they wished, but clans wouldn't want to share the same space. The peace enforced by the demon-kind was no more, and weaker clans would be swallowed by stronger ones if they tried to settle in the same place. The idea had been that by discussing it at the Gathering, bloodshed could be avoided.

What Nameless hadn't considered was how strong the pull of tradition was. He had thought perhaps the importance of their situation would have inspired the clans to a more forward-thinking mindset, but many of the clans had returned to the old ways. Few looked to the future of the People as a whole. Their thoughts were only for themselves.

Nameless didn't always blame them. In his calmer moments, he forced himself to remember they had all grown up in a time of hardship. They couldn't afford to look beyond their immediate clan and their immediate future. There hadn't been enough food to think of the People as a whole, not when your own stomach was constantly rumbling.

But here they were in a land full of food, full of resources. There was enough for everyone, and clans could afford to look beyond themselves. The only problem was that they couldn't. They never had before and they couldn't make the shift.

They also didn't see that the People were weaker than they ever had been. The move had cost them far more than Nameless had hoped, and it continued to cost them. There were barely enough demon-kind left to be with each clan, and the clan numbers had decreased substantially. Their new land was still hostile to them. If they didn't work together, they would all die apart.

But he might as well have been arguing to a group of trees for all the effect his words had. The largest and strongest clans claimed enormous amounts of land for themselves, much more than they would need for many cycles. Smaller, weaker clans felt as though they were being forced to settle in lands not much better than those they had left. They came to him, having grown used to the protection of the demon-kind, but no words of his would sway the larger clans. Unless he wanted to resort to force, there was nothing he could do.

Nameless considered returning to power. He still had the support of the demon-kind, and perhaps, if he could unify the clans, at least for another cycle or two, everything would work for the best. But the idea made Nameless sick. His only purpose had been to get them here. They needed to find the strength to survive on their own. They needed to be able to survive without him.

Day after day they met, but nothing changed. The weaker clans continued to approach Nameless, begging him to do something. Under his leadership, large-scale combat between the clans had come to a complete stop. The demon-kind had kept everyone in line. In Azaria, Nameless had known he needed every person alive he could. The weaker clans had appreciated the protection, and some had grown stronger under his leadership. They didn't see why he should give up his power.

So Nameless continued to be torn between two ideals. On one hand, he feared that if he allowed the demon-kind to assert their authority once again, there would be no turning back. The demon-kind would need to rule the clans from that day forward. They would be responsible for the welfare of all the clans, a responsibility that went against their traditions. Nameless had listened to all the legends growing up. There was a reason the demon-kind shunned authority. He knew how dangerous power could be. The demon-kind were stronger than anyone else, but the reason they had been successful was because they had been raised as servants. In this way, their power was channeled and controlled. Nameless had broken that tradition, but had only wanted to break it for a time. If the demon-kind remained in power, eventually disaster would befall them. The legends were clear on that point.

On the other hand, it seemed obvious that the People needed the demon-kind more than ever. Together they were strong, but if they allowed clan rivalries to dominate their time here, they might cease to exist altogether. They were balanced on the edge of a blade, and a fall to either side would kill them all. Nameless had no doubts about it, but few others seemed to agree with him.

In all this, Nameless had an unusual ally. Dorjee, the leader of the Red Hawks, was a vocal supporter of Nameless. Of all the clan leaders, he was the one who seemed to see the situation the same way Nameless did. They certainly didn't agree on everything, but they were united in the knowledge that the clans needed to work together.

It was a strange twist of fate that the man who had virtually led the rebellion against Nameless on the other side of the pass now urged his followers to unite. It was working, too. The Red Hawks had almost tripled in size since coming over to the Kingdom. Between marriages and other alliances, the Red Hawks had absorbed several smaller clans and were stronger than they had been in many, many cycles.

The greatest point of contention between Nameless and Dorjee was the method by which the People would come to live with the citizens of the Kingdom. Nameless believed the only way to get the people of the Kingdom in line was to intimidate them and make them understand who was strongest. Dorjee argued that the people of the Kingdom didn't think the same way the Azarians did. He believed that by moving into the land and making peace, much more could be achieved. Although Nameless hated to admit it, Dorjee's strategy had been successful for his clan. His clan was still strong, and didn't seem to have the never-ending problems with the native people that so many other clans had.

But Nameless couldn't quite bring himself to see facts the way Dorjee did. In his mind, strength was still paramount. If they didn't assert their strength, they risked finding themselves subservient to the people of the land. The moon was almost full, and the time of the Gathering was coming to a close. If he didn't find an answer soon, it would be too late.

Nameless still hadn't found his solution when he learned of the attack.

The news came from one of the demon-kind who had been riding far from the Gathering. He made his report in haste. "We will be under attack soon. I'd estimate about ten thousand, almost half of them trained soldiers. They'll be here tomorrow morning."

Nameless was surprised. He continued to underestimate the strength of the people of this Kingdom. Individually, they were weak, but they had strong leaders who brought them together. They were still outnumbered, but it was a substantial enough number that Nameless worried. They didn't have to kill every one of the People, they just had to get the People to shatter. Did the commanders of the Kingdom know how fragile the alliances of the People were?

"Send word around. Gather every fighter who will come meet them on the field. I'll gather the demon-kind."

The messenger left, and Nameless was left alone, his thoughts racing. It could only be King Akira, but it seemed unlike him. In all his time here, he hadn't known King Akira to make any foolish mistakes, and this felt like one. They had little hope of destroying the Gathering. Did they know how divided the clans were? Even if they knew about this weakness, an attack against the Gathering would only serve to unify the People. Were they just desperate?

There had to be something more happening. Akira was brave, not dumb. Nameless wished, not for the first time, that the old man was still with them. He could have warned them of this attack and let them know of any others.

It wasn't long before Dorjee came to visit him. "What's happening?"

Nameless looked up at him. "I don't know any more than you do. There's about ten thousand heading our way. They'll be here in the morning."

Dorjee didn't hesitate. "You should treat with them."

Nameless stood up straighter. The very idea was against every ounce of tradition. He didn't even stop to think through the proposal. "We are going to be attacked. There is no need to treat with them."

Dorjee yelled. "You fool! You sit here day after day and complain about how the clans can't break from our histories, but when faced with an opportunity to do just that, it's you who can't break from tradition! Don't you see that you're no different?"

He didn't give Nameless a chance to respond. "They have to know they are walking to their own deaths, but they do so anyway. Can't you see the strength of will they possess? Can't you respect that? You say every day that there is enough land for us all, and I agree with you. There is enough land for us all, including the people who were here before us. Why can't you see that?"

The old man had gotten much bolder in the past cycle. Last fall he had practically been on his knees begging for mercy. It was the nightblade, the one who had cut him. Her influence had grown on him. He saw a different future than Nameless.

"No. They are attacking us, insulting every one of us. I will not treat with a weaker force. Even if I wanted to, none of the clans would agree. No, we will fight, and I will crush them once and for all."

Dorjee hesitated for just a moment. "The Red Hawks will not answer your call."

Nameless towered over Dorjee, but the clan leader didn't back down. Nameless thought about drawing his blade and taking off the man's head, but perversely, he respected the man's courage. Dorjee spoke softly. "We have talked frequently these past few days. I know the clans are all you care about. It's the same for me. But talking isn't enough. We need to act, and that's what I'm doing. My men will stay by their tents. If they have the audacity to actually attack our tents, we will defend them with our lives. But we won't meet them in battle."

Nameless was filled with rage, but he took no action. As much as he wanted to kill Dorjee, he had no right. He had given up command of the People. Nameless watched the old clansman disappear into the darkness.

CHAPTER 35

Ryuu felt as though it had been ages since he had last rested. He had been on the road for so long. The journey had been a wearying one, but it was nearing its conclusion. That evening they would meet with the rest of the blades and plan their attack. He only hoped it would be enough.

Parting from Akira had been difficult. It was hard to believe that only a few cycles ago, Akira had ordered the deaths of both Ryuu and Moriko, an order only rescinded at the point of a blade. Now the man was a friend, and Ryuu was convinced he was the only one strong enough to lead the Kingdom on its new path. He was a strong leader, and a moral one.

When he first rode into view of the assembled nightblades, Ryuu had trouble believing what he was seeing. They camped in a valley, hundreds of men and women, all dressed in black. As much as he looked forward to finishing his journey, he stopped for a few moments to take in the sight. He thought of the history of the Three Kingdoms. Nothing like this had been seen in the land for dozens of generations. Whatever happened in the next few days, they were going to make history.

Ryuu shook himself out of his reverie and rode down towards the nightblades. The first two people he met were Rei and Shika. They rode out to greet him, and he met them with a deep bow.

"It's great to see you," he said.

Shika nodded. "It is great to see you as well. This is my first time in the land of my ancestors, and it is every bit as beautiful as I dreamed. If we live through this, I would like very much to explore all the land. And I don't think I'm alone in that feeling."

Ryuu thought he understood. For generations, the nightblades had been born, lived, and died on an island that one could walk across in less than half a day. By contrast, the Kingdom was enormous, full of varied geography and people. He had grown up here, and didn't think often about how fortunate he was, but he could understand how those who had grown up in a different place would find it incredible. It was a good reminder of what they were fighting for. There was much of the land he hadn't seen either. Perhaps Moriko would be willing to travel with him if they made it through the next few days.

Ryuu and Moriko joined the rest of the nightblades. They were still on the move, hoping to cover a final league or two before they rested for the night. When they set up camp, it was several leagues away from the Gathering. Ryuu and a few other nightblades used their ability to sense at a distance to keep everyone informed as to what was happening. A handful of dayblades who had joined the expedition wandered the camp, performing what minor healing they could so the nightblades were well prepared for the upcoming battle.

He never spoke of it, but Ryuu felt everything coming to its conclusion. So many threads were coming together, it couldn't be anything but fate. Akira and his men were on time, and they would launch their attack in the morning. The Gathering was in full swing, and although there were too many people for Ryuu to discern any details, he could tell the one thing that mattered most to him. Nameless was there.

That evening, before they retired, Ryuu spoke to Rei and Shika. "Our plan tomorrow isn't complicated. Our purpose is to draw the hunters away from the Gathering and Akira's assault. We don't know for sure how many hunters they have. It could be an overwhelming force, or it could be that we actually outnumber them. There is no way of knowing. But make sure everyone knows this: the weapons tomorrow are real. All of them have spent their entire lives in training, but real combat is different. They need to keep their heads and fight with their utmost skill. The hunters have grown up in an environment where they need to fight to survive, just like Moriko and me. They are talented and strong, and I don't want to see anyone making the mistake of underestimating them."

Shika frowned. "So you aren't planning on leading us?"

Ryuu shook his head. "I don't think it is my place. As welcoming as you all have been to me, I am still an outsider, and have no training in battlefield strategy. It is better that someone more qualified leads. Moriko and I are going to try to assassinate Nameless. Maybe, if we can cut the head off the beast, we'll have some leverage over the Azarians."

Shika nodded. "We expected you would want to do something along those lines. We'll play our part. Don't worry about that."

The nightblades all stood, and Ryuu spoke to Shika. "Good luck tomorrow. The battle will be hard, but I know you'll do well."

Shika grinned. "Stop making everything sound so serious. I still have a duel to win against you, so don't go dying on me." Without another word, she turned and walked away to her tent. Ryuu laughed softly to himself. She was a woman who would never change.

Ryuu turned to Rei. "What will you do tomorrow?"

Rei looked down at her useless arm and then grinned at Ryuu. "Actually, I'm commanding the blades. Shika might be a better commander, but she wants to fight, and I'm not good for much else. I'll be issuing commands from the back of the lines." Her smile disappeared, and Ryuu could see there was more to her orders.

Rei spoke softly. "If things go poorly tomorrow, my orders are to run and hide. No matter what happens, I'm supposed to report back to the island and let them know what occurred here."

Ryuu could see the orders chafed at her, but he understood their importance. The nightblades needed to know what happened. Rei could hide her presence, meaning she would have the best chance of escaping any wandering hunters.

"I think it is an excellent idea, although I understand why it upsets you."

They stood for a moment in silence. Then Ryuu looked at Rei's stomach and remembered there was something else he needed to ask. "Will you tell Akira?"

"When the battle is over. Until then, there's only one thing he needs to focus on."

Ryuu nodded, and Moriko wished Rei her own goodbyes. Then Rei also went back to the camp to start preparing for the battle the next day.

Ryuu took Moriko's hand. There wasn't much to be said. They found a clearing a ways away from the rest of the camp, and that evening they came together underneath the stars. He could sense and understand everything Moriko was. He could sense her fear, desire, love, and hate, and he understood the cause of each. She could do the same to him. When they were done, Ryuu felt a peace in his heart. He didn't know if they would live or die the next day, but his relationship with Moriko was strong once again, and if the end came, he could rejoin the Great Cycle with no regrets.

CHAPTER 36

It was a difficult decision, but Nameless decided to send only a few demon-kind to the battlefield. There were two factors influencing his decision. First, his instincts still told him something was off. The attack was too rash, and Nameless wanted to keep his demon-kind as his reserve. Second, the numbers of the demon-kind were being depleted too quickly, and there were groups of soldiers from the Kingdom who had proven adept at killing demon-kind. He wanted to risk as few of them as possible.

As the sun rose and Nameless walked towards the battlefield, he felt the pit of his stomach sink. For so long he had dreamed of a day when the People could be safe, a day they would be able to grow and prosper. They were strong, but this land was stronger than he had thought. He couldn't allow more harm to come to the People. They had to survive. They had to grow. This land was the answer.

But at the same time, the world seemed to be against them. The divisions in the clans ran deep, and they needed to unite behind a higher purpose. While they argued among themselves, their opponents banded together, using the last of their strength to fight the invasion.

Nameless arrived at the battlefield and was disappointed by what he saw. The soldiers of the Kingdom should have been far outnumbered by the clans, but they weren't. He wasn't an expert, but the number of his fighters seemed to only barely outnumber those of their enemies. The Red Hawks' refusal to fight had changed everything.

When he saw the troops of the Kingdom lined up against the clans, Nameless wondered if the People might fail. The troops they faced were outnumbered, but their banners snapped in the crisp autumn wind, and Nameless knew none of them would stop until they died. They were prepared to give everything, and he wasn't sure the clans were. He looked to his clans. It would be a close, vicious battle.

Nameless wasn't there to take command. They were back to the old ways, where each clan commanded itself. He was there to fight. He saw a man in fine armor across the field wave his sword and point it towards the clans. The screams of thousands of men, hungry for a fight, reached his ears. He memorized the armor of the man with the sword. It had to be King Akira. If Nameless could slay him, perhaps it would break the will of the troops they faced.

The morning sun rose bright, and Ryuu thought it somewhat ironic such a beautiful day would end up being so deadly. Under other circumstances, he would have gone with Moriko on a walk through the woods, enjoying the last warm days of autumn before the leaves began to fall.

But not today. Today the fate of the Kingdom and the Azarians would be decided. He had done all he could. He had brought the nightblades back to the Kingdom. Now it was no longer his responsibility. All he had to do was fight as hard as he could.

The nightblades met together in a loose formation. Ryuu and a few others knelt to the ground with their hands on the earth. Ryuu's sense traveled the few leagues separating them from the Gathering, and in a few moments he learned everything that was happening. The battle was about to begin. Akira and his men were lined up against the clans of the Azarians.

Ryuu was surprised so few Azarians had come to fight. There were far more Azarians still in the Gathering than outside defending it. Ryuu couldn't understand it, so he didn't try. The Azarians thought about everything differently. More importantly, there were only a few hunters in the battle defending the Gathering. Most of the hunters were still within the Gathering, clustered together.

Ryuu couldn't be sure, but he believed that Nameless suspected a trap. The man was smart and strong, and Ryuu wouldn't underestimate him. As soon as they moved closer, he expected all the hunters would swarm in their direction. It was possible they already knew what the nightblades planned. It didn't change their strategy. They still had to attack.

He felt the battle begin, and he waited nervously to see how the different groups would react. If there was a trap of some sort, it wouldn't be long before they sprung it. The nightblades held their positions, but still nothing happened. The battle raged, and the clans in the Gathering stayed within the Gathering. Ryuu even felt a few clans leave the battlefield and return to their tents. It was almost as though they didn't care about the Kingdom's assault.

When Ryuu came out of his trance, he saw most of the nightblades were waiting on him. They were a patient people, but he could sense their eagerness. They had waited their entire lifetimes for this moment. Rei had been waiting for some sign from him. He walked up to her.

"I say we go. The time has come."

She nodded. There was nothing else for her to say.

Ryuu stopped her just before she started shouting orders. "Be careful once the battle is joined. You carry a precious gift."

She reached down and lifted his hand off her reins, gently. "I will. Do what needs to be done."

Ryuu bowed. He was hers to command. He mounted his horse and rode into battle with the rest of the nightblades.

Akira stood in front of his men as the sun began to rise. After all the waiting it was time for the final push, their final effort. There was only one way forward. His words to Ryuu echoed in his mind. All they could do was all they could do.

It was surprising to see how few opponents they faced. They were still outnumbered, but not by as much as they should have been. Akira wondered idly at the reasons. Did the Azarians think so little of his force? Had the nightblades attacked too early? Ultimately, it didn't matter. It would still be a hard fight. Half of his soldiers were volunteers, and he had seen children and women among them. Every Azarian trained in combat. The same could not be said of his own force.

Akira mounted his horse and raised his voice. He knew his words would carry, and he hoped his men would pass them along to those he could not reach.

"We all know what is at stake today. This is not just another battle between lords for territory. We no longer play those meaningless games. Today we fight for our land and for our families. Everyone here has seen and heard the terror that awaits our people should we fail here today."

"You must fight with all you have! Your families and your descendants are counting on you! Think not of your own life, but of all the lives in the Kingdom. Think of wives and children. That is why we are here. If we fail today, there will not be another chance, so let nothing stop you! If you die, pick up your sword as a ghost and continue the charge!"

Akira drew his sword and spun it in an intricate pattern, a useless move in combat, but one that looked dangerous and impressive. A wild cheer came up from the men, and Akira pointed his blade towards the direction of the Azarian Gathering. His blood boiled, and for a moment, he was caught up in the emotions he had spurred in his men. His sword was all the command the men needed as they surged forward, the last army of the Kingdom. Akira kicked his horse forward, leading the charge as the lines came together.

The charge began, and Nameless watched as the clans and the troops of the Kingdom met. His experienced eye took in the sight, and he worried as Akira and his army penetrated deep into the Azarian lines. He watched Akira carefully and was about to wade through the battle towards him when he sensed something else, a feeling which left him cold inside. The power was incredible, and at this distance, there was no mistaking who it would be.

A few moments later Nameless was approached by one of his demon-kind. He came bearing dreaded news. "There is another force to the west. There are only a few hundred, but each of them is dressed in black robes."

For a few moments, Nameless couldn't even understand. It was too unlikely, too impossible. Renzo had told them there was no way the nightblades would ever leave their island. Was it a ruse? That would be the most logical conclusion, but his gut told him it was real. Either way, Nameless couldn't take the risk. He had left the demon-kind in reserve for just such an event.

"Give the command to all the demon-kind. Attack to the west."

Nameless worried. If the messenger was right, and these were nightblades, they outnumbered the demon-kind. He looked back to the battlefield, his heart torn. He could still see Akira's armor, cutting through the clans with remarkable ease. It would be good to kill him, but Nameless wasn't certain he had the time. He knew the boy was here, and if the boy was about, so was the woman. Akira was dangerous, but the two nightblades were the most immediate threat. They were also the people he most wanted to kill.

With a shout, Nameless turned from one battlefield for another. It was time to finish this once and for all.

The hunters met them on the fields to the southwest of the Gathering. Ryuu hadn't expected anything else. There were fewer hunters than nightblades, but Ryuu only found a small amount of comfort in that. He suspected the hunters were individually stronger than they were. It would be a close fight.

The battle was much smaller than the one happening almost a league to the east, but it was no less violent. Every person on the field was an expert, and their swords thirsted for blood. The nightblades never stopped their charge. They rode straight into the mass of hunters, steel pressing against steel.

As soon as they approached, Ryuu reached out and allowed the energy of the world to course through his body. It was becoming easier every time, and there was so much energy to draw on. Ryuu's muscles screamed with desire to attack his opponents as the energy flooded his body. Two hunters fell underneath his blade, taken by surprise in the sheer speed of his attacks. Ryuu's horse was cut down underneath him, but he leapt from the stallion and rolled smoothly away. He was better on his feet anyway, more connected to the ground beneath him.

Ryuu found his next opponent and lost himself in combat. The sun continued its relentless march across the sky.

Time didn't flow the same way for Ryuu anymore. His world moved slowly, as though everyone else was struggling to move through water. They were all so weak. Objectively, part of him knew he had been in combat for some time, but it didn't stop him. The thought of resting never entered his mind. He didn't feel tired, didn't feel pain. A part of his mind warned him that when he let this energy go he'd collapse on his face, but it didn't stop him. The power was intoxicating, and all he wanted was more of it.

Through it all, Moriko was at his side. They made a deadly combination. Ryuu attracted the hunters, and they swarmed around him like angry bees. They could sense him and rushed to attack, but the speed of his defense made him virtually invincible. And they were always surprised by the young woman who danced in front of them without warning, a woman they couldn't sense coming. Moriko never gave them a chance to learn from their mistakes. Between the two of them, they cut a path of death through the hunters.

The Azarians rode out to meet them, and in the time it took for the two forces to meet, Akira felt as though he had never been more alive. He thought he could see every blade of grass trampled underneath his horse, could smell the sweat and the fear of the man next to him. He felt detached as he saw arrows start to fall around him. There was no fear in his heart. His only concern was to bring vengeance down on his enemies. It was all he could ask for.

His calm was shattered when the two armies clashed, the relative silence of the field broken by the sound of steel clanging against steel, man clashing against man. Akira could hear the screams of horses and men as they were wounded and died, and gradually his attention shrank further and further, until all he cared about was the area within reach of his sword.

He was surrounded by his honor guard, the men who had fought so hard and sacrificed so much over the summer. This battle was what they had hoped for, what they had waited for. It was their chance to strike back in a meaningful way. Akira watched as guard after guard rode through the Azarians like scythes through wheat. Akira sent several Azarians to the Great Cycle himself, each cut a vicious victory over the enemy.

Unfortunately, they didn't have the momentum to carry themselves all the way through the Azarian lines. Their horses slowed, and as they did, more and more arrows found their mark.

Akira managed keep his mount for several precious moments before an arrow to the neck brought his horse down. Akira rolled from the saddle, coming smoothly to his feet, his blade flashing in the early morning light. He and his men were surrounded by Azarians, and although he took a few minor cuts, the cycles of training he had seen kept him safe. Azarians fell beneath his blade, and he and his honor guard were an island of destruction in the sea of the Azarians.

Although he couldn't see anything from his position on the battlefield, Akira suspected his honor guard had made it further into the Azarian lines than any other group. They would need to hold their ground until the rest of Akira's forces could reach them. He found Captain Yung in the commotion and together they ordered the men into a rough circle, maintaining a small safe space for soldiers to take a rest while they could.

For a while, the battle went smoothly for Akira and his guards. They formed a perimeter, with those on the outside being supported by those on the inside. Azarians fell beneath their blades, spears, and arrows, and his men cycled between the outer and inner rings of the perimeter.

Akira took a break from fighting in the outer ring. He took a moment to catch his breath. He tried scanning the battleground, but there was little he could see. His vision was obscured by the battle surrounding him. He scanned the area immediately around him. There was a shout from nearby, and Akira turned to see Yuki, the guard he had been locked up with at Hope, in trouble. Three Azarians were backing him up with spears, and no help was coming.

Akira glanced around and pulled a spear out of one of his men lying dead on the ground. He twirled it so its point was facing the right direction and gave a heave. His aim was true. The spear struck one of the attackers in the chest, knocking him backwards and dead. Akira joined Yuki at the line, his break over. Together, their swords penetrated the defense of the spears. The two remaining Azarians fell, but more were eager to take their place.

As the sun rose high in the sky, the battle started to turn against them. Akira's group of guards was drawing attention to itself, and the pressure on their perimeter grew. They fell back step by step.

Despite the skill of his men, no one could fight off a never-ending stream of opponents forever. One by one, his honor guard fell and they brought their perimeter in a step, continuing to fight almost shoulder to shoulder.

When Yuki died, it happened so fast, Akira barely even noticed it. One moment they were fighting side by side. The next, a spear was lodged in Yuki's throat, a look of surprise on his face. A memory of Yuki pacing their cell together flashed through Akira's mind, and he was overcome by rage and grief. He attacked without fear, slaying Yuki's killer and three other Azarians before finding his way back to the perimeter.

When all hope seemed lost, a force of soldiers from the Kingdom broke through, overwhelming the Azarians surrounding Akira and his honor guard. After a full morning of combat, there was a sudden break in the fighting. Akira fell to his knees, well past the point of exhaustion. It had taken half the day, but finally his men had caught up with him.

Suddenly Makoto, his giant general, was there at his side. He helped his king to his feet while letting him know what was happening.

"It is a hard fought battle, sir. The Azarians are better fighters, but they are even more disorganized than we are. Most of our volunteer units have been destroyed, but our own soldiers are doing well."

"Are we winning?"

Makoto considered the question for a moment. It didn't seem like a hard one to Akira, but the general always thought carefully.

"I don't think so."

Akira's heart sank, but Makoto continued.

"This battlefield is very much up for grabs. I don't know if you saw this, but a few of the clans we were fighting against broke early.

So, in a way, we actually outnumbered them for a while. We might still win here. But even if we do, we won't have any soldiers left. Even if we win, we'll have nothing left. The hunters are also a problem."

Akira's ears perked up. He hadn't spared much thought for the hunters, but then he realized he hadn't seen any all day.

"Have we seen any hunters yet?"

Makoto nodded. "Yes, but not nearly as many as I had expected. Also, the ones who are in the battle don't seem to have any coherent battle strategy. They are deadly wherever they go, but their actions seem very ineffective, especially considering what damage they could do."

That was good news, at least. "We need to keep pressing our advantage," Akira said.

Makoto nodded, but as he did, shouts of concern reached his ears. He looked up, and Akira wondered what it was he was seeing. His general stood a head above most others on the battlefield.

"The Azarians have organized a counter-attack. They are pressing this way. We should get you to safety."

Akira sighed. All he wanted was a break. Just to rest and lay down his head for a while, put all the worries of the world behind him. "No, I won't retreat. We've been through a lot, but my honor guard is still one of the strongest units we have here. We'll hold the center."

Akira saw his men nodding around him as they listened in. He was so proud to fight by their side. They all knew he was probably sacrificing their lives, but none of them hesitated. He would be honored to die in the company of such men.

He saw the indecision pass over Makoto's face. Makoto knew Akira was right, but he didn't want to sacrifice his king. But there was no choice, and they both knew it. "I will see you when this battle is over, sir."

Akira returned Makoto's bow as the general gave his orders. Units reformed around them, and Akira and his honor guard took their place in a much larger line. This was going to be the final push.

Ryuu was starting to lose his shadow as the sun rose higher in the sky. Time was meaningless, and he couldn't guess how many they had killed. All that Ryuu knew was that his blade was coated in the blood of his enemies, but its thirst was unquenchable. He had always been strong, but he had never experienced power like this. His rational mind was overpowered by a primal force inside of him.

Nameless didn't announce himself when he entered the fray. There was no polite exchange. Ryuu sensed him coming and turned his attention to the leader of the Azarians. He screamed in anticipation. The hunters were too weak. He wanted stronger prey. He wanted to taste Nameless' blood. Moriko dropped back a few steps. They had planned for this. Her responsibility was to guard him now. Ryuu had to trust Moriko completely if he was to have any chance of defeating Nameless. There was only one opponent that mattered to him.

Their swords met with bone-shattering force. Ryuu took the briefest of instants to size up his opponent. The man was the same as before, but this time, he was driven by even more rage. Ryuu had no problem sensing the strength of the hunter. Each of them was fully consumed by the power they possessed. Had he been given time, Ryuu was sure he would have felt fear, but no time was given. The battle was joined instantly, both men attacking with all their strength.

The two of them danced a duel that would have been legendary if anyone else had the ability to see it. The speed of their cuts was blinding, and Ryuu gave up on his vision completely. Only his gift of the sense gave him the warning he needed to react in time. Their swords crossed and crossed again, but neither could draw blood on the other.

The two of them passed again and again and Ryuu wondered how long the battle would last. He felt nothing, but he suspected Nameless didn't either. They were two of a kind. Neither was able to gain an advantage over the other. In the back of his mind Ryuu felt Moriko making short work of anyone who got too close to their battle. If this continued, soon it would be just the three of them.

Nameless must have sensed his distraction. Without warning, his speed seemed to increase. Ryuu thought such a speed impossible, that there was no way a man of such size could be so fast, but the reality was right in front of him, trying to kill him. Ryuu found himself on defense, dodging and deflecting the short black blade that seemed to be everywhere at once. He was cut half a dozen times, but there wasn't any way to retaliate. Ryuu was already moving as fast as he could, and it was all he could do to defend himself. Nameless was incredible.

Nameless made a mistake, a thrust that brought him just the slightest bit off balance. Ryuu didn't have time to strike with his blade, seeing that Nameless' blade was already coming back for protection, but he summoned all his energy and leapt forward, driving his elbow hard into the hunter's chest, knocking him back a few satisfying paces.

The thrill of victory surged through him. He was about to leap and make the killing strike when he saw that Nameless was poised and ready for the attack. It had all been a ruse to get Ryuu to over-commit, and it had almost worked.

The knowledge frightened Ryuu, and he stopped in his tracks. Sweat started to bead down his brow as Nameless stood there, perfectly still. Not only could he not penetrate the hunter's defenses, he felt like he was being played with.

Without warning, Ryuu lost his grasp on the energy that had been powering his attacks. He collapsed to the ground, falling to his knees. All around him, the battle continued to rage. Moriko was a blur, keeping him safe from other attacks. But she couldn't hold them back forever, and his most dangerous opponent was still in front of him. And he had no energy left. His body felt as though he had been run over by a whole herd of horses. Nameless looked at him and laughed. He took his stance, and Ryuu knew he was facing his last enemy.

The sun's heat was fierce for this season. The cold of the early autumn morning had given way to the warmth of a perfect fall day, without a single cloud in the sky. As the forces took a deep breath, Akira looked up and thought about how beautiful the blue sky was compared to the blood-soaked ground beneath him. It had been, he thought, a good life.

He heard the charge of the Azarians and brought his gaze back to the earth. He summoned what strength he had remaining and let out a primal yell, his own men rushing towards battle. The two lines met and bled into one long conflict.

In the midst of the battle, Akira lost all track of time and space. For a while they advanced, and the Azarians fell beneath his blade. At other times, they pushed back, and he would barely be able to keep his feet underneath him as he stumbled backwards over the bodies of his men. The combat raged back and forth. At one point, Akira looked up and was surprised to see the sun was still high in the sky. It seemed as though they had been fighting forever, but almost no time had passed. He was covered in blood, as was his blade, and a fair amount of it seemed to be his.

Whenever he got a moment, Akira looked up and down the line. The fight seemed to be stalled, going back and forth over the same ground again and again. Captain Yung was near him, fighting one handed, an arrow embedded in his left arm. Despite the handicap, the man fought as fiercely as ever.

And then Akira faced an opponent he had hoped never to meet in person again. He saw the tooth hanging from the leather strap around the man's neck, and knew he faced a hunter. A space cleared around them, other Azarians unwilling to interfere with the hunter. Akira saw Yung and some of his honor guard try to come to his aid, but the Azarians formed a circle around them, cutting Akira off from his men.

Akira took a deep breath. There was only one way forward, and he had no regrets. He had no further attachment to this life, but he would kill this hunter. He made a few tentative strikes, keeping his balance steady and his sword in front of him. There was no way he was going to give the hunter an easy opening.

The hunter deflected the strikes as though he was playing with a child. His sword was smaller and faster than Akira's, and Akira knew he had little hope of penetrating the hunter's defense. He had to try though.

The hunter went on the attack, and Akira brought his guard in close, managing just barely to block the hunter's attack. But it gave him confidence. He had survived a pass with a hunter. There weren't many who could say as much.

They passed again, and in this exchange, Akira left with a shallow cut on his neck. It wasn't fatal, but he was only alive by the width of a hair. He tried to think of some way to get inside the hunter's defense, but nothing came to him. The hunter was too fast.

On the third pass, Akira tried to go on the offense, stepping forward to strike, but the hunter leapt forward with incredible speed, and his short blade sliced easily through Akira's stomach. Akira didn't feel the cut itself, but he felt his organs trying to escape from the confines of his body. He felt himself going into shock, a comfortable numbness, but in that moment, the hunter turned around, his attention drawn by something off in the distance. Without thought, Akira stabbed out with the last of his strength, his sword piercing the hunter's back. Akira pulled his blade out and the hunter turned around to face him, a look of surprise on his face. It was the most satisfying sight Akira had ever seen. The hunter collapsed at his feet.

Akira dug his blade into the ground and supported himself on it. He didn't think he could fight anymore, but he didn't want to fall.

A shout rose up, but it wasn't from his own men. It was from the Azarians. Akira managed to raise his head and follow the gaze of the Azarians. Off in the distance, he could see people in black robes running down the hill, the glint of steel clear as day. Akira smiled. The nightblades would break what was left of the Azarian lines. His kingdom would survive.

Akira's strength left him, and he fell to the ground. His mind was still clear. He thought it silly that after all he had been through, it would end with a single cut on the battlefield. But, he supposed, that was the way it always was. They were all just hanging on by a thread, a thread that was all too easy to cut. Still, he had killed a hunter by himself, and there were few men alive who could say that.

He heard the sounds of his men retreating, and he hoped they would be okay. They had given everything for the Kingdom, and he would honor their memories forever. He hoped they would honor his.

And then his vision swarmed with black robes, darting all across the battlefield. Akira tried to smile, but the effort hurt. So he gave up and looked at the blue sky. And then Akira's world went black.

Ryuu struggled back to his feet, but there was nothing left. He had no energy, no strength to fight the monster of a man in front of him. Nameless knew it, too.

"Your strength is great, and your skill is similar to my own. But your body and mind lack the stamina for a fight of this magnitude. You cannot win."

Ryuu glanced over at Moriko. She was bleeding from dozens of small cuts, but still she circled, preventing any hunters from reaching the duel happening between the two warriors. But there was no way she could hold out much longer. This battle would be decided in the next few moments. Ryuu wanted to hold her one last time.

Nameless saw him looking at Moriko, and his gaze followed Ryuu's. Surprisingly, his attitude softened for a moment. "You are both very strong. This has been a good fight. It has been a very long time since I have needed to raise my blade against another."

Ryuu took it as a compliment. "Thank you. You are by far the strongest I've ever faced."

A hint of a smile played upon Nameless' face. "I did not believe such strength still resided in this land. The People will tell stories about you for generations. You were our final test."

Ryuu didn't know what he could do. He had done everything in his power, but he hadn't even gotten close to Nameless. And Nameless wouldn't give him a chance to figure out a new strategy.

Nameless attacked. Ryuu searched desperately for strength, leaping out of the way, running backwards, staying out of Nameless' reach. He was able to avoid being cut, but he couldn't evade forever. He would run out of space or strength, and it would all be over.

His mind raged against him. There was no way he could allow himself to lose! He had come too far, had accomplished far too much. There had to be a way to beat Nameless.

Nameless halted his attacks to taunt Ryuu. "What's the matter, boy?"

He pointed his sword at Moriko, still desperately fighting off hunters. "She can't hold out much longer, and all you're doing is running away. Is that all you have, after all of this?"

Ryuu's mind flashed back to his fight with Moriko in the woods, back when he had been without his sense. Then, he had found clarity of purpose. There was a reason for him to live. He thought of Takako, beautiful and innocent and dead. Shigeru, the man who had been much more than just an adopted father, who had been a master and a friend. Orochi had been a strong warrior, the man who pushed Ryuu to realize what he was capable of. He thought of Tenchi and Shika and Rei and Akira and everyone else who was depending on him. This fight was bigger than the two of them.

And there was Moriko. She was the strongest person Ryuu knew. More than anything, he wanted a future with her in it. She was worth it.

His mind calmed, and he found the energy that flowed around him. It had always been there. He just needed to move beyond the fear he felt. He summoned it, and his exhausted limbs filled with a newfound strength. Losing was not an option.

Nameless straightened up, sensing the difference in Ryuu. "Good. I was hoping it would be more of a fight."

It was all the warning he gave. He leapt forward, and he and Ryuu's blades met for the final time. Their first passes had been powerful and focused. These were still, but now they had a desperate edge. Ryuu knew if he lost his focus again he would never regain it.

Their swords clashed, and Ryuu kept himself low to the ground, slashing at Nameless' ankles. Like their first battle, Nameless danced backwards, but Ryuu didn't give him time to strike back. He kept attacking, kept Nameless moving. When he thought he had a chance, he cut upwards, hoping to catch Nameless off-guard. His hope was in vain. Nameless dodged the cut and got his blade in between them.

They passed again, Ryuu trying to make use of the extra length of his blade. He kept himself just outside of Nameless' range. But Nameless was patient and wouldn't make any mistakes. Ryuu couldn't get inside the hunter's guard.

Desperate for something, Ryuu closed the distance with a single thrust. Nameless slid to the side of Ryuu's blade, and a quick cut sliced into Ryuu's right forearm. It wasn't deep, but Ryuu grunted in pain. He couldn't bring his sword around in time, but his body was inside of Nameless' guard. He focused all his effort on driving his elbow into Nameless' chest.

The blow knocked Nameless backwards, and each of them took a moment to catch their breath. Neither of them had landed a fatal cut, but Ryuu was the one running out of time. The circle was closing around them, and Moriko and the other nightblades were having a hard time holding their ground. Already the battle was pressing uncomfortably close to Ryuu.

Ryuu didn't see any options. When all was said and done, Nameless was faster, stronger, and just as skilled a swordsman as Ryuu. He didn't see any way he could win. But he wouldn't give up.

Ryuu summoned more energy, afraid of what would happen when this battle was over. Even if he lived through the combat, his body might give up after this.

Nameless attacked, and immediately Ryuu found himself on the defensive. He kept his guard close to his body, favoring protection over a counter-strike. His only hope was to wait for Nameless to make a mistake. Nameless attacked and attacked, and although he was faster, he wasn't quite fast enough to make it past Ryuu's guard.

When it happened, Ryuu couldn't believe it. He and Nameless were engaged, their swords a furious blur of steel. And then she was there, behind Nameless, and a single cut was made. It wasn't deep, and Moriko went right back to defending against the hunters, but she had somehow found the time to cut Nameless.

Ryuu was astounded. She was fighting multiple hunters, and still had positioned herself behind Nameless. Her skill was beyond compare.

The cut slowed Nameless down, but more importantly, it made him wary. Ryuu took the advantage away from Nameless, pressing the attack. He summoned every bit of energy he could, cutting with all his speed. Nameless retreated, and Ryuu thought for a moment he would win.

Then Nameless exploded once again, an incredible burst of speed and energy, and Ryuu found himself on the defensive once again, doing everything he could just to stay alive.

When all of Nameless' focus was on Ryuu, she came again, her sword slicing through his calf. Nameless howled in rage and turned on her, but she had disappeared once more, placing a hunter between her and Nameless.

Ryuu seized the opportunity, thrusting his blade deep into Nameless' side. It wasn't necessarily a fatal blow, but it had the chance of killing him.

The giant hunter turned on Ryuu, his face a mask of rage and pain. Ryuu had never seen a sight more terrifying. Nameless swung his short sword with all his strength. It was an obvious and slow attack, and Ryuu got his blade up in time to block it. The attack hit with such force Ryuu's own blade snapped back towards his body, and he felt his wrist break as he held on to the sword. He flew backwards, struggling to push himself up on his good wrist. His focus fled, and he collapsed, unable to move his body.

Ryuu lifted his head and watched as Nameless approached him. He saw Moriko slay the hunter who had been a shield from Nameless' wrath. She leapt forward, and Nameless never sensed her coming. She was a ghost on the battlefield.

Moriko's sword went straight through Nameless, piercing his heart and coming through his chest. He looked down in surprise, the rage disappearing from his face. He tried to turn, but Moriko held the blade firmly, preventing him from turning.

Nameless fell to his knees, and Moriko pulled the sword from his chest. She didn't hesitate. As soon as her sword was clear she whipped the blade in one smooth cut, taking off Nameless' head.

Ryuu smiled at her. After all his preparation, she had been the one to kill Nameless. He wasn't dissapointed. They had won. He

CHAPTER 37

Moriko fell to the ground. She felt as though she had run the entire length of the Kingdom with a horse on her back. She never thought she could be so tired. Never before had she pushed herself so hard.

There was a satisfaction there, too, the pleasure of a job well done. She had never put forth so much effort, but never had the results been so pleasing.

All around her, the hunters broke and ran. The death of Nameless threw them into utter chaos. His passing was a shock, even to her. He had possessed so much power. In a moment, it had all disappeared, and to everyone gifted with the sense, it was as though a deep blackness had suddenly opened up in the middle of the battlefield. She didn't blame the hunters. If she possessed any strength, she would flee the battlefield, too.

It was all over. All the fighting, all the killing. The desperate desire to survive. All of it was gone. In its place was a simple peace, a relief that she had survived.

Ryuu was unconscious but alive. She couldn't believe what she had witnessed. His power had grown, much more than even the last time he had fought. He truly was a remarkable man. She may have made the killing blow, but it was only because he was strong enough to stand toe-to-toe with Nameless.

She watched the nightblades as they pursued the hunters. She didn't care. The spine of the Azarians had been broken, and she and Ryuu had given more than enough. She crawled over to him, unable even to stand on her own feet.

She sat down next to him and lifted his head up onto her lap. Gently, she felt his forehead and extended her sense. He was weak. Much weaker than she had initially thought. He had told her he feared using too much power, and perhaps his fears had come true. But there was nothing to be done about it now. She had no ability to heal him, not from this.

Eventually, with nothing to do, she lay down next to Ryuu and stared into the blue sky. It really was a beautiful day. She closed her eyes and rested.

Her sense warned her awake. Two people were approaching. She sat up and saw that it was Rei and Shika. She cursed softly to herself. They were both fine people, but she was enjoying the peace.

It was Rei who spoke. "How is he?"

"Very weak. He used up everything he had to fight against Nameless. I think his wrist is broken, too."

Rei flared her energy. "There should be a dayblade here shortly."

Shika spoke softly. "He did it. He actually killed Nameless. From everything I heard, I wasn't even sure it was possible. I could feel his strength all the way across the battlefield."

Moriko thought about correcting her, but abruptly decided she didn't want to. She didn't want the recognition as the one who had killed Nameless. Ryuu knew, and that was all that mattered. She was happy with as little attention as possible. Anyway, he had done the hard work.

Shika and Rei continued their rounds of the battlefield, trying to aid as many nightblades as they could. As promised, it was only a matter of time before a dayblade came to Ryuu's side. She laid her hands on Ryuu and focused.

"I've never felt anything like this before."

"What do you mean?"

"It's hard to describe. Imagine him as a candle. He has burned himself all the way down. He's recovering, but I think he's very close to dying."

"His wrist?"

"A clean break. It will be easy to fix."

The dayblade began to work. Moriko watched, but there was little to see. She could sense the connection between the dayblade and Ryuu, but nothing else was apparent to her sense. She lacked the finesse with the ability the dayblades possessed.

A little while later, the dayblade opened her eyes and looked up at her again. Sweat was on her brow, and she looked exhausted.

"This is more than I can handle on my own. He's dying from lack of strength. His body is completely burnt out." The dayblade flared her energy, calling for help. "When they come, let them know what I told you. I'll need them to join me."

Moriko didn't have time to respond. The dayblade closed her eyes and focused on keeping Ryuu alive. Fear clutched at Moriko's heart. Had Ryuu pushed himself too far this time? He couldn't die, not now, not when they were finally safe. She wouldn't allow it.

It seemed an eternity before three other dayblades appeared. Moriko told them what the first dayblade had said. They looked skeptical, but knelt down and went to work without question.

Moriko stared, wishing there was anything she could do. She had never seen the dayblades work in unison before. She panicked when the first dayblade collapsed next to Ryuu. One moment she had been kneeling down and healing Ryuu. The next she was unconscious next to him. A few moments later a second dayblade fell. Her heart raced. What was happening?

Finally, the two remaining dayblades opened their eyes. One looked at her. "He should live now. I don't know how long it will be until he wakes up, but his body should be healed."

"What happened?"

The dayblade spoke slowly. "I'm not sure. I've never felt anything like it before. He used all of his strength and more in his last fight. We had to find a way to give him more strength, and the only place we could find it was within ourselves. It took all of us to pull him back, but still he's weak."

The dayblade saw Moriko's concerned glance at his companions. "They'll live. They just need to recover. Like he does."

She bowed slightly, and the dayblade moved on to the next patient, stumbling as he went.

The sun was beginning to set when Ryuu finally awoke. He looked up at Moriko, affection and relief in his eyes. "I didn't think we were coming back from that one."

She looked down at him. "You almost didn't. It took four dayblades to bring you back."

Ryuu laughed and sat up. He grimaced, and Moriko thought it took him more work to sit up than it should have. He was alive, but exhausted. "Better than Nameless having the pleasure."

He surveyed the scene around him. "You were amazing. I don't know how you managed to defend me and attack Nameless at the same time. I owe you my life. The Kingdom owes you."

Moriko shook her head. "No, they owe you. I told them you killed Nameless."

Ryuu looked puzzled for a moment, and he looked as though he was about to ask her a question. But then he thought about it. Of all the people in the world, he understood Moriko best. He nodded. "I see."

"The hunters all scattered after Nameless died. I think it's all over now."

Ryuu looked off into the distance. "I hope you're right."

The sun was starting to fall when Rei, Moriko, Shika, and Ryuu met again. They had saved all the injured they could, but still their losses had been substantial. They had come into the Kingdom with three hundred and seven blades. There were a hundred and three left. Moriko didn't underestimate the strength they had remaining. It was still the strongest force the Kingdom had seen in over a thousand cycles. But it was a third of the strength they had come with. Each death weighed heavily on her mind.

Ryuu had been meditating, extending his sense, trying to find out what was happening. Nameless' death had had a cascading effect. The hunters had panicked and run back to the Gathering. When the hunters scattered, the nightblades swept down on the main battlefield, breaking the lines of the Azarians who still fought against the Kingdom. Losses had been tremendous on both sides, but all the Azarians had retreated back to the confines of the Gathering.

They had to decide what to do next. Ryuu's worry was the Gathering itself, and he was trying to use his sense to determine what was happening. They were waiting anxiously for his information.

He came out of his trance and looked around. He fixed his gaze on Moriko. "Moriko, you know the Azarians best. How will they react to their losses here?"

His tone was serious, and she guessed he was hoping her opinion would help him understand what he was sensing. She thought carefully, aware her answer might have serious repercussions.

The problem was, it was hard to generalize the Azarians. Although they claimed a single heritage, clan loyalties were stronger than loyalties to the People as a whole. Each clan would react differently. But what would be the dominant reaction?

They wouldn't leave the Kingdom. Every single Azarian knew how rich the land they had come into was, and they had sacrificed too much to get here. Even with their defeat, most Azarians would view the citizens of the Kingdom as weak, and wouldn't hesitate to attack. They certainly wouldn't run with their tail between their legs. The Kingdom had won today, but the Azarians would only view it as another setback, a challenge to be overcome.

She spoke carefully, considering her words. "I'm not sure what they will do, but if you forced me to guess, I would guess they would take one of two actions. They won't consider themselves beaten, and their reaction will be fierce. They will either use today to unify to a degree we haven't yet seen, or they will split for good and cause chaos throughout the Kingdom. Nameless held their alliances together, and I'm not sure exactly how they will react to his death."

"Either way, it sounds as though you don't think our mission here is accomplished yet," Rei said.

Moriko shook her head. They had dealt the Azarians a blow, but it wasn't enough.

"I fear they are attempting to assemble," Ryuu said. "I can sense a collection of hunters near the center of the Gathering, and they are attracting many of the Azarians. I fear our attack will only provoke them."

Moriko wondered if their attack had made the situation worse. Had they managed to do what Nameless never had? Had they truly started the unification of the clans?

The nightblades sat around the tent in silence, each lost in their own thoughts. Moriko tried to think of a way to save the situation, but nothing occurred to her. She raged at fate. After all their sacrifice, they still hadn't accomplished what they set out to do. It wasn't fair.

The silence stretched out, and eventually Ryuu stood up. Moriko studied him carefully. His face was a mask, but she had lived with him too long. He had a solution, but he didn't like it. She wasn't even sure he was going to share it with them. Understanding dawned on her. She couldn't believe what he was thinking, but there wasn't any other way. It was beyond horrible. It was unspeakable. But maybe it was necessary.

"Ryuu, you need to tell them."

The nightblades from the island looked up, questions on their faces. Her eyes met his, and she offered him what strength she could. He needed to speak up. He shook his head.

"We need to attack the Gathering itself."

Rei didn't understand. "What do you mean?"

Ryuu crouched down, and Rei worried he was about to explode. "Look, we know the Azarians respect one trait above all others. They respect strength. The reason we haven't succeeded yet is because despite our best efforts, the Azarians still believe they are stronger. As long as they believe that, the Kingdom will always be in danger. It isn't enough for us just to beat them. We need to put so much fear in them they never threaten the Kingdom again."

Shika's and Rei's faces fell. They began to understand what Ryuu was suggesting. Rei shook her head. "I can't order the nightblades to do this, Ryuu."

Ryuu considered his words carefully. "I can't think of another way to bring peace to the Kingdom."

Rei was adamant. "Ryuu, this goes against more than a thousand cycles of history. Nightblades are protectors. We've beaten the hunters. We've done what we set out to do. There are only a few left in that Gathering who can defend themselves against us. You're not talking about warfare anymore. You're talking about a slaughter. Most of those people didn't even participate in the battle against the Kingdom today."

Ryuu shrugged. "I know. I hate it, too. Fighting hunters is one thing. This is another. But I don't see any other way. If any of you do, please speak up. I would rather do anything else than this."

Shika spoke up. "Why not send the remainder of Akira's units? They've been victimized by the Azarians for an entire season. I'm sure they're itching for revenge."

Ryuu shook his head. "That's exactly why it can't be them. And they aren't strong enough. If they attack the Gathering the Azarians will destroy them. It needs to be us."

The silence spread again, oppressive. Moriko knew it was their only path forward. She just wondered if the nightblades from the island would realize it too.

Moriko looked up as she heard a sniffle. Tears were streaming down Rei's face. "We came here to protect those who were weak from those who were strong. If we do this, we're no better than the Azarians. I can't order this, Ryuu. I won't."

Ryuu spoke softly, and Moriko's heart broke when she realized he had made his decision. His voice was firm. "You don't have to. Put out a call for volunteers. We will do all we can to save those who hope for peace, but I need nightblades who are willing to shoulder this responsibility."

Shika stood up. "I will join you. You don't have to bear this alone."

Ryuu nodded. Moriko spoke up. "I will join you as well."

Ryuu shook his head. "No. I need you to do something else. If we have any hope of salvation, it lies with you. You know a clan leader. I need you to bring a message to him. You need to find him and tell him we attack tonight. All those who are willing to live in peace should remain in their tents. No livestock will be harmed, but any soul who is out tonight when the moon is high in the sky will be slain. We will treat with those who remain in the morning. With any luck, most will stay inside tonight."

Moriko studied him carefully. She didn't want to leave his side, but he wasn't in any physical danger. If she wanted to save him, this was what she needed to do. With a sigh, she nodded. She would try to find Dorjee, if he was even still alive. Perhaps she could convince him to put a stop to the madness. She stood up and left the tent to make her preparations for going into the Gathering once again.

Moriko ran as fast as she could. Thanks to the care of a dayblade, she had regained most of her strength, but still it felt as though she couldn't run fast enough. The nightblades had set up their tents about a league to the west of the Gathering, but no matter how fast she ran, she felt like she was running in place. She kept her focus on the sun, watching as it continued to approach the horizon. There was time, but it didn't feel like it was enough.

A variety of emotions tore through her. She was glad they were alive. They hadn't expected to make it out of that battle, but together they had. It was an unspeakable relief. But it was overshadowed by the dread growing inside of her. The worst part of it was that she agreed with Ryuu. They needed to take an action to prove their strength to the Azarians. Try as she might, she couldn't come up with a better solution. They needed to break the Azarians for good.

The price was too high, though. When she and Ryuu had fought in the clearing against each other so many moons ago, Ryuu had found the purpose he was looking for. He had discovered he was willing to kill to protect the Kingdom. He would go as far as was necessary. Though he had found his purpose, he was still a kind man, and she feared this action would destroy him.

Their only chance was her. If she could somehow convince the Azarians not to put up a fight, to spend the evening in their tents, perhaps Ryuu's actions wouldn't ruin him. She had to get to Dorjee, convince him and give him the time he needed to spread the word throughout the clans. Everything required time, the one thing she didn't have much of.

Although she covered the league to the Gathering quickly, her eye was always on the sun. Most days she welcomed the coming of the night, but today it was coming too fast. She abandoned all attempts at stealth, running straight to the crest of a small hill that overlooked the Gathering.

It was so much smaller than it had been last fall. She remembered the Gathering stretching almost as far as the eye could see. It was still a tremendous collection of people, but it lacked the scope of the previous one. The Azarians really had been decimated by their invasion of the Kingdom. Her eyes scanned the tents, trying to make out the emblem of the Red Hawks that would be painted on their coverings. Her first glance didn't reveal any familiar symbols.

She considered her options. She could run directly into the Gathering, although she knew she would attract unwanted attention. She could fight quite a few people at once, but if everyone in the Gathering was focused on her, it was only a matter of time before she would fall. Stealth had to play at least a small role in her movements.

Moriko ducked beneath the hill and started running around the Gathering. Last autumn the Red Hawks had been near the very edges of the Gathering, a statement against Nameless and his ideas. She assumed they would be on the outer fringes of the Gathering again this cycle, but it was an assumption. A lot could have happened between now and then. Perhaps the Red Hawks had been killed.

She refused to give in to despair of any kind. Dorjee was a strong leader. There was no way he would allow his clan to perish. But no matter how many times she came within view of the Gathering, she couldn't see the tents of the Red Hawks. Either they were closer to the center of the Gathering or they were dead.

The sun was beginning to set, and Moriko faced a choice. She hadn't run around the entire Gathering yet, but she was running out of time. She needed to go in. It wasn't the smartest idea, but she didn't have time for anything else.

Moriko studied the tents below her. She didn't recognize the symbols on their tents, but there weren't many people out and about.

Ryuu had said they were beginning to gather near the center of the camps. Perhaps it would be easy to sneak in.

She didn't have the time to think it through. Instead, she ran straight down to the nearest tent. Her sense told her the tent was empty and she stepped inside. She tore the tent apart searching for clothes. She found some that were too large for her, but she threw them on over her black robes. There was no way she would pass as an Azarian under scrutiny, but if no one looked too closely, she should do pretty well. She stepped out of the tent and went towards the center of the Gathering.

Her luck changed just as the sun was hitting the horizon. She had only encountered a few people on her way towards the center and they had paid her no mind. But without warning she found herself among tents decorated with the Red Hawk she had looked so long for. Dorjee and his clan had moved towards the center of the Gathering. Moriko didn't have time to question why it had happened. She just needed to find Dorjee.

A young man stepped out of the tent next to her. He looked familiar to Moriko. With a start, she realized he was one of the young men who had tried to attack her when she had entered the camp last fall. She laughed, drawing his attention to her.

He had changed. Last fall, when they had met, he had still been a boy. But now he had the eyes of a man, the eyes of one who has seen war and death and survived it. He held himself straight, and this time he didn't attack Moriko without thinking. Moriko could see he was on his guard, but he spoke before attacking.

"Why are you here?"

"I need to see Dorjee. Something horrible is about to happen."

Doubt flickered across the young man's face, but he made his decision quickly. "I can't take you to Dorjee, but I can take you to Lobsang."

Moriko didn't ask questions. Any progress was worthwhile. "That's fine."

The young man turned and started walking briskly deeper into the camp. His attitude welcomed no questions, and Moriko didn't ask any. She understood she was a victor walking into the camp of the recently defeated. It would be hard for her to find a welcome here. She was fortunate as it was.

The Red Hawk came to a tent and spoke loudly in Azarian. Moriko could hear the noises within, and in a moment, Lobsang appeared at the front of his tent. Despite everything, he was grinning from ear to ear. "Moriko."

She bowed to him. "Lobsang. I regret the circumstances that bring me here, but it is good to see you again."

He motioned her inside, and she went into his tent. Most of his large family was there, and Moriko was surprised at the trust he showed her. "Lobsang, I am sorry I don't have time to catch up, but my task is urgent. Something horrible is about to happen, and I need to speak to Dorjee."

He frowned. "Dorjee is in a meeting of all the clan leaders as we speak. Taking you to him would be a death sentence for you, for him, and the messenger. As you can imagine, you and your people are not welcome here right now."

"I understand. But the Gathering is going to be attacked."

Lobsang's eyes rose in surprise. "It would be suicide. We know you don't have the strength to attack the Gathering. That's why they are planning a counter-attack."

Moriko was confused for a moment, but realized they were speaking at cross purposes. "I'm not talking about the army from the Kingdom. I'm talking about my people, the nightblades. The ones as strong as your demon-kind."

Lobsang's doubt was replaced by fear. "We hadn't been told there were more of you."

"There are. Many more. Enough to cause terrible harm. I've come to try and save as many of the People as I can."

Lobsang hesitated and Moriko pressed him.

"Take me to where Dorjee is. If you fear for your life, simply point the way. I can find it on my own. Just, whatever happens, don't leave your tent tonight."

Lobsang stood up. Something Moriko had said made up his mind for him. "I won't hide while a small woman risks everything. I would never live it down." He smiled at Moriko and grabbed his blade.

Together they moved towards the very center of the Gathering. Moriko kept her head down, trying her best to be invisible next to Lobsang's bulk. As they walked, Lobsang tried to fill her in quickly on what was happening.

"Much has changed since you left. Dorjee has become respected once again, and strangely enough, he was on good terms with the leader of the demon-kind. They both see far into the future, and they shared a common goal in helping the People. Dorjee has gained much respect, but I fear it isn't enough. He argues for peace, but his voice is overpowered by others on the council. The death of the leader of the demon-kind was a blow to him, and he fears we will march to war until there are none of us left to march."

Moriko took it all in. Dozens of questions raced through her mind, but there wasn't any time to ask them. She simply had to take Lobsang at his word.

The center of the Gathering was well guarded, but Lobsang was able to get them in with the correct passwords. Moriko knew he was risking his life by bringing her in this far. Lobsang tried to get Dorjee's attention from across the fire, but Dorjee was engaged in a passionate argument in Azarian with another man.

The sun had set below the horizon, and its last orange rays were disappearing. Moriko didn't have time to wait. Impatience seized her and she broke into the center of the ring surrounding the fire. The council was surprised, but not as much as when she threw off the garb of the Azarians and stood before them as a nightblade. A roar came up from the council as swords were drawn all around her.

Moriko was about to draw her own sword when a commanding voice shouted. "Stop!"

Everyone paused, responding to the authority of the voice. It had been Dorjee who shouted, who stood a pace in front of his companions. He looked at Moriko and she couldn't decipher the look on his face. A combination of surprise, fear, and awe.

Dorjee seized the moment. "This is the woman who cut our leader last fall. If she has come this far, it is with good reason. Let us listen to her before we slay her."

"Nonsense!"

The scream came from a man to Moriko's right. He leapt towards her, and Moriko sensed that he was a hunter. Perhaps one who sought to replace Nameless. His sword was high as he charged towards her, all technique forgotten in his rage at seeing a nightblade in the center of a meeting of the council.

The hunter never had a chance. Moriko stood still, and he couldn't sense her at all. He swung wildly and missed, and with one smooth cut, her blade leapt out of its sheath, severed his head, flicked off the blood, and came back home to its sheath. It was a more powerful statement than if she had stood there and argued all evening. The Azarians responded to strength, and that she had plenty of.

"I did not come here to fight or kill," Moriko began. "I came here to save your lives, if I can. My kind, the people you call demon-kind, are camped just outside the Gathering. They know you mean to counterattack, and they will not let it happen. All of us wish for peace."

She paused, realizing it was difficult for her to find words. She wasn't a diplomat, but a warrior. The only way she could speak was bluntly.

"Tonight, a collection of my kind will attack the Gathering."

There was a roar of voices, but Moriko drew her sword and silenced them.

"It may be hard to believe, but they do not wish to kill. Yet they will protect this land and the people of the Kingdom. Tonight, if you stay the night in your tents, you will be spared. But if you believe you are still stronger than the warriors of the Kingdom, try and prove it tonight. They will come when the moon is high in the sky, and should you be outside, you will die. Let all your people know not to leave their tents! Tomorrow, our leaders will treat with whoever is left, whoever is willing to live in peace."

There was a stunned silence all around her, and Moriko seized the opportunity to exit the circle. She had delivered her message and everyone had heard it. There was no reason for her to stay. It would only complicate their discussion. She gave a short bow of her head to Dorjee and escaped before they could organize a hunt for her. She met up with Lobsang and the two of them left for the tents of the Red Hawks.

Lobsang had heard her message, and Moriko could tell he was full of questions, but the moon was quickly marching up the sky. It was time for her to leave.

"Lobsang, I hope we meet again under better conditions. I would love for us to be at peace. But please, whatever happens, don't leave your tent tonight."

Lobsang nodded, and Moriko left. She had done everything she could. She hoped it would be enough.

CHAPTER 38

The moon was high in the sky, but Ryuu hadn't ordered the attack yet. It was the action he needed to take, but he couldn't bring himself to do it, not quite yet. Behind him stood almost sixty nightblades, shuffling nervously in the light of the moon. Every one of them had volunteered.

Ryuu was exhausted. He had been healed, but it had been close. He could feel the energy surrounding him, begging him to accept it, but he had to remain distant. If he allowed too much into his body he wouldn't see another sunrise.

Shika stood next to him, offering her silent support. Ryuu appreciated it. Like Moriko, she had a strength he admired.

"Do you think there is forgiveness for something like this?"

Shika considered his question thoughtfully, understanding the importance he placed on it.

"I don't think it is about forgiveness, or even the idea of right and wrong."

Ryuu frowned. "What do you mean?"

"The histories will always talk about who did what, and I have no doubt they'll place a value on whatever is done here today. But that isn't for us to know or even to worry about. In my mind, the only question is: do we have the strength to do what is necessary?"

She paused before continuing. "There isn't a person here who wants to do this. None of us are monsters. But we have agreed we need to act, and so we will. Our burden isn't light, but we must be strong enough to carry it. If we don't, think how many more people in the Kingdom will die. We are causing suffering, yes. But we are preventing much more."

Her words steeled Ryuu. Perhaps it was a thin justification, but as she said, it was what needed to happen. He turned around to the assembled nightblades. There was no need to yell or to encourage them. Everyone knew what needed to be done. He spoke in his normal voice. "Let us begin."

With that, they ran towards the Gathering. They had elected not to ride into battle, being less experienced mounted. Moriko had not returned to the nightblade camp, but she had allowed Ryuu to sense her. She had gone into the Gathering and left it, so he assumed she had completed her mission and was staying away until the business was concluded. He hoped she had convinced many of them not to fight. He had no idea what kinds of debates they would be having in the Azarian camp.

They ran, their robes and footsteps no more than a whisper in the night. They crested the final hill before the Gathering and ran down it, blades drawn as they neared the first line of tents. As they got closer, they spread further and further apart from one another. Their plan was simple. They would spread out and charge straight through the Gathering, from east to west. Anyone standing outside was a target. They would meet again on the other side of the Gathering.

As the others fell away from him, Ryuu focused on summoning all of his own physical strength. He couldn't risk absorbing energy, not if he could help it. He ran among the tents and was relieved when he saw the walkways between tents were empty. His sense told him he was surrounded by people, but all of them were huddled together inside. A small wave of relief washed over him.

He moved further into the Gathering, walking slowly. Tents were everywhere, and it would be an easy matter for someone to jump out and attack him. He kept his sense alert. In the distance he could hear the sounds of steel on steel and knew not everyone was hiding. There were still those who fought.

Ryuu encountered his first attackers as he neared the center of the Gathering. A small group of men stood around a campfire, their swords ready. Ryuu approached them without fear. They weren't hunters. His blade cut them down, moving so fast they didn't even have a chance to meet steel. He didn't think about what he had done. He just kept moving forward.

In the very center of the Gathering he found four hunters patiently awaiting his arrival. They had sensed him coming, hoping to spring a trap on him. He walked into it without hesitation. They charged in unison.

Ryuu allowed himself to bring in some of the energy surrounding him. He wanted it all, but he didn't allow himself. To do so would mean death. He brought in just enough to rejuvenate his exhausted limbs and give him the speed and strength he needed.

At the last moment, Ryuu dashed to the right, throwing off their attack. They were strong, but so was he, and he was much faster. His move brought him one-on-one with the hunter farthest to the right. The hunter swung too early, his shorter blade passing a hair's width in front of Ryuu. Ryuu cut across, a deep cut against the hunter's arm and chest. The hunter's left arm went limp and blood poured out of his chest. He had a few moments to live, but Ryuu moved on to the next hunter.

By the time they met, the other hunters had regrouped. Ryuu turned away one cut with his blade and stepped towards the middle of the three remaining hunters, dodging an attack from another one. He rotated inside of the center hunter's guard but didn't strike him. For the moment, he was safe from the middle hunter's blade. He continued his rotation, swinging his sword with all his strength against another hunter. It was a strong, slow attack. The hunter got his blade up in time to block it, but Ryuu had hoped he would.

Ryuu's cut knocked the hunter a few steps off-balance, taking him out of the fight for a few precious heartbeats. He finished his rotation by driving his elbow deep into the stomach of the center hunter, knocking him backwards as well. The third hunter, still balanced and on his feet, saw an opportunity and struck.

Ryuu swung his blade up and easily parried the thrust. His blade was inside the hunter's, and with a quick flick of his wrists, he rotated his own blade and cut down and across the hunter's throat. Two down, two to go.

The hunter Ryuu had knocked backwards with his sword was quick to recover. He slashed at Ryuu, forcing him to dance backwards over the bodies of the other hunters. This hunter was focused, keeping his balance as he unleashed a devastating flurry of attacks. Ryuu kept giving up ground, allowing the hunter to tire.

Abruptly, he stopped retreating and parried a strike instead of dodging it. The hunter had sensed it, but he had grown accustomed to the pattern. Ryuu's block left him in an indefensible position, and Ryuu saw the hunter's eyes widen as he realized he had lost. Ryuu thrust his blade through the hunter's heart just in time to meet blades with the final hunter.

Alone, the hunter didn't have a chance. Ryuu cut him down in two passes. He scanned the area around him, making sure there were no more hunters out to spring a trap on him. Confident, he faced east and continued moving.

The way out of the Gathering was more crowded for Ryuu than the path in. He encountered three more groups of Azarians, one as large as twenty people. In later cycles he would be haunted by the vision of a lone child who attacked him. Ryuu easily knocked the blade out of the young girl's hands. He kicked her, once, viciously, to ensure she stayed down.

He didn't encounter any more hunters. The Azarians who raised their blades against him fell. Not one of them was even able to scratch him. His power and ability sickened him, but he kept putting one foot in front of the other, always moving to the east through the Gathering.

When he came out the other side of the Gathering, he saw he was one of the last to arrive. Many others were already there. He looked down and saw his blade was slick with blood. He wiped it off as best he could, but there was no way to get all the blood off. There was no telling how many people he had killed. Fifty maybe? It was far fewer than it could have been, but it was still far too many.

He felt empty inside, as though his soul had departed his body. The moon was out and almost full, but still the world seemed bathed in shades of gray. He shook his head, but nothing seemed to change. His body felt heavy and slow, and his body felt tired in an unfamiliar way.

Ryuu met up with the other nightblades and together they waited for others to join them. He thought about trying to use his sense at a distance, but he couldn't summon up the energy to care. They would come or they wouldn't. He wasn't going to go back. They waited, and a few more came. But not everyone. They had lost friends, too. With a silent look at Shika, Ryuu turned and led them away from the Gathering, their black robes disappearing in the night.

CHAPTER 39

Akira opened his eyes and swore as pain tore through his body.

His mind raced to catch up with what was happening. The last thing he remembered was looking at the blue sky and thinking he was dying. He had been at peace. But if he was still in pain, he was still in this world. There wasn't any way it should be possible. He had felt his guts leaking from his stomach.

Another wave of pain crashed across his body, and Akira's eyes were drawn to a man kneeling next to the cot he was laying on. Step by step, Akira's mind tried to start. The man seemed familiar. When the memory came to him, he understood everything at once. The man was the same one who had come to take Rei away. He was a dayblade. If he was here, he was attempting to heal Akira's wound.

Akira managed to get some words out. "How am I?"

The man started. He hadn't realized Akira was awake. Akira noticed the dayblade's face was covered in sweat. Whatever he had done, or was doing, he was working himself to exhaustion.

The man's voice was steady, but Akira noted a hint of sorrow in his voice. "I have done all I can. I can keep you alive for a while longer, but you are going to die before the sun sets again. Some wounds can't be healed."

Akira's heart sank. The pain was bearable if it meant life, but without life it was meaningless. Why was this man torturing him? He had been ready to die an honorable death. His mind latched onto fear and wouldn't let go. Had he misjudged the nightblades?

"Why?"

The man frowned, confused by Akira's question. "Why am I keeping you alive when you are still going to die?"

Akira nodded, sending another wave of agony down his spine.

"You still have work to do, although I know little of what that may be. More importantly, he told me to." The dayblade pointed his thumb back behind him. Akira's focus widened, and he saw that the dayblade was pointing towards Ryuu.

Almost everyone he cared about was in the tent with him. Ryuu and Moriko were there, and Captain Yung as well. Yung looked as though he'd been on the wrong side of a fight. He had a patch over one eye and his left arm hung limply from his side. Makoto was there too, seemingly whole and healthy despite the battle they'd just fought. All of them were covered in blood. Only Sen was missing. Akira would have liked to have seen him one more time. And Rei. It would have been good to see her again too. The thought of her made him smile.

"Did we win?"

It was Ryuu who spoke into the silence that answered Akira's question. "Your Kingdom will be safe. Makoto has come to terms with the Azarians. Don't worry about anything else."

Ryuu's answer confused Akira. A simple yes would have sufficed. Something had happened, but if Ryuu said the Kingdom was safe, and everyone was here, Akira believed him. He didn't need to know anything more.

Akira turned back to the dayblade. "I want you to heal Captain Yung when I die. He deserves your care more than I do."

He saw a tear come into Yung's eye. The dayblade bowed. "It will be as you wish."

Yung stepped forward, and Akira could see his captain was ashamed. He smiled. "Yung. You did all you could to protect me from myself. Have no regrets. You have been the best captain of the guard I could have asked for. If I could bow to you, I would. Thank you."

Yung lost all control of his emotions. Tears streamed down his face, and his body was wracked by sobs. It made even Akira tear up to see such a strong man weep. After a few moments, Yung got control of himself and straightened up. He made no move to wipe the tears from his face. "It was an honor to serve you. I couldn't have asked for a better king. I will miss you, Akira."

Akira laughed, causing him to cough up blood. The dayblade gave him an evil look. In the end, all it had taken for Yung to call him by his name was his imminent death. Their eyes met, and there was nothing more to be said. Yung retreated to the rear of the tent, where he dried his tears.

Makoto came up next. There was a sadness in the giant's eyes, but he composed himself well. "Thank you for everything. I will always honor your memory."

This time it was Akira who teared up. He was the one honored to have commanded men of such skill and strength. "The honor was mine. If I still have any authority. . ." Akira glanced around. Was he still king? Makoto nodded.

Akira started again. "Then I promote you to commander of whatever forces remain. Lead them as well as you have, and the Kingdom will be strong again. It was an honor to serve with you."

Makoto bowed, and also backed to the edge of the tent.

Ryuu advanced next. Akira wasn't sure what to say to the young nightblade, and when he looked into his eyes, he saw something new there, something that hadn't been there before. It was more than sadness. It was a deep sorrow. Akira knew, deep in his bones, that Ryuu had done something that had changed him. Something he would carry for the rest of his life.

"What did you do?"

Ryuu's eyes met his. "Everything that was necessary."

"Will you tell me?"

Ryuu thought for a moment and shook his head. "The Kingdom is safe. Don't carry your concerns for those of us still living with you into the Great Cycle."

Akira reached out towards Ryuu, and Ryuu took his hand in his own. Akira's own hands were rough, but Ryuu's were even more calloused. The two of them locked eyes. Akira searched for the perfect thing to say, something that could express how he felt. Everything seemed wrong, pathetic compared to the depth of his true emotion. But he couldn't think of anything else to say. "Thank you, for all you've done."

Ryuu nodded. "And you as well. May your rest be peaceful."

Akira spoke to the group. "Someone write up an edict. Nightblades and dayblades are allowed in the Kingdom once again. Write it up and I'll sign it."

Makoto stepped out of the tent to make it happen.

While he was gone, Moriko came up to Akira. It didn't look like she wanted to, but everyone else had. Akira smiled. He didn't know her well, but if she was with Ryuu, she was a good person. She spoke to him. "Akira, I misjudged you when we first met. You are a good man and a good king. I will miss you."

"Coming from you, that means a lot. Thank you, Moriko, for all you've done. I know you have also made many sacrifices for a Kingdom you don't care for."

He beckoned her closer and whispered in her ear. "I don't need to know what Ryuu has done, but will you look after him for me?"

She stood up and nodded. It was good Ryuu would have someone to watch over him.

There seemed little else to do, but Ryuu spoke up. "There is someone else you should see, Akira. We will give you a moment."

They all walked out of the tent. The dayblade, the nightblades, even Captain Yung. He was left completely alone, but then the tent flap opened and Rei stepped in.

Akira could have sworn his heart skipped a beat. His eyes were drawn straight to her belly, full with child. There was only one conclusion, but he couldn't believe it.

"When?"

She smiled, and Akira could see she had grown up in the moons since he had last seen her. "Just before I left, I think."

Suddenly, the enormity of what he was looking at hit him. Right in front of him was the heir to the Kingdom, the offspring of nightblade and royalty.

"This child is the future. It will unify us once and for all."

Akira was at a loss for words. To think that at the end of his life he would discover he had a child.

"It's going to be a son," Rei said with a smile.

Akira frowned, a small effort that still caused him to grimace.

"How do you know?"

"We have our ways."

Akira didn't seem pleased with the answer, so she continued. "Different sexes usually give off a different energy. I can sense the life inside of me, and I can assure you, it's going to be a boy."

A wave of sadness crashed over Akira. He had always been driven primarily by the needs of his kingdom, but there had always been a part of him that had wanted to start a family. Now, at the end of his life, he finally had his chance. Tears streamed down his face.

"I wish I could be there to see him grow up. I wish I could spend more time with you, help you to raise him."

Rei quieted him. "It's okay. I know the type of man you are. I will raise him as a nightblade, and he will know the strength of his father."

Akira made a decision. "You will raise him as a king, too." He called for everyone gathered outside his tent. They all came in. He figured Ryuu and Moriko knew already, but it would be quite the surprise to Makoto and Yung.

"Rei is carrying my son." Akira spoke with a direct tone that accepted no argument.

"I have decided that my child will not grow up as a bastard in the new Kingdom. I know we face an uncertain future, but you can accept this and deal with it as you will. I hereby bequeath all of my titles and all of my land upon my son. Until he reaches such age as he is prepared to rule, I ask that Sen act as regent in my stead. Makoto, write out the edict."

His general and captain couldn't have been more surprised, and Akira enjoyed looking at the expression on their faces. "It is a good thing, here. Perhaps he can be the one who finally bridges the divide between the blades and the citizens of the Kingdom. Yung, Makoto, please, protect him and train him. Make him worthy of the crown."

They both bowed to Akira, and he waved everyone out of the tent except Rei. "Thank you, Rei. You've given me hope as I pass into the Great Cycle."

Rei embraced him, an awkward affair with him flat on the cot, but a gesture Akira appreciated. She held him tightly, and he treasured his final moments against her.

"Rei, will you stay with me until the end?" He was seized by a sudden fear. He didn't want to die. He wasn't ready to leave, not anymore.

She nodded. "I will. We all will."

She sat down next to him and propped his head on her lap. It was a painful transition, but he couldn't think of a better way to spend his last moments.

Rei called everyone back in. They all knelt down by Akira's cot, and together they talked of meaningless things. At one point Makoto had Akira sign and seal the edicts he had proclaimed. Akira studied each face, so that he could take their memories with him. There was sorrow in the eyes around him, but there was hope too. He had heard once that the quality of one's life was determined by the quality of those one surrounded themselves with. He agreed.

That evening, as the sun began to set, everyone was still next to him. But he was tired. More tired than he had ever been. His spirit was light, but his body was unbearably heavy. He got their attention, interrupting a conversation debating different sword styles.

"Thank you, everyone. Now it's your job to lead the Kingdom."

His comment was met by solemn nods, but when it was clear he wasn't going to add anything else, they resumed their conversation, knowing it was what he desired.

The world slowly faded away from him, his world gently consumed by darkness and silence. In his last moments, he imagined he could feel the entire Kingdom breathing a great sigh of relief. They were safe and whole after a thousand cycles. Perhaps it was real. Perhaps it was in his head. Either way, he died with a smile on his lips.

EPILOGUE

That autumn was a busy one. Makoto had hammered out the details of the peace treaty in the days following the nightblades' attack. The Azarians wouldn't return to Azaria, but that had never been expected. Makoto knew they were still too strong to be forced out, and there was plenty of land for everyone. The Azarians were allowed to settle wherever they wanted, provided the land wasn't already in use by another.

In exchange, the Azarians agreed to obey the laws of the Kingdom and submit themselves to the justice of the king. Ryuu feared that it would be a difficult transition, but some groups of nightblades were starting to return to the Kingdom, and many of them were taking the roles of regional guards. It would be their responsibility to enforce the peace during these turbulent days.

There were few hunters left from their battle with the nightblades and the nightblades' subsequent attack on the Gathering. Those that remained joined clans and helped them rebuild. Ryuu and the other nightblades who could sense at a distance kept a wary watch on them.

After a small debate, Ryuu and Moriko decided to visit Shigeru's hut one last time. It wasn't a far journey from where the Gathering had been, and Ryuu wanted to see the home he had grown up in.

Returning to the hut opened up a host of memories for Ryuu. He spent two days just wandering the surrounding forest with Moriko. He thought a lot about Shigeru. The man had given up everything for a young boy he had saved from bandits. Ryuu thought back to those early days, wondering what Shigeru would think of him now. His master had also carried a heavy burden. Would he understand?

When Ryuu was older, Shigeru had told him he was destined to do something great. Ryuu wasn't so sure he was. He had brought the nightblades back, but he had also initiated a massacre. It was a far cry from the legends he had dreamed of living as a child. He would be happy to fade into obscurity.

Moriko was more content than Ryuu could ever remember seeing her. She loved being in the old woods. She always had. He was still a little surprised she was so eager to leave for an island that had so few trees. At times, he considered trying to convince her to stay, but he knew his efforts would be in vain. Her heart was set on returning to the island, and even he had to admit he was starting to acknowledge the wisdom of her decision.

He wasn't sure what to do with the hut. A part of him wanted to burn it down, to burn any connection he had with his past. He was ready for a new start. But Moriko argued against it. The hut was important to both of them. Ryuu had grown up there, and he and Moriko had lived there together for several cycles. It was as close to a home as either of them had in the Kingdom.

Instead, they cleaned it well, emptying it of any goods they wanted to keep. They harvested what little of their garden had survived their absence and prepared the ground for anyone who might return. They would leave the hut in pristine condition. It was unlikely anyone else would come across it, but if they did, it could be a home for someone else, too.

With a fond farewell, they departed the hut and walked until they found the river. Ryuu purchased passage on a boat going up the river to Highgate. They had talked about exploring more of the Kingdom together, but had decided against it. Winter was coming, and soon transportation to the island would be a lot more difficult. They made good time and were in Highgate in a few days.

Ryuu was pleased to see that life in the Kingdom was slowly returning to a new normal. Many people still lived at the monasteries, but every day people were coming back. News of the nightblades was spreading, and while none wore the black in public, whispers could be heard. There was fear in the whispers, but there was hope too. The nightblades had saved the army in their final battle against the Azarians, and word of their deeds was starting to take hold. Ryuu wondered how long it would be before the public learned of the other events of that evening.

Highgate was also returning to the city it had been before the war. It would take more time to heal, but the process was beginning. Ryuu and Moriko enjoyed a delicious meal, and Moriko begrudgingly admitted it was one of the best she'd ever tasted, far better than the fare at the inn the last time they had passed through.

The next day they caught a ship to the island. They were delayed by a storm, but came to the island without further incident. They made their hut on the island their home, and as the days passed, they tried to start their new lives.

One night, just over a moon later, Ryuu and Moriko were asleep when both awoke to the feeling of someone running towards their hut. Ryuu sensed it was Rei, and his heart sank. There was only one reason why she would be running here at this time of the night. He looked over at Moriko and saw understanding in her eyes as well.

They were both up and dressed by the time Rei got to their hut. She was ready to give birth any day now, and she moved slower than she once had. The look in her eyes said it all, but she spoke anyway. "He's dying. He wants both of you."

They walked quickly towards Tenchi's hut, indistinguishable from the others on the island despite his position. While on the way, Ryuu asked a question.

"Rei, how is it that he knows he's dying? Did something happen?"

Rei answered without looking back. "You may have already figured this out, but the line that separates dayblade and nightblade is fairly ambiguous. In general, nightblades are able to manipulate the sense externally, while dayblades manipulate it internally. But there isn't any rule or natural law that prevents one from doing both. Generally, it's just a natural limitation we all deal with. Tenchi is able to utilize the sense in both ways, at least to a degree. He can sense what's happening in his body, and he knows he's dying."

Moriko spoke up. "If he can sense what's happening, can't he fix himself?"

Rei's smile was sad. "Healing doesn't last forever. Dayblades can heal, but we can't cheat death. I have little doubt that his vitality, especially considering his age, is due in large part to continual self-healing. But no one lives forever."

Rei stopped at Tenchi's door. "This is as far as I go. He has already spoken his last words to me." She glanced at Ryuu with a look he couldn't comprehend.

Ryuu and Moriko stepped into Tenchi's hut. It was as bare as ever, filled with only the minimal essentials for living.

"Come in, come in." Tenchi's voice was strong. It wasn't what Ryuu had expected, but with his new knowledge, he expected that Tenchi would push himself to the very end. He would go out strong and quickly. Ryuu's respect for the old man only deepened.

"It's good to see you both. Thank you for coming."

Ryuu couldn't help but tear up. "I'm going to miss you very much."

Tenchi's grin was sad but wide. "And if I'm being honest, I expect I'm going to miss you both very much as well. Your presence here hasn't always been comforting, but you've changed our future, and for that, I'll always be grateful."

Tenchi fixed Moriko with a stare. "Moriko, please take care of Ryuu. You can see as well as I that he hasn't healed yet, but if anyone can help him, it will be you. Don't give up on him."

Moriko nodded, tears starting to stream down her face.

"And one last warning. The skill you possess, the skill that makes you so dangerous, comes with its own danger. You're not the first with your skill, and I imagine you won't be the last, but I don't know of anyone whose talent exceeds your own, living or dead. Your ability to go so far inside yourself and live there constantly, it can cause a person to cut themselves off from the world. I know you struggle with it already, but never give up on the world. It's a good place, no matter how much evil happens here."

Moriko bowed deeply, tears dripping from her eyes. Ryuu didn't understand exactly what Tenchi was saying to her, but it affected her deeply.

Moriko stepped away and Tenchi turned his attention to Ryuu. "Ryuu, I've never met anyone with as much strength as you have. Already you are the best warrior I've ever met, and you still have many cycles of development left. Don't let the power get to your head. Keep learning and stay humble. Come here."

Ryuu did so and Tenchi held out his hand. Ryuu took it and the world fell away. He recognized the technique instantly. He and Tenchi were as one. It was how he had learned to sense at a distance so quickly.

At the time, he had simply been absorbing one skill, but when he touched Tenchi's hand this time he experienced it all. A part of his mind realized Tenchi was pushing skills into him as fast as he could, but it was all a jumbled mess to him. One moment he felt like he could block someone's distance sensing, another moment he could feel every single muscle twitching in his body. Skill after skill embedded itself in his mind. Then it was over. He rocked backwards.

Tenchi grinned, although it was obvious the effort had taken its toll on him. "You won't understand it now, but with study, all the pieces should come together and you should be able to get quite the jump on others. There's so much we don't know. You've told me that you've considered sheathing your sword forever, but I would ask you not to. Perhaps you will never have to kill again. I hope for your sake you don't. But the sword is a tool that illuminates all other teachings and philosophy. Continue to study. Continue to grow. Let your knowledge become a beacon for future generations. And show the other old men how much they have yet to learn."

Ryuu grinned, but Tenchi turned serious. "Ryuu, I know you're still torn about what you've done. I understand. I am, too. I can't help you to find peace, but you must. Find it and move on, otherwise it will hurt you forever."

Ryuu nodded through the tears and Tenchi spoke again. "Call Rei in."

Moriko went to go get Rei. The two women helped him to his feet, and together they walked slowly. At his direction, they stepped out of the hut and sat outside. The sun was rising in the east.

"I just want to see one last sunrise. Then I'll let it go."

The sun rose slowly, burning the ocean and night away as it rose.

Tenchi looked at each of them in turn. "I have been fortunate. I'm dying in the company of the three I love most, watching a beautiful sunrise. Thank you."

They watched until the sun completely rose above the horizon. Around them, the island was slowly coming to life. Tenchi smiled. He looked around and took a deep breath. Ryuu saw that his face was dry and he was calm.

Tenchi closed his eyes and was gone.

It had been over a cycle since Tenchi passed away. Ryuu still thought about him often, but the grief was getting more bearable every day. Moriko was his constant companion, for which he was extremely grateful. There were good days and there were bad days, but he wasn't sure he would have made it through the bad days without her.

They had asked Ryuu, after Tenchi's death, if he was interested in coming onto the council or becoming head of the island. They had asked Moriko as well, but both of them had refused. Moriko wasn't interested in guiding the nightblades, and while Ryuu did have some interest, he didn't believe he was worthy to lead. Not yet.

Elections had been held, and it was no surprise when Shika won them. Support for returning to the Kingdom was at an all-time high; and in a reversal of fortune Shika spent her time trying to convince them they needed to take it one step at a time. It was quite the change for a woman who had been willing to go to almost any length to return to the Kingdom.

Both Ryuu and Moriko gave Shika a lot of advice in that cycle. The two of them had grown up in the Kingdom, and combined with Moriko's firsthand knowledge of the Azarians, there were many questions that could be answered. Even if they weren't in charge of the island, their knowledge and advice guided many of the council's decisions.

Beyond that, life settled into a predictable routine. Ryuu and Moriko both continued training every day. Ryuu sought out teachers among the elders and books in the library. Never before had he read so much. Moriko told him he was getting soft. He didn't agree, but there was no arguing that life was much easier than it ever had been.

Tenchi had been right, of course. With the knowledge Ryuu had been given he learned much more quickly than others. His base of knowledge was growing faster than anyone expected, and already he was developing techniques previously thought impossible. When he wasn't training or learning, Ryuu was often trying to pass the knowledge on to others. He was also trying to develop a new sword style based on everything he learned.

Relations with the Kingdom continued to evolve. Rei had become the blades' ambassador to the Kingdom, and more and more of them were working their way over to the land they had once been exiled from. Progress was slow, and it was only Rei's influence and Sen's wisdom that prevented the entire idea from collapsing all around them. The situation was delicate, and it would be for a long time. Turning away from over a thousand cycles of tradition would take several lifetimes.

The Azarians were becoming integrated with the citizens of the Kingdom, one agonizing step at a time. Most of the clans had found places to settle, and while conflict was still common, there hadn't been any outbreaks of violence strong enough to cause the treaty to be questioned. Dorjee had become the unofficial ambassador from the clans, and he and Sen were in frequent contact.

The monasteries were disappearing from the land. When the war ended, Sen had cut them off from his treasury. Their purpose had been to protect the land from nightblades, but now that nightblades were allowed back in the land, there was no reason for them any longer. Some monasteries managed to scratch out a living on public donations, and some of them had become hotbeds of discontent, but Sen and the nightblades kept a close eye on them.

Rei had given birth to a strong baby boy. She named him Akira, and the child was truly a child of the new world. He knew his heritage as a nightblade, and Ryuu had already promised to train him personally. Sen would train him in the ways of the Kingdom, and Dorjee was willing to teach him the ways of the Azarians. He was the future, and they all knew it.

Most importantly, Moriko was finally happy. She was glad to be on the island and safe from harm and persecution. The Kingdom was safer than it had ever been for a nightblade, but it was still far more dangerous than the island. Her belly was also starting to grow, and Ryuu was both excited and terrified of the future.

Even though everything was improving, Ryuu still felt a lingering discontent. Over and over he tried to figure out what was bothering him, but the feeling was too vague to be pinned down easily. When at last he understood, it happened in an instant.

Most days he didn't think about the war or the role he'd played. Over a cycle had passed, and life continued. But he couldn't hide from the guilt he felt. Despite taking action he was still convinced was necessary, he wasn't convinced it was right. He needed to find atonement.

Unsure of what to do, he decided to write, to try to make sense of what had happened. He wrote about his life, how he had come to be the sort of person who could make the decision to kill so many. He didn't have any answers. No matter how long he thought about it, he could never come up with another path he could have chosen that night. Perhaps someday someone would read his words, learn from his mistakes and find a better way. It didn't seem like much, but perhaps it would be enough.

He wasn't a writer. Some days the words came easily, other days it felt as though he were pulling his stomach out through his mouth. But he persisted, working through his life and his decision every day.

One day Moriko came up to him as he was writing. He hadn't allowed her to read anything he had written yet, but the time was coming when he would. He looked up, smiled, and rubbed his hand against her swelling body. The dayblades said the girl would come in about two moons.

"How's the writing coming?"

"Slow, but I'm almost done. I don't know if it will prevent another tragedy from occurring, but more understanding is always better."

Moriko nodded her agreement. They had had this discussion a hundred times, and she was always supportive. It meant more to him than she realized.

She pulled gently on his hand and together they walked to the edge of the plateau. The sun was setting, blood red against an incoming storm. They held hands and watched as the sun dipped below the horizon, throwing a blanket of darkness across the land and sea. Ryuu looked at Moriko, and in the light of the stars he saw her smile. He returned the smile and looked back over the sea, enjoying the peace he had found.

AUTHOR'S NOTE

I've learned that finishing a story (or in this case, a trilogy) is much harder than starting one. When you start, a whole world of possibility awaits, and you can take whatever direction you like. Every blank page is an opportunity. But finishing a story is just the opposite. With few exceptions, a good ending doesn't leave the reader hanging. It answers the questions and closes the loops.

With The Wind and the Void, I've finished telling the story I originally set out to tell. I've never had more fun than I've had writing these stories, and sharing them with all of you has been a privilege. I always thought it was a good story, but I never thought it would excite and engage so many. I've treasured every email, Facebook post, website comment, and tweet. I love stories, and its awesome to interact with so many of you who do too.

Ryuu's and Moriko's stories, for me, are done. I suspect that in the future I will return to the world of the Kingdom, but it will be with a new story and new characters and a new place in the time line.

More than anything, I wanted to thank all of you who have read the books and joined me on this adventure. Endings are challenging, but I hope the journey was a worthwhile one.

Until we meet again,

Ryan Kirk
March 2016

Acknowledgments

With the final book in the trilogy complete, I felt like it was time to give credit where credit is due. Few deeds in life take place without the help of many, and these books are no exception.

First, I need to thank you, the reader. Without your support, there's no way I could continue to write. I'm grateful for each of you, and your emails, comments, reviews, and tweets have meant the world to me as I've started writing. Thank you for taking a chance on a new, unknown writer.

Second, no single person deserves as many thanks as my gorgeous wife, Katie. I could write an entire book on the ways she's made this possible. She's my first reader, my developmental editor, and my greatest supporter. She allowed me to quit my job and write full-time, even though the future was very uncertain. There's no way I can thank her enough.

I wanted to take a moment to say thank you to Andrew Tell, the producer of the audio version of these stories. Andrew took a huge risk when we first started producing these books, and I'm grateful for the countless hours he's spent bringing these books to life.

Thanks to Sonnet Fitzgerald, the editor for this final book. Her work and dedication have been awesome, and any mistakes that remain are solely my own.

Thanks to Justin and Christine for being beta readers. And finally, thanks to all my family and friends for all the support they've provided along the way. There's far too many to thank here, but I'm grateful for you all.

If you've read this far - congratulations! If you've enjoyed the books, there are a number of ways to get even more involved. Reviews are always appreciated, but if you're interested in learning more about me, the worlds I've created, or any of my other work, head on over to www.waterstonemedia.net. There's a whole lot of information on there, with more being added all the time. Also, take a moment to subscribe to my email list on the site.

Email subscribers get chances for free stories, sales and discounts, and can participate in giveaways and contests.

As always, thanks for reading!